A Christmas to Remember...

The strong, dreamy scent of pine made Eve shake her head. Roarke had gone wild for tradition on this, their first Christmas together. Who knew what he had paid for the live trees he'd placed throughout the house. And this one, the one that stood by the window in their bedroom, he'd insisted they decorate together...

"Tree lights on," she ordered, and smiled a little as she watched them blink and flash.

She was sitting on the arm of the sofa taking off her boots when Roarke came in... She angled her head and studied him as he stood just inside the doorway. She let her second boot drop and stood up slowly. "Come here."

Recognizing the glint in her eyes, he felt the light tingle of lust begin to move through his blood. "There?"

"You heard me, slick."

Keeping his eyes on hers, he walked across the room. "What can I do for you, Lieutenant?"

Traditions, Eve thought, had to start somewhere...

—from "Midnight in Death"

SILENT NIGHT

J. D. Robb

Susan Plunkett

Dee Holmes

Claire Cross

JOVE BOOKS, NEW YORK

SILENT NIGHT

A Jove Book / published by arrangement with the authors

PRINTING HISTORY
Jove edition / November 1998

ISBN: 0-515-12385-4

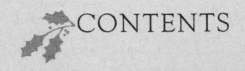

CONTENTS

SILENT NIGHT

A BERRY MERRY CHRISTMAS

Claire Cross

PROLOGUE

Toronto—December 18, 1996

Drew Sinclair sat in the vinyl-upholstered chair and watched the tiny figure in the hospital bed. Swathed from head to toe, she was unrecognizable as his niece, Natalie. For the umpteenth time Drew hoped she didn't remember anything about how she had gotten here.

Then he also hoped, one more time, that the scars from her burns wouldn't leave her marked for life. The last thing he wanted was Natalie thinking of what—or who—she had lost every single time she looked in the mirror.

Who could have guessed that the mice in his brother's rambling country house would chew through the electrical cable that strung the Christmas tree lights together? Drew would have checked them—it was in his nature to double-check everything—so seriously that Greg would have teased him about it.

But Greg would never tease Drew about anything again. A week had gone by, but Drew still couldn't completely accept that his happy-go-lucky younger brother was gone.

Forever.

Drew watched Natalie's little chest rise and fall, knowing without a doubt why Greg and Winona had never bothered to trap the attic mice. Natalie thought they were cute, and everyone falsely assumed that anything cute must be harmless.

Drew guessed that it had been Natalie who wanted the Christmas lights left on all night and that her parents had seen no harm in indulging her.

And Drew had awakened to his phone ringing in the middle of the night. In no time at all he was driving north through the snow to the hospital nearest the old farmhouse that Greg had been renovating.

Old wiring, was the conclusion of the fire inspector. Not up to code. And the mice had been busily chewing on more than the string of Christmas lights. The older man had shaken his gray head while giving Drew the news this very morning, and Drew had realized that it wasn't the first time this fire inspector had delivered such news at this time of year. And not only did the older man know it wouldn't be the last—he knew there was precious little he could do about it.

Any way you sliced it, it was one hell of a Christmas present.

Drew gave thanks that he could afford the very best. If he had anything to say about it, Natalie wouldn't have a single physical scar.

The scars on her heart, now, were something he wasn't sure he'd be able to fix.

But he would bloody well try.

The monitor beeped quietly, the red lights all doing what they were supposed to do. The silence of the night permeated the hospital ward, and darkness pressed against the window. Drew leaned his elbows on his knees, templed his fingers together, and watched for some tiny sign that Natalie was still in there.

"Mr. Sinclair! You're *still* here." The nurse who was always on duty in the evenings hovered in the doorway. "Have you gone home at all?"

Drew barely glanced her way. "I need to be here."

The nurse bustled into the room and gave him a stern glance. "Have you eaten?"

"Enough," Drew lied. The truth was, he wasn't the least bit interested in food.

"Mr. Sinclair, it's been seven days. This could go on for a long time. You have to take care of yourself—after all, Natalie has no one else left."

A pang shot through Drew's heart at the reminder that he didn't really need. "I know," he said softly, his gaze still fixed on the bandaged figure on the bed. Natalie looked so much smaller than he knew her to be.

It was the unnatural stillness of her, he guessed: Who ever knew a four-year-old who stopped moving for even a moment? And Natalie had been the busiest—and the happiest—of little girls.

Would Drew ever see her smile again?

"She needs me here," he said when the nurse seemed to be waiting for him to say something. And the funny thing was that as soon as Drew said the words, he knew them to be true.

That gave him an idea. The nurse made another comment or two, but when Drew didn't answer, she left the room, scanning her clipboard as she went. As soon as the echo of her heels on the linoleum faded, Drew pulled his chair closer to the bed. His heart was racing, and he didn't know if he was about to do the dumbest thing he'd ever thought of, but it had to be worth a try.

He was not, after all, an impulsive or whimsical man.

Despite that, Drew reached down and extracted a stuffed animal from the bag the fire inspector had brought. Even though it didn't look its best, Drew knew it was a teddy bear, none other than Mr. Bumbles.

Mr. Bumbles had been in pretty rough shape before the fire, having been loved and squeezed by a certain little girl until he was a mere shadow of his former self. Winona had patched him up more than once, but still he was missing an eye, and his fur was worn away in several much-adored spots.

Now the bear had a few scorch marks to add to his battle scars, but he was still unmistakably Mr. Bumbles. The fire inspector had evidently heard about Natalie's condition and guessed the ownership of Mr. Bumbles in his search of the site. Mr. Bumbles had a couple of jazzy new bandages and a little sling, and the charred fur had been mostly trimmed away.

The fire inspector hadn't said anything at all when he gave the bear to Drew, but Drew was touched by the compassionate gesture. Complete strangers did the damnedest things this time of year.

Now he gently lifted a small bandaged arm and tucked Mr. Bumbles in the crook of Natalie's elbow, where he rightly belonged.

Drew waited with bated breath, but nothing happened. Unable to account for his sense of failure, he settled back into his chair and pressed his fingertips together once again.

And Natalie moved.

Drew's eyes widened in shock. He blinked, he looked again. Natalie's grip on the bear changed ever so slightly, and her bandaged face turned as though she would brush the tip of her nose across Mr. Bumbles. Her little fingers clenched the bear's paw and she snuggled him close.

Drew knew he didn't imagine her little sigh of satisfaction. One of the monitors, after all, had picked up its pace. His heart danced around his chest like a wild thing, and he couldn't help but grin idiotically.

Natalie was going to be all right.

A week later, on the day of Christmas Eve, the doctors took off another round of Natalie's bandages.

It was a challenge, given her death grip on Mr. Bumbles.

Drew was a bit startled to see his niece with her blond corkscrew curls gone, even though he knew that some of her hair had burned in the fire and the rest had been shaved away to treat her burns. One cheek and temple were still an angry red, but the plastic surgeon was confident that the damage could be repaired.

She was still a pretty child, with her heart-shaped face

and Greg's dimple right in the middle of her chin. She had Winona's blue eyes, their luxuriant lashes gone now. Drew remembered all too well how merrily those eyes had danced when Natalie made some mischief.

He hoped desperately that one day she would laugh again.

It took Natalie a few minutes to get used to even the dimmed light in the room, then her serious gaze zeroed in on Drew. The doctor stepped back into the shadows and shooed the nurse away, leaving the two with a comparatively private moment.

Drew's mouth went dry, and all the words he'd composed to explain the truth to Natalie completely fled his mind. He stared back at her, feeling more helpless than he ever had in his life.

"Unca Drew?" Her voice was so much more fragile than Drew remembered, but at least she recognized him. The psychologist had been uncertain how heavily traumatized Natalie would be.

How much did she remember of that awful night? All Drew wanted to do was scoop up his niece and protect her from everything nasty in the world, but he was terrified of frightening her. After all, he was just an uncle who visited half a dozen times a year.

Drew forced a little smile. "Yeah, punkin." He had always called her that, and he hoped the familiarity would reassure her in this very unfamiliar place. "I'm here."

"You were here before," she said with eerie certainty. "You gave me Mr. Bumbles."

Drew caught his breath. "Yeah, I did. He wanted to help you get better."

Natalie hugged the bear closer, licked her chapped lips, and scanned the room. She solemnly eyed the doctor before looking at Drew once more.

"Mummy and Daddy aren't coming, are they?" she whispered.

Drew tried very hard to swallow the lump in his throat and failed. He wasn't sure he could summon a word, so he simply shook his head.

Natalie's brow furrowed and she watched the doctor for a moment that stretched long. Her thumb stroked Mr. Bumbles' paw with an intensity that would soon wear off what little fur remained on it.

"Not tomorrow neither," she finally said, a soft ring of conviction in her voice. Her clear gaze swiveled to lock on to Drew's once more, as though this tiny child would will him to tell her the truth.

It seemed that Natalie remembered quite a lot.

Drew inched his chair closer, never breaking her gaze, then reached out to gently touch her hand. "No. Not tomorrow either, punkin," he confirmed quietly.

Natalie's bottom lip trembled ever so slightly, then a tear cascaded over her cheek. Her mouth worked for a moment, her vulnerability tearing at Drew's heart. It wasn't fair that a small child should have to come to terms with such a loss!

Just when Drew thought he could stand it no longer, Natalie took a deep breath and impaled him with a piercing look. "Are you going to be my daddy now?" she demanded hoarsely.

Drew's heart clenched. He immediately captured Natalie's tiny hand, liking how her fingers curled reflexively around his. He looked into her too serious eyes, willing her to understand how hard he was going to try to make everything right in her world.

His voice was surprisingly husky, even to his own ears. "You can count on it, punkin."

ONE

December 17, 1998

> *Dear Santa,*
>
> *Can you bring me a new mommy? I have been very, very, very good. Mr. Bumbles says so.*
>
> > *xoxox*
> > *Natalie*

Holly read the note twice, trying desperately to figure out what this had to do with her. Being called into Mr. C.'s office wasn't usually a good moment for her—and she *had* mucked up the paint on those new toy dump trucks this morning.

It wasn't as though she tried to do things wrong—just the opposite, in fact—but Holly simply wasn't mechanically minded at all. The elves in charge of the North Pole workshop kept inventing clever new devices, almost as though they meant to spite her. It seemed to Holly that those gadgets took one look at her and went wild.

The last time she had stood in this very same place—after the tragic doll-with-three-eyes incident—Mr. C. had told her she would have another chance. There was no doubt that Holly had blown that chance today. Her mouth went dry. What was going to happen now?

She wasn't sure she wanted to know.

Holly peeked over the note and met the very serious gaze of Mr. C. himself. She tried to swallow the lump of dread in her throat but failed. Mrs. C. was even there—less of a good sign, to Holly's mind—and both of them wore unusually grim expressions.

Holly waved the note. "I, um, I don't understand."

Mr. C. breathed deeply, straining his red suspenders. "Holly, there's no two ways about it. You just aren't working out among the elves on the floor."

He frowned and pushed his spectacles further up on his red-as-a-cherry nose. Holly had never seen him so solemn, not even that time when she had entangled the strings of four hundred and twelve brand-new marionettes.

Three weeks ago.

"We can't have elves who don't contribute to the bottom line," he continued, "especially at this time of year, when we're heading into very heavy production."

"It's bad for morale, dear," Mrs. C. interjected. "And we can't have *that* when everyone has so much work to do."

"Please, Holly, we're asking you not to go back on the production floor," Mr. C. said.

"Ever," Mrs. C. clarified.

"Under any condition."

Holly's heart sank like a stone. That could mean only one thing.

She was being fired.

From the North Pole workshop. Holly was quite certain that elves didn't get work anywhere else.

"Now, don't look so crestfallen, dear. We know that it isn't really your fault," Mrs. C. continued quickly, wringing her hands in her apron. "We know you have a heart of gold, Holly. Perhaps you just haven't found your *niche*." She licked her lips and frowned in turn. "There's just something about you that makes everything run amuck. You have some kind of . . . *gift*, dear."

It didn't feel like much of a gift to Holly.

"Damnedest thing." Mr. C. scowled. "And very inconvenient."

Mrs. C. gave her a sympathetic smile. "So, dear, you'll just have to stay out of the workshop for good."

Holly finally found her voice. "But what will I do?"

"Well!" Mrs. C.'s expression brightened considerably. "We've found just the thing for you, dear. Tell her, Noel."

"Very tricky job," Mr. C. said gruffly. "But you just might have the necessary talent to get it done."

Holly wondered whether they needed something broken somewhere.

Mr. C. took off his glasses and fixed Holly with his blue gaze, pointing at the note she held. "Charming little girl, this Natalie. Orphaned two years back, adopted by her bachelor uncle. As you can see, she wants a new mommy."

Mr. C. cleared his throat when Holly said nothing. "I suspect he's afraid to continue on with his life, now that the niece is his responsibility. Drew Sinclair seems to be the kind to take responsibility very seriously. Could stand to lighten up, actually, although that isn't exactly what we want you to do."

Holly knew she looked blank.

Mrs. C. leaned forward, her eyes sparkling. "You see, dear, we're quite certain there's just a little mix-up here. Tell her, Noel."

Mr. C. put his glasses back on and scanned a fax on his desk. "Well, there's a certain Katherine O'Neill who has some idea about marrying this uncle." Mr. C. flicked Holly a stern glance. "I discovered this through quite unorthodox channels, by the way, and I'd like to keep the whole thing very hush-hush."

"Of course, sir."

Mr. C. nodded. "The way I see it, the bottleneck here is

Mr. Drew Sinclair. What we want you to do is go on down there to Toronto and set things in motion." He checked his watch. "It's the seventeenth of December, and Christmas is an awfully nice time to propose marriage, after all. Wouldn't you say, Noelle?"

"Oh, Noel!" Mrs. C. blushed like a schoolgirl. "Holly doesn't want to know about all *that*!"

A merry twinkle took up residence in Mr. C.'s eyes. "What do you say, Holly? This could be the beginning of a bright future for you."

"I can't imagine how *anything* could go wrong!" trilled Mrs. C. with obvious excitement. "It's so perfectly simple!"

Holly, though, had her doubts. "Won't they notice that I'm an elf? I mean, the ears do give it away." She fingered the telltale points on her ears, then held up a foot. The bell on one toe jingled. "Not to mention the shoes."

"We can conceal the ears, dear, and I've had a mortal wardrobe prepared for you."

Mr. C. shuffled through the paperwork on his desk. "And we've worked out a cover for you. Oddly enough"— he winked—"Natalie's nanny quit suddenly just this morning. Mr. Sinclair is in a bit of a fix, since he does have a day job where a six-year-old child would get in the way. He's interviewing nannies at this very moment—we've prepared an excellent résumé for you, complete with impeccable references."

He looked Holly dead in the eye. "You'll get the nanny job, that much I can ensure."

"But the rest, dear," Mrs. C. added softly, "is entirely up to you."

As she looked back at them, Holly knew that she held in her grasp what was truly her very last chance. She had to make this work or she would be a very unemployed, yet still immortal, elf.

It would be tough to scrape by for all eternity.

Holly *had* to succeed.

She swallowed and nodded with false confidence. "I'll do it. When do I start?"

The pair before her smiled with satisfaction. "Right now," Mr. C. confirmed. Before Holly could say anything more, he lifted his hand, with his palm flat. She saw the glitter of fairy dust for just an instant before Mr. C. pursed his lips and blew.

Then Holly was surrounded by dancing crystals, not unlike swirling snowflakes. A warm wind picked her up and tumbled her along with them as though she weighed no more than a snowflake herself. She rolled helplessly, surrounded by fluttering silver and light, and wished with all her heart that she would succeed.

Holly landed square on her feet on the sidewalk in front of a brick house. It was not unlike the houses on either side of it. The well-tended lawn and garden were brown and waiting for spring, the cedars bound in burlap, although there was no snow just yet. Holly looked down to find her clothes completely changed.

She was wearing a dark green jacket that was nice and warm, and a peppermint-striped scarf wound around her neck. Her slim-fitting trousers were a deep shade of red, and she peeked under the jacket to find herself wearing a lovely creamy sweater that was embroidered with prancing reindeer. She had a large black purse slung over her shoulder and neat black boots on her feet. A small black suitcase rested beside her on the sidewalk.

The combination would go well with her dark hair and gray eyes. And goodness knew, Holly wanted to look her very best for such an important job. The little black boots didn't even have pointed toes.

A glitter caught her eye, and she discovered a merry Santa brooch pinned to her jacket. Just the sight of it made Holly smile. She reached up and found the peaks gone from her ears, much to her relief. And little earrings, although she couldn't tell what shape they were. They jingled when Holly moved her head.

All in all, Mrs. C. had done quite well. Holly glanced up and down the street and imagined she looked perfectly mortal. A thrill of anticipation swept through her.

Maybe she really *could* do this job!

She looked back at the house, not quite sure how to proceed. Was this the right place? Bay windows flanked the front door, and she noticed that this house—unlike its neighbors—had absolutely no Christmas decorations at all.

How odd.

Maybe they just hadn't gotten around to decorating yet. After all, Mr. C. had said that this uncle had his plate full with the nanny leaving so suddenly. The front door was a cheerful bright red, though, and with her keen elvish vision Holly could see the name engraved on the brass door knocker.

Sinclair.

This must be the place. She took a deep breath and hoped desperately that she wouldn't screw this up. That resolved, Holly marched right up the path and rang the bell.

The door cracked open just an instant later, although it moved slowly, as though someone was having difficulty pulling it wide. When the crack increased to about a foot, a head poked out in the vicinity of the doorknob.

It was a little girl, her curly hair cut short around her head. The light from the house got caught in the fair curls and made her seem to be wearing a halo.

What a darling child! Holly would have cast her as a cherub in the angelic host without a second thought.

This must be Natalie.

Holly smiled, quite genuinely pleased to meet the girl who had written to Mr. C. It took some gumption to ask for what you really wanted, after all.

Natalie's eyes went big and round as she scanned Holly from head to toe. "You're Christmas!" she exclaimed.

Holly laughed lightly. "No. Just Holly. Holly Berry."

Before Natalie could say anything else, the door was quickly opened from behind. Holly's gaze rode up, way up, until she met the steely blue eyes of the very tall man standing right behind Natalie. His shoulders were broad, his navy pin-striped suit trim, his burgundy tie crisply knotted. A white handkerchief peeked out of his pocket at the perfect angle.

His hair was a chestnut brown, his temples touched with just the right measure of silver to make him look distinguished. His jaw was square and his nose straight with aquiline precision. In fact, he might have been a very handsome man if he hadn't looked so grim.

Holly had a funny feeling that the exactitude of his profile suited him perfectly. His eyes were so relentless in their appraisal that Holly felt herself flush a little. She was pretty sure she hadn't measured up to his first survey of her assets.

And she knew without the shadow of a doubt who he was. Because if ever there had been a man who needed to "lighten up," it had to be the one standing right in front of her.

This was Drew Sinclair.

Even though he was much younger than she had anticipated, Holly guessed that he was somewhere in his early thirties, mortally speaking. She took another look. Here she had been expecting a sweet and kindly older man who would take readily to her suggestion that he pop the question to the equally sweet and kindly older Katherine O'Neill.

But Holly couldn't even begin to imagine how she would make this man do anything he hadn't already decided to do.

It seemed she *could* screw up this job, after all.

And that conclusion made Holly's heart sink straight to her toes.

Drew Sinclair was fed up.

A dozen nanny interviews already this morning, and not a single applicant with sufficient sense that he would entrust Natalie to her care. In fact, he wasn't sure the women he had met could be trusted to find their own way back home without incident.

He had kept Natalie home from school so he could see her response to each applicant, but he was starting to feel as though the entire morning had been an exercise in futility. Drew was certain he wasn't being overprotective.

He was just being *sensible*.

It could have been his middle name, after all.

Natalie's greeting of this candidate had brought Drew's protective instincts screaming to the fore. Christmas! The last thing they needed was any reminder that it was Christmas—and an anniversary of sorts. Drew was prepared to dislike this Holly Berry on sight when he pulled open the door.

But he didn't.

In fact, Drew found her very attractive.

And that was so remarkable, so ridiculous, so utterly illogical that it made him frown. Since Drew had long ago abandoned his quest to find a suitable life partner, it was a bit startling to find the most intriguing woman he'd seen in years standing right on his doorstep.

He didn't quite know what to do.

So he took a better look, certain that the nonsensical attraction would just go away at second glance.

But Holly Berry was tall and trim, with curves in what looked to be all the right places. Her dark hair was neatly cropped at her chin, and its waves bounced with a life of their own. She apparently wore no makeup, at least none that Drew could discern, and he noted with approval that her prettiness needed no such accent. Her full, ruddy lips curved as though she was on the verge of laughter.

It was her eyes, though, that ensnared Drew's attention. They were thickly lashed and tipped up at the outer corners with delightful femininity. That in itself would have been interesting enough, but their color was incredible: Ms. Berry's eyes were the most unusual shade of silver-gray, and they sparkled as though they were filled with stardust.

That was by far the most whimsical thought Drew had ever permitted to invade his orderly mind, but it was exactly right. He stared and he marveled and he knew that he would never see another pair of eyes so beautiful.

And that was just plain nuts. Drew frowned a little more severely, just for good measure.

Amazingly, Ms. Berry didn't seem to pick up on his sour mood at all. Her smile was unfailingly sunny. The longer Drew looked at her, the better he felt, although he knew that was crazy. He had the weirdest urge to smile right back.

"Hello. I'm Holly Berry," she repeated for Drew's benefit. Her voice was low and curiously pleasing. The promise of laughter clung to her words in a most intriguing way. "And you must be Mr. Drew Sinclair."

Drew tried to look stern but was pretty sure he didn't quite pull it off. "Yes, I am."

Ms. Berry held his gaze for an intoxicatingly long moment, then those full lips quirked. "Might I come in?" she asked mildly, then glanced at Natalie and back at Drew before raising a dark eyebrow. "We wouldn't want anyone to catch cold."

Belatedly, Drew realized they were still standing on the front step. Good thing someone was thinking! What had happened to his solid good sense?

Not to mention his manners.

He must be losing it.

Drew shook his head as though to clear his thoughts of such nonsense, then stepped back and gestured to the foyer behind him. "Won't you come in? Perhaps I could see your résumé?"

She stepped over the threshold, that smile faltering momentarily when Drew extended his hand. Ms. Berry frowned, then grasped at her purse as though it were a life preserver. "It *must* be in here," she declared cheerfully, then rummaged in the bag with purpose.

Drew blinked. How could she not even know whether or not she had brought a résumé with her?

That couldn't be a good sign. Not at all. Maybe she really wasn't any different from all the other candidates. Drew glanced at his niece to find her staring avidly at the woman.

Now *that* was something. Natalie hadn't been nearly so interested in anyone else. Drew looked back to the potential nanny and deliberately gave her the benefit of the doubt.

Anyone could have a moment's disorganization. Couldn't they? Drew wasn't entirely sure, not being able to recall ever having had one himself.

Ms. Berry gave a cry of delight and victoriously produced a creamy envelope from the depths of her bag. She smiled with her previous confidence and presented it to Drew with a flourish.

Her hands, he noticed immediately, were slender and long-fingered. Her nails were carefully trimmed and buffed, her fingers were free of rings. And Drew liked those hands very much, though he didn't dare to examine precisely which aspect of them prompted his approval.

But Drew *never* noticed people's hands. Obviously, the inconvenience of this morning was getting to him. He accepted the envelope quickly, minimizing the moment their fingers brushed.

But his hand still tingled slightly from the warmth of Holly's fingertips. And Drew felt as though he had lost an opportunity for . . . something.

He had definitely been working too hard.

He gave the envelope his most forbidding survey to get his mind back on track. Drew's name was neatly typed on the front, his address below. The stationery was a nice choice, a good-quality stock but not too expensive, one that he couldn't help fingering. Drew was impressed.

Even though there was still one thing bothering him. "How could you not know that you had this with you?"

Ms. Berry laughed, a sound that made Drew think of hundreds of silver bells pealing simultaneously. Or a sparkling mountain waterfall. "I'm sorry, but it's been a very odd morning," she said and smiled right into his eyes.

The foyer suddenly seemed a little bit warm to Drew.

Oddly reassured and wanting to reassure her in turn, Drew let his lips curve just a little bit. "It's been a bit hectic here this morning, as well, Ms. Berry," he acknowledged.

"Ms. Berry!" she echoed and wrinkled her nose in a charming way. "Everyone just calls me Holly, Mr. Sinclair. You have to do the same. I insist."

Drew found himself clearing his throat. He had called the other nannies by their first names—why did Holly's suggestion seem so . . . intimate?

"I'm not certain that would be appropriate, Ms. Berry,"

he began in his best banker voice, but his niece wasn't going to let him finish.

"I'll call you Holly," Natalie interjected from the region of Drew's knees. Drew looked down in surprise. She didn't usually take to strangers that quickly.

But then, Holly was so engaging that she didn't really seem like a stranger.

"Good!" Holly declared before Drew could come to grips with the fact that he was already thinking of this woman in such friendly terms. "You must be Natalie," Holly said and turned her smile on Drew's niece.

Drew's heartstrings tugged when Natalie nodded shyly and said, "I am." The little girl's brow puckered for a moment.

"What is it?" Holly prompted with concern before Drew could ask. Natalie bit her lip and Holly leaned closer, raising one fingertip to her lips. "You can whisper it to me," she confided, "if you need to."

Natalie glanced at her uncle, then stepped toward Holly to do exactly that. Drew's chest clenched.

"Do those bells ring?" Natalie pointed at Holly's earrings.

Holly smiled. "Let's find out." She deliberately shook her head. The movement filled the foyer with the sparkling sound of tiny bells ringing, and Natalie gasped with delight.

Then Holly laughed again as she tugged the earrings from her earlobes and held them out to Natalie.

"Here. You can have them."

"Can I? Really?" Natalie's eyes were round with wonder.

"Of course!" Holly fitted the clip-ons to an enraptured Natalie's tiny ears with nimble fingers.

But Drew couldn't let her do this. "Ms. Berry, you're very generous, but . . ."

"But nothing," Holly interrupted Drew flatly. "Natalie likes them and I want her to have them." She closed the clasp on the second earring and sat back on her heels. Natalie shook her head tentatively, her eyes shining when that sound filled the foyer once more. Her lips parted and Drew held his breath.

But Natalie bit back what might have become a smile. Drew's heart sank as his niece danced away, shaking her head to make the bells ring even more.

It was a lovely gesture, but he couldn't let Natalie accept the gift. It was inappropriate.

Drew lowered his voice so that his niece wouldn't hear his protest. "But Ms. Berry, I really must insist . . ."

Holly straightened, brushed off her trim burgundy trousers, and met Drew's gaze steadily. She was nearly as tall as he and she smelled faintly of peppermint.

Drew's heart chose this very illogical moment to skip a beat, and his words, quite uncharacteristically, faltered in mid-argument.

"Mr. Sinclair," she said firmly, her voice pitched low. "This has nothing to do with whether or not you choose to hire me." She looked into his eyes and Drew saw sincerity shining in her face. "Natalie can have the earrings either way."

"But"—Drew frowned—"you don't need to do this."

"Of course I don't!" Holly's lips curved into a beguiling smile. She leaned closer to tap a fingertip on his perfectly knotted tie, and Drew caught his breath. "Haven't you heard, Mr. Sinclair? It's *Christmas*, a season of giving, a season for making little girls and boys smile."

Could Holly really make Natalie smile again? It had been so long, Drew was halfway certain his niece never would smile, much less laugh, again.

But she had already taken to Holly in a big way.

Natalie came running down the hall at that moment, the tinkling of the bells along with her. "Can I keep them, Unca Drew? Can I?"

The last of Drew's resistance to the gift disappeared when he noticed the shine in Natalie's eyes. "That's what Ms. Berry says," he conceded gruffly. "Now, remember your manners."

Natalie turned to Holly and folded her hands before her. "Thank you very much, Holly, for the jingle bell earrings," she said, then reached out and impulsively touched Holly's hand. Her gaze met Drew's and then flicked away, as her words fell in a breathless rush. "I hope you stay *forever!*"

As though embarrassed by this confession, Natalie fled into the kitchen. Drew blinked and watched her go.

It seemed that Holly already had one vote in her favor.

Holly smiled. "She's absolutely adorable," she murmured and turned that smile on Drew as though giving him the credit.

It made absolutely no sense, but Drew felt warm right to his toes. He wasn't impulsive, of course, but there was something about Holly—and Natalie's response to her—that made Drew suspect that she might be the perfect candidate for this job. Naturally, he'd have to take a few moments to check Holly's references before making his decision.

But a part of Drew knew the decision was already made. He ushered Holly into his office and hoped fiercely that there were no surprises in the envelope he held.

Oddly enough, the fax machine began to beep an error message as soon as Holly stepped into the room. Drew apologized and crossed the room to reset the machine.

He arrived just in time to catch the blank sheet of paper that the machine spewed onto the floor. To his astonishment, that was just the beginning of a barrage of sheets that spilled out in rapid succession. He snatched them out of the air and pushed the Reset button, but the machine beeped merrily and kept on flinging paper at him with what seemed to be joyful abandon.

Drew pushed Reset again and again, but to no avail—paper continued to cascade out. He wondered what sort of an idiot Holly must think he was. He felt his ears grow hot and bit back a curse as the machine blithely ignored his efforts to silence it. Finally Drew bent and pulled the plug out of the wall socket.

To his relief, the machine subsided with one last defiant beep.

He turned to Holly, only to find that she looked more

startled than he was. When their gazes met, Drew indulged his urge to smile at her.

He did so only to reassure her that this sort of thing didn't happen all the time, of course. The last thing he wanted was for her to decline this job.

In fact, Drew felt a sudden urgency to hire her as soon as possible. It must be because Natalie liked her so much. Or because he had already moved his nine-thirty business appointment twice and couldn't possibly do it again.

Or maybe it was because Holly Berry truly had the most intriguing eyes of any woman Drew had ever met.

"I'm sorry about the interruption," he said with all the charm he could muster. Drew knew he didn't look quite as credible as he would have liked, what with all the loose paper clutched in his hands. "I don't know what went wrong."

To Drew's disappointment, Holly didn't smile back. She bit her lip and took the seat he indicated, her glance darting to the subdued fax machine.

Almost guiltily.

But that made no sense at all.

Maybe she was just nervous.

Well, he could do something about that. Drew decisively chucked the paper into the recycling bin and set about getting the formalities out of the way.

TWO

An hour later, Holly was still shaken by her response to Drew Sinclair's smile. It was just because she had never seen a mortal man smile, she told herself as Natalie waved good-bye to her uncle from the living room window.

It was just because Holly hadn't expected this man to *ever* smile. It must have been surprise that made her heart go *thumpity-thump* in her ears.

It wouldn't happen again. Holly just knew it. She was here to do a job, and she was going to do it right. All the same, the house felt oddly empty once Drew's car had disappeared around the corner.

Natalie didn't seem to share Holly's view. She took Holly's hand and tugged her toward the stairs. "Come on! I'll show you your room."

Holly scooped up her bag on the way through the foyer and followed the little girl to the third floor of the house. Natalie ran ahead on the last flight of stairs and disappeared into the only doorway at the summit. Holly followed and caught her breath on the threshold.

One big room filled the space beneath the eaves, and

winter sunlight slanted through the skylights. The ceiling
was sloped, all of it wallpapered in a yellow-and-blue floral
print. The furniture was bleached pine, the mood welcom-
ing.

"This is for me?"

"And you have a bathroom, too." Natalie indicated the
bath en suite, then bounced on the bed. Holly unpacked her
things and tried to look as though this was perfectly normal
for her.

Even though she didn't know what was in her bag. It
was hard to keep from gasping with delight as she unfolded
each garment Mrs. C. had provided.

"I'm hungry," Natalie declared abruptly.

Holly vaguely recalled something about mortals *needing*
to eat. Elves merely snacked when the mood struck them
and often went for months—particularly during the demanding pre-holiday season—without eating anything at
all.

Holly wondered *what* mortals ate.

And how often.

She tried to sound nonchalant. "What would you like to
eat?"

Natalie didn't even need to consider this. "A peanut butter sandwich."

Whatever peanut butter was. Holly glanced around her
room and couldn't see anything that looked edible, much
less that could have been called peanut butter.

Natalie snorted. "You're being silly," she charged. "We
have to go to the *kitchen*!"

Ah, the kitchen. But where was that? Fortunately, Natalie
headed for the stairs, apparently intent on showing the way.

The kitchen in question proved to be a white expanse of
surprisingly alien territory lurking behind the swinging door
at one end of the foyer. Gleaming gadgets with coiled electrical cords lined the counter, there were stacks of dishes
of varying sizes within the cabinet that Holly opened, and
a good dozen more cabinets lined the wall.

Holly was overwhelmed. The occasional steaming mug

of reindeer-milk cocoa had never required so many tools to make.

But there wasn't even one reindeer in the carefully cultivated backyard, and Holly wasn't quite sure how to proceed.

Natalie seemed to have no doubts, however. She opened a door in the front of a large white box—not without some difficulty—and stretched up on her toes.

"It's back there."

Holly was surprised to find the machine lit inside and full of all sorts of tempting tidbits. At the back was a jar with little bears on the label, which said "peanut butter."

Aha!

"I have to have milk for lunch, too."

Reindeer milk was good for little elves, so it made sense that it was good for little mortals, too. Holly reached for the carton of milk, grateful that she didn't have to hunt down those missing reindeer to milk them.

"I can help," Natalie insisted and pulled a stool up to the counter. She reached into a bag and pulled out two slices of bread, laying them flat on the cutting board. "You, too?"

Holly opened the jar and took a sniff. This peanut butter smelled wonderful! She nodded agreement. "We'll have lunch together."

Natalie began busily spreading the peanut butter on the bread, apparently the first step in making sandwiches—which was a good thing, since Holly knew nothing about the construction of peanut butter sandwiches.

It looked as if she would have to learn.

Over the crumbs and empty milk glasses, Natalie met Holly's gaze. "What should we do this afternoon?"

What exactly did nannies do? Holly wished, a bit too late, that she had read her résumé before handing it over to Mr. Sinclair. It might have provided a few much-needed clues. "What do you usually do in the afternoons?"

"Go back to school," Natalie said with a little frown. "But Unca Drew said that I could stay home all day today to see the nannies. Tomorrow I have to go back.''

''Hmm.'' Holly smiled. ''Maybe we should take the chance to get to know each other a bit better, then.''

Natalie's face brightened at the prospect, but she simply waited expectantly. Holly suddenly recalled the little girl's delight with the earrings and had the perfect idea. ''You don't have your Christmas decorations up yet.''

The little girl's gaze slid away. ''Unca Drew said he didn't have time,'' she admitted in a small voice. Natalie shrugged as though she were indifferent, but Holly wasn't fooled.

And she wasn't amused in the least.

No *time* for Christmas! Of all the selfish excuses! What kind of person would deny a child the joy of the holidays for the sake of his own convenience?

Holly had a sneaking suspicion that she had just been hired by exactly that kind of person. After all, she had already had to explain the meaning of the season to the man.

Oh, she could just spit! Her first impression of Mr. Sinclair had been exactly right!

And that was not good news, Holly realized with dawning horror. Because if Drew Sinclair didn't believe in Christmas, would he believe in love or marriage? Holly couldn't imagine that he would.

And if he didn't believe in *that*, why would he ever ask Katherine O'Neill to marry him?

Oh, no! Faced with the distinct possibility of failure, Holly took a deep breath and squared her shoulders. Mr. C. had trusted her with the job, after all. Holly could do it.

Holly *had* to do it.

For Natalie.

And she would have to start at the very beginning. Holly got up from the table and collected the dirty dishes, fighting to hide her annoyance from a little girl who she suspected was very perceptive.

''Fortunately, *we* have lots of time today,'' she declared with cheerful resolve. ''Let's do the decorating, just the two of us. That way, your uncle won't have to worry about a thing." She winked at Natalie. "We'll surprise him."

Natalie frowned with unexpected concern. "But we don't have any money."

Holly blinked. "Money?"

"We need money," Natalie insisted with a solemnity beyond her years. "Unca Drew didn't give you any."

That he hadn't.

Whatever money was.

The gleam of hope in the blue glance the little girl slanted through her lashes made Holly determined to find some. She wondered whether she would be lucky enough that Mr. and Mrs. C had planned for this eventuality.

After all, that résumé had been tucked inside her purse, just waiting. Could she have been granted a magic bag, one that conjured up anything she might need? Holly retrieved her purse and rummaged in it, hoping she looked purposeful. There were tissues, a few mint candies, a comb, and a small leather folder with a clasp.

Nothing else. Holly's heart sank. This wasn't a magic purse, after all.

Just when she could have really used one.

Natalie peered into the purse with open curiosity. "There's your wallet," she contributed with the seriousness that Holly was beginning to associate with the child. When Holly looked up, Natalie pointed to the leather folder.

Holly dug the wallet out and opened it, almost afraid to look. There was a slot along one side, and she cracked it open enough to peer inside. A lot of pieces of green paper were tucked neatly in there, but before Holly could wonder, Natalie gasped.

"You have *lots* of money!" she said with evident awe. Then she raised shining eyes to Holly. "This could be the *bestest* Christmas ever."

Holly decided at that very moment that she would make it so.

She smiled. "Then we'd better get started. This is a big house and there's a lot to be done."

Holly carried the dirty dishes to the sink and hesitated. There was no hand pump for water and no bucket. But

Natalie opened a door in the lower cabinet with the familiarity of habit and reached for the plates. Holly eyed the stainless-steel interior dubiously.

Her charge evidently noticed her surprise.

"Don't you have a dishwasher?" Natalie asked, seemingly unable to imagine such a possibility. Holly shook her head, knowing she'd never seen such a contraption and instinctively distrusting whatever it might do.

Even without her influence.

"It washes the dishes for you," Natalie explained. Holly had never liked washing dishes, and so was fascinated despite herself. She had a good look from a few steps away, not wanting to tempt the machine to do anything bizarre.

"I thought *everybody* had a dishwasher." Natalie stacked the dishes inside as though she did it all the time.

She probably did. Natalie closed the dishwasher door and Holly braced herself.

But nothing happened.

Nothing at all.

And the kitchen was sparkling clean once more.

Holly could definitely get used to peanut butter sandwiches and dishwashers. In fact, the mortal world had definite promise—the marked exception being Natalie's curmudgeon of an uncle.

Well, Holly would have him straightened out in no time at all. This house would be more festive than the North Pole workshop itself by the time she was done.

Drew Sinclair didn't have a chance.

It had been a miserable day.

And Drew was bone-tired. He supposed everyone had rough days, but he didn't like having one himself. As Drew drove home in the early-winter darkness, tired from conference calls and confrontations, too late for a decent dinner, he had a sense that there was something missing in his life.

He still believed with all his heart in the initiative he had personally begun within the bank, even if it wasn't easy. Maybe *because* it wasn't easy.

Drew believed in lending to small businesses. He loved their enthusiasm, their dedication, their creativity. He liked making his bank a part of their success.

All the same, Drew took it as a personal failure whenever a loan went sour. He didn't like making mistakes, and he didn't like being wrong.

Not one bit.

Not that he hadn't tried. He had worked like a dog the last two months to help this business succeed. But the fact was, Drew couldn't solve O'Neill Leathergoods' cash flow problems alone.

But Drew didn't have to like it.

He also didn't like being told that something he had seen with his own eyes was "impossible." That's what the fax machine service guy had said. Drew ground his teeth and turned the corner to his street, resolving to fix the damn thing himself this weekend.

It was especially irritating that he had missed dinner with Natalie tonight. Drew had felt guilty calling to tell Holly he would be late—it was her first day, after all—and he knew he shouldn't have been surprised to find her tone a bit frosty.

He certainly shouldn't have been disappointed.

And after this, Holly probably thought he was some kind of a workaholic. That bothered Drew as much as being late did, although there was absolutely no reason why he should worry what the new nanny thought of him.

But it bugged him all the same. He hadn't been able to stop thinking about the sparkle of her unusual eyes all day long.

All in all, Drew was *not* in a good mood as he pulled into the driveway. He sat for a moment and studied the house that he called home.

It didn't look very homey. In fact, it looked a bit austere. All those softening touches that made a house feel like a home just weren't Drew's forte.

He sighed and leaned back in his seat. He didn't like being single, he didn't like going to bed alone, he didn't like that there was no one he could talk to about whatever

had happened in his day. He certainly hadn't planned for
life to work out this way.

But Drew had just never met the Right Woman.

And he sure as hell wasn't going to spend his life with
the wrong one.

He gave his head a shake and reached for his briefcase.
One bad day didn't make his whole life a failure. The emptiness in him was just in his belly, he was sure. He had
forgotten to eat lunch, after all, and it was late. Drew hefted
his briefcase and trudged up the steps. Too bad he was too
late to read Natalie a bedtime story and tuck her in. He
grimaced and his mood soured a little more.

Those moments were precious to him.

Drew unlocked the front door of his home and was struck
by a wave of cinnamon, cloves, and allspice. He took a
deep breath and halfway smiled. The scent conjured memories of himself and Greg tumbling into the kitchen after
school to find freshly baked Christmas cookies.

But no one baked cookies in this house.

Especially not Christmas cookies.

Drew frowned. What was going on? He pushed the door
fully open and was stunned by the sight that met his eyes.

His tastefully conservative hall had been decked out in
cedar roping hung with big red-plaid bows. The same festive garland wound its way around the bannister and up the
stairs, with candy canes and Christmas balls spaced along
the length of it. The door to his office sported a wreath with
brass bells and another fat red bow that Drew knew hadn't
been there this morning.

None of this had been here this morning, and none of it
had been dragged out of his basement storage. Drew's lips
thinned. He set down his briefcase with a thud of disapproval and hauled off his topcoat, determined to get to the
bottom of this before things got worse.

Because someone had been busily breaking the one un-
alterable rule of his household.

And Drew had a very good idea who it was. He should
never have hired a nanny impulsively!

Drew stormed toward the kitchen, purpose in every step,

and flung open the swing door. In the nick of time he saw Natalie and bit back his expletive, quickly swallowing another right after it.

What was she doing up at this hour? His whole household had gone to hell while he was at work!

"What in the heck is going on around here?" he roared.

Silence descended on the kitchen with breathtaking speed. Drew scanned the damage. The usually gleaming expanse of marble countertop was generously littered with half-finished popcorn strings. Trees cut from green construction paper, with rows of sparkles and stars haphazardly glued onto them, were scattered everywhere.

Some of the sparkles had stuck to Natalie, who was sitting at a stool on the other side of the counter, and an errant gold star clung to her cheek like a distinctive freckle. There was a smear of chocolate on her chin, and in one hand she held a gingerbread cookie shaped like a heart.

Her expression was alarmed, her eyes fixed on Drew, but his argument was not with his niece.

It was with the faintly flushed nanny who held a steaming tray of cookies, her hands encased in oven mitts shaped like Rudolph's head. Holly had sparkles in her hair and flour across her sweater, but the laughter that had tweaked her ruby lips this morning was absent.

She looked even softer and warmer than she had this morning and was without a doubt the most perfectly alluring woman Drew had ever found in his kitchen. He clamped down on his inappropriate response before it, too, could get out of hand.

Holly stared at him as if uncertain what he would do.

"I asked you what was going on," Drew repeated coldly.

Holly licked her lips, glanced around the kitchen, then summoned a defiant smile. "We're getting ready for Christmas," she declared, then squared her shoulders.

There was a glint in her wondrous eyes that told Drew she had already guessed that this would not go uncontested. He was forced to admire the fact that she held her ground and was apparently ready to fight for what she thought was right.

But Holly Berry was dead wrong.

And Drew was going to make sure she understood that. Right now.

"We don't decorate for Christmas here," Drew informed her, his tone positively glacial. "Period."

A frown flickered across Holly's brow, but she lifted her chin. "Natalie said you didn't have time. I thought that she and I could take care of things today, and we've made great progress . . ."

"I *make* time for the things that matter," Drew retorted. "And this isn't one of them." He glared at Holly, willing her to accept his house rule without further argument.

They had had a full year without Natalie's nightmares, and Drew intended to keep it that way.

But the new nanny wasn't going to let the matter go.

"Not one of them! How can you even say such a thing?" Holly dropped the tray of cookies on the stove with a bang.

"We have one rule and one rule only," Drew retorted. "We do not celebrate Christmas."

"That's cruel!" Holly propped her oven-mitt-encased hands on her hips and her eyes flashed. The move accentuated the narrowness of her waist, and the bit of flour on the end of her nose made her look far from a worthy adversary. "That's unfair and it's *wrong*!"

Drew had to admire how she stuck to her guns. He folded his arms across his chest and summoned his fiercest glare.

Holly advanced on him, clearly undeterred. "Mr. Sinclair, I have to disagree with you on this. Surely there's no harm in enjoying the spirit of the season . . ."

"There *is* harm. Plenty of it."

"Mr. Sinclair! You're being unreasonable!" Holly yanked off the oven mitts and closed the distance between them with quick steps. Her voice lowered in appeal. "Christmas is for children, Mr. Sinclair, it's a magical time of the year. Whatever your own memories are, think of what this means to Natalie!"

"I *am* thinking of Natalie!"

Holly paled and she held herself stiffly. "That seems unlikely," she challenged softly.

Drew ràked a hand through his hair, feeling like the grinch caught in the act of stealing Christmas. But he had no choice.

"Get rid of it all," he said grimly. "Now."

Holly's eyes widened in horror and she backed away. The way her eyes darkened told Drew that she did not think much of his attitude.

Or of him.

But he was doing this for Natalie! Drew took a step in pursuit, suddenly needing to explain everything, to make Holly understand the reason for his concern. He'd gone about this all wrong, courtesy of his hellish day, but surely Holly would agree with him once she knew . . .

"Unca Drew!" Natalie wailed and Drew remembered— too late—that the object of his concern was still in the kitchen.

How could he have forgotten that she was listening?

Drew turned to his niece, hoping that he could somehow make this better. "Natalie," he said in a softer tone, "I think it's for the best."

Natalie's bottom lip trembled and her eyes filled with tears. "But Unca Drew, I'm having fun!"

Drew's heart wrenched, but he couldn't let her have those nightmares again. He loosened his tie and squatted down beside her.

"Punkin, I don't want you to be afraid . . ."

"I'm *not* afraid!" Natalie cried. "I like Christmas. And I hate that we don't have it anymore!"

And with that she flung herself past Drew and ran out of the room. He hung his head in defeat as her footsteps pounded on the stairs.

Oh, he had handled that well, there was no doubt about it. It had been a four-star kind of a day—and it wasn't getting any better soon.

"Afraid of what?" Holly demanded softly.

Drew looked up to find the condemnation had melted out of Holly's expression, and was replaced with curiosity. That alone made him feel a little better.

"Why on earth is she afraid of Christmas?" The uncertainty in Holly's words made Drew realize that she already cared about Natalie.

Holly had just tried to do something festive with a little girl, a little girl who otherwise would have every reason to be excited about Christmas. Holly hadn't known the reason why that couldn't be.

She *couldn't* have known—because Drew hadn't told her. It was his own fault, for not explaining things this morning. Drew sighed, stared at the floor, and decided it was better late than never.

"Two years ago, my brother's house burned to the ground," he confessed flatly. Holly caught her breath, but Drew didn't even glance up. His chest was tight with the memory of that night and what had come after it. "He and his wife were killed, but Natalie escaped, with very serious burns."

Holly gasped softly but didn't interrupt him.

Drew swallowed and resolutely kept his gaze on the floor. "It was Christmas."

"Oh, Mr. Sinclair. I am sorry." There was no doubt in Drew's mind that Holly's apology came from the heart. He looked up now and saw the dismay in her eyes. "I never imagined . . ."

"No, you couldn't have known." Drew pushed himself to his feet and shoved his hands into his pockets, feeling that familiar emptiness flood through him one more time. He had never talked to anyone about that night.

There had never been anyone to talk to.

Drew frowned, shoving his own wounds aside, and forced himself to continue, matter-of-factly, "We don't have Christmas because I don't want to remind her of it all."

Holly crossed the floor quickly and laid a hand on Drew's arm. He felt guilty for treating her unfairly and wished he could just start all over again.

"I'm sorry," he said quietly and stared at his wing tips. "You didn't know. I shouldn't have lost my temper."

Holly smiled. "Don't apologize for being protective of someone you love, Mr. Sinclair."

He did love Natalie. And Drew found himself very relieved that Holly understood exactly what had made him
angry. Her words eased Drew's conviction that he had
screwed up every single thing that had come his way today.

Maybe hiring a nanny impulsively was one thing that
had come out right.

Holly turned and spread her arms wide to take in the
whole room. "Mr. Sinclair, if you had come in here a bit
differently, you would have seen what a wonderful time
Natalie was having. Look at all she's done today!"

At her urging, Drew did look.

This time, instead of seeing a broken rule, he saw all the
hours Natalie had spent cutting out trees and sticking on
sparkles. A lump rose in his throat when he realized that it
had been a small helper who decided that chocolate sprinkles had to be on every single cookie.

"She said she missed Christmas and that you were
busy," Holly said quietly. "I'm sorry. I thought you just
couldn't be bothered, and it was so very important to her."
She took a breath. "I just wanted to make her happy."

Had she been happy? Drew knew he had to ask the question—just as he knew Holly would tell him the truth. "Did
she smile?"

Holly shook her head slightly, then frowned. "A couple
of times, I thought she might, but she never did." She
looked into Drew's eyes with concern. "Does she? Ever?"

"Not since that night," Drew admitted and felt better
just having the opportunity to voice his concern. He had
had no one to ask, no one with whom he could compare
notes, and children certainly didn't come with instructions.

Surely if Drew had been a good enough "father" to
Natalie, she would have smiled *once*?

Holly leaned closer, her silver eyes shining with reassurance. "None of us can erase the past, Mr. Sinclair, but
we have to go on to the future. Natalie *is* healing."

Drew frowned. "I'm not so sure."

"You should be, Mr. Sinclair. It says a lot that Natalie's
ready to have Christmas again, and she is." Holly paused
for a telling moment.

Then she tilted her head to watch his response to her next softly uttered words. "But the question is, are you?"

Drew scowled and surveyed the kitchen once more. It seemed very important that he answer Holly honestly. But he simply wasn't sure how much of his anger had been protectiveness of his niece and how much had been his own pain resurfacing.

Finally, Drew shrugged and met Holly's unswerving gaze. "I don't know." He ran a hand through his hair. "I just don't know."

Holly smiled, a soft smile that seemed just for him, and Drew felt a little less empty inside. Her fingers tightened on his arm and he was suddenly very glad that she was here.

His worries seemed a little less daunting now that he had voiced them.

"I'm sorry that I didn't know the whole story sooner, Mr. Sinclair. Believe me, I would never have surprised you this way."

"I do believe you." As soon as he uttered the words, Drew knew they were true. Their gazes held for a long, breathless moment that awakened a tingle of awareness within Drew. He eyed those fragile fingers against the navy of his suit, the softness of those lips that could not seem to stop smiling, the warmth and caring shining in those silver eyes.

He wondered suddenly what it would be like to kiss Holly Berry.

Drew frowned at the inappropriateness of his thought. "I should go to Natalie," he said gruffly and stepped away.

But Holly's allure did not diminish with distance.

"Give me a moment with her," Holly suggested easily. "Take off your jacket and have a cookie." Her smile broadened. "Mr. Sinclair, Natalie will be just fine." Holly exuded such certainty that Drew actually believed her.

Not only that, he found himself tentatively smiling back.

"Call me Drew," he said impulsively.

Before he could wonder what had gotten into him, Holly's smile widened and a dimple made an appearance in one cheek. Drew was sure he'd never seen anyone so pretty in all his life.

"Drew, then," she said and wrinkled her nose playfully.

Drew liked the sound of his name falling from those red lips. Holly winked and brushed past him, calling "Natalie!" as she darted up the stairs.

Her light footfalls echoed on the hardwood floor overhead as Drew looked around the kitchen once more. The funny thing was that the familiar ache inside him didn't seem to be quite so hollow as usual.

Nor nearly as big. In fact, Drew decided he *would* have a cookie. They smelled awfully good.

And they *were* good. Drew leaned against the counter, loosened his tie, and let a deluge of memories tumble through his mind as he chewed. He let himself think of Greg, of snowball fights on the way home from school, of a thousand precious moments, and found himself smiling at the memory of his brother for the first time in two years.

Drew treated himself to another cookie, shaking his head at someone's diligence—he could guess whose—in providing the snowman with eyes, nose, mouth, eyebrows, ears, and hair.

All in chocolate sprinkles. These were probably the most enthusiastically decorated cookies Drew had ever eaten. But he ate the second and a third nevertheless, savoring their taste as well as the care with which they had been made.

And as Drew stood in his unusually chaotic kitchen, he had a sudden thought. Maybe, just maybe, Natalie wasn't the only one around here who had been missing Christmas.

THREE

Holly leaned around the doorjamb and watched her tiny charge sniffle. She was humbled by the concern she had seen in her new employer's eyes and felt horrible that she had so impulsively jumped into the middle of a situation that she didn't understand.

Drew wasn't coldhearted—he was just very protective of a vulnerable child. And Holly found herself admiring him for that.

It seemed that her talent for making a muddle of things was getting even worse.

"Natalie," she murmured softly, hoping she could make this right. The little girl sat up at the call, clutching a very well-worn teddy bear to her chest as though he would protect her from harm.

She looked balefully at Holly. "You made Unca Drew mad," she accused.

"I did." Holly nodded and stepped into the room. She put her hands in her apron pockets. "I'm sorry, Natalie. I made a big mistake."

Natalie hugged her bear tighter, and Holly, thinking a

change of subject might be in order, asked, "Who's that?"

To Holly's relief, Natalie brightened. "It's Mr. Bumbles. He's my bestest friend in the whole world." She fiddled with the bear's paw for a long moment.

When she finally continued, her voice became so quiet that Holly had to bend down to hear her words. "Sometimes Mr. Bumbles has bad dreams about the fire."

Holly guessed that Mr. Bumbles hadn't had those nightmares alone and only now understood the fullness of Drew's concern. She couldn't blame him in the least for being angry.

"That's terrible," she said quietly. "I sometimes have bad dreams too, so I know how he feels."

Natalie looked up. "You do?"

Holly nodded. "It can be pretty scary."

Natalie looked back at the bear. "When I was little, I used to have bad dreams too, but not anymore."

"Good for you."

"It's 'cuz of the magic chair."

Holly's eyes widened in surprise. She didn't realize that mortals knew how to work magic. "You have a magic chair?"

"Uh-huh." Natalie pointed to an old white rocker in the corner of her room. It didn't look very magical to Holly, but you could never be sure. "When I had my bad dreams, Unca Drew would come and I would sit on his knee in the magic chair and he would tell me how it would make all my bad dreams go away." She lifted her chin proudly. "And they did, just like Unca Drew said."

At Natalie's words, any lingering reservations Holly had about Drew melted away. There were a lot of elves in this world who wouldn't have been so thoughtful of a child's fears, never mind busy mortals.

Holly perched on the side of the bed. "You're very lucky. Magic chairs are hard to find."

"I know." Natalie nestled closer to Holly. "If you have a bad dream, you can come and use my magic chair. I don't mind."

"Oh, that makes me feel much better." Holly smiled at

· this unexpected offer. Now she was doubly determined to see that Natalie's Christmas wish for a new mommy came true. "Thank you."

Holly leaned toward the little girl and put a tentative hand on Natalie's shoulder. To her relief, Natalie snuggled in closer. "And if you ever want anyone to sit in your magic chair with you, or with Mr. Bumbles, you can call me," Holly murmured. "It doesn't matter when."

Natalie looked up, then nodded. "Okay. But only if Unca Drew can't come. He knows how to make it work best."

Holly's heart twisted. Could she possibly have misjudged Drew any more seriously than she had?

Low words from the hall interrupted Holly's thoughts.

"Maybe we could finish those decorations together this weekend."

Holly looked up to find Drew in the doorway. He had loosened his tie and discarded his jacket. His chestnut hair was tousled, and his eyes weren't quite as shadowed as they had been in the kitchen.

He really was quite an alluring mortal. Holly's mouth went dry. The corner of Drew's lips tugged upward slightly, his gaze dancing between her and Natalie, and he almost smiled.

They were a pair, these two, with their hard-won smiles! Holly fervently hoped that Drew had overheard Natalie's testimony of his magic-chair competence.

"Finish them?" Natalie echoed as though she were afraid to hope.

Her uncle nodded firmly. "If we don't finish them, how can we hang them up?"

"We can hang them up? Really?" Natalie erupted from the bed and crossed the room in a flash. "Really? Can we? We don't have to get rid of them?"

"Not if you don't want to."

"I don't want to!" Natalie crowed with delight.

She latched on to Drew's leg and hugged him tightly. When he crouched down beside her, Natalie smiled.

Holly saw Drew's eyes widen, saw him try to hide his astonishment so he wouldn't startle his niece. His gaze flicked to meet hers and Holly let her delight show in her own smile.

Drew cleared his throat and tousled Natalie's hair with one affectionate hand. "Maybe we should have Christmas again this year," he suggested.

Natalie's approval of that was more than clear. "I already wrote Santa!"

"You did. I hope you've been good."

She smiled again. "Mr. Bumbles said so." Natalie's response should be more than enough to reassure Drew that his niece truly was ready for Christmas again.

"Well, then," Drew said sagely, "we can't have Santa coming to a house that isn't ready for Christmas. Good thing Holly's here to help." And when Natalie hugged him tightly, Drew winked at Holly with a playfulness so unexpected that her heart skipped a beat.

A most alluring mortal indeed. And it wasn't just his smile.

Drew's voice lowered as he set Natalie on her feet, and his gaze rose once again to meet Holly's. "I'm sorry I got mad, punkin."

The light in his eyes told Holly that this apology was for her, too. She felt herself flush a little bit at the warmth in Drew's gaze and she smiled at him, hoping he understood that she understood.

Natalie nodded, then bounced Mr. Bumbles on her uncle's knee. Her mind was clearly on more important matters than apologies. "Can we hang the decorations in the kitchen? Can we? And some more in the hall? Holly liked those plant ones, but I wanted to make some *special* decorations. Can I, Unca Drew, can I?"

"Sure." Drew's grin flashed at his niece's enthusiasm. He tapped a fingertip on her nose. "You can do anything you want."

That smile took a curtain call. "I'll make the very bestest one of all for your office, Unca Drew!" Natalie punctuated her declaration with a wet kiss on his cheek.

Drew's smile flashed more broadly than it had thus far, and the tension eased out of his shoulders. Holly's heart did its *thumpity-thump* again and showed no signs of calming down anytime soon.

"You've got yourself a deal, punkin. Christmas is back." Drew stood up and propped Natalie on his hip. His manner turned serious as he held up a finger. "But we've got to have one rule that no one can break, okay?"

He impaled Holly with a look that told her not to cross the line he was going to lay down.

She nodded mute agreement to whatever his terms might be. If nothing else, Holly already knew Drew would be fair and his request would be justified.

"No lights," he said firmly. "All right?"

Natalie seemed untroubled by this demand, and Holly quickly acquiesced.

Drew winked at her, then frowned with mock sternness at his niece. "Isn't it awfully late for you to be up? Tomorrow's a school day, after all."

"But I had my bath!"

"I can tell." Drew wiped the smear of chocolate off Natalie's chin with one strong fingertip and gave her a wry smile. "And what did you have for dinner?"

"Peanut butter sandwiches. Holly makes the bestest ones."

"I'll bet she does," Drew said softly.

To Holly's surprise, her new employer's gaze turned to her. The way he smiled directly into her eyes made Holly feel very feminine. And now there was a funny tingling in her belly.

Never mind the pounding of her heart.

She obviously wasn't used to mortal men. Or maybe this strange feeling was just because she was relieved.

That must be it! After all, Holly didn't have to thaw Drew Sinclair out—which meant she could move right along with making Natalie's wish come true.

First thing tomorrow morning, Holly was going to find Katherine O'Neill. The good news was that she wouldn't have to be up half the night washing up the mess from making those cookies.

Because Natalie had shown her the dishwashing machine.

The next morning, Drew did something he couldn't remember ever having done before.

He overslept. It was true that he and Holly had taken a while to clean up the kitchen after Natalie was in bed—just as it was true that Drew hadn't rushed the process.

A kitchen couldn't be too clean, after all.

And it was true that Drew had found himself thinking about a certain intriguing nanny long after he should have been asleep. Clearly, he was just impressed that Holly had so quickly coaxed a smile from Natalie.

Clearly, Drew had just been rethinking his strategy with his niece. Holly's arrival had shown him that maybe he hadn't been quite playful enough with Natalie. Playing wasn't something that Drew did instinctively—in fact, it had always been Greg who started their snowball fights.

Maybe it was time he lightened up.

Of course, he had only lain awake to plan an effective strategy for that course of action. His inability to sleep hadn't had anything to do with a certain pair of silvery eyes or a very kissable smile.

That wouldn't have been logical.

The sound of Holly's laughter in the kitchen was what finally awakened Drew that morning. He smiled and stretched leisurely as he opened one eye to glance at the alarm clock.

Drew saw the time, swore, and lunged for the shower.

In record time he was trotting down the stairs, thanking the powers above that this was Casual Friday. Drew glanced in the hall mirror on his way past and straightened his collar, feeling oddly nervous about stepping into his own kitchen.

He opened the door just in time to hear Holly's question.

"What would you think if your Uncle Drew got married?"

He froze on the threshold and watched as Natalie considered the question. The pair were apparently unaware of his arrival. Natalie was already dressed for school in her favorite denim pinafore, and she perched on her stool, watching Holly at work. Holly wore jeans that showed her slender curves to advantage and a red sweatshirt embellished with dancing candy canes.

It looked like Holly was making peanut butter sandwiches again. Drew stifled a smile. Maybe she couldn't cook.

Since Drew loved to cook, that was a flaw he could live with.

Or maybe he could teach Holly.

It would take a very long time, Drew was certain. These things had to be practiced, over and over again.

"I would have a mommy then," Natalie said finally.

Holly wrinkled her nose in the playful way that Drew was starting to find very sexy. "Well, not exactly. An aunt."

"But Unca Drew is my new daddy, so she would be my mommy."

Holly smiled, maybe at the same ring of conviction in Natalie's tone that made Drew smile. "But what would you think of that?"

Natalie nodded vigorously. "I'd like it."

"Maybe someone should ask what Unca Drew thinks of that," Drew interjected. Holly pivoted and flushed, her guilty reaction making Drew wonder why she was even asking such a question. Her gaze met his and danced away, her blush deepening in a most interesting fashion.

Could Holly possibly be interested in *him*? Drew's pulse quickened as he watched her fidget.

"We're having peanut butter sandwiches!" Natalie informed him, unaware of any adult subtext.

Drew raised his eyebrows. "Again? You're going to start to look like a peanut." He crossed the room and peeked under her pinafore, as though afraid of what he would see. When he saw she was wearing her striped green leotards, he made a face. "Oh! Remember the picture of the peanut plant in your book? You've got little roots just like it!"

Natalie squealed and examined her legs, her expression

turning tolerant. "Unca Drew, those are just the line things on my leotards."

"Phew!" Drew wiped his brow in mock relief.

"You're silly." His niece giggled. Drew caught his breath at the sound. He looked at Holly, and she smiled encouragement in a way that made him feel giddy and young again.

Then Holly bit her lip. "You don't usually eat peanut butter sandwiches for breakfast?"

"No." Drew tousled his niece's hair. "I think you've been getting biased information."

Natalie grinned and bit into her sandwich. "Holly likes them too."

"For breakfast?" Drew had to ask.

Holly flushed again as she nodded, then an enchanting smile curved her lips. She was definitely a woman challenged on the culinary front. Imagine, living on peanut butter sandwiches!

Natalie would be in seventh heaven.

"Once in a while, I guess it can't hurt." Drew accepted the sandwich Holly offered and took a bite. "You know, you were right, Natalie," he said a moment later. "Holly does make awfully good peanut butter sandwiches."

Holly looked self-consciously pleased. "It's not that hard . . ."

"Ah!" Drew lifted a finger. "Don't be giving away your secrets," he teased, then winked at her.

And Holly not only smiled, she laughed out loud. Then she winked at Natalie. "Your uncle is teasing me," she informed the little girl, who beamed at them both.

"He only does that to people he likes," Natalie declared.

Holly's glance flew to Drew, and he felt the back of his neck heat up. "Don't worry about dinner tonight," he said as casually as he could. "I'll cook."

Holly's eyes widened.

"Don't look so surprised." Drew pretended to be insulted. "I'm a man of many talents. Right, Natalie?"

"Unca Drew cooks nice food."

Holly looked skeptical at this endorsement, then her lips

quirked as she met Drew's gaze again. "Peanut butter sandwiches?"

Drew laughed in turn. "Not a chance. Chinese food."

Holly looked suitably surprised. It wasn't a common
thing to do, Drew knew. "I went to cooking class once,"
he explained. "Szechuan and Cantonese 101. I thought it
would be a great place to meet interesting women." Holly
raised a questioning brow, and Drew's lips twisted at the
memory. "So did the other sixteen guys in the class."

Holly's dimple appeared. "There were *no* women?"

Drew shook his head. "Not a one. Evidently, they were
down the hall in Small Engine Repair." Holly laughed and
he shrugged. "It wasn't such a loss. I still meet a couple
of those guys for racquetball once in a while." He winked.
"We compare brands of oyster sauce."

Holly's eyes continued to shine in a most intriguing way,
but unfortunately Drew couldn't linger here all day. He
glanced at his watch and grimaced. "Do your best at school
today, Natalie."

"Uh-huh. You do your best, too, Unca Drew." Natalie
slipped off her stool to give Drew a sticky kiss good-bye.

"I'll try." Drew found his gaze rising to meet Holly's.
"You'll do your best, too?" he murmured and she grinned.

"I'll try."

Drew nodded and made for the door, pausing halfway
there to glance back, hoping against hope that he could
sound nonchalant. "Oh, and Holly, I think marriage is a
great idea. Always have. I just never found the right woman
to share it with."

Their gazes held for an electric moment, and the stardust
in hers seemed to shimmer. Drew wanted to sit right down
at the kitchen table and spend the entire day talking to
Holly, to hell with loan applications and business plans. He
wanted to watch her smile, he wanted to make her laugh,
he wanted to give her that kiss.

And Drew knew that if he didn't leave right this minute,
he wouldn't be able to leave at all.

Tonight couldn't come soon enough, to his thinking.

At least it was the beginning of a weekend. Drew consoled himself with that thought—and immediately tried to think of a way to persuade Holly to spend her days off with them. He waved and left the kitchen quickly, well aware of Holly's gaze following him.

But Drew wasn't aware of his niece's gasp of delight—much less the little half-smile of anticipation that she kept to herself.

That little girl was quite certain she had just gotten a glimpse of something she wasn't supposed to see.

Natalie was sure that what she'd seen was part of a special Christmas secret that Santa was making just for her. She couldn't imagine how she would be able to wait for Christmas Day.

Because it was clear to Natalie Sinclair that Santa was reading his mail and checking it twice.

Good thing she'd been nice.

Holly opened the dishwasher and made a face at all the dirty dishes still there. "You said it washed the dishes."

Natalie bounced across the room and pointed to the little dish inside the door, more than willing to explain. She liked Holly. A lot. And she especially liked what Holly was going to *be* on Christmas Day.

It wasn't Holly's fault that she'd never had a dishwasher.

"You have to put soap in there and then you close it"—Natalie demonstrated—"and you turn it on with this button." She fixed her nanny with a serious look. "But you have to wait until it's all the way full of dishes, 'cuz Unca Drew says so."

Holly nodded, then peeked inside once more. "It's not full yet," she determined and Natalie had to agree. Holly wrinkled her nose and smiled in that way that made Natalie want to smile back. "We'll let it do its magic tonight."

"Okay." Natalie skipped off to get her coat, convinced that Santa was bringing her the bestest Christmas gift ever.

She had a feeling that Unca Drew was going to think so too.

• • •

Natalie introduced Holly to her teacher, a lovely mortal with golden skin, then ran off to play. Ms. Monteray had eyes so dark they seemed to go on forever, and her manner was so tranquil that Holly was certain she had just met a being of rare wisdom.

After all, Ms. Monteray was a *teacher*.

And finding her was a good thing. Because Holly had a real problem.

She didn't know where to find Katherine O'Neill. Maybe Mr. C. had engineered this encounter as well.

"It's a pleasure meeting you, Holly," Ms. Monteray said smoothly. "I'm glad Mr. Sinclair found you so quickly. Will you be meeting Natalie at noon?"

"Oh, yes, I'll be here." When the teacher nodded and might have stepped away, Holly blurted out her question. "Do you know Katherine O'Neill?"

Ms. Monteray repeated the name, then frowned. "No, I don't think I do. Should I?"

"I don't know. I need to find her."

"Ah!" The teacher smiled. "You're supposed to look someone up. Are you new in the city?"

Holly nodded.

"There's a telephone book in the office." Holly's confusion must have been obvious, because Ms. Monteray pointed to the building entryway. "Right through there, turn right, it's a black door on the left. Ask Marianne for the telephone book."

Thanking the teacher so profusely that the woman looked a little alarmed, Holly dashed off as bidden. The office was a small, drab room in the precise location Ms. Monteray had specified.

"Can I help you?" A silver-haired woman perched before a humming machine peered over her glasses with an unwelcoming look.

"Are you Marianne?" The woman nodded but otherwise did not move. "I'm Natalie Sinclair's new nanny. Ms. Monteray said I could ask you for the telephone book."

The woman's chilly demeanor thawed slightly. She got up, retrieved a thick book, and put it on the counter between them with a thump. She didn't appear to be ready to relinquish it. "Who are you looking for?"

Holly silently sighed with relief. It was no small triumph to have assistance with unfamiliar things. "Katherine O'Neill."

Marianne flipped open the book and fanned through its pages. Holly was amazed by the thin white paper and no less by the tiny type that covered each page. Elvish vision was clearly going to be an asset here.

She squinted and realized that each column sported a name linked to a sequence of numbers. It must be a magic code!

Ms. Monteray was indeed wise to send her this way.

Marianne spread the book open on the counter and ran her fingertip down a column. "Here. O'Neill. Oh, it says to check 'O'Neal' and 'O'Neil.' " She peered over her glasses again. "Do you know which way it's spelled?"

"No."

"Hmmm." Marianne pursed her lips. "Do you know whether it's Katherine with a *C* or with a *K*?"

"No, I don't."

Marianne rolled her eyes and pushed the book toward Holly. "Well, then, you've got a lot of phoning to do. There are fourteen C. O'Neills, twelve K. O'Neills, three C. O'Neils, and four K. O'Neils." Marianne smiled primly. "You're lucky. There were no C. or K. O'Neals."

"Oh." Holly scanned the listings and realized that Marianne was right. She must have looked particularly dejected, because the woman reached over and patted her hand.

"It won't take that long, dear. Here, use the office phone."

And she patted a black device sitting at the end of the counter.

It was clearly a machine.

Holly licked her lips and felt an inkling of dread. What would go wrong when she touched this phone? She hesitated, and Marianne cleared her throat with a trace of her earlier cold manner.

"Honestly, you'll never get finished if you don't get

started.'' She marked the first possibility with her fingertip, picked up the crescent-shaped part of the phone, and put it to her ear. ''You've got to dial a nine first,'' she said matter-of-factly, then poked the button marked ''9.''

Marianne said the numbers out loud from the book and poked them into the machine in sequence. ''There. It's ringing.'' And she handed the crescent-shaped part of the phone to Holly.

Holly gingerly took hold of it and held it to her ear. She had just enough time to be confused by the periodic ringing that came from the device before things got much, much more confusing.

Every single phone in the office began ringing simultaneously. Marianne jumped in alarm, but before she could pick up even one, they all stopped. Then they started again. Within moments the office was filled with a cacophony of phones starting and stopping intermittently, each screaming for attention.

It was enough to make Holly want to cover her ears. She could hear more phones ringing throughout the rest of the building. She strained her elvish hearing and discerned the ringing of phones in the houses that surrounded the school. It seemed that every one of them had come to life at the same time.

Just as suddenly as it had begun, the noise stopped.

The office seemed eerily still after all that ruckus. Even the phone Holly held made no noise at all now.

Marianne picked up the phone on her desk, listened, and frowned. ''There's no dial tone. Something's gone wrong with the service.''

And Holly had a very good idea what that was.

Or at least who was responsible.

Marianne muttered something unflattering about telephone companies, and Holly took the chance to thank her. She scurried away from the school guiltily, wondering how on earth she could fix whatever she had done to the phones.

Let alone how she was going to find Natalie's new mommy.

•   •   •

Drew found himself watching the clock all afternoon. For the first time in a long time—perhaps ever—he couldn't lose himself in the business plans piled on his desk.

His mind kept wandering back to a pair of silvery eyes.

And to precisely what he would make for dinner. He had a funny urge to impress Holly with his cooking. It had been a long time since he'd been looking forward to a woman's company this much. Drew skipped out early to go to the market, the vision of the meal crystal-clear in his mind. He arrived home in record time and practically bounced up the steps.

The wreath on the front door of the house made him smile—Holly and Natalie had been busy again. Drew could see his niece's hand in the glitter glopped onto the pinecones and an artistic sense that he was beginning to associate with Holly in the clustering of those cones.

They made a good pair.

And that thought made his smile broaden. Drew juggled the groceries, managed to extract his keys, and got the door open without dropping anything.

"I'm home!" he called, unable to explain the lightness that had taken his heart hostage.

Drew kicked the door closed just as Holly came out of the kitchen. She seemed to be deliberately avoiding his gaze, but before he could ask what was wrong, she tilted her head toward his office.

"Someone's here to see you," she said softly. Her gaze flicked suddenly to his, and Drew caught a glimpse of unexpected concern. He stepped forward, wanting to solve whatever was bothering her, but Holly simply lifted the groceries out of his hands and stepped away. She looked to the office pointedly once more before disappearing into the kitchen.

Drew frowned, then turned to find the last person he wanted to see waiting in his office.

Katherine O'Neill unfolded her legs and rose elegantly to her feet, her reddened lips curving in a smile that Drew could only call predatory. As always, her suit was impeccable designer fare, every hair was in place, and her accessories were of the finest Italian leather.

Of course.

"Drew!" she chided, as though they were more intimate than they ever had been. "Tsk, tsk! You haven't been returning my calls."

FOUR

Drew snorted, ready to nip this visit right in the bud. "What else do you expect when you default on your loan? It's too late for excuses, Katherine. We've been around and around on this." He noted with satisfaction that her smile faltered ever so slightly. "It's out of my hands now."

"But, Drew, I'm certain we can work something out!"

"I'm not." Drew deliberately did not step across the threshold to enter the office.

"I am," she breathed. Katherine's smile turned sultry, and she stepped close enough for him to catch the scent of her perfume. She was so polished, as perfect as a magazine model, that he wondered whether there was anything real behind the carefully maintained facade.

She fingered his sleeve. "Why don't you and I go for dinner?" she purred. "Just to discuss the possibilities. I've made a reservation at my favorite little French bistro. We can have a less formal chat there." She wrinkled her nose, but the gesture didn't look nearly as sexy as when Holly did it.

The reminder made Drew impatient to get into the

kitchen and begin the evening he was looking forward to. "I have plans."

Katherine arched a brow. "Dinner at home with the child and the nanny?" Her disapproval was more than clear, her own objectives becoming more obvious as her fingertips walked up his sleeve. Her voice lowered. "Come for dinner, Drew. Come play with the adults."

Drew shook off her touch. "We've nothing to talk about, Katherine. We've spent the last two months trying to put together a package that would work and you've missed every single commitment. It's over."

Katherine lifted one brow again. "Unless I can come up with a payment for the bank," she mused.

Drew folded his arms across his chest. "But you don't have the cash. You know it and I know it. That's it, Katherine. They won't play anymore."

"Even if I get a personal endorsement?"

Drew's lips thinned. "At this point, you need cash."

"A loan, then," Katherine murmured with a seductive smile. "A quiet little loan from a very personal friend." Her fingertips traced circles on his sleeve and she leaned closer.

Drew finally did the math. He stepped back in horror. "I'm not lending you any money!"

Katherine pouted. "But Drew . . ."

"But nothing! Katherine, you're way out of line." Drew couldn't believe her nerve. "After what just happened with that loan, how could you imagine that I would *personally* lend you any money?"

"Drew, it wouldn't be much and it wouldn't be for long," Katherine practically begged, her eyes wide with appeal. "Just three months, then my receivables will come in and there'll be the increased sales over the holidays . . ."

"Followed by the retail doldrums in the winter. Forget it, Katherine." Drew shoved a hand through his hair. "I can't believe you're even asking me this."

"It wouldn't be much. Just fifty thousand dollars."

Drew choked on that figure, but Katherine rushed on. "I

know you can afford it—just look at this place. It would be nothing to you and everything to me.''

She gripped his arm and stared deeply into his eyes. ''Drew,'' she whispered, ''you have the power to make my dream come true.''

It seemed rather pedestrian that the dream at the root of this performance was a leather-goods store.

Drew moved away from her. ''I said no.'' He gestured to the door. ''As I mentioned, I do have plans for this evening.''

Katherine straightened, brilliantly playing the role of the wounded innocent, betrayed by a trusted ally. She even managed to summon a tear of disappointment, presumably for his lack of faith.

Drew wasn't impressed.

''I could make it worth your while.''

Drew opened the door.

Katherine's bottom lip trembled. ''It's the only thing I ever wanted,'' she confessed unevenly. She reached for his sleeve. ''That is, besides . . .''

But Drew didn't care about Katherine's dreams. ''Then you should have managed the books better and kept your word, instead of running around spending money that wasn't yours to spend,'' he said quietly. ''Good night, Katherine.''

Katherine inhaled sharply, and Drew thought her eyes flashed. She spun around and snatched up her fur coat, then marched to the door with less than her usual grace.

But by the time she met Drew's gaze, her eyes were softly luminous. He wondered if he had imagined her anger.

''I can't believe you've become so coldhearted, Drew,'' she whispered. Her lashes fluttered to her cheeks and before Drew could fathom what she was going to do, Katherine stretched up on her toes and pressed a kiss to his cheek.

''Think about it, Drew, please.'' She raised one hand and touched his chin as Drew stared at her. ''For *me*.'' Katherine's hand trailed to his chest, her eyes filled with tears, and Drew felt as though he'd been dropped into a play without a copy of the script.

Then suddenly Katherine was gone, leaving Drew blinking on his own doorstep at the strange turn their conversation had taken. He shook his head, locked the door, and
headed for the kitchen.

Enough business already. It was time to get cooking. He
pushed up his sleeves and strode into the kitchen with an
expectant smile.

Holly couldn't explain her lousy mood. She had spent most
of the day unsuccessfully seeking Katherine O'Neill and
was beginning to despair as to how she would fulfill her
mission.

Yet when this gorgeous mortal showed up at the door
and introduced herself as the woman in question, Holly
hadn't been glad to see her.

Not in the least.

It must be because of Natalie. After all, Holly had a hard
time imagining that this woman was mommy material. The
way Katherine had turned up her nose at the sight of Natalie
and instructed Holly to keep the "brat" away from her was
a big clue.

But when Drew strode into the kitchen with a red lipstick
kiss on his cheek and a smile on his face, Holly knew that
the way her heart sank to her toes had nothing to do with
Natalie at all.

It was a relief for Drew to step into the warmth of the
kitchen and put Katherine and her visit behind him. She
was so typical of the women he met—all polish and insin-
cerity, expensive dates each and every one.

Holly, though, was completely different. In the wake of
Katherine's visit, Drew realized that was part of what had
intrigued him about Holly from the very beginning. She
seemed so natural, so sweet and giving, so different from
self-motivated women like Katherine.

And he liked that very much. Natalie launched herself
across the room and gave him a big hug, and he scooped
her up to swing her around. Drew snuck a glance at Holly
and saw that her features were pale and her eyes averted.

What was wrong?

"You've got icky stuff on your face," Natalie accused.

Drew touched his fingers to his cheek, and they came away adorned with red lipstick. He rolled his eyes, swallowed something unflattering about Katherine, and tore off a paper towel. He scrubbed at his cheek, then presented himself to Holly for inspection. "Gone?"

She didn't smile or meet his eyes but simply shook her head no.

Drew rolled his eyes, unwilling to leave the kitchen so soon after he had arrived. "Can you get it for me?"

Holly wet the paper towel and scrubbed off the lipstick with quick gestures. The move brought her close, and Drew smiled as the scent of her skin wound into his nostrils. He was fiercely glad to be home—and determined to convince Holly to spend the weekend with him and Natalie.

Even if she still wouldn't meet his gaze.

Something *was* wrong.

Holly lifted her hand and forced a prim smile. "All gone." She would have moved away, but Drew captured her hand in his and pulled her to a stop.

"What's wrong?" He ran his thumb across Holly's palm, instinctively liking the soft smoothness of her hand in his. "Did something happen today?"

Holly licked her lips and flushed. "Nothing important."

"Tell me," he urged softly.

Holly flicked a glance up at Drew. "Well, I *did* break the phones at the school," she admitted quietly, as though fearful of how he would react.

Drew frowned, not certain that he understood, but Natalie was ready to supply details. "All the phones started ringing all at once when Holly took me to school."

"When I touched one," Holly clarified dejectedly.

She had touched a phone at the moment the system went down and thought herself responsible. Drew's lips twitched despite himself. "But you didn't do it," he assured her and squeezed her fingers.

"Oh, I think I did."

It was hard to fight his smile, but Drew saw that Holly was convinced of her own guilt. "But, Holly, that's impossible. You're blaming yourself for something completely out of your control. Phones *do* stuff like that.''

A hopeful light dawned in Holly's eyes, and Drew caught his breath when she looked up at him. ''Really? Often?''

''Well, no,'' he had to admit. ''Hardly ever, actually, but it happens.'' Drew smiled for her and pulled her a little bit closer. ''And you couldn't possibly have done it.''

''Oh.'' That seemed to reassure her slightly.

Eager to take advantage of the moment, Drew found himself speaking with uncharacteristic haste. ''Holly, I was wondering what your plans were for the weekend.'' She looked perplexed. ''You know, Saturday and Sunday should be your days off and if you have any plans, I certainly would understand, but I was wondering whether you'd like to spend some time with Natalie and me.''

''I have no plans,'' Holly conceded and Drew grinned.

''Well,'' he said, forcing himself to sound stern, ''we have a very serious problem, and it might just be the kind of thing you could help us with.''

''We have no problem,'' Natalie declared loyally.

''Oh, yes, we do, punkin. Have you seen that living room of ours?'' Both nanny and child looked blank, and Drew leaned closer to Holly as he lowered his voice. ''I'm certain it's missing something, but I'm not sure what it is.'' He pursed his lips. ''Something big and green and pine-smelling with shiny stuff all over it.''

''A Christmas tree!'' Natalie squealed. She dove off her stool and danced around the end of the counter. ''We're getting a Christmas tree. Holly, you *have* to help!''

To Drew's relief, Holly didn't look dismayed at the prospect.

In fact, she lifted a warning finger for Natalie. ''But no lights,'' she reminded the little girl, her silvery gaze rising to meet Drew's.

His heart began to pound in a most erratic manner. ''We'll have to go out to a tree farm,'' Drew said and pulled a newspaper clipping from his pocket without releasing Holly's hand. ''And it just so happens that there's one not too far away." No one had to know how long he'd looked to find it. "One with sleigh rides, I'm afraid."

"With horses?" Natalie's eyes went round.

Drew nodded. "With jingle bells." He grimaced. "Probably a lot of candy canes, too. And Christmas cookies."

"And reindeer milk cocoa?" Holly breathed.

Drew laughed. "Well, cocoa of some kind." He gripped her hand tighter. "Will you come?"

Holly smiled so warmly that Drew's uncertainty dissolved. "I'd love to." Drew stared into the shimmers of Holly's eyes and was quite certain there was nowhere else in the world he wanted to be. Her lips parted ever so slightly, and that inappropriate urge to kiss her came back with a vengeance.

Then Natalie interrupted the course of his thoughts. "Who was that icky lady?"

"Someone from work." Drew was dismissive. "She shouldn't have come to the house."

Holly flushed in a most flattering way and actually fidgeted. "She said the phones were out when she tried to call ahead."

This time Drew couldn't stop his chuckle. Holly fought her own smile but lost the battle, and her dimple finally came to light.

"I don't like her," Natalie asserted and stuck out her tongue as though her statement weren't clear enough. "And she didn't like me neither."

Holly clicked her tongue disapprovingly, but Drew spoke up. "Well, she's gone now, punkin. What do you say we start dinner?"

Natalie glanced up. "Holly lets me help," she declared archly, an obvious reference to Drew's usual practice of cooking alone.

But Drew just grinned. "Well, then," he sighed in mock concession, "I guess I'll have to make room for two helpers tonight." He looked at Holly, sensing her uncertainty. "If you want," he amended and won another bone-melting smile.

"I'd like to learn," she admitted shyly, and Drew knew everything was going to be just fine.

Chicken in black bean sauce was much, much more interesting than even peanut butter sandwiches. Not to mention the Cantonese chow mein. Drew was clearly a master at this cooking business.

Although it did seem that he had used every single pot and dish in the kitchen. Thank heavens for the marvel of the dishwasher. Holly lay in bed and patted her full belly, admitting that mortals and their ways could certainly grow on an elf.

Or more specifically, Drew and Natalie were growing on Holly.

But soon Holly would be leaving. Soon Katherine O'Neill would move into this house, and Holly would be on her way northward. Disappointment coiled within Holly, but she knew it wasn't justified.

Katherine had kissed Drew, after all, and Drew had smiled about it. So, the romance was on track and Holly was doing her job.

Then why did she feel so irritable about it? Maybe this was what "success" felt like—goodness knew, Holly had no experience with success.

But that didn't seem quite right. Holly frowned and watched the stars. She liked how she could lie on the bed and see the stars through the overhead skylight in her room. It was very peaceful to simply lie here through the night and watch the stars dance around while the mortals slept.

Of course, Holly was spending a lot of that time thinking about one particular tall and handsome mortal with a very engaging smile. She sighed and refused to worry about Katherine for the moment.

Fact was, Holly liked Drew better without his suit—he looked less dauntingly formal. She liked when his hair was more disorderly and his eyes sparkled with mischief. He seemed more playful each time she saw him, his antics as he cooked tonight making Holly laugh out loud more than once.

She liked Drew Sinclair.

And she didn't like Katherine O'Neill.

That was the meat of the matter. Holly frowned. But it wasn't up to her. She had been sent to do a job and by all appearances, it was getting done. Maybe she should just trust Mr. C.'s instincts and enjoy the fact that for once in her life, everything was going according to plan.

Because in one short week she would be back at the North Pole.

The prospect of that seemed a bit flat. Holly sighed. She chewed her lip, wishing she knew what Drew really thought of Katherine. Did he know something about this woman that Holly didn't? It wasn't an unlikely possibility.

Holly swallowed, remembering the seriousness in his eyes when he had asked whether she could spend the weekend with the two of them. She hadn't anywhere else to go, but Holly knew that wasn't the reason she had agreed.

She wanted to know more about Drew Sinclair. And in the darkness of her room, Holly admitted to herself that it wasn't so that she could make sure he married Katherine O'Neill.

But no one else had to know that, did they?

Drew dreamed of ocean waves. They rolled in from the horizon and pounded on an endless beach in rhythmic succession, they roared and foamed and lapped against his toes, and dripped.

Dripped?

Drew woke suddenly, the unmistakable sound of incessant dripping in his ears. The shards of his dream scattered, the familiar silhouettes of furniture surrounded him, but the dripping didn't fade away.

Drew sat up and frowned. The sound didn't stop. He sighed. If there was a leak, he'd better find it now. He tugged on a sweatshirt and track pants and stepped out into the darkened hall.

The Little Mermaid night-light glowed orange from the electrical outlet by Natalie's room. The rest of the hall was shrouded in shadows. Drew could hear the gentle rhythm of his niece's breathing.

Punctuated by that relentlessly steady drip.

Drew listened. Definitely not the bathroom. And not from the third floor. It might be coming from the kitchen. He trotted down the stairs, strode down the hall, and flung open the kitchen door for the second time that night.

The suds surged forth to embrace his legs and rolled on into the foyer.

Drew surveyed the kitchen in shock. The room was knee-deep in soapsuds, frothing over the counter from the sink. The dishwasher churned merrily away, no doubt making even more suds. That steady drip echoed in the room, and he wondered just how much water had leaked into the basement.

Drew waded through the foam and turned off the dishwasher with a twist of his wrist. It fell silent with a grumble, and Drew surveyed the damage.

He could make a good guess what the problem was. Drew opened the cupboard below the sink, eyed the relative positions of the contents, and knew exactly what Holly had done.

It wasn't the first time it had happened here. Drew's lips curved in recollection.

The dishwasher inexplicably chose that moment to spew one last volley of rinse water into the overloaded drain. Suds exploded out of the drain and rained down over Drew like big snowflakes. They spread across the kitchen counter. The geyser even splashed the ceiling.

By the time it stopped, Drew was not only soaked to the knees but dappled with water everywhere else too. It was a hell of a way to wake up at—he looked at the clock on the stove—1:14 in the morning.

And the worst thing was, he couldn't help but grin at the absurdity of it all. He leaned against the counter, tipped his head back, and roared with laughter.

•   •   •

Holly had heard the dripping and had hoped desperately that nothing was wrong—or more important, nothing for which she could be deemed responsible.

She had a funny feeling that Drew wouldn't be as understanding about her foibles as even Mr. C. had been. Holly chewed her lip and waited, her dread rising with every passing moment. Until suddenly she heard the unmistakable sound of Drew Sinclair.

Laughing.

Holly sat up in the darkness, confused. She listened again, but there could be no mistake.

He was *laughing*. And something was still dripping.

Holly couldn't deny her curiosity. She slipped out of bed, crept to the top of the stairs, and listened. Gradually she moved to the first landing, then the second. The deep sound of Drew's laughter made Holly's own lips twitch.

But what was so funny?

She moved down to the foyer, where any tendency to laugh was immediately dismissed. The golden light from the kitchen was spilling into the hall—along with a considerable quantity of soapsuds.

Holly bit her lip and remembered the fax machine.

And the school phones. She should have known that the mortal world would be a veritable minefield for her.

She figured she might as well get the worst over with. She took a deep breath and stepped into the suds, putting herself in clear view of the man in the kitchen. Drew's laughter slowed to a chuckle as he saw her.

The gray sweatpants that he wore were wet and clung to his muscled thighs in a way that was decidedly distracting. His faded red sweatshirt emphasized the breadth of his shoulders, and the opening at the front revealed a bit of very masculine chest hair. His hair was rumpled, his eyes twinkling, and Holly had a very hard time concentrating on what she had to say.

"I'm sorry about the mess, Drew," she said quietly, and he sobered. "I just have this thing . . ."

"This *thing*?" Drew leaned against the counter and

looked as though he was fighting against a smile.

And losing very badly.

Holly cleared her throat and stared at her interlaced hands. "Yes. It's terrible. You see, machines just don't like me."

Drew said nothing. No doubt he was coming to terms with this enormous flaw. If Holly's pointed ears hadn't been safely concealed, she knew they would have been glowing red.

She cleared her throat and continued. "It's very embarrassing, but I can't do anything about it. Machines just take one look at me and go crazy."

Holly flung out her hands, more than a little disconcerted by Drew's silence. "In fact, it's awful. Mrs. C. said that I have a gift, but I don't think so, not at all. It's always the same. And there's nothing I can do!"

"Oh, I think there is." Drew folded his arms across his chest as Holly watched. To her surprise, even in the wake of her confession there was an undeniable thread of humor in his low voice.

"You could, just for example, not put the liquid dishwashing soap into the dishwasher."

Holly blinked. "I don't understand."

"Obviously," Drew snorted, but there was a teasing glint in his eyes. Holly stared at him, unable to explain his response. "Holly, you have to use the special dishwasher soap because it doesn't foam as much. Didn't you see the box?"

"Um." Holly licked her lips. "No."

Drew grinned. "It's a mistake anyone could make, Holly, especially if it's all new to you." Holly was so astounded that she could have made a forgivable blunder that she didn't know what to say. "I did it myself once, a long time ago, and my brother never let me forget it."

Holly could barely grasp that astonishing admission.

Drew had made such a mistake?

But he did *everything* right! Holly felt a sudden and very strong alliance with this mortal, who otherwise appeared to be different from her in every conceivable way.

And she did like how he smiled.

"You?" she echoed incredulously.

Drew smiled right on cue. "Oh, yeah. I was worrying about something else and grabbed the wrong container." He shook his head and rolled his eyes. "Unfortunately, there were witnesses. You should have *heard* Greg."

Holly instinctively knew that he referred to Natalie's father, the brother who had died.

"I mean, he was the one who was always getting into a muddle," Drew continued. "He just loved that *I* had screwed up, and in such a big way. It gave him something to tease me about for years. He actually accused me of having done it on purpose to make sure the kitchen was *really* clean."

Holly smiled at the affection in Drew's tone. "You must miss him," she ventured, and Drew's smile immediately faded.

"I do." He looked around the kitchen, eyeing the suds, and frowned thoughtfully. "I really do."

"Why don't you tell me about him?" Holly suggested, startled at the speed with which Drew's gaze locked on hers.

Then his eyes darkened. "I'd like that," he said huskily. "I'm guessing that you're a good listener, Holly Berry." The conviction in his low voice made Holly's heart skip a beat.

Then it skipped another just for good measure. The kitchen suddenly seemed very warm as the two of them stared into each other's eyes.

Holly decided she must be very, very unaccustomed to mortals. Or maybe all elves felt this way around men.

Or maybe it was time she got this floor cleaned up and stopped staring into a certain man's eyes. Holly stepped forward with purpose.

And slipped in the suds.

Holly squealed. Drew called her name and jumped forward. He caught her around the waist, then slipped himself. They went down together, in a flurry of arms and legs and soapsuds, and landed with a thump.

Holly was in Drew's lap, his arms around her waist, her breasts pressed against his chest. There were soapsuds on the side of her face and she could feel the dampness soaking through her clothes. She was very aware of the muscled thighs that had kept her from landing on the floor.

Then she made the mistake of looking up.

And then Holly was aware of nothing beyond Drew's warm gaze. Her pulse began to echo in her ears when he lifted one strong hand to gently wipe away the suds that adorned her cheek.

"Not your color," he teased and Holly felt herself flush.

She caught her breath as Drew studied her features, a wonder dawning in his expression that Holly knew couldn't be associated with her. She was just a perfectly average and slightly unlucky elf, after all. But Drew's slow smile made her tingle right to her toes.

"You have the most amazing eyes," he murmured. "And you always look like you're ready to smile." The warmth of his fingertip slid across her lips as though he couldn't stop himself from touching her and Holly had a sudden—and very unelvish—urge to have this man touch more than her lips.

She impulsively reached out and mimicked his gesture, running her fingertip across his firm lips. His eyes darkened, then he captured her hand. The way Drew cradled her hand in his made Holly feel very tiny and feminine, though all of this was very new to her.

Drew pressed a kiss into her palm, his gaze unswerving from her own. Holly's eyes widened at the shiver that rolled over her skin from that one featherlight touch.

Maybe mortals did understand something about magic, after all.

Or maybe just this one did.

Holly watched, breathless, as Drew slowly leaned closer. It was as though he was afraid she would pull away, but Holly had no intention of going anywhere. He paused, his lips a finger's-breadth away from hers, his gaze searching. Holly understood that Drew was waiting for her agreement to continue.

So she smiled.

Drew smiled back. He eased the last vestige of suds from her cheek, then his hand slid along her jaw and into the hair at her nape, awakening an army of tingles along the way.

Holly had never felt anything quite like this. Drew put her hand on his chest, and Holly was astonished to feel his heart thundering at the same accelerated pace as her own.

They had more in common than using the wrong dishwasher detergent. Holly caught her breath.

Drew whispered her name, then his lips brushed across hers. She closed her eyes as starlight sparkled through her veins, and she leaned a little bit closer.

Drew needed no more encouragement than that. He gathered her against his chest, his strong arms encircled her, his mouth slanted over hers with purpose. Wonder coursed through her at his touch. She felt safe and secure within his embrace, cherished and desired, in a way she never had before. She understood as Drew kissed her just how special this man's protection could be, and she never wanted to leave his arms.

Rather inconveniently, she thought of Katherine at that very moment. Holly broke away from Drew's kiss and bounded to her feet, leaving him looking more than a little astonished.

It was Katherine, after all, who was destined to be protected and cherished by this man. "You were going to tell me about your brother," she said hastily.

Drew got to his feet more slowly, his gaze steady upon her. "I will," he said solemnly, then half smiled as he brushed the suds off her sweatshirt with a deliberation that made Holly's heart skip again. "Why don't we clean this up first?"

FIVE

Drew awakened to the enthusiastic bouncing of his niece on his chest. "Unca Drew! It's snowing!"

He opened one eye and grinned at Natalie's delighted smile. One glance out the window revealed big, fat flakes wheeling out of the sky. "Looks like a good day to find a Christmas tree," Drew declared, and Natalie gave him a kiss.

He wiped at the residue on his cheek. "Let me guess. Holly made breakfast."

Natalie giggled and nodded. Then she squirmed off the bed, heading for the kitchen and, no doubt, more peanut butter.

The change in his niece was amazing. And it was all because of Holly. Drew rolled out of bed and trotted to the shower, unable to stop the whistle on his lips. He winked at his reflection and conceded that Holly was working her magic on everyone in this household.

Drew had been amazed at how much he had told her the night before about Greg. It seemed that once he started talking, he hadn't been able to stop. Two years of holding back his grief hadn't diminished it in the least.

And Holly, lovely Holly, had patiently listened to it all. Just sharing his burden had lightened it beyond belief—and in the wee hours of the morning, Drew had found himself eating Holly's Christmas cookies and even telling her about those old snowball fights.

Holly had helped him work past the painful memories to the good ones. It was the most wonderful Christmas gift anyone could have given Drew—that and Natalie's redis-covered smile.

It paid to be patient, Drew decided. He had waited a long time to find the right woman to share his life, and now he had found a woman more right than he ever could have expected.

It was time, Drew informed his reflection, to start build-ing some new good memories. And he had a very strong feeling that Holly Berry was the one he should be sharing them with.

Holly had never imagined that finding a Christmas tree could be such fun. She refused to worry about the fact that Katherine apparently wasn't going to be joining them and forced herself to believe that her mission was on schedule.

It was hard to be anything but happy in the company of these two mortals. The tree farm was a delight, the snow absolutely perfect. A pair of massive horses, their harnesses jingling merrily, hauled the sleigh out into the fields as all the mortals aboard sang Christmas carols.

Drew swung Natalie onto his shoulders when they set out in search of the perfect tree, to ensure that she had a good view. It took a long time to find just the right one, what with the snowball fights that kept erupting and the angels Natalie had to make in every expanse of snow.

By the time they cut down their choice and dragged it back to the sleigh stop, Holly suspected she wasn't the only one thinking longingly about peanut butter sandwiches.

But the little shop by the parking lot had cocoa and cook-ies, which hit the spot. There were even a few reindeer, although they weren't inclined to confide their names to

Holly. She did ask politely, much to her companions' mutual amusement.

But reindeer could be testy, Holly knew, particularly this
close to their big shift of the year.

Drew lingered in the shop on their way to pay for the
tree, and Holly wondered what was taking him so long. She
retraced her footsteps, Natalie trailing behind, and found
Drew frowning at a box of several hundred tiny white fairy
lights.

He must have heard her coming, because he spoke without looking up. His tone was thoughtful. "Holly, do you
think I'm being too tough about the lights?"

Holly bit her lip, not entirely sure why he was so ada-
mant about them. "You seem to feel pretty strongly about
it."

Drew turned an intense glance her way. "The fire was
started by a short in the Christmas lights," he said in an
undertone.

That fire. Holly eyed Natalie, who was more interested
in reindeer made of clothespins than in any adult conversation. All the same, she took a step closer to Drew. She
still didn't completely understand. "What's a short?"

Drew rubbed his brow. "When the wires rub together
wrong. There were mice in the attic—they'd chewed the
electrical wires in the lights." He grimaced. "Actually, in
a lot of the house."

"Oh." Holly peered at the box. "Have these been
chewed by mice?"

Drew's smile was fleeting. "No. Of course not."

"Are there mice in your house?"

"No."

Holly met Drew's concerned gaze. "And the wire in the
house?"

"I had all the wiring replaced when I bought it years
ago. Along with the plumbing and just about everything
else." This time Drew's smile lingered a little longer. "Just
to be sure. You can't be too careful, you know."

Holly smiled back at Drew, understanding that he was
referring to his own cautiousness. Then he turned the box

over slowly in his hands and cleared his throat. "But maybe I'm being a bit too careful about this," he mused. He impaled her with a glance. "What do you think?"

Holly had to be honest with him. "I cannot understand— if all the wires are new and there are no mice—how there could possibly be the same problem."

Drew slowly smiled. Holly loved how gradually his expression changed, how he could summon a smile from the depths of serious consideration. She felt like she was watching a sunrise.

"You're right, Holly," he agreed warmly. "I'm being too cautious again. And what's a Christmas tree without lights?"

"It would still be a Christmas tree."

"But not as pretty a one." Drew's gaze flicked over Holly's head and his smile widened. A mischievous glint lit his eye. "Look!" he murmured. "You're standing under the mistletoe."

Holly only had a moment to look and see that he was right before Drew kissed the tip of her nose. Tingling warmth shot through her from her nose right to her toes. A few people near them applauded and laughed, then Natalie tugged at Holly's sleeve. Holly, grateful for the distraction, turned her flustered attention to the child.

"Me, too!" she demanded, and Holly bent to kiss the little girl's cheek under Drew's watchful eye.

"Now, then," Drew said with mock ferocity, "don't we have some serious decorating to do?" Natalie cheered, Drew winked, and Holly couldn't help but smile brightly.

Drew took Natalie's hand in his, put Holly's hand in the crook of his arm, and led them to the checkout station. She blushed furiously when the computerized cash registers immediately started to malfunction, spewing tape and adding everything up wrong, but everyone else took it in stride.

In fact, the clerk confided with a smile that she preferred to add things by hand. "Better for the old noggin," she declared and Drew laughingly agreed.

Holly just tried to keep a low profile until they were safely out of there.

• • •

By Monday night, Drew knew the truth. He was smitten, and he wasn't going to fight it.

He whistled as he strode through the underground mall from his office to the parking lot, knowing he hadn't felt so optimistic in years. They had had a great weekend, real family stuff, the kind of close camaraderie he'd missed the last two years. Natalie had been as busy as a bee with her decorations, and the tree was virtually overwhelmed by her efforts.

They had made popcorn garlands and eaten a good part of the stock. Holly had made perfect little bows for the pinecones Natalie had rescued from the backyard. They had gone tobogganing on the fresh snow and had stopped for latte and cocoa on the way home.

And most precious of all, Drew and Holly had already developed a routine of sitting in the kitchen after Natalie went to bed. Holly never seemed to get tired of talking or of listening, she always was ready to laugh. Drew had taught her to play Scrabble—and Holly had promptly beaten him.

All in all, it had been an absolutely perfect weekend. Now the thought uppermost in Drew's mind was how to ensure that they had many, many more of them. He noticed a Christmas display at a florist's shop and paused to buy a sprig of mistletoe.

Natalie's reaction to him kissing Holly at the Christmas tree farm had been everything Drew could have hoped for. In fact, Holly was everything Drew had ever hoped for in a partner. She was clever and playful, she had a sense of humor, she was warm and giving, she cared deeply about Natalie's welfare. There was a sincerity about Holly that was tremendously appealing to Drew—he knew instinctively that she would always tell him the truth. The fact that he had never been so physically attracted to a woman before was just a wonderful extra.

Drew Sinclair was falling madly in love for the first time in his life, and he didn't care who knew it. Holly made him feel lighter, made him laugh more, made him concentrate on what was really important.

He had called home twice today—for no good reason at all—just to hear Holly's voice. Drew had even left work early tonight, just so he could get home and see Holly again.

Yes, he was definitely smitten. Drew grinned, took his Christmas acquisition, and headed for the garage.

He could only hope that this feeling was mutual.

By the time Drew came home Monday night, Holly was not nearly so convinced that things were going according to plan. In fact, it seemed to her that Katherine O'Neill should have been around sometime during the weekend if Drew was going to propose to her in five short days.

It also seemed to Holly that Drew shouldn't have been kissing her with such enthusiasm if he was going to marry someone else.

And she was quite convinced that she shouldn't have enjoyed those kisses at all.

But she had.

She slathered peanut butter onto bread with a vengeance, biting her lip when Drew called from the foyer. Natalie danced out to meet him, her Christmas poster for his office finally complete.

It was a drawing of Mr. C. himself, lavishly adorned with sparkles and sequins, in the very moment before he dove down a chimney. His impatient reindeer pranced on the roof behind him, and Holly had helped Natalie write their names above them. It was snowing, and the sky was filled with very large stars. Natalie explained that Santa was holding a finger to his lips, "Shhhh," so that no one woke up the children.

And in big letters of her own, Natalie had written BELIEVE above the entire scene. Holly listened as Drew admired the marvelous drawing, then the pair's voices faded as they went into his office.

No doubt to find the perfect place to hang it. Holly smiled despite herself at Drew's obvious love for his niece.

Before she could completely erase her expression, the two came into the kitchen.

"Aha! What's Holly smiling about?" Drew teased.

"Peanut butter sandwiches for supper, that's what," Natalie crowed with obvious anticipation.

Drew soberly regarded the sandwiches Holly was making for dinner, but the twinkle in his eyes belied his expression. "I think"—he said with utmost seriousness—"that we'll have to seriously consider expanding your culinary repertoire." He arched a brow as his gaze locked with hers. "Over the long term, of course."

Holly's breath caught in her throat. Here was her chance to find out what he was really thinking, although she had a hard time forcing the words from her throat. "Won't Ms. O'Neill want to cook herself?" she asked in a strained voice.

Drew frowned. "What?"

"Ms. O'Neill. When she moves in," Holly's voice faltered, but she forced herself to continue. She concentrated on making the sandwiches, but was unable to completely blink away her disappointment. "Surely she'll have plans of her own."

"I'm sure she does, but they have nothing to do with me, or you, or Natalie, or certainly with moving into this house." Drew's words were resolute.

They didn't? Holly slanted a glance to a very watchful Natalie and took precisely too long to come up with her next question. "But . . ."

"But, obviously you've been working too hard," Drew murmured, intent glowing in his eyes. "Making sandwiches. You need a little relaxation, Holly." He paused, and she caught a glimpse of a mischievous twinkle in his eyes. "Maybe some Christmas decorating."

Drew stepped closer and conjured a familiar piece of greenery from a shopping bag. "Any ideas where we should hang this? Oh! How about right here?"

Holly knew what Drew was going to do the barest instant before he did it. But when he flicked the mistletoe over her head, she couldn't escape because of the counter beside her.

And she couldn't argue because his lips were locked on hers.

At least that was what Holly told herself as she closed her eyes and leaned into Drew's kiss.

Drew had hung the mistletoe in the foyer, and he had been diligent in catching Holly each and every time she passed beneath it. She had to be honest with herself and admit that she quite enjoyed the way he kissed her, the way he held her, the way his touch made her heart skip in an uneven kind of way. She liked talking to him, she liked how delighted he was when she surprised him. In fact, she knew she more than *liked* Drew and his kisses.

But she wasn't here to kiss Drew Sinclair. She wasn't even here to fall in love with this tough and tender man, which was what she was afraid was happening. No, sir. Mr. C. had entrusted her with a mission and she had to see it through.

After all, she couldn't stay here forever. She was an immortal elf, and immortal elves belonged at the North Pole workshop. And Holly wouldn't be allowed back there unless she made this work. What she needed was a little job security—and that could only come from getting Drew to marry Katherine, regardless of what Holly thought of the matter.

In four very short days.

Desperate times called for desperate measures. As soon as Natalie was safely at school the next morning, Holly raced back to the house and pushed up her sleeves. She had to get Katherine back in the picture—because Drew clearly wasn't going to do it.

Holly had a feeling that that had been a "farewell forever" kiss she had seen on Drew's cheek.

She had to work fast! With grim determination, she practically ripped the house apart that morning, looking for some reference—*any* reference—to Katherine O'Neill. She poked through the files in Drew's office, she rifled through the papers neatly stacked on his desk. She pitched order into chaos.

And shortly before lunch she found it.

Katherine's name was written on a little card attached to a row of other similar cards, apparently organized alphabetically. Below was inscribed "O'Neill Fine Leathergoods" in a decisive handwriting that had to be Drew's own. Holly ran a fingertip across his script, then frowned. Immediately below Katherine's name was an address and a telephone number.

Holly knew better than to touch the phone. She memorized the address and resolved to find it this very afternoon, after lunch, once Natalie was safely back at school.

There wasn't a moment to waste.

Katherine O'Neill wanted to sit down on the step and weep.

But she couldn't, because the movers would have just trampled right over her. They were here at the behest of the bank, doing their job in laying claim to everything of value inside her shop. Every dream she had ever had was walking out the door, and there wasn't a damn thing Katherine could do about it.

But she had worked so hard! It wasn't fair.

Damn Drew Sinclair and his bank anyway.

Left with no other options, Katherine stood in the corner, folded her arms across her chest, and sulked. In fact, she was so busy feeling sorry for herself that she barely noticed a slender dark-haired woman slip through the doorway and scan the shop.

When the woman smiled tentatively and headed for Katherine, the former shop owner bristled at the interruption. She glared at the approaching woman and realized she was a vaguely familiar, if rather plain, person.

The woman smiled.

Katherine did not. "Do I know you?"

"Oh, yes. I'm Holly Berry."

That meant just about nothing to Katherine. "We're closed," she snapped. "As if you can't tell." And Katherine turned away, wanting only to brood over her misfortune in privacy.

"No, you don't understand. I'm not here to buy anything. I'm Natalie Sinclair's nanny, but I have a mission to fulfill.'' Katherine's ears perked up at the mention of that familiar surname, and she turned back to find the woman blushing. "That is, I've come to get you.''

"Me?''

The woman cleared her throat. "I know that you have a certain affection for Drew—I mean, for Mr. Sinclair.''

"What are you talking about?'' Katherine demanded frostily.

"Just that I've been looking for you. That you and he . . .'' The woman frowned and swallowed awkwardly. "Mr. Sinclair said he was very interested in marriage.''

That got Katherine's attention. "To me?''

The woman's cheeks pinkened again. "To the right woman, he said.''

Katherine clutched the woman's sleeve. "When? Precisely when did he say this?''

"On . . . on Friday.''

"Ha!'' Suddenly Katherine's future seemed much brighter. She had seduced shy men before, and she would do it again. Although she never would have imagined that Drew Sinclair would be anything but blunt about his feelings on any subject, this cast a very different light on matters.

Obviously he was just playing hard to get. And she— foolish, trusting Katherine—had thought him disinterested in her many charms. Apparently she had retreated from the game too early.

So, Drew had sent a message. The wily devil.

Katherine set to thinking. Imagine, if she married Drew, her shop could be a little joint venture. In fact, all that lovely money Drew refused to lend to her would be half *hers*.

At least, it would be after she got him to sign a nice little prenuptial agreement. Katherine nearly rubbed her hands together with glee. She would have fine-leathergoods stores all around the globe! She'd be a success! She'd be a leathergoods mogul.

They would fete her in Italy, throw roses when she ar-

rived to spend her semi-annual budget in Milan. She'd dine
with all the famous designers and have each and every one
of them begging at her slender feet for her endorsement.
She would make or break manufacturers on her whim
alone.

She would be the queen she deserved to be.

It was all within reach.

"Stop!" Katherine cried as the movers hefted another
box of perfectly divine ostrich evening bags. She pushed
past Drew's messenger, intent on seeing results, and the
sooner the better. "Stop right there and put it all back,"
she commanded. "There's been a new development."

The supervisor of the movers frowned. "But ma'am, we
have instructions . . ."

"Forget them! I'll contact the bank myself."

And the men, hesitantly, put down that box of ostrich
purses. It was but the first victory of many. Why, the tide
was turning, even as Katherine watched.

What she needed was a plan. It wouldn't do to run
straight to Drew. No, that would make her look *biddable*.

And Katherine was anything but biddable. She really
ought to get the legal docs drawn up first. Yes! That would
be a perfect strategy. Then Drew could sign before she
finished seducing him, while he was still overwhelmed by
her charisma.

Perfect! Katherine was so busy getting her lawyer on the
phone that she didn't even notice a forlorn figure ease her
way out of the store and run down Bloor Street.

Holly sighed and watched the clock that night. Both Drew
and Natalie apparently noticed her mood, because they exchanged a concerned glance. They set out as one to cheer
her up—in fact, they were so thoughtful that Holly wanted
to sit down and cry.

She knew, deep down inside, that Katherine would never
appreciate this pair the way they deserved. Holly braced
herself for the inevitable moment of that woman's arrival,
trying to bolster her conviction that Mr. C. had it right.

But the minutes passed and Katherine didn't come.

Natalie demanded that Holly help tuck her into bed and even offered Mr. Bumbles to console her nanny. Holly did cry then, just one or two little tears, which her charge sweetly kissed away. Drew watched carefully from the hall, and Holly couldn't meet his eyes when he eased past her to tell Natalie her bedtime story.

Holly sat in the kitchen and watched the clock tick as the low rumble of Drew's voice carried through the house.

Katherine still didn't come.

Holly was so busy puzzling over this that she jumped when Drew appeared. "Want to talk about it?" he asked quietly, but Holly shook her head.

She was quite proud of herself for managing to summon a smile. "It's not important."

"Hmm," Drew said and sat down beside her. Holly found her fingers captured within his hand and his gaze boring into hers. "You listen to me, I listen to you," he declared in a low voice. "That's the deal around here, okay?"

Holly shook her head, but before she could protest, Drew laid a warm fingertip across her lips.

"No rush," he said gently. "But I'm here when you're ready."

Holly knew that Drew would always be there for anyone who relied upon him. That was one of the things she admired about him. He was so steadfast and protective, so gentle and yet strong. But Holly wouldn't get to rely on him, not after Katherine became his wife.

Not after Katherine became Natalie's new mommy.

Holly blinked back her tears and stared at their entwined hands, not having the will to pull her fingers away from Drew's. She had a feeling she was going to treasure this moment for a long time.

"Hey," he said softly and squeezed her fingers. "Why don't you beat me at Scrabble?"

Holly nodded agreement, grateful for anything that would take her mind off the scene ahead. Drew winked and

pulled out the board. Holly knew he was trying to make
her laugh and eventually, he did.

But Katherine still did not come.

Drew didn't know what was bothering Holly, but he knew
what was bothering him. His growing feelings for his
niece's nanny were quite inappropriate under the circumstances.

Drew didn't think it was right to continue this way. He
wondered if that was what was troubling Holly.

She must be wondering what his intentions really were.
After all, she had asked about Katherine moving into the
house, which was a laughably remote possibility.

But then, it wasn't laughable that Holly was concerned.

Drew didn't want Holly to have any doubts because he
didn't have a single one. He paused before a jeweler's window, an artisan whose work he had always admired, and
eyed the rings displayed there. Drew shoved his hands into
his pockets and considered the matter.

It wasn't like him to be impulsive. He had only known
Holly Berry for a week.

On the other hand, Drew had been looking for the right
woman long enough that he figured he ought to be able to
recognize her when she showed up on his doorstep.

And he really didn't want Holly worrying about the future.

Impulsiveness did have its benefits. After all, Drew had
hired Holly impulsively and she had made Natalie smile in
short order. That was an encouraging thought.

And Greg had always told Drew that he could stand to
lighten up a bit. Drew grinned at the recollection, decided
his heart was probably going to keep skipping as long as
he thought about Holly, and stepped into the jeweler's shop.

Because Drew intended to think about Holly for a very
long time.

By Christmas Eve, Holly was really worried. Katherine still
hadn't come. When the doorbell rang in the late afternoon,
Holly ran down the hall and practically flung open the door.

Instead of the relief she expected to feel at the sight of Katherine's cool smile or her elegant little black dinner suit, all she felt was a crushing disappointment. That disappointment quadrupled when she saw Drew's car pull into the driveway a moment later.

Holly swallowed. It seemed that her job here was going to be done all too soon.

Katherine waved her red-leather-gloved fingertips. "Hello, Drew! What perfect timing."

"Katherine." Drew frowned and slammed the car door a bit more loudly than he usually did. To Holly's surprise, when he strode closer, it was clear he wasn't very glad to see their visitor. "What are you doing here?"

Katherine chuckled. "A little early Christmas present, Drew." She wrinkled her nose. "Just for you."

Drew grimaced. "I've heard about the runaround you've been giving the auditors this week. It won't get you anywhere, Katherine, and I'd strongly advise you to give it a rest." He saw Holly and smiled, just for her. "Hi, Holly."

Holly's heart fluttered in response to his greeting.

"Doesn't the *child* need you?" Katherine asked Holly pointedly.

The child in question poked her head around Holly, her hand gathering a fistful of Holly's skirt. Holly was struck by the way Natalie hovered behind her, exactly as she had lurked behind Drew just a week before.

"You're the icky lady," Natalie said bluntly. "Unca Drew said you shouldn't have come here."

Katherine's lips thinned. "Well, I am here and I'm back to stay."

"What?" Drew was clearly incredulous.

Katherine sniffed. "We've just had a misunderstanding, Drew, that's all it is. I know that you want me and I certainly"—she smiled with more than a vestige of her usual composure—"want you. It's perfectly understandable that you'd prefer not to lend money to someone outside of your family."

Drew blinked, clearly blindsided by this development, while Katherine hauled an envelope out of her alligator purse. "I've taken the liberty of having my lawyer draw up an agreement for our . . . merger."

"What merger? What the hell are you talking about?" Drew took the envelope with a frown, pulled out a document, and scanned it. Horror dawned on his face. "This is a prenuptial agreement!"

Katherine smiled. "All standard and customary for the modern wedding, my dear." She pointed to the bottom of the document. "You just need to sign right down there . . ."

"But I'm not marrying you!"

Katherine blinked. She glanced at Holly and gritted her teeth. "But *she* said that you were interested in marriage."

Drew's lips set grimly. "I am. To the *right* woman." He stepped onto the porch. "Sorry to be blunt, Katherine, but that's not you." He handed her document back to her, took Holly's elbow, and stepped into the house. "Good night, Katherine. Have a merry Christmas."

"You!" Katherine let loose a string of profanity, but Drew shut the door decisively in her face. He looked down at Holly, who was struggling to quell her guilty relief at Katherine's departure. She had the distinct sense that she had mucked something up one more time.

And this time she had done a particularly good job.

Without a single machine in sight. It seemed that her abilities were expanding in a most disconcerting way. She swallowed carefully.

"Natalie," Drew said softly, "can you go and color in the kitchen, please? Holly and I need to talk."

Oh, this was going to be bad. Drew looked very grim. This was a hundred times worse than being called into Mr. C.'s office, that was for sure.

Natalie scampered away, but Drew didn't loosen his grip on Holly's elbow. There was no escape.

"Holly, did you really have anything to do with that?"

Holly felt her cheeks burn and knew she couldn't possibly conjure up a plausible explanation in time.

But she could still try. "Well, I thought when you talked about marriage . . ." Holly took a deep breath, knowing that route wouldn't lead anywhere helpful, and tried another tack. "Natalie would like a new mommy and I . . ."

"Don't worry, Holly," Drew said so confidently that Holly had to look up and meet his gaze. He smiled slowly. "I've found the perfect candidate."

Who? Holly was confused. There were no other women around, and Mr. C. had put his vote on Katherine.

Drew released Holly's elbow and pulled a small box out of his pocket, a shred of doubt filtering into his eyes. He caught her hands in his and leaned toward her.

Holly braced herself for very bad news.

When Drew spoke hastily, she knew he wanted to get the worst over with as well. "Look, Holly, I know this has happened really quickly, but I don't want to continue on like this and have you worrying about the future."

"You're going to fire me," Holly whispered fearfully.

"No!" Drew shook his head. "Well, not exactly. That is, there's"—he hesitated and rolled the tiny box in his fingers, then suddenly looked intently into Holly's eyes— "there's another job I'd like you to consider."

Drew put the little box into Holly's hands and folded her fingers around it. "This is for you," he murmured.

Holly took it because she didn't know what else to do. Drew was so serious. She certainly didn't understand. Holly nibbled her lip, eyed the gift, then decided she'd might as well open it. Maybe it was a farewell gift of some kind.

But inside the box there was only a golden band nestled in the deep-blue velvet lining.

And Holly knew exactly what kind of ring it was. Her heart stopped cold and she stared at it, unable to believe even her keen elvish vision.

"Holly, will you marry me?" Drew said quietly. "I know we've only just started to get to know each other, but I'm already falling in love with you. I think it's only going to get worse," he added with a tentative grin.

Holly couldn't help but smile back.

Drew seemed to find her response encouraging. "Holly, I want to spend the rest of my life learning more about you and laughing with you. I want to come home, knowing that you're here, I want to teach you to cook and talk to you all night. I want to catch you under the mistletoe when you're not expecting it, I want to let you beat me at Scrabble over and over again.''

Holly gasped. ''You did not let me win!''

Drew grinned. ''Maybe just the first time.''

Holly laughed out loud before the need to confess her fatal flaw made her smile disappear. ''But, Drew, I'm always messing things up,'' she protested.

He smiled with an affection that couldn't be denied. ''On the contrary,'' he said smoothly. ''It seems to me that you've been very busy *fixing* things since you got here.''

Well, she had brought Christmas back to this house. Natalie did smile now, and Drew, well, Drew had lightened up in a most interesting way.

Maybe this was her niche.

Holly ran her fingertip across the ring and stared into Drew's eyes as a lump rose slowly in her throat. Nothing would make her happier than to accept Drew's proposal. Seeing Mr. C.'s mission complete, even having a permanent job at the North Pole workshop, just couldn't compare to what she had found here.

The only thing Holly wanted was what Drew was offering. She wanted to stay in this house, she wanted to be Natalie's new mommy more than she'd ever wanted anything before.

''I know it's sudden,'' Drew said urgently, as though he felt the need to convince her. He folded her hand into his. ''But it's *right*, Holly. I know it, and I hope you feel the same way.''

Holly did feel the same way. She knew that this man was absolutely the most perfect companion she could ever have.

But no matter how much she wanted to, Holly knew she couldn't marry Drew. He was a mortal and she was not.

Holly swallowed and looked down at the ring, wondering how on earth she would explain that to Drew.

Somehow she had to find a way to tell him the truth.

She parted her lips, but Drew silenced her with one fingertip. "Just think about it," he urged. "I don't want to rush you, Holly. I just want you to know that I'm serious about this." Drew smiled with rare uncertainty. "Just promise me you'll think about it until the morning."

Drew kept his fingertip pressed to her lips, as Holly nodded.

"I love you." Drew smiled into her eyes, and Holly decided in that moment that she wasn't going to just think about his proposal.

She was going to *do* something about the only thing that stood between them. It took a lot of gumption to ask for exactly what you wanted, but Holly now knew what that was.

Fortunately, she knew exactly who could make her only wish come true—and this was the night to ask.

SIX

Holly sat beside the Christmas tree, watching all those little white fairy lights twinkle in the darkness. She had promised Drew that she wouldn't go to bed and leave the lights on, but Holly had no intention of going to bed.

She was waiting for someone.

And she would wait all night.

When a distinctive prance sounded on the rooftop, Holly clenched her hands tightly together and once again re-hearsed what she was going to say. There was a *pouf* of ash in the fireplace, then a familiar grunt reached her ears.

And a great jolly elf landed behind the brass fire screen with a resounding *thump*. Mr. C. shook out his hat and brushed off his jacket, hefted his sack—and saw Holly.

He froze for a long moment. His red lips pursed, and the apples in his cheeks dimmed ever so slightly. Mr. C. ad-justed his spectacles and peered through them at Holly once again.

"Hmmm," was all he said.

Holly didn't need Mrs. C. to tell her that Mr. C. wasn't pleased. She pushed herself to her feet and folded her hands in front of her, but her little speech wasn't going to have a chance to be heard.

"You're still here," Mr. C. accused quietly.

"Well, yes. I mean, the job isn't done."

"Ah!" Mr. C. eyed the tree, the garlands, the decorations. He peered toward Drew's office, and Holly knew that his elvish vision was as keen as her own. She could barely make out Natalie's picture, fastened in a place of pride, and knew she didn't imagine the little smile that curved Mr. C.'s lips.

It seemed to Holly that his gaze lingered on the mistletoe hanging from the light fixture in the foyer. She had the distinct impression that it was tattling on what it had witnessed.

She blushed.

Mr. C.'s eyes twinkled so briefly that Holly thought she might have imagined it.

He pivoted abruptly, without saying anything, then moved deftly toward the Christmas tree, acting for all the world as though Holly wasn't even there. He cleared a space beneath the tree with businesslike ease and deposited an array of parcels covered in glittering paper.

Just when Holly was wondering whether he would even acknowledge her again, Mr. C. glanced over his shoulder. His twinkling gaze met hers, and he deliberately winked.

And when he turned to face her, Holly saw why.

Mr. C. was holding out a tiny parcel wrapped in shining gold paper. Perched atop it was a golden bow that was much too large. He held it out toward her, and Holly's heart started to hammer.

"You might as well have your Christmas gift here and now," Mr. C. rumbled, laughter hiding in the depths of his voice.

"For me?"

"Are there any other elves named Holly Berry here?" Mr. C. looked so pointedly under the furniture that Holly had to smile.

"But I didn't even ask for anything."

Mr. C. smiled and his dimples danced. "Didn't you?" he mused.

Holly looked into his eyes and suddenly understood. "You knew!" she breathed.

"Holly! How could I do this job if I couldn't hear the secret whispers in every heart?" He leaned closer and tapped a gloved finger over her own heart. "Even elvish ones?"

And Holly knew that was true.

She accepted the parcel, which was no heavier than a feather in her hands. Holly was dying of curiosity to open the box, yet afraid it contained something other than the only thing she really wanted.

She met Mr. C.'s gaze. "I love him."

That smile broadened, and the understanding and tenderness in it made Holly's vision blur. "I know." Mr. C. nodded. "Didn't Noelle say you would find your place?"

Holly shifted the parcel from one hand to the other, trying to compose one last appeal. She was sure it couldn't be very easy, even for Mr. C., to give her what she wanted. "But, Mr. C. . . . ."

"Holly," he interrupted sternly, "open it."

Holly took a deep breath and did what she was told. She tore off the bow and ripped open the paper.

Only to find that there was nothing inside the wrapping at all.

Holly gasped and looked at Mr. C., whose smile did not waver. "Wish, Holly!" Mr. C. advised. "You have only to *wish* for your heart's one desire."

"I want to be mortal," Holly said without hesitation, but just uttering the words did not seem to be enough. "I want to be mortal!" she said more loudly. "I want to marry Drew. And I want to be Natalie's new mommy."

"Then you have only to believe," Mr. C. whispered. "Natalie already knows that." He winked confidentially, then leaned forward to blow gently.

And a thousand tiny snowflakes took flight from the wrapping paper clutched in Holly's hands. She saw now that there was a sprinkling of fairy dust there, the same dust that had sent her spinning from the North Pole workshop to this house, the same dust that could make a million dreams come true in a single night.

As it would make hers.

Holly laughed as the shimmering light surrounded her, as the flakes swirled and danced. They reflected the light from the Christmas tree and put her in the middle of a crystal snowstorm. The flakes landed on her lips, her cheeks, her hands, her brow. They melted against her skin, and Holly felt a subtle change roll through her body.

Holly understood exactly what that change was. She knew with sudden certainty that the only magic in her life from this point on would be the magic that Drew awakened with his touch.

And that suited Holly just fine.

When the last flake of fairy dust shimmered to nothing and Holly Berry turned to thank Mr. C. for his gift, he was gone.

There were new parcels beneath the tree, and the stockings on the hearth were stuffed. The cookies and milk that Natalie had left out had disappeared, but otherwise the room looked just the same as it had before Mr. C.'s visit.

But Holly could feel within herself that there had been a real change. In fact, she felt tired in a way she never had before. She sat down in an armchair opposite the tree with a yawn. Holly picked up Drew's gift and closed her fingers around the box as she smiled in anticipation of what the morning would bring.

But her newly mortal body was a little less enthusiastic about staying awake that long. Despite Holly's best efforts, when the clock struck three, her eyes drifted closed.

And for the first time ever, Holly Berry fell asleep, only to find sugarplums dancing in her dreams.

"Santa was here!"

A certain six-year-old's cry of delight awakened Holly with a snap. She rubbed her eyes and sat up, blinking when she was confronted by Mr. Bumbles himself, not six inches from her nose.

Lurking behind the bear was a golden-haired cherub wearing jingle-bell earrings, a flannel nightie, and big, fuzzy slippers. Natalie's eyes were wide.

"Are you going to be my new mommy?" she asked in a stage whisper, as though she didn't dare to hope. "I asked Santa and you're here now."

Holly smiled. "Maybe more like an auntie," she answered, then wrinkled her nose playfully.

Natalie's eyes went round, and she threw herself into Holly's arms with unrestrained glee. Holly laughed and hugged the little girl tightly, feeling as though her own heart would burst with happiness.

She looked up to find Drew leaning in the doorway, his arms folded across his chest and a smile tugging at his lips. Holly's heart clenched, then took off at a gallop.

"Unca Drew! Holly's going to be my new mommy!" Natalie raced across the room as her uncle chuckled and scooped her up high.

"So I hear," he murmured. "Merry Christmas, punkin." Drew managed to kiss Natalie's cheek before she squirmed to be set down.

"I have to look in my stocking right now, Unca Drew!"

"Of course." Drew set Natalie down and she dashed to the tree.

But Holly had eyes only for Drew. He strolled across the room and retrieved the box that had fallen out of her hand while she slept. He opened it as he sat down beside her and removed the delicate ring.

Drew held it an inch away from Holly's hand and looked into her eyes. "Sure?"

"Absolutely," Holly declared, then pushed her finger through the golden circle. Drew grinned and caught her chin in his fingertips, then bent to kiss her.

"Merry Christmas, Holly," he said softly, just before his lips closed over hers. Holly twined her arms around his neck and kissed him back, knowing without a shadow of a doubt that she had made the right choice.

"There's no mistletoe here," Natalie protested long moments later. Holly and Drew parted reluctantly, then both turned to the little girl.

"Sometimes you don't need mistletoe," Drew said solemnly.

"Unca Drew, you just want to kiss my new mommy," she accused with childish conviction.

Drew feigned sheepishness at being caught, but he didn't let Holly go. "Caught me, punkin." He winked at Holly. "That's *exactly* what I want to do."

Holly sighed with contentment and nestled against his warmth. "I suppose we should look under the tree," she teased.

"I've already found the best present," Drew declared and gave Holly a squeeze.

"Me, too!" Natalie declared. The little girl, with Mr. Bumbles in tow, wriggled in between the two of them. She granted Holly and Drew each a wet kiss, then sat back with a delighted grin to survey the shambles she had made of her stocking contents. There was still a gleam of anticipation in her very blue eyes.

"Mr. Bumbles says this *is* the bestest Christmas ever," she said with satisfaction. "I told him it would be."

And Holly could only agree.

THE
UNEXPECTED
GIFT

Dee Holmes

ONE

"Mommy, Mommy, there's a dead man in the yard!"

Sabrina McKay slid the hot mincemeat pie onto the top of the stove and turned off the oven. The dessert was a family tradition and her father's favorite, but she should have waited until she was less rushed to bake it. She took off the oven mitt and turned to her son. "Honey, please, no games. Not today. If we don't get to the village to buy the tree, there won't be any left."

It was two days before Christmas in Pine Falls, Vermont, and Sabrina's original plan had been to take Josh to cut down their own tree. She'd wanted to create their own traditions and emphasize that the season had meaning beyond the busyness, the buying, and the stressful hassles. So far, as indicated by her treeless living room, her efforts were a bust. Plus she had packages to wrap, and more cooking to do in preparation for her parents, who would be arriving on Christmas Eve. This was the first Christmas since her divorce, and she wanted the celebration to be smooth and special.

"Mommy, you gotta come and see."

The five-year-old tugged on her arm. He was bundled in a fleece jacket, his cheeks were cherry red, his brown hair going every which way. "Where's your hat?" asked Sabrina. "Oh, Josh, you didn't lose it, did you? If it's not mittens, then it's hats."

"I didn't lose it."

She grinned at him, ruffled his hair, and said, "Good. Then why don't you get it while I get my coat?"

"I can't."

"You can't?"

"I put it on the dead man. His head was cold."

"Josh, really. Your imagination is a little too imaginative." But a slight tremor ran through her.

"Not my 'magination. It's true."

She paused in the process of buttoning her coat. Her son's blue eyes were round and wide, his mouth unsmiling. He was headed toward the front door. "He's in the yard near the bushes. I'll show you."

She grabbed Josh's jacket to stop him. Could it be Robert? Good God, if it was her ex-husband playing some stupid joke . . .

"I want you to stay here," she said to Josh. If it was her ex, she intended to deliver some choice words that her son didn't need to hear. Since the divorce had been final in June, they'd spoken twice. Oh, yes, Robert Townsend had a dozen excuses for ignoring his son, and all were about as convincing as that silly hairpiece he'd taken to wearing. Maybe he'd been seized by holiday guilt and wanted to make a dramatic appearance.

"I know how to call 9-1-1," Josh said, heading for the phone.

"I know you do, but wait until Mommy comes back into the house."

Sabrina opened the front door and walked outside. Brown spots poked through the half-inch layer of snow. The bushes along the front of the yard maintained a pristine white coating. She noticed a dark green Ford Explorer parked slightly askew by her driveway, but with the holidays and families having company, there were often unfamiliar cars in the neighborhood. Robert drove a small sports car, but then again, he changed cars the way he did girl-friends. *Maybe that's why he's dead in the yard,* she thought, her fury now gathering for a confrontation. Perhaps one of his girlfriends had gotten fed up with his quirky habits, finished him off, and dumped him back into her life.

No way. Her Christmas spirit didn't extend that far.

She made her way along a row of bushes, turned—and there he was.

For a full five seconds she stared.

It wasn't Robert.

It wasn't even some poor stranger.

Sabrina bent down to make sure, but she knew by the way her heart kicked into racing speed, knew by the way her pulse jumped, knew because no one else had ever had quite that effect on her. The man sprawled halfway under the bushes was the town's onetime bad boy—and her old boyfriend—Zach Danforth.

Always the rogue, Zach was the unpredictable rebel, too dangerous for Pine Falls girls. A poster boy for reckless behavior, yet there was a charm about him that made him hard to forget. Just last week the principal at the grammar school where Sabrina taught third grade had asked her if she ever heard from Zach, remarking that he'd always had a way of popping up unexpectedly.

"And this is definitely unexpected," she murmured, feeling her breath hitch in her throat. A small spill of bubbles fluttered deep within her, an instant reminder of past passionate encounters. Now she could smell alcohol, and her instinct told her he was more drunk than dead. She touched his whiskery cheek, running her hand inside his coat collar to feel the pulse in his neck. At her touch he groaned and curled up, as if trying to get warm.

She knelt beside him, noting the knit cap that Josh had stretched over his head. His black hair was shaggy, poking out from under the knit, and Sabrina had little difficulty recalling the last time she'd felt that hair in her fingers.

Her cheeks warmed at the clarity of that memory—the fraught encounter on her wedding day just moments before the ceremony. Zach invading the church foyer, his eyes dark and dangerous, his figure clad in leather and faded denim. Her mother's carefully applied makeup couldn't hide her paleness. Onlookers stared with mouths agape. Sabrina's own expression had been confused. She was foolishly intrigued by his outlandish behavior.

She should have fled, backed away, something, anything. Instead she presented her most fiercely independent glare. Zach ignored it. In fact, he discounted everything and everyone, his hands drawing her close, his mouth at her neck searching for her skin behind the lace and the flowers in her hair. She stiffened, but her protest was lost under his lips.

"Don't do this," he murmured against her ear. "Come with me. Run away with me."

"But you don't love me."

"I want you."

She shivered from her own disappointment at his response. For the year that they'd been lovers, she'd hoped to hear him say he loved her. He never had. And now, only moments before she was to marry someone else, his silence remained. He didn't love her. "Oh, Zach, you know that sex isn't enough."

"I'll make it enough, babe, make it more than enough . . ."

The moment was erotic but also bizarre and frightening, for not only did she feel consumed by his sudden reappearance in her life at such an inopportune moment, she was terrified that if he lifted her into his arms and carried her out of there she would not protest.

"Zach, let me go."

He stared down at her, his eyes seeming to search through their past intimacies, recalling the walks in the woods, the funny gifts, the range of their feelings from teasing to intense. All the memories sifted, then spilled, and then sadly slid away, like the ghosts of yesterday.

"No one ever kissed me the way you do," Zach said, startling her with that peek into his soul. "I want one more."

And before she could speak or protest, he kissed her,

assaulting her mouth, dragging her into the dark swirling space of them alone with an arousing hold that took her too many moments to resist. But resist she finally did. And a moment later he had gone, the taste and smell of him lingering along with the question: What if she'd fled with him?

She sighed. Zach and her ragged emotions were a volatile combination. One moment she'd demanded that he say he loved her, and the next, love notwithstanding, she'd been plagued by the question of whether to run off with him. Talk about tugs from opposite ends of a slippery rope. If he'd swept her up and carried her away . . . She shuddered. That was a question she'd never allowed herself to answer, and now was certainly not the moment to be considering it anew.

Zach groaned, the sound reminding her she couldn't leave him here on the ground. Whether she wanted to admit it or not, she was curious about what had brought him back to Pine Falls and to her house.

She shook his shoulder. "Zach? Come on, let me help you. You can't stay out here."

He mumbled something, then muttered, "Go away. It's over . . . all over."

Sabrina frowned. "What's over?" But before she could press him to answer, she was interrupted.

"Mommy?" Josh stood a few feet away.

She started to scold him for not waiting in the house, but he looked worried and scared. "It's okay, sweetheart. He's not dead, but if you hadn't found him, he would have gotten very cold."

Josh eased closer, still appearing anxious. "He looks dead."

"You remember the man we saw on TV last night that was staggering?"

"Uh-huh."

"He'd had too much to drink and it made him sick."

"Is the dead man sick?"

"Yes. And he's cold. We have to get him into the house." Her son remained uncertain. She added, "It's okay. I know him. His name is Zach and he travels all over the world taking pictures like the ones in the newspapers.'' She didn't add that she had kept up with his career despite telling herself it was a silly waste of time.

"Did he take the one of Santa you showed me?''

"No. He takes 'news' pictures.''

At Josh's puzzlement, she said, "Not important now. Are you strong enough to help me?''

Josh nodded, but after a couple of tries, it was clear that they needed assistance. "Honey, go next door and get Byron and Chris.''

In a few minutes Josh was back with the two teenagers.

The boys stared down at Zach, refusing to get too close.

"Is he dead?'' Chris asked.

Byron shuddered. "Hey, man, I'm not touching no dead dude.''

"Come on, guys,'' Sabrina coaxed. "If he were dead I'd have called the police. He's just drunk. Help me get him into the house.''

The two teenagers blinked at her like she'd lost her mind. "Geez, Sabrina, that's not a cool idea.''

"I know him. Come on. He will be dead if we don't get him warmed up.''

It took some minutes, but with the help of the two boys, she got Zach inside and on the couch.

The teenagers didn't leave. "Want us to call somebody to come over here?''

"No.''

"Want us to take Josh with us?''

She started to say no to that, too, but then changed her mind. It might be good if her son wasn't here when Zach woke up. "You know what you could do? You could take Josh into the village to get a Christmas tree.'' So much for her idea of making that chore a family one, she thought unhappily. She got her purse and gave Byron some bills.

"You gonna be okay? Mom would fry our asses for leaving him with you if you got hurt.''

Sabrina appreciated their concern. "I'll be fine.''

But would she?

TWO

After the three trooped out, she braced herself, then went back to the couch, where Zach was sprawled. For a few moments she stood with clasped hands and concentrated on getting her breathing even. Part of her was anxious, part of her uneasy, but the part that worried her, the part that questioned whether she would be okay, was her growing excitement at unexpectedly finding Zach back in her life.

Which was ridiculous. She'd just begun to recover from a bad marriage and a stressful divorce. The last thing she needed was wondering about taking a jaunt down lovers' lane with an old boyfriend.

Pretend he's just a friend temporarily in need of some help, she reminded herself.

She reached down and removed the knit hat. Then she saw the blood.

She looked closely at the wound along his hairline, feeling it with her fingers. It didn't appear to be serious; it was a nasty cut rather than a deep gash, and the blood had dried. She got a hot, soapy washcloth and cleaned the area, then rinsed it and patted it dry. She applied some antiseptic cream, and when she glanced back down at his face, his eyes were open and he was staring at her.

That blue-gray, smoky stare bore into her with the same hypnotizing effect as the one that had goaded her to hop on his motorcycle when she was nineteen and feel reckless and flattered enough to ride off with the "bad boy" in town.

She blinked and concentrated on getting the cap back on the antiseptic cream. She took a step back, determined to stay indifferent. "The cut isn't bad. It probably won't even leave a scar."

"Sabrina?" His voice was raspy, and with some effort he managed to sit up amid a chorus of groans. He leaned forward and plowed his hands through his hair. "God, my head feels like a battered drum."

He wore boots, jeans, and a heavy blue knit shirt beneath a dirty but obviously expensive suede jacket. In the jacket pocket was an empty flask.

"Hung over is a better explanation," Sabrina observed.

"Jack Daniel's. The bottle was full. I remember that much. How did I get here?" He glanced around and then resumed staring at her. "How did *you* get here?"

"I live here." She was proud of the way she was handling this. None of the bubbly breathlessness that she'd too often displayed when Zach simply entered a room back when they were lovers.

He glanced around, looking genuinely stunned, then his gaze came back to her again. "This is Pine Falls? The last thing I remember was a redhead in Rutland who sent me out for condoms."

"Then I guess you wasted a trip. I'm all out," she said, pushing at the sleeves of her sweater and getting up from the edge of the coffee table, where she had been perched. She certainly wasn't interested in his relationship with some Rutland redhead, but more alarming was the little scrap of jealousy that rose out of nowhere. She had no right or reason to be jealous.

"The bar was, too," he added, pressing his fingers into his temples.

"They don't sell condoms in bars."

He looked at her. "You've been in Pine Falls too long. Bars give them away. Any color, any flavor."

Sabrina stepped back from the couch. Only from Zach would a bald statement about flavored condoms not seem odd. His straightforwardness was vintage Zach, and this particular habit of his was one she'd always admired. Well, she could be straightforward, too. She'd done her good Christmas deed and brought him in from the cold. She hadn't seen or heard from him in more than six years, and given the range of emotions that he'd awakened in her since she first recognized him, she decided it was time to send him on his way.

"You seem to have sobered up a little. My son found you on the ground by the bushes. I presume you have some clothes in your car. That is your Explorer, isn't it?" Her pulse had begun to pound under his gaze, and she knew she was babbling. He rose, not answering her question but staring at her so hard that she was sure he saw her heart thumping in her chest.

Sabrina backed up, the words spilling out. "Well, of course it's your car . . . Isn't it?"

"It's my car." He moved closer.

Her palms were damp and she pressed them against her wool slacks. From outdoors came the sound of a dog barking, the buzzing of a chain saw, and the muted ringing of church bells. Inside her soul she was a mass of old memories and new possibilities that were so ridiculous she fought to discount them. My God, this is so dumb, so foolish, so outrageous.

She cleared her throat, refusing to look at him. "If you want to take a shower and get cleaned up before you leave, you can."

"Thank you."

"You're welcome." Were they really having such an inane conversation?

He grinned, and for just an instant she remembered how devastating his smile had always been to her. And damn him, she thought suddenly, so did he.

Despite the rumpled clothes, the whiskers, the walk that was a bit unsteady, she was struck by how utterly he dominated the room. The moment. And her. She swallowed, breathless at the inner conflict she felt. She wanted to run from him. She wanted to run to him.

He was so close now, close and hot and . . . "What are you doing?" she whispered.

He reached out for her, and she jumped back.

"Watch out."

But it was too late. Her foot had already stepped on one of Josh's plastic trucks, propelling her body forward. Her arms flailed as she tried to get her footing, and just as she was sure she would fall in an ungraceful lump, he caught her. In a matter of seconds she was flat against him, her face pushed into his shoulder.

One hand supported her and the other smoothed her hair. "I was trying to get to the truck before you stepped on it," he murmured into her hair. It was far too reminiscent of the moment on her wedding day. Trying to save her from Robert then, saving her now from a fall.

Never mind that both times were all his fault, she decided illogically. Then, if he'd said he loved her she wouldn't have married Robert. And now, if he hadn't totally unnerved her by moving so close, she would never have stepped on the truck. She was a mother, for heaven's sake, she was used to sidestepping toys.

Suddenly he released her, turning away so that his face was averted.

Sabrina reached for him, but he waved her away.

He went back to the couch and sank down, looking a little woozy.

Immediately she was beside him. "You look awful."

"Believe me, I don't look as bad as I feel." Once more he tried to get to his feet. It didn't work. He sank back down like a stone. "I could use a drink."

Sabrina stared at him as if he'd lost his mind. "How about some coffee? The last thing you need is more alcohol."

Then he pulled the flask from his pocket, opened it, lifted

it to his mouth, scowled, and returned it. "I got a bottle in the truck," he said, this time making it to his feet. He looked fierce in his determination and managed a few steps before he grabbed for a chair. Sabrina moved instantly, steadied him, then staggered when he leaned on her.

He was over six feet and lean, but she could feel tight muscle, the wound-up tension when he tried to straighten and move on his own. Sending him on his way suddenly seemed more reckless than sensible. She steered him back to the couch.

"I can't stay here. Gotta go."

"You can't drive, Zach. You can barely stand up."

"Doesn't matter. Nothing matters. Being dead or alive, drunk or sober. It's over."

"What's over?"

"Everything. Every goddamn thing." He pushed away her steadying hands, shuddered, and then managed to get to the front door.

On a maple table was a red wicker basket full of greens and silver and red balls. Poked among the ornaments were candy canes. He took one of them and turned to Sabrina. "You always were a sucker for Christmas."

"At one time you were, too." She still had the furry white-plush bear with the red ribbon that he'd bought for her the last Christmas they were together. She'd seen it in a store window, and Zach had laughed, saying she was too old for stuffed toys. But the next night at the Festival of Lights he'd presented it to her, then taken her picture with the bear in her arms.

"Time long past," he murmured, returning the candy cane to the basket.

Desperate now to get him to stay, for she honestly feared he wasn't capable of driving, her mind scrambled for something to distract him. "Zach, what made you come back here? It's been more than six years since you've been in Pine Falls. Why now? What happened?"

For a moment he looked puzzled as if it was beyond his ability to give a cogent answer. Then he sagged against the door, and almost in a whisper said, "Out of work, out of hope, and out of guts.'' He opened the door, shivered against the burst of wind, but then straightened as if shaking off any reluctance.

She didn't want him to leave. She didn't know why, but suddenly she felt compelled to keep him here. Maybe his desolation, maybe old memories of happier times with a charming Zach, maybe the Christmas season of hope and faith and believing that doing for others was a tradition that no season could ever have enough of.

But convincing him to stay? A possibility flitted through her mind. She dismissed it, and then just as instantly grabbed it back.

It was bold and outrageous, but the alternative was hitting him over the head and, well, she couldn't do that.

''Zach, you have to stay here.''

He slowly turned, his gaze settling on her, and she was suddenly filled with second thoughts. ''Why?''

''Because I want you.''

THREE

Zach stared at her, suddenly feeling more sober than he'd been in the past week.

"Don't you think Robert might object?"

"We're divorced."

Don't go there. Don't ask. He tried to sound casual. "His loss."

"I don't think he sees it that way."

"Then he's an idiot."

Sabrina grinned. "No argument from me."

He scowled, glanced outside and then back at her. "Do you usually haul drunks into your house and then convince them to stay by offering sex?"

She slipped her hands into her pockets and walked closer to him, looking, he decided, far too sure of herself. "Only you."

"I'm flattered."

"No, you're not. You're trying to figure out what happened to the naive, shy, wide-eyed Sabrina," she said with such confidence that Zach felt a bit overwhelmed.

"So—what happened to her?"

"She grew up and learned how to be a woman and make her own decisions."

"I thought you did that when you walked out on me."

"But you walked back into my life. I think that's not just an ordinary event."

Zach had to admit this was a different Sabrina, a very tempting Sabrina, but he was different, too. And not in a good way.

He pulled the door open, then turned. "As appealing as the invitation is, I don't want you to be sorry in the morning." He started out the door, and Sabrina rushed forward to stop him.

"I'm serious."

"Then you're a desperate woman."

"There are thousands of front yards in Vermont that you could have passed out in. You chose mine. I think that's significant."

"Or stupid."

She looked as if he'd insulted her.

He reached out and palmed her cheek. "It's too late to rescue me, babe. You probably knew that when you left me to marry Robert, the promoter of social acceptability. Now you're suffering from a bout of seasonal charity. It will pass."

He looked deep into her eyes and felt a sense of loss and regret far beyond any of the screwups and failures that he'd experienced in his work in the past year. But she didn't need some has-been photographer hanging around, waiting for the best camera shot. Zach had little use for people who felt sorry for themselves, but then, he had little use for bums and drunks either. Yet since he'd returned to the States and gone on this weeklong binge, he had adopted all three.

He wanted to kiss her, but he probably smelled like a stale barroom, and besides, he wasn't sure he knew anymore how to kiss a woman like Sabrina.

He whispered, "You don't want me here, babe."

"I want you to be okay."

They watched each other for a long, tense moment. He

tucked a strand of hair behind her ear. "Tell you what. I'll call you later and let you know I'm alive."

"You promise?"

Her question dug itself deep within him and took root. It had been a long time since anyone had asked him for his word. "Yeah, I promise."

He walked across the yard, hurrying now, fearful that he would change his mind. He climbed into the Explorer, fished in his pocket for his keys, and found them dangling from the ignition. On the passenger seat was his camera equipment, a satchel of film, and that unopened bottle. He reached for the liquor, uncapped it, took a long swallow, and then made a whopper of a mistake.

He looked back toward Sabrina's front door.

She stood there, her arms crossed over her slender body to ward off the cold, watching him as if he was going away on a trip and she wanted to assure him she'd wait for him.

The whiskey turned sour, churning, rolling down to his belly with a sickening lurch. He capped the bottle and shoved it into his duffel, then saw the newspaper jammed between the console and the seat. He blinked, trying to recall when he'd bought it.

Zach had been a newspaper freak long before he sold his first shots to the Associated Press. Whatever town he was in, he would buy the local newspaper. At one time it was to see if any of his work had been picked up, and later he wanted to stay aware of his competition. Lately it had been just a bad habit.

This was a four-day-old Rutland newspaper. Zach believed in neither coincidence nor spiritual reckonings, but abruptly he remembered. He'd bought it to read Vermont news, but instead of tossing it away afterward he'd kept it because of the photo on page two of Sabrina and two other women surrounded by cans and boxes of food. Zach felt as if he'd been socked in the gut. The caption read, "Rutland grocers choose Pine Falls the winner in a holiday turkey lottery. Locals donate time to help fill baskets for the needy." Seeing the unexpected photo of Sabrina doing the exact same thing she'd been doing when he met her years ago twisted the cap off of a dozen memories.

His mother had been the recipient of one of those baskets, and he'd been dispatched to pick it up. When Sabrina came over to assist him, he'd been gripped by lust so fierce he'd actually felt his own cheeks color. He got out of there, arranged his "stay cool" attitude, found out who she was, and had her in bed by the New Year.

Now he stared at the photo for a long time, eyes welling up by the nostalgic punch to his booze-soaked gut. Pine Falls had been the village of his childhood, where he'd raised hell, worked his way through the community college, and watched his mother be buried at the local cemetery. Pine Falls was where he'd won his first photography contest, where he'd seduced and fallen in love with Sabrina McKay, and where he'd lost her to Robert Townsend, the mayor's son.

"Too many memories, too much time passed," he muttered. "Coming back to this one almost got you killed."

He fired the engine, shoved the stick into gear, and drove away determined not to glance back at her again.

He checked into the only motel in town, ignoring the wary look of the clerk when he paid cash. The room looked out on the village square with all its lights and decorated windows. Her words—*I want you*—came back to him, curling around his needy heart with such greed that it terrified him. He was too old, too cynical, too far beyond redemption for such outspoken softness. Damn.

Zach yanked the drapes closed.

Opening his duffel, he pulled out clothes and another bottle of Jack Daniel's. He'd get clean, he'd get drunk, then before dawn tomorrow he'd be on his way out of town.

He eyed the phone, his promise tugging at his thoughts. Calling her was stupid. Remembering the feel of her hands on his head, her body in his arms, and the worried look in her eyes was idiotic. What dumb fate had so possessed him that he drove from Rutland to Pine Falls to pass out in her front yard? His head throbbed too much to think. His heart beat too wildly to consider.

Taking what she offered would be dumb. Insane. Stupid.

Like he believed she really meant it. Like he believed in anything at all.

Only in keeping promises.

He jerked open the drawer of the night table and scowled his way through the thin phone book. The numbers blurred, and he cursed when he couldn't find hers. "How the hell am I supposed to call without a number?"

He tossed the book aside, then instantly grabbed it back, turning pages. Divorced. Not Townsend anymore. Living in the house where her parents had once lived. Questions piled up in his mind; he shook them off. He found the McKay on Laconia Street, and punched out the number, feeling as if he'd accomplished a momentous deed.

"Promise kept," he growled when she answered. "I'm at the motel and I'm okay."

"Hold on a minute, Zach." He waited, hearing a child crying, and then she was back. "I'm glad you're settled."

Settled? God, he couldn't remember the last time he'd felt settled. He wasn't going to ask, but the kid was blubbering louder and louder. "Look, sounds like you got your hands full. Is everything okay?"

"Josh is upset about the tree."

"Josh?"

"My son."

Her son. The kid who found him. "What's wrong with the tree?"

"That's the problem. We don't have a tree."

"Why not?" He winced the moment the question was out. Was he nuts? Asking her questions meant he cared. It meant he wanted answers. It meant he was curious.

"It's a long story."

Say okay and say good-bye. "I got time."

There was a crash, and he heard her curse, which made him smile. When they were seeing each other, she was always telling him he swore too much. "I have to go, Zach. Josh just dropped a box of glass decorations. I'm glad you're okay. How long are you going to stay?"

Stay? What did she think? That he was home for the holidays? But he had no idea where to go when he did

leave. "I'm taking off shortly. Thanks for everything."
And he hung up before she could say anything more.

When he emerged from the bathroom some time later,
someone was banging on his door. He ignored it, pulling
on briefs and jeans. The knocking continued.

"Who is it?"

But there was no answer. He yanked open the door. She
wore a black coat and a plaid scarf and smelled like lilacs.
Her mouth was red, as were her cheeks. Every thought in
his head sprinted for his groin. "Didn't anyone ever tell
you it's dangerous to come to a man's motel room?"

"But I know you."

"No, you don't."

"Then maybe we should get reacquainted."

His eyes widened at this second forthright answer. No
coyness, no flirting for amusement. She was serious.

"I'm out of condoms, remember?"

"I know a drugstore with a magnificent assortment," she
said so matter-of-factly that he scowled. He wanted to ask
how she knew and how often she purchased them, but just
as quickly he reminded himself he didn't care and it wasn't
his business. "Can we come in? It's freezing out here."

"We?" His head was a pounding tangle of confusion
and pain. He felt as if he'd missed an important thread.
From her saying good-bye on the phone to simply appearing and wanting to get reacquainted made his head hurt.

Had she held out the possibility of sex or had he imagined it? He shuddered. Don't ask. Just enjoy the meager
hope.

"This is my son, Josh." Sabrina presented the small boy,
who eyed Zach with some degree of reserve. He had huge
blue eyes and shaggy brown hair and stood close to his
mother, but at the same time his hands were balled into
fists as if holding her hand would make him look like a
sissy.

Zach offered his hand. "Glad to meet you. Guess I owe
you my life, don't I?"

His eyes got even wider as he shook Zach's hand.
"Mommy said you were sick not dead."

Zach eyed Sabrina. A matter of word choice, yes, but to Zach it carried enormous meaning. Drunk was crass and disgusting. Sick was, well, it was just sick. Sweet Sabrina, who always looked for the best in people. "Well, thanks to you, I feel pretty good now."

He didn't, but the small lie brought a grin to Josh's face.

The motel clerk had come out of his office and stood in the brisk wind watching them. Zach opened the door wider and stepped back so the clerk could see that Sabrina and Josh were coming into his room on their own.

She passed by him, leaving that haunting scent in her wake. Josh followed and perched on the edge of a chair. Zach turned on the television for him and in a few minutes he was involved with a Christmas cartoon.

"I have a proposition for you," Sabrina said, pulling off her gloves and stuffing them into her pockets.

His eyebrows shot up. "Is this another proposition?"

"I talked it over with Josh."

So much for sex, he thought, more disappointed than he would have thought possible.

"Are you interested in hearing it?"

"No."

Josh asked, "Doesn't he like us, Mommy?"

"Of course he likes us. He's just being stubborn."

"He won't have to sleep in the yard."

Zach looked at the boy and then at Sabrina. "I won't touch that one."

Sabrina laughed. "We want you to spend Christmas with us. Josh and I talked about you. His kindergarten teacher has been emphasizing that the true meaning of Christmas is in giving, not in getting. I explained to Josh that you used to live here and that you were my friend."

"An apt choice of words," Zach commented.

She shrugged. "We have a pull-out bed in the den that you're welcome to."

He walked to Josh and knelt down. "That's a very generous offer, Josh, and I really appreciate it, but I have some things to do."

"What things?"

"Uh, just some personal things." Like figure out what I'm going to do with the rest of my life.

"But you have to stay for Christmas. We're going to have presents and turkey and Mommy said you'd take pictures."

Zach was touched by the boy's earnestness and surprised at the deep inner tug he felt. It had been a long time since he'd taken pictures just for the enjoyment of the moment. "Well, pictures are pretty important at Christmastime."

"Mommy said that if you stayed—"

Sabrina moved closer to her son and whispered, "I only said it was a possibility."

Zach intervened. "This conversation is between Josh and me." He gave the boy a serious, man-to-man look. "So what's up? Why do I have to stay?"

"To cut down our Christmas tree."

"Hmm, that's a big job. Don't they have trees already cut in the village that you and your mommy can buy?"

"Not like in the woods. Byron and Chris and me couldn't find one."

He glanced over at Sabrina.

"I promised him a big tree, and we were going out to one of the tree farms to cut down our own. Then I got so far behind that I decided to get one here in town. But it's so close to Christmas that there aren't any big, bushy ones left. The McKay property behind the house extends a couple of hundred feet into the woods, and there are a lot of trees. We just need someone with the muscle to cut one down and haul it to the house."

Zach knew those woods. Once he'd hidden from an abusive father in them. Once he'd collected pinecones for a school project. Once he'd kissed Sabrina under an oak tree. "What about those two kids I vaguely remember? Can't they cut one down?"

"That was Byron and Chris. Actually, they're going to their grandmother's house in Maine as soon as their dad gets home from work."

"Well, I guess that answers that. No friends? No other

strong-backed neighbors?'' At her shrug, he asked, ''What about an artificial tree?''

Sabrina paled. ''In Vermont? You're not serious.''

''Sorry.''

''Are you gonna cut down our tree?'' Josh asked, as if Zach would be the sole cause of a lousy Christmas if he said no.

''It seems to me it's a simple request, seeing as how Josh saved your life,'' Sabrina said, amusement curving her lips just enough for him to know that tree-cutting and life-saving were not the issues. Sabrina wanted him to stay, and as much as he hated to admit it, he wanted to as well.

He pulled on a heavy shirt. ''Axe or chain saw?''

Sabrina grinned. ''Your choice.''

Josh jumped up and down. ''Can we go now? Can we?''

Zach glanced outside, swinging his camera bag onto his shoulder. ''We'll have to hurry. It will be dark in an hour.''

Sabrina touched his arm as they headed out of his motel room. ''Thanks.''

''No way. I get to choose how and when you say thanks.'' He deliberately hesitated, then added, ''And I think that when we're alone would be a good time to explore your gratitude.''

Then she tossed him a curve he hadn't expected. ''I look forward to it.''

FOUR

Because of the gathering darkness, a chain saw was the tool of choice. It had been a few years since Zach felled a tree, but the rules he'd learned on how and where to cut to determine where the tree would fall came back as though he'd learned them yesterday.

He handed Sabrina his Nikon, telling her to take some shots of the tree before it came down. Josh wanted pictures, so they needed to be in a sequence, to tell a story.

"I can take them to school for show-and-tell," Josh said in an excited voice.

"Sure can. After the tree is down, we have to shoot the stump, too, so everyone will know where it came from."

"So they'll believe me."

Zach grinned and ruffled his hair. "You got it."

With the early shots taken, Zach made sure Sabrina and Josh were on the opposite side of the marked landing spot before he started the saw.

The tree, a long-needled pine, was bushy, thick, and a little over six feet. Josh had picked out an eight-foot spruce that would never have fit in the house. While his mother explained that they would have to cut off the top branches with that tree, Zach steered the boy to a smaller pine.

When the tree hit the ground at the exact point that Zach had said it would, Josh was wide-eyed. Zach let him take some pictures, and the boy was fascinated with the camera and awed that Zach allowed him to touch it. While they dragged the tree back to the house, he chattered about a friend whose father cut down a tree one spring and it landed on their garage.

"Zach knows what he's doing," Sabrina said.

And when the tree was in the stand, and placed in the living room, Josh eyed the bushy branches and Zach took more pictures. "It's so big," Josh said in awe.

"Good thing we didn't cut down that other one, isn't it?"

The next hour was spent putting up lights, hanging the decorations, and taking more pictures. Sabrina served eggnog and Christmas cookies. Carols played softly, and Josh sat beside Zach and listed all the things he wanted for Christmas, including "a camera just like yours." Zach watched Sabrina roll her eyes as the list got longer and longer.

"Maybe I should just buy Toys 'R' Us, wrap it up, and put it under the tree."

"It wouldn't fit, Mommy," Josh said seriously. "Like the other tree wouldn't fit."

"Smart kid," Zach murmured.

"What do you want for Christmas, Zach?" the boy asked.

The question threw him, and the answer that popped into his mind wouldn't have been appropriate. "I think I got my present when you found me, Josh."

"Is finding sick people a present?"

"Yes," Sabrina said. "And it's time for you to put the angel on top of the tree and then get to bed. It's late."

Zach lifted him up and the gold mesh angel was put in place—a bit crooked, but looking regal and proud.

They all stood back while Sabrina turned on the lights.

Josh clapped his hands and jumped up and down. "This is the best tree in the whole world."

"Absolutely."

"Thanks, Zach," Sabrina whispered, drawing close to him.

He slipped his arm around her for just a moment before drawing back. Then he reached down and lifted Josh up into his arms. "I'm glad you asked me to help," he said to the boy.

Josh only nodded, but he gave Zach a huge hug before going off to bed with Sabrina.

Zach stepped back, looking at the tree, feeling good about the soreness in his hands from dragging the monster back to the house. He sat down on the couch, looking around at the homey touches, which went beyond the festivity of the holidays. Family photos, a small piano with sheet music of "Silent Night" open and ready to be played, and a basket of well-read children's books.

Zach stretched his legs out and closed his eyes. An inner contentment that he hadn't felt in years blossomed inside of him, and he folded his arms across his chest to keep it there.

Fifteen minutes later Sabrina returned to the living room. "Zach, you made this a wonderful tree-trimming celebration—" She cut off her words when she saw that his eyes were closed.

She moved quietly to his side and simply looked down at him. How vulnerable he appeared now compared to the way the troubled man she'd tended earlier had looked. The years had matured him, and she had no doubt that some of his experiences shooting pictures in the world's hot spots had made him wise as well as cynical.

She wondered about the drinking and his early pained declaration, "It's over."

He looked too comfortable to disturb, and she reached for a wool throw to cover him, but he suddenly opened his eyes.

"I'm sorry. Did I wake you?"

He simply looked at her for a few silent seconds as if considering the question. Sabrina's heart and her breathing collided, tangled, and made her dizzy. She started to retreat.

"No. Come here."

"I am here."

"Not close enough."

Her knees were mere inches from his thighs, and when her gaze slid up that long body to his almost smile, she found her own pulse pounding into overdrive. Zach hadn't touched her—he hadn't even moved.

Eyes meshed. Bodies remained still—hers standing and his still sprawled with legs stretched out, arms folded. Silence hummed louder than the soft ticking of the mantel clock.

"The last time I kissed you was on your wedding day."

"In the foyer of the church a few minutes before I was to walk down the aisle."

"You kissed back. Why?"

"I never could resist you. You know that."

"But you blew me off to marry Robert."

"Because you didn't love me and you didn't want any commitment that would tie you down."

"So you got tied-down commitment with Robert and it didn't work. Doesn't sound like much of a trade-off."

She stepped away. "It's a dreary subject. I'd rather talk about you."

"That's an even drearier topic." He straightened, snagged her wrist, and pulled her down so that she sat on the edge of the coffee table facing him. Their knees brushed; hers moved away until he effectively caged them with his own. "Why did you divorce him?"

"He neglected Josh. Never had time for him unless it was some business function where he needed a family scene to make him look good. In public relations looking good and projecting a positive image is a career necessity." She paused, her voice growing softer. "And he cheated on me."

"Why am I not surprised?" Zach murmured. "He always did like women fawning over him. Tell me, how does he explain the absence of you and Josh when someone asks about his family?''

She took a deep breath, the words snagging in her throat. ''He lets anyone who asks assume that I'm selfish and want to live here rather than be in Albany with him. He plays the role of the abandoned husband.''

''And you haven't tried to counter that?''

''It doesn't matter. No one here in Pine Falls believes him, and I don't care what his associates think. I divorced him, and Josh and I have our lives here. I have a good teaching position and Josh is happy. What Robert does or says isn't important.''

''I wish I'd known,'' Zach muttered. ''I would have come back here and wrung the bastard's neck.''

She lowered her head, recalling Zach's telling her she was making a mistake in marrying Robert. On the other hand, she hadn't wanted to hear it and so had avoided directly asking what Zach thought of him. She'd convinced herself that Robert was the man she wanted, the man she loved. And for a little while things had worked out okay. For a little while . . .

Then she felt his hands at her waist, felt him pull her forward. ''What are you doing?''

''Getting Robert out of our conversation and putting you where I want you so you can thank me for my tree-cutting expertise.''

Where he wanted her was straddling his lap. Other times of being in just this position with him tumbled back into her thoughts. Then, as if on automatic, her knees folded, her calves tucked close to his thighs, her breasts brushed high on his chest. And his arousal was evident.

''Just like old times,'' he murmured, sliding his hands up her back.

''Not like old times. Then we made love. I don't think I can do that.'' She felt the familiar needy itch, the heightened awareness that being with Zach had always produced. A need that was hot, deep, and draining.

''Okay,'' he said easily. ''Can you kiss me?''

She blinked at the question. So simple and honest. No

pushy, crass seduction, no arguing with her, no dumping her off his lap because she said no.

But when she looked full into his eyes, she saw the amused smile. "You are a trip, Zach Danforth. You want sex, not a kiss, and you figure if you can't get me in bed directly then you'll just work up to it."

"I always honor the word 'no,'" he said, even as he was drawing her closer, brushing her lips with a teasing madness across her mouth. Never grabbing, but touching her enough to make her ache.

She wanted this. She wanted to be with Zach with an eagerness that astonished her. "Just one kiss."

"Then we'd better make it good."

His mouth angled over hers, dragging her spinning thoughts into a pinwheel of need. She pushed closer to him, pressing her body tight, opening her mouth at his urging. And when his tongue slipped inside, tangling with hers, mating, dancing, flirting, and then devouring, Sabrina felt her attempts at control slip beneath the seduction of every memory she had of him.

Their mouths twisted for deeper sustenance, their bodies arched for maximum indulgence; they embraced, their mutual desire making their mouths do what their bodies craved. Intimacy and fulfillment.

Finally, Sabrina drew back. Zach's head rested against the back of the couch. His eyes were closed, his breathing erratic.

She started to move.

He held her fast.

She ached in her breasts, in her womb, in her heart. Just arousal, she reminded herself, while at the same time knowing that arousal with Zach was unlike what she'd experienced with anyone else, including Robert. And it was too soon, she was too vulnerable, too wary of beginning anything with a man. Especially a man like Zach, who would be gone in a few days, leaving her hurt and lonely.

Zach skimmed the sides of her breasts with his hands, the wool of her sweater a hindrance that she wanted to tear off. Crazy, foolish, outrageous. Hours ago he was a drunk passed out in her yard, and now she wanted to follow through on her earlier statement of wanting him. Perhaps her offhand invitation had been reckless and unwise, but that didn't change the growing realization that she'd accidentally stumbled upon the truth. She wanted to make love with him. She shook her head to clear it of the rampaging thoughts.

"Tonight when you're curled up in your bed, I want you to remember this."

She blinked. Was he serious? He'd just sent rockets off in her heart and he had to remind her to remember? Then with an ease that was so characteristic of him, he lifted her off his lap, set her on the couch, and rose to his feet.

When he reached for his jacket, she felt panic. "Where are you going?"

"Back to the motel. I appreciate you and Josh asking me to stay here, but I don't think it's a good idea."

"Am I—uh, I mean, are we going to see you tomorrow?"

He looked down at her, looking lonely and sad but resolute. "I don't think so. I'll send the pictures after they're developed." He leaned down and dropped a kiss on her forehead. "Thanks for everything, especially that kiss."

And a few moments later he was gone.

FIVE

At eleven o'clock on Christmas Eve morning, Zach parked in front of her house, adjusted his sunglasses, and tried to ignore the battalion of knots in his spine.

He got out of the Explorer before he could change his mind and grabbed the two packages, which now felt awkward and cumbersome. When was the last time he'd done something like this? He couldn't recall. When was the last time he'd watched a sunrise instead of cursing the intrusive morning light? Never. When was the last time he'd walked out on a woman when five minutes more of kissing her would have had her in bed? Once. When she told him she planned to marry Robert Townsend.

Okay, so the tree-cutting, the wide-eyed kid, and yes, Sabrina, too, had caught him up in all the Christmas shit. It didn't mean anything—just an emotional aberration that would go away as soon as he got out of Pine Falls.

Just get it done, he reminded himself, and make your exit.

He seriously considered putting the packages down, ringing the bell, and fleeing. "Coward," he muttered under his breath. But he didn't run, and when she pulled open the door he savored her look of surprise.

"Zach! I didn't expect you." She wore a long red sweater and black leggings. Her hair was swept back with combs and her mouth was red and moist. Her scent circled around him, making his blood rush and his mind dizzy.

"I didn't expect to be here, either. Bad time? You on your way out?" He expected Josh to come racing around the corner, and when his gaze came back to Sabrina she was folding and unfolding her hands. Nervous, uneasy, or both. Suddenly he wished he'd called first. Now he damned his impulsiveness. "Where's Josh?"

She pulled the door open wider, albeit reluctantly, and gestured him inside. "He isn't here, but he should be back soon."

Her standoffishness made him scowl. "You don't need to use your son to warn me off, Sabrina. I didn't come here to finish what we started last night." Although doing just that appealed mightily.

"What?" She looked confused. Then, "Oh, no, I wasn't worried about that."

For reasons that made no sense, her dismissal wounded his ego. Keeping his tone easy and distant, he said, "If I'd intended to seduce you last night, I would have."

If he'd expected to get a denial or a blush or even an argument, it didn't happen. Instead, as though she hadn't heard him, she glanced at her wristwatch, obviously gauging the time she could spare. "Would you like some coffee?"

He stared at her, and when she wouldn't look at him directly but again checked her watch, Zach figured he knew a brush-off when he saw one. "No, thanks. Look, obviously you're on your way someplace. This isn't a big deal. I brought the pictures for Josh."

"Already?"

"I went to a place that develops them in a couple of hours." He handed her a fat envelope.

"You didn't have to do that." She walked into the living room, and with an eagerness that had him wondering if

Townsend ever took pictures of his son, she opened the envelope. "He won't have show-and-tell until after the first of the year. Take off your jacket and sit down."

"I had to make sure they were okay. Wouldn't do to have heads cut off or out-of-focus and blurry shots."

She glanced up with a kind of amazed astonishment that actually embarrassed him. "Blurry shots? You? Don't be ridiculous."

"They're in order," he said, tossing his jacket on a chair. At her puzzled look, he added, "Photos relive the experience better when they're looked at in the order the shots were taken. Old habit of mine. In the news business, putting the photos into a story unit adds cohesion, plus it has a calming effect on a frazzled editor who freaks if he has to sort out what came first. Sometimes some of the best shots are not the before and after, but the emotional experience of what took place in the process."

Her eyes were wide, her attention fully on him. "I never thought of keeping photos in order, but it makes sense."

He shrugged, wondering what had possessed him to say so much. As she began to look through them, Zach felt like this was some supreme test of his work. Which was totally insane. His expertise, or at least it used to be, was in blood-and-glory shots, not wide-eyed wonder in a kid and interesting light-and-shadow angles on his mother. These were snapshots, for God's sake. Even so, they were good; he knew it, and he wanted her to like them too.

She looked at each one closely before moving to the next. She took a longer time with some, and Zach imagined those were the ones of Josh. When she was all finished, she looked up with tears in her eyes.

"These are incredible."

"Thanks. They were easy to take. You and your son were expressive and relaxed."

"Have you thought about doing this kind of photography professionally? Family shots, emotional moments captured on film win prizes all the time."

"My prize-winning days are over." Actually, selling them had been a consideration when he'd realized how poignant they were; for a little while, he'd wrestled with the potential success of the photos against the sentimental silliness of just handing them to Sabrina. Then again, seeing the look of pleasure on her face gave him an unexpected joy that he'd never gotten from the sale of a photo. Maybe there *was* something to all the Christmas shit.

"I love this one of Josh climbing over the stump to get to the tree after you cut it down. With the setting sun coming through the woods, it has a whimsical yet spiritual quality." She studied it. "And you know what? You're right. Seeing the picture in the order in which it was taken makes it more powerful than if I'd seen it first."

"Yeah, context makes a difference." Zach took a Christmas-wrapped package from a bag and placed it under the tree. Then he took out a smaller one and slid it in, too.

Sabrina gave him an amused look. "For someone who was so bah-humbug about Christmas yesterday, here you are with fabulous pictures and presents."

"I figure I owe you something for dragging me out of the cold. Better go."

He reached for his jacket. A white envelope fluttered out of a side pocket. When Sabrina picked it up, two photos slipped out.

Zach snatched up the photos.

"I want to see them."

"No."

"Why not? They look like the ones you took last night."

"They're not very good."

"You aren't capable of taking a bad picture. Let me see them."

"They're out of order. They won't make any sense."

"You're stalling."

"Damn right."

They stood almost toe to toe. Her head was tipped to the side, her eyes determined and warm and working crazy magic on his senses. One of the combs in her hair had slipped, and Zach pushed it back in place. "It's time for me to go."

"Please let me see them."

Her words brought her breath puffing across his mouth and he rubbed his thumb just under her bottom lip. "You disturb me, you know that?" he whispered. "You make me want things I forgot about a long time ago."

"Like being with people who care about you at Christmas?" she murmured.

"Like being with you."

She touched her finger to his cheek, and Zach would have sworn that every nerve in his body jumped. "I never forgot you, Zach. I never wanted to."

He drank in those words like a parched man would drink water. He hadn't come here to have his heart melt, or to break up that hard shell he'd put in place so long ago.

"When you walked away from me for Townsend, I convinced myself it was the best thing. I was too hard-edged, too wild, and I had nothing to offer you. I've probably lost most of the edge, and acting wild—well, you see where that landed me. Drunk, in your front yard. But I still have nothing to offer you. *That* hasn't changed."

"Robert offered me a lot of things, and in the end those things were meaningless. Just stuff. I don't want stuff from you, Zach."

He scowled. Things were moving too fast, and the look in her eyes was too sincere. Don't be an idiot, he told himself. This isn't the place for you; this isn't the woman for you. Not Zach Danforth who had blown a lucrative career because of boredom. Or perhaps "idiocy" was a better word. He couldn't sort that out and have it make sense; as for sorting out his feelings for Sabrina . . . oh, hell.

Zach took her arm and pulled her closer. He could feel her heat and was too aware of the sizzle of arousal that singed his nerves. He needed to bring some sanity and reasoning into all of this. "Okay, Sabrina, time to quit the dancing around, time for some truth. What do you want? Sex the way it used to be between us? An affair? Some payback to show old Robert you can do what you want to do? That you can woo back the guy you walked away from?"

She backed away. "Is that what you think of me?"

"I don't know what to think. I don't know you. Hell, you don't know me. We're two people who once were lovers and we're cruising around one another like a couple of heat-seeking missiles."

"Maybe we need to give ourselves a chance to find out."

He looked at her a long time, then laughed. "Where have I heard that before?"

She didn't laugh. "I don't know what you mean."

"Don't you? You don't remember the sleigh ride when I told you that if I got you into bed we'd burn up the sheets, and you said . . ." He paused, waiting for her to catch up.

"Oh, God."

"Yes, indeed."

"I can't believe you remembered that."

"It was a momentous statement, and it led to a weekend of great sex." Not much about you that I've forgotten, he mused silently, which, now that he thought about it, was odd indeed. His memory of the women he'd known since Sabrina was sketchy at best. And then there was that small detail of how despite being drunk, despite his intentions of not going to Pine Falls, he'd ended up there. And in her front yard.

She paced the room, circling the furniture, fussing with an ornament on the tree, glancing down at the packages he'd tucked among the others. "I don't know what to say."

"And you don't know what you want." He straightened and moved to the door.

"Wait." She grabbed his arm, pulling him around to face her. Softly, she brushed her hands over his jacket, resting them against his chest. "Tonight is the Festival of Lights. I mentioned it before, but now I'd like you to come with me and Josh. Then"—she took a deep breath as if laying hold of a new decision—"after Josh is settled and asleep, then we can, uh, well, we can spend time together alone and . . ." She glowered at him. "Don't just look amused. You know what I'm saying."

"I haven't a clue."

"Damn you, Zach."

"There's that."

"You won't make this easy for me, will you?"

"Ah, easy I can do." Without a moment of hesitation, his mouth enveloped hers in a hot, wet kiss that made the one of the previous night seem almost prim. His hands gripped her hips, bringing her against him, and her arms circled his neck tightly. Tongues tangled, mouths twisted, nipping, searching for more. Zach leaned against the door, taking her weight as she practically climbed into his clothes.

"I like this," she murmured. "I want more."

He wrapped his arms around her, held her snug against him, slowing her down. "You want too much, baby . . ."

Her mouth was nibbling on his chin and his neck and searching lower. He held her, eyes closed, enjoying the feel and the scent and the eagerness.

"Well, now. What have we here?"

Zach's head came up and Sabrina froze. She tried to untangle herself, but Zach held tight.

The man standing across the room, his eyes narrowed in judgment, his hand gripping a bag of Christmas packages, was Robert Townsend.

SIX

Urbane, sophisticated, pinched nostrils flaring, he entered the room like a king peering in disgust at his servants. "Is this the kind of lewd behavior my son is exposed to?"

Sabrina, Zach noted, made herself not run her hands down to check her clothes or reach to secure the combs in her hair. She'd done nothing wrong, and obviously she wasn't about to give her ex the pleasure of seeing her nervous guilt. Zach was impressed.

"Where's Josh?" she asked, and he guessed now that Townsend was the source of her earlier nervousness. He'd shown up unexpectedly and taken his son Christmas shopping. No doubt Sabrina worried he would return and find Zach there. Zach scowled. What the hell was she worried about? She didn't have to answer to Townsend.

"He's in the kitchen," Josh's father said. "He bought those Christmas cookies you like and he's putting them in the cookie jar." He knelt down and placed the packages beneath the tree, tossing the bag aside. Standing, he took off his coat and hung it in the closet. It was a territorial gesture, Zach decided, clearly saying, *I belong here and you don't.*

"Well, Danforth, what brings you back here—besides my wife? Last time I checked, Pine Falls wasn't a hot place for news. You didn't tell him I was in town, did you, Sabrina? Afraid he'd embarrass you like he did last time? Then again, from what I've heard he's been an abject failure of late. Out of work, drinking, bumming around. No secrets in the news business, are there, Danforth? An executive at CBN in New York told me about your fall from grace."

Zach kept his face bland and dipped his hands into his pockets.

Sabrina glared at her ex-husband. "You just couldn't resist, could you?"

"Darling, I'm just trying to save you some future grief."

"You mean worse than I had from you? Impossible."

"You had everything you wanted from me," Townsend remarked, lifting a table ornament and examining it before setting it down.

"Except your attention and your time."

Time to split, Zach decided. He zipped up his jacket, aware of the smirk of satisfaction on Townsend's face. The jerk figured he'd won. He assumed Zach was leaving because he was too indifferent to bother interjecting himself into the fray, either with a defense of Sabrina or himself. Truthfully, Zach didn't see the point. And what did he care what Townsend thought? The guy was a jerk. However, he was Josh's father, and Zach wouldn't have faulted him for wanting time with his son. What pissed him off were his barbs, his gossipy judgments, and—most of all—his nastiness toward Sabrina. That obviously was not new, and not his problem, Zach reminded himself. He had only stopped by to give her the pictures and leave the two presents—he was on his way out of town.

He pushed his hands into his jacket pockets. His keys were in one, the envelope with the two photos in the other. It was all he intended to take. Nothing more, nothing less. Damn. "I'll say good-bye to Josh."

"No, Zach. I don't want you to leave."

Townsend sat relaxed on the couch, arms extended along the back, feet propped on the coffee table. Sabrina moved the photos before he knocked them off. He peered at Zach. "Before you go, tell me—did you come back to Pine Falls and my wife for some solace and sex, or just sex?"

That pushed him over the edge. "You know, Townsend, I thought you were an ass before you married Sabrina. Now you've removed all doubt." He paused. "By the way, you have pink lipstick on your collar."

Townsend gaped, then sagged a moment before he recovered. "I ran into an old friend at the drugstore and she hugged me."

"Gee, and lipstick got all the way through your coat collar to your shirt. Powerful lipstick they're making these days."

"Now wait a goddamn minute," he said, rising from the couch. "I come in here and find you two feeling each other up and I'm the one who has to explain?"

"Josh was with you, Robert," Sabrina said, her voice brittle. "Your son. How could you? And lipstick on your collar is such a cliché." She turned away, but not before Zach saw the disgust on her face.

"I certainly don't have to explain anything to you after what I just saw," Robert snapped, getting to his feet and turning away from her as if to say the matter was closed.

Sabrina reached out and pulled him back around. His look of astonishment at her action amused Zach.

"When Josh is involved you couldn't give me an explanation that would be good enough. But then, why am I not surprised at your behavior? You sure didn't think about Josh when you were doing overnights with all those other women. And when you had excuses for missing his birthday, and you didn't have time to talk to him when you called me. And this morning you show up here like some devoted father and give me a story about how you want to make things right with your son. Now this."

"For God's sake, Sabrina—"

"Mommy?" The boy eased into the room, clutching the

huge green-and-red bell-shaped cookie jar. "Hi, Zach. I didn't know you were coming back today. Are you going to stay with us now?" He scowled. "Is Daddy going to stay, too, Mommy?"

"That's what they're trying to work out, Josh," Zach said, moving to the boy and placing a hand on his shoulder. "Your dad can't decide whether he wants the front yard or the back."

Josh giggled. "Daddy, you want to stay out in the yard?"

Townsend huffed. Sabrina palmed her own mouth to hide her grin, and Zach swept up the photos. "You going to hog all those cookies?"

"They're Mommy's favorite."

"Mine, too. While your dad is trying to decide, let's you and I go into the kitchen and check out the pictures."

Josh went ahead, and Zach turned back. "Hey, Townsend, just for your information. I quit CBN. And as for Sabrina, she's too good for either of us."

Sabrina watched Zach and her son saunter into the kitchen. She took a deep breath and forced herself not to follow. She would much rather eat cookies and look at Zach's pictures again than deal with Robert.

"I don't like this, Sabrina. He's not the kind of man I want around my son."

"Really. And what kind of man would suit you?"

"Well, now that you ask . . ." My God, she thought, he thinks I'm truly asking for his opinion. "I was thinking that we should reconsider this divorce."

She blinked, and blinked again. "What?"

"Josh needs a father, and you and I should be thinking about what's best for him."

"I always think about what's best for him. In our case, reconciliation would not be."

"You won't even give us a chance?"

The pitiful tone in his voice brought her up short. Robert, who usually demanded and lectured, suddenly needing something from her? It was too strange. She ventured her own question. "A chance to do what?"

"Really, Sabrina. Don't be obtuse. A chance to be a family again." He approached her and took hold of her shoulders, his hands moving in a kneading motion. "We were happy once. We can be again. Josh and I had a great time today, and I . . ." He paused long enough to clear his throat. "Well, I realized that I have to be with him, to show him what it means to have a full-time father." He brushed his mouth across her forehead. "He needs more than a mother, he needs both of us. And I know you, darling. You want Josh to be happy and well adjusted."

Her head was reeling. "He is."

"Of course he is, but think how much better it would be for him if we're together." He pulled her into his arms, murmuring into her hair. "I'm asking you to marry me again. We could announce the news when your parents come. You know your mother was never happy with the divorce. Maybe a New Year's wedding. A new start in a new year. Yes, that would be perfect."

Whether it was the sound of Josh and Zach laughing in the kitchen or the uneasy sensation of Robert's hands on her or the sudden about-face in his attitude, she didn't know, but Sabrina stepped away, ducking his attempt to bring her closer to him.

"You know, Robert, if you had said all those things to me a few days ago, I might have at least given them some consideration. You are Josh's father, and you have every right to see him."

"And what about us? Darling, think how Josh would love having us together again."

"To be honest, it all sounds a little too desperate."

It was his turn to blink.

"Desperate?"

"Yes. You show up here unannounced, wanting to take Josh Christmas shopping. That was fine, but from that to remarriage . . . What pieces am I missing here?"

"Don't you believe I'm sincere?"

"Yes, as a matter of fact I do. I think you honestly want

what you're asking for, but what I don't know is why.''

"Why? Christ, did you ask Danforth why he was drunk in the front yard? Oh, yes, Josh told me all about that scene. Have you asked him why he has no job? Why in hell is he here, for God's sake."

"No."

"No? That's all you can say—no?''

"I didn't ask him because I know he wouldn't tell me. And not because of some ulterior motive. He'd be afraid I'd feel sorry for him, and Zach hates to have anyone pity him. He needed us for a few days and we needed him. Christmas is about giving. And you know I've always believed that nothing happens in life without a purpose. Zach ending up here has a purpose. In time I'll know what it is. You have a purpose in wanting Josh and me back. And that's where I have a problem with you, Robert. Nothing is ever unconditional, and the efforts you've made in the past toward us as a family have been to benefit you. You haven't explained how this time is different.''

Robert rolled his eyes. "And what about the scene I walked in on? Danforth's purpose was to get you in bed. A blind man couldn't have missed that.''

"Actually, you're wrong," Sabrina said, straightening the couch pillows. "I was trying to get him into bed.''

He glared at her, his face paling, than reddening. "You're covering for him. You always did have this weakness for protecting him like he was some lost child.''

"Maybe because he needed me," she said quietly, glancing toward the kitchen and listening to the happy sounds of her son giggling. Josh had never been happier than he'd been since he'd found Zach. For that matter, neither had she.

"I need you, too.''

"For what?''

Robert hesitated, rubbing his hand across the back of his neck, apparently searching for the appropriate words.

"It seems a fairly simple question," Sabrina said. "You need me for what?''

Silence engulfed the room. Sabrina waited.

"I can answer that." Zach leaned against the doorjamb. Sabrina looked up and Robert scowled as he turned around, his body visibly stiffening. In the utter stillness, Sabrina held her breath.

SEVEN

Robert Townsend narrowed his eyes, his resentment unmistakable. "This isn't your business, Danforth."

"Nope, but it's Sabrina's question that you haven't answered. Figured I'd give it a try. Since Pine Falls isn't a hot place for news, as you so adroitly pointed out, I've tried to keep informed by reading the bigger newspapers. I picked up an upstate newspaper this morning when I was getting coffee, and what do you know—I found this interesting political scene section with a small paragraph about prospects for candidates. The name Robert Townsend was mentioned for the state senate." Zach grinned. "May I be the first to offer congratulations. You know what they say. There's no secrets in the news business."

"Now just a minute," Robert began. "Sabrina, I can explain all of this. I was approached by the party as a possible candidate, but nothing is settled."

Sabrina crossed her arms. "Oh, yes, something is settled. Your phony attempt to convince me you wanted Josh and me for ourselves. This is the why, isn't it, Robert? You need a family to bolster your candidacy, and what better

way than to reconcile after a divorce? You are beneath con-
tempt.''

"Danforth, this is all your fault," Townsend snapped.

"Hey, I only reported what was in the newspaper. Call
them and complain. You can always deny the story or say
that after serious reflection, you're withdrawing your
name.''

Sabrina took his coat from the closet and handed it to
him. "Good-bye, Robert."

He shrugged it on.

Josh scooted around Zach, his eyes wide. "Daddy, are
you leaving?"

He knelt down and ruffled Josh's hair. "Got to go, but
I'll call you after Christmas to see what Santa brought."

Then he reached beneath the tree and retrieved a small
box, slipping it into his pocket. He gave Zach a contemp-
tuous look, ignored Sabrina, ruffled Josh's hair again, and
walked out.

"Daddy, wait. I want to give you a picture." Josh followed his father out to the kitchen.

Sabrina looked at Zach. "What's your guess of what's
in the package?"

"A ring."

She nodded. "He really thought he could convince me,
and if not, opening the box with my parents and Josh here
would have been a very awkward moment."

"He was counting on it being awkward, but you would
have said no."

"Oh, Zach, I don't know. It would have been hard. My
mother would have been thrilled, and he *is* Josh's father."

"Fatherhood doesn't equal sainthood. He's still an un-
derhanded jerk, and he just proved it."

She looked at him. "If he hadn't found you here, and
discovered us—"

"With you feeling me up," he added, taking considerable satisfaction in recalling the scene. "That's an important element."

She chuckled. "Oh, definitely. But if he hadn't, he would

have poured on the charm and used Josh as a wedge and maybe worn me down.''

Zach shrugged. ''Well, he didn't, and you're still standing and I have to go.''

''What about tonight? The Festival of Lights?''

''I think I better pass.''

''No, I want you to come with us.''

''Look, I'll stop by before I leave town.''

She lowered her head, hiding her expression, but he heard the sniffle. He cupped her chin and tipped her head back, lowering his mouth and kissing her.

''I want more than kisses,'' she whispered.

''More makes it tougher to leave.''

''I know that.''

He kissed her again, then opened the door and stared at the couple coming up the walk.

From behind him, Sabrina gasped. ''But they're not due until late this afternoon.''

''It's called a surprise. The second one today.''

Zach nodded to the McKays, said Merry Christmas, and walked to his Explorer.

Caroline McKay, wearing real fur and flawless makeup, looked aghast at her daughter. ''Wasn't that Zach Danforth?''

''Yes.''

''I understood that he was fired from his job. Didn't we hear that at the drugstore, Warren?''

''Yes, we did.'' Sabrina's father, carrying two bags of wrapped gifts, didn't bother to argue. He'd learned years ago that it was less stressful to agree with Caroline.

Sabrina watched the Explorer move down the street and disappear. ''He wasn't fired. He quit.''

Her mother raised her eyebrows. ''But that's worse. Isn't it, Warren?''

''Depends on why.''

Sabrina smiled. She loved her mother, but she adored her father, and she immediately decided that he, too, would have questioned Robert's motives for remarriage.

''And why are we standing out here in the cold?'' He

nudged her mother forward. "Got any hot coffee, Sabrina? How about the mincemeat pie you promised me?"

"I have both," she said, holding the door.

"Do you know why he quit, Sabrina?" her mother asked, still frowning.

"Not yet, but I will."

"That sounds dubious at best."

"Caroline, can we continue this in the house? The neighbors are going to start wondering why we're huddled around the front door."

That moved her mother. "He always was an unconventional sort of boy," Caroline said as she delicately hugged Sabrina. "Darling, the combs are coming out of your hair. And no makeup, not even lipstick. Does she look pale to you, Warren?"

"She looks well-kissed."

"Kissed?" Caroline's eyes widened. "Kissed? Not by that Danforth boy?"

"Oh, Mother, please stop calling Zach a boy."

Caroline lowered her voice as if the neighbors might hear her. "Sabrina, you didn't allow him liberties, did you? You know how he used to chase after you years ago, and then coming to your wedding on that dreadfully loud motorcycle and acting so barbaric by kissing you seconds before you walked down the aisle. It was a scandal."

Warren McKay rolled his eyes. "It was a kiss, Caroline. And any man my daughter kisses isn't barbaric or scandalous, he's privileged." He winked at Sabrina, setting the bags of presents beside the tree.

Sabrina grinned. "Thanks, Dad."

Caroline sniffed. "He just seems inappropriate for Sabrina, while Robert is—"

"Unacceptable," Sabrina interrupted. "I don't love Robert." The moment she verbalized her disinterest in her ex-husband, her heart felt as if it had found solid ground. Of course she didn't love Robert. Perhaps she never had in the way she should have. She'd been in love with the idea of love. She was young and impressionable, and Robert was charming and approved of by the family. Zach was a rogue, a rebel, and she'd feared that her feelings for him wouldn't last. But now she knew they were real. They might have been dormant, they might have been but a flicker for the past six years, but despite time and separation the love she had for Zach had never gone away, it had never died. It was alive and powerful and filled her with joy . . . and resolve.

At that point Josh came rushing in, hurling himself at his grandfather and then at his grandmother. While Caroline was led to the kitchen to look at pictures, Warren McKay took his daughter into his arms.

"So, is this serious with Zach?"

"I hope so."

"Your divorce isn't a year old. You don't want to be too hasty."

"Believe me, Zach isn't pushing me into anything. By the way, Robert was here," she said in a low voice so as not to alert her mother.

"And?"

"He wanted to reconcile."

"And what do you want?"

She shook her head. "I can't."

"Good."

"I thought you liked Robert."

"Your mother liked him, and it was easier to agree than point out that he was shallow and prissy and lacked character."

"Oh, Dad—"

"Now before you get all enthusiastic, Danforth isn't any prize either. No job, dresses too tough, and your mother would be a hard sell to gain approval of him for you."

"I'm a grown woman. Well past the necessity for parental approval. Besides, we're moving way too fast here. I can't even get Zach to take us to the Festival of Lights tonight, so any hope of something more involved is remote at best."

"Have you asked him for Christmas dinner?"

"Actually, I asked him to stay here. I think he was either

worried about my reputation or afraid he might like being part of a family too much.''

Her father took the gifts he'd brought and placed them under the tree. Afterward, he stepped back and, with hands on his hips, said, "Say, this is quite a tree."

"We cut it ourselves. Out back in the woods."

Her father walked all around it and peered at Sabrina through the branches. "Zach do the cutting?"

She nodded.

"Seems he bought you a present, too. And one for Josh. That doesn't sound like a guy who's not involved."

"Well, maybe he's a little involved." She told her father of Robert's less than forthright attempt to convince Sabrina to remarry him and the news that Zach had seen in the newspaper.

"Political office for Robert, huh? Not surprising, but isn't it a bit odd that Zach intervened? I mean, you would have figured out Robert's motives in a few days. Political aspirations are rarely kept secret for long. Seems to me Zach kept himself very much in your life by finding a way to keep Robert out."

Sabrina absorbed this, amazed as usual by how her father could get past the obvious reasons for decisions to the deeper issues behind them.

"Warren, you have to see these pictures!" Her mother came into the living room waving a handful of photos. "They are really quite good."

He looked at Sabrina. "And he took pictures?"

"Yes. For Josh. For show-and-tell."

Her father pursed his lips and looked through the photos. "You're right, Caroline, they are good. Exceptional, in fact. But then, we shouldn't be surprised. Zach is a well-known photojournalist."

"Perhaps, but that still doesn't make kissing Sabrina all right."

"Oh, Mother, for heaven's sake."

Warren put an arm around Caroline and the other around Sabrina and walked into the kitchen. "I'm still waiting for my coffee and homemade mincemeat pie. Hey, Josh, heard it's going to snow tonight. What do you say to going sledding tomorrow after you open all your presents?''

"Yes!"

The pictures were put away, coffee made, and the mincemeat pie brought out. Her parents each had a piece, but Sabrina ate Christmas cookies with her son and thought about Zach. He had kept himself in her life by finding a way to keep Robert out. Dad, she thought, you are simply brilliant. She reached over and hugged him.

"What's this for?" he whispered, patting her arm. "Not that I'm complaining."

"Because I love you."

"I love you, too, honey."

Josh chattered nonstop about Zach and going shopping with his dad and how Zach told him about needing good subjects to take good pictures and that he'd said kids and moms made the best pictures. The afternoon wore on, while Sabrina's mother caught her up on what they'd been doing.

The McKays had talked Sabrina into taking the house to keep it in the family. They had moved closer to their favorite ski area. Her father was the skier, while her mother preferred the warmth of the lodge with other wives. Warren McKay filled Sabrina in on the new shelter for women in crisis that he'd invested in. As a retired attorney, he preferred putting his money into local projects so that he could become involved if he so chose. Sabrina had told him about this particular program in October, and his contribution had given the project a certain credibility, thereby bringing in more donors.

Sabrina fixed Buffalo wings for supper and once the dishes were cleared away, she went into her room to dress warmly for the Festival of Lights.

While she was standing in front of the mirror debating what to wear, her father's comment about Zach continued to roll through her mind, and she decided to call the motel.

"Zach Danforth's room, please."

Five rings later there was still no answer. She scowled, then redialed the motel office. "I'm not getting an answer in Mr. Danforth's room. Could you look out and see if his car is still there?''

Moments later, the clerk said, ''Yep, the Explorer is there. Looks like he's packing it up. Just saw him put something in the back.''

Sabrina's heartbeat tripled. Packing? He was leaving and probably had no intention of stopping by to see her.

She pulled on a heavier sweater over wool slacks, brushed out her hair so that it was loose, and applied a small amount of makeup.

Ten minutes later, as they were climbing into her father's car, she said, ''Would you mind taking Josh and going on without me? I'll meet you there. I have an errand to run.''

Her mother turned in the seat, a frown pinching her forehead. ''Really, Sabrina, can't it wait? You always go with us to the Festival of Lights.''

''This is important. Would you mind taking Josh with you?''

''Of course not, but I don't understand—''

''Caroline, you don't need to understand. You need to say, 'Go do what you have to do.' ''

''But it's Christmas Eve!''

''Well, maybe this errand needs her more than celebrating Christmas Eve.'' He winked at Sabrina.

''Thanks, Dad.''

At the motel she parked beside his Explorer. In the distance she could hear the ringing of church bells and the strains of Christmas music. The lights in Pine Falls were glorious, and their illumination streamed down the streets and around the corners. The residents had begun to gather for the last and final display of lights on the town square. Carolers would begin the singing, and eventually all of Pine Falls would join in.

Sabrina experienced the same fullness in her heart she felt every year—the festival always did that—and yet Zach's unexpected arrival had opened up a part of her that she had thought was long ago closed and locked.

Despite realizing that she was in love with him, she didn't expect any long-term promises from him, and since he wasn't answering his phone, she wondered if he would answer the door. She knocked anyway.

"Go away."

"No. And I'm going to stand out here until you let me in."

To her astonishment he flung the door open. "I don't need this, you know." His eyes burned into hers, and she forced herself not to step away from their intensity.

She wasn't going to be intimidated by him, and dammit, she wasn't going to just walk away because he didn't want her here.

She slipped past him and into the room. His duffel was all packed and ready to be put into the Explorer with the other things. If she'd waited until after the festival, he would have been long gone. "You knew that was me calling, didn't you? You knew, and you deliberately didn't answer."

"It seemed easier, and it avoided this kind of scene." He closed the door and leaned back against it. His chest rose and fell, and he crossed his arms. "You don't get the message, do you? I'm not the man for you."

She slipped off her coat and laid it across a chair. "Why not? Because you quit some high-paying job? Because I found you drunk in my front yard and you have no faith in yourself? Because I broke off with you once and you're afraid that I'll do it again? So to avoid facing any of those questions, you're running away?"

"I'm leaving town. You want to call it running away, call it that."

"You weren't going to stop by like you promised, either, were you?"

"I was going to call."

"Uh-huh. Is that what you were waiting here for? To make sure I'd gone to the festival?" She paced the room, her hair flying every time she turned quickly and glared at him. She pulled off the heavy sweater, plunked her hands on her hips, slipped out of her shoes, and took a step closer to him.

He took a deep breath. "Jesus."

She traced a finger along his jawline. "Then if I wasn't home you could very conveniently say good-bye on my answering machine."

"It just seemed easier."

"You're a coward." She opened the buttons of her blouse.

"Damn right. What the hell do you think you're doing?"

"Taking off my clothes."

"Sabrina, for God's sake!"

He sucked in his breath when her blouse came off, followed by her slacks. She stood before him in a lacy demi-cut bra and panties. His head dropped forward and his body slumped against the door.

Then she walked forward, tucking her fingers into the waistband of his jeans. His skin felt hot and tense. Her own body felt rigid and uneasy. What if he pushed her away? What if he turned away? But her anxiety dissolved when his hands circled her throat, tunneled beneath her hair, and tipped her head back.

"God, this is insane." Then his mouth crushed down on hers.

EIGHT

Insane and idiotic and stupid, but never in his entire life had he craved anything or anyone more than Sabrina. It was as if every decision he'd made since quitting CBN had been a simplistic no-brainer. But now, with her warm body pressed eagerly against him, a reason to resist taking her was as elusive as his control. Her arms climbed around his neck and she sealed her body to his, sending pinwheels of desire spinning through his gut. He swore he could feel her skin even through his shirt and jeans.

He tore his mouth away and held her at arm's length so he could look, so he could allow his senses the feast of pleasure. Her mouth was wet, her green eyes dark and aroused, her breathing as ragged as his. Longing pounded with greedy impatience. He moved his hands down her shoulders to her breasts, then unhooked her bra.

Her breasts spilled into his hands, and Zach shuddered when he cupped the warm flesh. That elusive scent of summer flowers enveloped him as he bent his head and took first one nipple and then the other lightly between his teeth.

She murmured her gratification, her hands grasping his head to hold him against her.

"How can you make that feel so good . . ."

Zach soothed and nipped lightly, murmuring, "My masterful knowledge of your body."

She laughed. "It's been years."

"Some things I couldn't forget." His mouth moved, kissing, tugging, his hands sliding to her bottom and pulling her up against him. Then he lifted her and carried her to the bed, following her down onto the rumpled sheets. He pressed against her so that there was no mistaking his arousal. Denim nudged against her silk panties, with intoxicating friction, and Sabrina began to wiggle.

"Easy, babe," he whispered into her mouth, only to have her wrap her legs around his and trap him in a provocative prison that he gladly accepted. He blew across her lips and didn't miss her shivery gasp. "You're going to come . . ." he felt her tighten and draw back, and he stroked her until she began to whimper.

"You do this to me . . . you always make it happen . . ."

It was her awe, her recognition that he still had this skill with her, this entrenched knowledge of her body, that humbled him. He sucked in a breath, feeling his own frenzy burst from smolder into flame. Their mouths came together, tongues dancing, tangling, tantalizing, and finally languishing into a sultry simulation of the intimacy they both hungered for.

Sabrina wasn't sure what to embrace next—the clamoring swell building low in her tummy or the hunger of his mouth and the dexterity of his tongue. She was whirling precariously close to an orgasm and he wasn't even undressed. His clothes against her nudity increased the erotic friction, yet she wanted to feel his heat, his skin. She reached between them and gloved her hand around him, causing him to jerk up, then roll away from her. But instead of getting rid of his clothes, he kissed his way down her body, sliding across her panties. Her body arched and she groaned.

"Wait." She tried to pull him away. "I want you with me."

"First time is for you. First time is always for you." He tugged her panties off, tossing them aside, and then cupped her. His gaze was riveted on her face, on the tinge of pink that had climbed into her cheeks, at the slight glassiness in her eyes, at the way her tongue rubbed across her lips. His hand lifted and then pressed, lifted and pressed. Dampness. Heat. Trembling. Her arms were flung out above her head, her eyes now closed, her breathing a fast pant. Vulnerable and dazzling and endlessly delightful, he thought, with a reverence that made him too aware of how weak in resolve she made him. He leaned down and kissed her, and she murmured his name as he slipped a finger inside her and felt her burn into his palm.

She pressed once more into the circle of coming fulfillment that was winding tighter and tighter . . .

"Oh, Zach, my God . . ." Then a breath-stopping burst filled her with spirals of color that shot in a million directions. For a few moments she hung there, her back arched, her hands clutching fistfuls of his shirt, her skin flushed, her eyes dazed.

Zach leaned down and nuzzled lightly between her thighs. "I love watching you," he murmured, as she slowly came back down, her body relaxing, her sigh of satisfaction audible.

She lay in a boneless afterglow while he rose to his feet and began shedding his clothes. She felt drugged and lazy, and his motions seemed slow, his eyes fondly watching, a slight smile curving his mouth.

He tossed his shirt aside, the dusting of dark hair on his chest making her fingers itch with the need to touch. He opened his jeans, tugging the zipper down.

She grinned, feeling silly and lightheaded and not even caring. "That's very sexy, you know."

"You always had a thing about watching me undress."

"I always had a thing about you," she said softly, her eyes heavy with overflowing emotion. "I love you."

He went still, turned away so she couldn't see his expression.

She knew it was dangerous to say the words aloud, she knew it wasn't even fair. He was vulnerable and unlikely to turn around and walk away, yet it was also the perfect time, because the declaration was true and joyous and momentous for her.

Watching him, hearing the drone of silence that hummed with increasing tension, she rose up on her elbows. "Zach?"

He turned back, naked, aroused, and quick. He reached down, pulled her across the bed, and then leaned over her, his hands fisted on either side of her body to hold himself above her but not touching. His eyes were dark and fierce, his jaw tight, and his hair delightfully rumpled. She would have smiled at his resistance, at what she knew was coming, but his grim expression caused her to stay still and wait.

"You planned all this, didn't you?" he asked in a gruff voice.

"Going to bed with you? Yes."

"And making some declaration."

"No. I didn't plan to tell you I love you."

"What's going on here isn't love."

"Ah, are these words from the expert on the subject? Or denial because the words scare you?"

"This isn't love," he snapped.

"So if I'd said I love sex with you, that would have been okay."

"Oh for chrissake."

"And what about you telling me on my wedding day that you wanted me to run away with you. It wasn't love, but it was more than you'd ever offered before. As I recall, I didn't force those words out of you."

"That was my ego. You'd left me for Robert and I was pissed."

"And because I was moments from getting married you knew I wouldn't do it. You knew it was safe."

"Yes, goddamn it, it was safe!"

But his eruption didn't phase her, and he was already

sorry for the outburst. He was in the throes of making love—no, no, having sex, the best sex he'd had since the last time he'd been with her—and what was he doing? Arguing about the meaning behind his intentions years ago.

"Well, you're not safe now," she whispered. "I have you where I want you."

"I should blow you off, you know that. It would serve you right," he grumbled.

"But you won't. You want me too much."

She put her arms around his neck and urged him down, opening her legs and wiggling to bring him into position.

He kissed her shoulder, her neck, her chin, and her mouth. "You're too good at this, you know that?"

"Only because I love you."

"No more, okay?"

"Why?"

He blew out a breath. "Because I don't want to hear it."

"Tough. Because I like saying it."

"Making you come was a mistake," he complained. "This time I'm going to return the favor."

She moved in some sultry magical way, and his body responded like he was born to be where he was. She kissed him, stroked her hand down his hip, and ran her foot up the back of his thigh.

"Very nice, very sexy." He slid into her in one fast, hot stroke.

"Oh . . ."

"No?" He started to pull out, and her hands tugged him back.

"Don't even think about it, Zach Danforth."

He began a slow rhythm within her that made his eyes dark and drowsy. Sabrina felt the winding spiral of arousal begin again. Zach felt hot and eager and more intoxicated by her body, her scent, and her eagerness than by anything the best whiskey could offer. Greed seized him with new resolve—he wanted her, craved her, hungered for the sweet silk that enveloped him so tightly.

His body burned, hers was sleek and electric as the ancient rhythm of joining blazed between them. Zach felt the climb begin, and it wasn't slow and deliberate, it wasn't steady and relentless, it was dangerous and fierce and fast and threatened him with much more than the savage peak and roll of consummate satisfaction. He squeezed his eyes closed, whipped his head back, and felt Sabrina hold him steady. His mind, his heart, his very soul bonded with her and he knew he'd come home. Her own climax came just seconds before his, and for a moment they grasped that mysterious and ultimate joy in unison before their bodies collapsed in exhaustion.

A minute or two passed, with only the sounds of uneven breathing, a groan and a shudder from Sabrina. Zach moved a little, his face buried in her shoulder, his body satiated.

Sabrina whispered, "That was incredible."

"Am I dead or does it just feel like it?"

"I feel great."

"You came twice, you better feel great."

They laid tangled in silence for a few moments before she kissed his rumpled hair and wiggled out from underneath the leg that was tossed across hers. Suddenly he felt cold.

"And if we hurry, we won't miss it."

He lifted his head and squinted at her. "Miss what?"

"The final lighting of the Festival of Lights. Afterward, I want you to come back to the house. Josh is going to open two of his presents." She had her bra and panties on, and she was tugging her slacks on. "He's so eager to see what you gave him."

He'd turned onto his back, crossed his ankles, and laced his fingers behind his head. His eyes were narrowed, but only from his unsmiling mouth did she have any sense of his distance.

"In fact, I want to open the box you brought to me."

"I'll save you the trouble. It's a stuffed bear."

"Like the one you gave me before?"

He shrugged.

"I wish you hadn't told me." She slid her arms into her blouse, buttoning it, and when she glanced at him, he was glaring at her. "What's wrong with you?"

"Not a thing. I always like to have great sex and then have my lover leap up and announce she wants to be somewhere else."

"It wasn't as if I was just going to run out. I want you to come with me."

"I already did that," he said succinctly. He rose and strode to her, causing her to take a step back. He gripped her shoulders and pulled her against him, and this time she was dressed and he wasn't. He leaned close, his breath against her ear. "You came here to seduce me, declare you loved me, and hope I'd see the light and return the words back to you. That was the plan, wasn't it? First you save me from freezing in your front yard, and then you lure me with all the Christmas shit, from cutting down a tree to taking pictures. I even got rid of Robert for you. You figured if I did all those things I must be in love. All I needed was the release of great sex, and magically I'd declare that I loved you and we'd live happily ever after. Have I got it about right, Sabrina?"

She tried to pull away, but he held her fast.

"Answer me."

"You make me sound so calculated."

"You learned well from your ex."

"Dammit, Zach, that's not fair."

"Fair? Fair? Christ, what you pulled tonight wasn't fair. I didn't want to need you." Abruptly he went still, then swore vividly before he released her so suddenly that she staggered back. His hands tunneled through his hair. He snatched up his clothes, among them her sweater. He tossed that to her. "Turn the lock on your way out." Then he stalked into the bathroom and slammed the door.

Sabrina clutched the sweater, fighting back her tears. She pulled it on, her heart heavy with regret. Not for what she'd done tonight. She'd never regret that. Her regret was that she couldn't make him understand that she truly loved him and that she believed he loved her.

NINE

In the town square, the crowd gathered for the lighting of the huge Scotch pine that had been planted in the mid-1800s. Lighting the tree as the finale had been a tradition in Pine Falls, a symbol of completion, of gathering all the varied spiritual beliefs and cultural customs together in one grand unity.

But tonight, for Sabrina, the ceremony was just a tinny whine of noise and a blur of intrusive lights. She held Josh's hand, stood straight, and smiled when spoken to, but inside she was a churning mass of heartbreak and confusion. How could she have so misjudged him? She was sure he loved her, sure that all he needed was assurance that she loved him, wanted him.

She'd asked no questions about why he quit his job; she cared about him, not about what he did for a living. She had once deferred to her mother, believing that the first standards for a successful relationship were a socially proper family and a prosperous career. She'd had both of those with Robert, and she'd been miserable.

What she had with Zach was love. But what good did it

154

do her if he wouldn't accept that? Now he was no doubt driving God only knew where just to get away from her.

Josh tugged on her hand. "Can we go home? I want to open my presents."

"In a few minutes. Look, they're going to light the tree."

"Where's Zach?"

"I don't know."

"Didn't you go to get him?"

Sabrina knelt down. "Honey, Zach was just visiting. He helped us with the tree, but he has his own things to do." The words trembled, and she hoped her son didn't notice that she hadn't answered his question.

"But didn't you ask him to come? He wouldn't say no."

Sabrina sighed. *Not to you, sweetheart, but he said no to me.* Just then, all attention turned toward the tree. The switch was thrown and the massive Scotch pine came to life in red, green, and white lights. Murmurs of awe went through the crowd, and a few moments later carolers began to sing "Silent Night." Soon everyone joined in.

"But why didn't you ask him, Mommy?"

"Josh, that's enough," she said irritably. "No more questions."

His mouth trembled, and she drew him close to her. "I'm sorry, honey."

Her own throat was tight, her eyes filled with tears. All she wanted was to go home, close herself in her bedroom, and curse her idealism for putting so much faith in Zach's unexpected appearance. She'd honestly believed his ending up in her yard wasn't a coincidence; she'd honestly believed that it meant he'd come home. Home to her. Home forever.

An hour later, they were back home and Josh was trying to decide which two presents to open. Sabrina's father was relaxing in the lounge chair with a glass of brandy and a cigar. Her mother wrinkled her nose at the smoke but didn't object; long ago she had promised not to complain about special-occasion cigars.

Sabrina had changed to jeans, thick red socks, and a University of Vermont sweatshirt. Her hair was tied back with a red ribbon. She sat beside her son on the floor.

"It's getting late," she said to Josh. "Better choose."

He chewed his bottom lip, touched one box and then another. "I could open them all tonight, then go to bed early and play with them in the morning."

"Good try." Sabrina grinned at his impatience. "And what about Santa? If he comes and sees all the packages are open, he's going to be disappointed."

"But the ones he brings won't be opened."

Warren McKay laughed. "The boy has a point."

Sabrina eyed her father. "You're a big help." To Josh she said, "Two presents tonight. No exceptions."

Finally resigned, he pulled out the present from Robert and the one from Zach. Tearing off the paper on the one from his dad, he studied it for a few seconds, clearly confused.

"It's a chemistry set, honey," Sabrina said, wondering what Robert could have been thinking. The gift was too old for Josh. When he began to pull at the plastic covering to get to the small bottles, Sabrina eased the box away from him. "Let's not take it apart tonight. We need to be at the kitchen table and read the directions first."

Josh didn't argue, and Sabrina guessed he was a bit overwhelmed by a gift he didn't know what to do with. She put the lid on the box and tucked it behind her. With any luck, the other gifts would occupy him enough that she could hide this one away.

"Mommy, Mommy, look!" He held up the opened gift from Zach. "It's a camera with real film and a case and everything. Zach got me just what I wanted."

Caroline McKay frowned. "Why in the world would that Danforth boy buy such an inappropriate gift?"

"As compared to a chemistry set," Warren murmured.

"But a real camera? What would a little boy do with a real camera?"

"Take real pictures. As I recall, Zach does all right with a camera. Maybe he planned to teach Josh."

Caroline sighed. "Well, I suppose it's better than one of

those air rifles or some such thing. And the Danforth boy does take wonderful pictures.''

Sabrina was barely listening. She couldn't help but note that Robert was Josh's father and had no clue what to get him, yet Zach had known exactly what to buy for a little boy he'd known for less than two days.

She watched Josh examine the camera and then deftly load in the film. "Did you tell Zach you wanted one?''

"Uh-huh. When we cut down the tree and he let me hold his. Then he showed me the pictures that I took.''

Sabrina scowled. "Pictures you took? I didn't see those.''

"They were of you and Zach.''

"But I saw the pictures, and I didn't see—'' Realization rushed through her. The two pictures that Zach wouldn't let her see. Two pictures of them.

"Zach, come on in. Josh just opened your present.''

Sabrina turned around, her heart flopping like a fish. He stepped into the house, looking sexy and handsome. His suede jacket was open, collar flipped up, his eyes intense. His smile was visible but uneasy.

Sabrina got to her feet, determined to appear cool and as though she'd expected him. "I thought you'd never get here. Josh is just thrilled with the camera.''

"Sorry I missed the unwrapping.''

Josh rushed to him, eyes wide with delight. "Zach, I put the film in all by myself.''

"You made sure you did it like I showed you?''

"Yep. Just like you showed me.''

Zach ruffled his hair, his gaze meeting Sabrina's.

Why did you come back?

I couldn't stay away.

Sabrina slipped her arm through Zach's, feeling the strain in his body. She urged him toward the kitchen, saying to her parents, "We'll be back in a few minutes.''

She closed the door, and before she could turn fully around, his arms were around her and he was crushing her to him.

"Don't send me away," he whispered. "I'm sorry. I'm so sorry."

Her head was reeling with joy and confusion, her body humming, and her heart almost too afraid to hope. "I would never send you away. Never."

He touched his forehead to hers, whispering so quietly that she couldn't hear him. He took a deep breath, pressed his mouth to her hair, and then slowly released her. He stepped back. "I need to tell you something."

"Oh, Zach . . ." She felt her throat tighten and pressed her fingers to her mouth. She couldn't stop the surge of hope swelling deep in her soul.

He leaned against the counter, hands jammed in his pockets. "There's a reason I quit my job at CBN—"

"You don't have to tell me. It doesn't matter."

"It matters because it's why I quit on you. Why I didn't want to need you."

She started to object again, but something more profound was at work here. He'd come to her, not drunk and unwilling and denying he felt anything, but to give her answers that would affect their relationship. The risk here wasn't in his explanation but in his decision about the two of them.

"Tell me," she said softly.

"The work I'd been turning in for the past six months was getting some criticism from my editors. Too soft, the shots had lost their edge. I thought it was just some bum assignments, but then I got sent to a Third World country that had just gone through a horrendous political uprising. Everywhere I looked were bodies, blood, and evidence of torture. Instinctively I knew these would be pictures that would get me back on top."

She shuddered, but kept her silence.

He didn't miss her reaction. "Exactly."

She frowned.

"I had the exact same reaction. People had been brutally killed, and all I could think about was the boost it would give my career. The work I would have turned in would have killed any idea that Zach Danforth had lost his edge, gotten too soft.''

Sabrina's eyes were riveted on him, on the obvious inner turmoil he was experiencing. "What happened?"

"I froze. I couldn't take the shots. The guy with me who was doing the story freaked out, contacted my editor, who pulled me from the assignment. Before I could be summarily fired, I quit. I wasn't even sure what the hell was wrong with me, but I knew it was over.''

"Those were the first words you said after we brought you into the house," she said softly. "It's over."

He nodded. "In some ways I was glad. I was burned out, tired of taking grisly photos, and quitting rather than trying to save a job I no longer loved seemed like the right thing to do. But after my surge of rebellion passed, I realized I'd thrown away a career, and I had no clue what I wanted to do. I was still wrestling with whether to find another career or figure out a way to take pictures that were more than grit when you came to the motel.''

She watched him, waiting for him to go on. Instead he paced the length of her kitchen. Finally, when Sabrina thought she would explode from the unending silence, he said, "I didn't want to make love to you because my life was in such chaos and I knew that once I crossed that line you would have to be part of any decision I made. So I wanted to get all the other stuff straightened out so that I could offer you more than life with an out-of-work photographer.''

Sabrina pressed her lips together to keep from crying out, but there was no stopping the tears in her eyes. "And I didn't help when it seemed to you that I was pushing you into something too soon."

"If you hadn't said I love you—'' He turned and took her into his arms. "I was furious that you said the words and furious at myself that I didn't have the guts to say them back to you.''

She hugged him. "Oh, Zach. I knew. I knew when you chose my yard to pass out in.''

He reached into his pocket and took out the pictures he'd refused to show her.

"Josh took these of you and me," he said.

He handed them to Sabrina, and when she looked at them, her eyes grew moist. They weren't good photography, but they were wrenching in their simplicity. Zach with his arm around her, and she leaning against him.

"I knew when I saw these, but not until I was forty miles out of town did I realize that I'd left part of myself with you. I wanted a future with you. I felt empty and cold and lonely, and as special as pictures of us in my pocket were, they weren't enough. I wanted you, I wanted to be with you and I wanted to tell you that I love you."

"Oh, Zach, you couldn't say anything that would make me happier." She slipped her hands inside his open jacket and around his waist. "Years ago my heart told me I loved you, and I ignored that. When I found you in the yard, it was like a second chance, an unexpected gift. I didn't want to lose you again."

He lowered his head and kissed her, then whispered, "You make me whole again, you make me full and complete."

Later when they were alone in the living room with only the Christmas tree lights blinking, she curled into his arms. "This is the best Christmas," she whispered.

"Hmm, but I still have to win over your mother."

Sabrina grinned. "When she calls you 'Zach' instead of 'that Danforth boy,' then you'll know."

He chuckled, then tucked her closer. "With you, Josh, and your dad on my side, I can't miss."

"I love you," she murmured.

"Tell me again. I can't ever hear it enough." And when she did, his heart closed over the words and sealed them forever. "Merry Christmas, my love. Merry Christmas."

CHRISTMAS PROMISES

Susan Plunkett

ONE

Marne York punched off the alarm and opened her front door to a pair of icy gray eyes, the same eyes she'd avoided for four years. Before the full impact of the shock settled, Jake Rimsa moved through the doorway, caught her in a rib-cracking embrace, and seized her astonished lips in a heated kiss. The carnal exploration of her mouth left no doubt that he hadn't forgotten what they'd once shared. The way he kissed her warned he wanted it back. And a lot more.

Arms dangling at her sides, she closed her eyes; and, just for a second, was consumed by the violent awakening of desire that she'd thought was slain in a Denver hotel room. The feeling frightened her enough to push against him, then tear her mouth free.

"Merry Christmas, Princess," Jake breathed against her mouth. "Long time no see."

"Why are you here? Where's your sister?" Concealing her emotions was something she was good at—most of the time. She turned away, freeing herself from his lingering embrace.

"Alice went ahead. I'm your ride. Are you packed?" He shut the front door against the damp California afternoon. The air currents sent the tinsel on the flocked Christmas tree dancing.

She studied him as he surveyed her pine-scented living room. Amid the white walls and antique furniture, Jake appeared taller than the last time she'd seen him. His shoulders filled the doorway. Time had sharpened his chiseled features into dangerous good looks. There was nothing pretty or soft about him. Judging from the way his black hair curled around his ears and neck, the FBI had looser grooming rules than did the Navy SEALS.

Although Jake had matured, she realized he hadn't really changed. There was still an air of determination about him. The way he studied her and the room made Marne uncomfortable, made her feel like he was here on a mission and he aimed to succeed. "Was this arrangement your idea, Jake?"

"I figured you must be ready to see me if you agreed to come on the same Christmas I was coming. But picking you up wasn't my idea. Alice asked. Hell, I haven't seen her for a year, how could I say no?" His gaze roamed toward her white kitchen.

Jake never could say no to his sister. Marne could. The next time she saw Alice, she was going to rake her over the coals for this little one-on-one holiday surprise.

The phone rang. "I sincerely hope that's Alice." Marne stormed through the living room and into the kitchen. "I don't appreciate being manipulated."

Within seconds of answering the phone, Alice was forgotten. Marne's pencil flew across the tablet kept beside the phone. By the time she hung up, she had new reasons to hate holiday surprises. She folded the paper and grabbed her Gore-tex jacket from the back of a kitchen chair. She started for the garage before remembering that she'd lent her car to Maria Sandavol until after Christmas.

"How badly do you want to get to the Christmas reunion on time?" She pulled her house keys from her pants pocket. "Where do you need to go?"

"County Hospital." She hurried across the living room. "Why?"

The man always did ask a thousand questions. "Just give me a ride or get out and I'll call a cab."

Jake hesitated, then opened the door. "Let's go."

Despite her rush, she took the time to lock the front door and activate her security alarm.

"That system wouldn't keep a hungry rat out," Jake grumbled. "I'll put in a good one after Christmas."

"I don't need anything from you, Jake." She hurried down the walk.

"So you've said." He caught her arm, then steered her to his car. "There's nothing worse than relying on something, or someone, that fails when you need it. Consider a better security system a Christmas present."

She got into the car. "What do you want in return?"

"Not a goddamn thing." He slammed the door.

"Right," she murmured before he opened the door on the driver's side. The kiss still tingling in her veins proved him a liar. He wanted something all right. The same thing he'd wanted twelve years ago. But she wasn't a love-struck seventeen-year-old anymore. This time, he wouldn't get the Christmas gift he wanted. Not from her.

He started the car. "Put your belt on."

She complied, bit back her agitation, and changed tactics. The car was a new Lincoln, not the usual wheels for a truck man. She guessed his tastes had changed. "Nice car."

"Rented."

"Figures."

He pulled away from the curb. "You didn't think I drove from Virginia, did you?"

She wished he had driven. There was a helluva snowstorm shutting down the interstates in the Midwest. "Why'd you come, Jake?"

"Probably the same reason you're going. I promised that nothing short of my own death would keep me away this Christmas." He accelerated onto the freeway and wormed the car into the endless stream of traffic. Riding with him prompted an episode of déjà vu. He treated the Lincoln like an oversized race car and took advantage of any space greater than ten feet to change lanes. "Besides, I wanted to see you."

"You've seen me. Drop me at the hospital, then go on. Tell them I'll be there as soon as I can."

"Thought you didn't have a car." He glanced over his shoulder, then changed lanes.

"I have a car." It was none of his business what she'd done with her car.

"Yeah? You always did have an eye for the expensive ones." The hint of disdain for her automotive tastes in her early twenties rang out loud and clear.

She looked out the side window and ignored him. The days of BMWs and Mercedes died four years ago. Today she drove a cheap, reliable compact. Unobtrusive beige. A car the women she rescued through the Grayson Foundation felt comfortable borrowing in a pinch, like Maria had done for Christmas.

"I'll wait around until you're finished at the hospital."

"I'd prefer you didn't. I'll make a call, rent a car, and drive up." That's what she should have done in the first place. But then, she'd had no idea Alice would stoop to backing out of giving her a ride and send Jake in her place.

The exit ramp to the hospital was stop and go through the traffic light.

"What'd I do to you, Marne?"

"Nothing."

"Was that the problem? Something I didn't do?"

"No."

"I didn't make enough money? Didn't fit into the social set you and my sisters belonged to? Had the wrong job?"

"Drop it, Jake. It isn't open for discussion. I've moved on. So have you." She turned on the radio. "You want nostalgia, listen to the oldies station."

The tires squealed as he accelerated through a left-turn yellow light. He reached down and turned off the radio. "I don't want nostalgia. I want you. In bed. Breathing hard. Wanting me as much as I need you."

"I don't want you." Her voice was steady despite the

images and old memories he dragged through a crack in the door she'd slammed shut years ago.

"The hell you don't. Christ, I felt it when I kissed you."

"You surprised me. Is that the only way you get a woman to kiss you these days?" One glance at his dangerous, dark gray eyes denied her goad. Four years, and he was still as devastating to look at as ever.

"What do *you* think?"

"I don't think about you at all," she lied.

He maneuvered the car into a tight parking spot in the crowded hospital parking lot. "Not even at Christmas?"

"I don't think on Christmas. It's my day off." She let the seat belt clasp snap back, then got out of the car. "Thanks for the lift. Good-bye, Jake."

Jake got out and slammed the door hard enough to rock the entire car. Goddamn it, she was not going to tell him good-bye again. Not this time.

He watched her hurry through the parking lot. Gone were the trademarks of her privileged upbringing. Jeans, running shoes, and a worn jacket had replaced the Neiman Marcus designer clothing he'd associated with her for the last twenty years. Her blond hair hung straight to the shoulders of her oversized all-weather jacket. Time had hardened her fine pixie features into a more classic beauty that she no longer enhanced with cosmetics. The more impassive her blue eyes became, the more uneasy Jake felt.

Whatever had changed her mind about wanting him four years ago had also changed damn near everything else about her. After banging his head against a wall of silence for a couple of years, he'd tried to walk away, reasoning that he would be a fool to want someone who didn't want him. Especially when he knew that no amount of education or sophistication could change the fact that he had grown up on the Great White Way, the ugliest, richest drug and sex strip in the valley. She had grown up surrounded by culture and steeped in class.

God help him, he still wanted her.

Well, they had a long drive ahead. The heavy traffic two

days before Christmas worked to his advantage. She would be a captive audience and have to talk to him. Finally.

He followed as she dodged cars on the way to the emergency room. Inside, the crush of humanity filling the small space promised a miserable afternoon for the hospital staff. Violins cried "Silent Night" through the waiting room speakers. Two children wailed an off-key duet from opposite sides of the room's long lines of worn plastic chairs. They passed a purple-faced man coughing into a handkerchief. The smells of disinfectant and vomit stung Jake's nostrils. Ignoring the throng clustered around the information desk, Marne rounded the partition.

She seemed at home, unaffected by the sights and sour smells. This was a new side of Marne, an unexpected one.

"Marne." The sound of her name brought her around sharply.

"Where is Angela Tomari?" Marne asked the nurse who'd called her name.

Jake recognized the name from the past and an image of a vivacious teenager with dark hair and dark, laughing eyes popped into his mind. Hell, it couldn't be the same nymphet. Or could it?

"Sixth-floor surgery. She's in bad shape."

"Thanks." Marne threaded through the minor injuries crowding the waiting room. At the elevators, she turned to Jake. "You don't need to come. Go do Christmas with the families. I may be here for a while."

"I'm stickin' around." She wasn't going to get rid of him that easily.

"Your choice."

"Finally," he said under his breath. It was about damn time he had a choice.

They rode the elevator to the sixth floor in charged silence. The doors barely opened, and Marne rushed to the nurses' station.

"I'm Marne York. Angela Tomari asked to see me before surgery."

A doctor dressed in greens looked up from the chart he was examining. "What the hell took you so long?"

"I stopped for a burger and fries. What do you think?" she snapped.

He eyed her warily, then looked at Jake. "I'm Dr. Kulick. Come on." He started down the hall. "She's touch and go. We're almost ready to take her into surgery."

Jake followed the pair down the corridor. Marne was much too comfortable here. When he was told that she was working with battered women, he had assumed she had an office job and spent all of her time organizing elaborate parties to benefit some charity.

"How long ago was she brought in?" Marne matched the doctor's long strides.

"We've had her an hour. She didn't want any anesthesia until she talked to you." He scowled. "Who are you, Marne York, that she would refuse painkillers to talk to you?"

"A friend. How bad is she?"

"Broken leg, shattered left forearm. Two broken ribs. Internal bleeding. Her face has severe trauma."

Marne swore under her breath.

"Wait here," she told Jake as she followed the doctor into a room.

He shoved his hands into the front pockets of his jeans and stayed put. He'd seen enough broken bodies over the years and had no desire to confront a ghost from the past in a hospital bed.

The fires of outrage, helplessness, and sorrow roared through Marne when she saw Angela surrounded by a medical team. Julius Tomari had outdone himself this time. Angela's ex-husband's fists had reshaped the left side of her face. The lopsided swelling of her mouth indicated he'd knocked out several teeth. An IV needle protruded from the back of her black-and-blue right hand.

"Angela?" Marne said softly. "I'm here."

"Claritha," Angela rasped, her right eye spilling a river of tears along her temple. "Find her. I put her out the window. Ethcaped. Before he broke th' door."

"I'll find Clarissa and bring her to you. Jesus, Angela,

let them get you into surgery." It hurt to look at the young woman's battered body. She rested her hand on Angela's arm.

Angela caught her fingers and squeezed. "He thaid . . . he'd kill you. Before Christmath."

Marne swallowed. The lump in her throat compounded the bile in her stomach. "Thanks for the warning. I'll be careful. Let them take you into surgery now. I'll take care of Clarissa. I'll find her, Angela. I promise you'll have your daughter with you before Christmas."

A wildness in Angela's eyes sent ripples of gooseflesh over Marne.

"Don't trust . . . copth." Her message finished, Angela exhaled in relief.

"OR-6 is ready. Let's go, people," the doctor called. In a heartbeat, the room came alive. Before Marne could ask what Angela meant about trusting cops. She probably meant the cops hadn't protected her as they'd promised when she testified against Julius after the divorce.

Marne walked out of the room and right into Jake's solid chest. He had been watching the scene in the room, and now he looked at Marne warily.

"Angela Tomari? Jesus, she used to be such a pretty girl."

"You know her?" Jake was full of surprises.

"Yeah. Long time ago. She married Julius, hell, sixteen years ago. We were kids then."

"She grew up and divorced him." Marne led the way down the corridor and toward the elevators.

"And he beat the shit out of her when he caught up with her?"

"That was two and a half years ago. She pressed charges, and he went to jail for felony assault and battery." She glanced at the thunder in Jake's face. "His second felony. This will be his third."

"I remember Julius as a hard, sneaky bastard."

"He hasn't mellowed with age, just gotten meaner."

Jake shook his head. "He won't be easy to find, even if the cops actually look for him."

"They'll look for him," she murmured. Julius Tomari's promise to his ex-wife meant he'd be looking for Marne. He wasn't the first man to threaten her life. He probably wouldn't be the last. But he was more dangerous than most. He had more to lose. "Once they catch him, he won't be home for Christmas for a long, long time. He's on parole with two felony battery convictions."

As they crossed the parking lot to the car, Marne took her cell phone from the inside of her jacket and punched in a number.

By the time she tucked the phone into her pocket, Jake was steering the car onto the street.

"Where to? Angela's apartment?" he asked.

"It's her sister Lucinda's, but yes. We go there next." Frustrated, Marne pounded her fist on her thigh. "Why the hell didn't Angela stay in Boise? Why'd she come back into Julius's territory when she knew he'd been paroled?"

"Maybe for the same reason we've changed everything around for the next few days. Christmas. Family."

Lucinda Gigliotti's apartment was in the heart of the territory Jake had left behind fifteen years ago when he'd joined the Navy at eighteen. A man who worked as hard as he had to change his destiny had no intentions of ever going back. All he left on the mean streets were bad memories and hard times.

As a Navy SEAL, and more recently a special agent in communications security for the FBI, he'd roamed the dark corners of the world. But no place had triggered anxiety twisting in his gut like driving through his old turf.

Other than the few new buildings—fruitless attempts to revive the inner city—the neighborhood hadn't changed. The years had just brought more of the same. The graffiti on the buildings and tattered fences carried the same dismal messages. Drugs and sex were still sold on the streets. Now, the drugs were stronger, the stakes higher, and the sex more deadly. The faces had changed, but the attitude was the same.

Jake parked the car beside a police cruiser, then got out.

Marne didn't wait for him to open her door. A sense of loss rippled through him. Before she'd ended their relationship, she would have sat in the car a damn hour before opening the door herself.

"What the hell happened?" he murmured. Before he returned to the East Coast, he was going to get to the bottom of this; he'd learn the truth about why she slammed the door on their relationship and what caused her to change so much.

Angela's sister lived in a dilapidated apartment building on one of the worst streets in the neighborhood. The sirens screaming down the freeway reminded Jake of how close and yet how distant the law was on the fringes of the Great White Way. He followed Marne around a rise of slab steps leading to the second- and third-floor apartments. Tucked beneath the stairs was a broken garbage bag of dirty disposable diapers. The smell conjured the dingy rooms he'd called home after his mother divorced his father. Jake's staying with the Old Man had been the price of freedom for his mother and two sisters.

The front door of the apartment hung by one hinge to the right of the steps. Inside, a patrolman and two plainclothes officers compared notes in the busted-up living room. Ornaments and lights from the Christmas tree crunched beneath their feet. Blood spatters decorated the walls. Julius Tomari hadn't left a single stick of furniture unbroken.

"Marne, come in. We're about done here," said the man who appeared to be in charge. "I figured you'd show up."

"Great deductive thinking, Lieutenant Peterson. Bet my phone call tipped you off." She shoved her hands into her jacket pockets and surveyed the ruins as though she saw this kind of destruction on a regular basis. The realization that Marne roamed such scenes with familiarity sickened him. This wasn't her world. She didn't belong here.

He didn't understand why she had chosen this profession. He had turned his back on the bleakness, the violence, the hopelessness of the life he'd left behind. Marne—she'd sought it out. Why?

"Angela's lucky she survived this," Marne said after completing her survey of the small, ruined apartment.

"We'll interview her when she can talk. Meanwhile, we'll keep an eye on her. From the looks of this mess, Julius may be pissed enough to want to finish the job. Who's your friend?"

Jake had already sized up the plainclothes detective as a mediocre cop too damn interested in Marne. Women usually went for his type of clean-cut, blond, blue-eyed good looks. He wondered if Marne went for the flashy suit and golden looks. Why the hell a cop wore a designer suit in the field defied logic.

Ever the professional, Jake extended his hand. "Jake Rimsa, Marne's ex-fiancé," he said with deliberate casualness.

"Jeezus, Jake," Marne muttered.

"No shit?" Peterson asked, dropping Jake's hand. "What're you doing here, then?"

"Taking her to a family Christmas." Jake watched the way Peterson's sharp blue gaze darted to Marne, then back. He would bet his last nickel the bastard was more interested in laying Marne than in preserving the crime scene.

Jake snorted and started toward the bedroom where Marne was examining the window. Peterson grabbed his arm. Jake froze and slowly turned his head toward the golden detective.

"Make sure that's the only place you take her."

"If you like your fingers, you'll take them off me."

"You threatening an officer?"

"I take exception to cops who use their badges as weapons." Jake raised an eyebrow and looked pointedly at Peterson's hand.

"Did you find any of Angela's things?" Marne asked from the window.

"On the bed. He cut everything up." Peterson released Jake's arm.

The fine hair at the nape of Jake's neck rose. "Which proves how dangerous Tomari is."

"He's a punk." Peterson squinted, openly assessing Jake. "You a punk too, Rimsa?"

Jake turned away before he slugged the guy. "Nope. Just a Fed who specializes in putting away cops who cross the line."

"My ass," Peterson spat.

"It will be if you don't back off." The asshole wanted to play King of the Mountain. If he didn't back off, Jake might be forced to oblige him by showing him who owned the mountain.

"How many men do you have looking for Clarissa?" Marne interrupted, brushing past Jake on her way to Peterson.

"Two." He glanced over his shoulder at the patrolman. "I'll send Hopkins after we seal this place up."

Jake saw the color rise in Marne's cheeks. She was ready to blow. That much hadn't changed. He folded his arms over his chest, ready to enjoy Marne's explosion at the lieutenant.

"She's a ten-year-old kid, for God's sake. Her mother was practically beaten to death. The man who cut up her clothing is out there looking for her. And you've got *two* men doing a search? Where the hell do you think we are? Mr. Rogers' neighborhood?"

Peterson retreated a step. Jake suppressed a smile. The horny bastard wasn't going to get into Marne's bed by pissing her off. Whatever charged her protective streak had been etched into her spine with a diamond-tipped bit. The former kindergarten teacher from the rich side of town had grown a lethal set of fangs. Jake kind of liked it.

"It's the holidays, Marne. There's a limit to the resources the department can allocate," Peterson shot back.

"How many more will they *allocate* after Clarissa Tomari's little body is found in a Dumpster? Or after she's raped? Or kidnapped? Oh, but she couldn't be kidnapped, could she, Lieutenant?"

"Marne—"

She advanced on him, her cheeks crimson with fury. "Not kidnapped. That would be too resource-intensive to pursue. What will you do? Classify her as a runaway?''

"I'd do more if I could. As far as the department is concerned, Clarissa is a potential witness to an attempted murder. We're looking for her and will continue to do so.''

If Peterson hadn't been such a prick, Jake might have felt sorry for him. Facing down one of Marne's displays of temper was not for the fainthearted.

A closer look at the crime scene—clothing strewn throughout the tiny apartment, broken furniture, holes in the walls from a head or a fist, telltale blood spatters—told him that Peterson was sloppy. He didn't wear gloves when handling what could be evidence. Where the hell was the forensics team? A good lawyer would get half the physical evidence in the place tossed out of court.

Figuring he couldn't make the situation worse, Jake picked up a child's pink backpack from the floor beneath the bedroom window. Maybe there hadn't been enough time for Clarissa to take it. He searched it, frowning when he found a scrap of paper in the side pouch.

"Have you got a picture of Clarissa?'' Jake asked.

"Here you go.'' Patrolman Hopkins offered a five-by-seven school photo scarred by broken glass. "We've already got dupes of her.''

"Thanks.'' Jake put his arm around Marne's shoulders and tugged her away from Peterson. "Let's start here.'' Before she could shrug him off, he shoved the paper scrap in front of her face. "I found it in the kid's backpack.''

"Let me see that.'' Peterson snatched the paper. Jake let him have it. He'd already memorized the information.

"This isn't your job, Jake. You don't have to help—''

"Damn it, Marne. Somebody does.'' He guided her toward the door. "It'll be dark in a couple hours. She's alone, and she's gonna be cold.'' He stopped short of adding what they both knew: The night belonged to an even harsher lifeform.

"Stay out of this, Rimsa,'' warned Peterson. "This is an ongoing police investigation.''

"Thought you boys and girls were always looking for community support and assistance. Why not do a little door-to-door—unless you're not afraid of getting your suit wrinkled.'' Before Peterson could respond, Jake led Marne out of the apartment.

"You know where St. Mark's is?" Jake asked her as they approached the car.

"Sure."

He tossed the keys to her. "You drive." He reached inside his jacket and withdrew a cell phone and an electronic organizer. "Let's see if I have better luck at rounding up some resources than your lover lieutenant."

"He isn't my lover." She rounded the car and opened the door. "But he *is* a friend."

"I could tell."

She started the engine. "Helping look for Clarissa doesn't change anything between us, Jake. I can't be bribed."

He punched in a telephone number. "Don't judge me by Lieutenant Lover. He's the one looking to crawl into your pants."

"Oh, and you're not?"

"I've been there." He punched in the last number, then shot a glance her way. "First."

The tires squealed as she pulled away from the curb. "And for the last time."

Before he could ask if she was willing to place a wager on it, Tony Prine's voice on the phone widened the opening door to his past.

 TWO

The north wall of St. Mark's Church was the battlefield of a spray-paint war. Cost prohibited the parish from getting rid of the turf war proclamations more often than once a year. Within the chain-link fence of the parking lot, half a dozen cars clustered around the light poles. They reminded Marne of lambs waiting for the wolves of the night.

"Well?" Marne turned off the engine and handed the keys to Jake. "What's the deal?"

"Same as always. When money talks, assholes walk. I'll need an ATM before we cruise the Great White Way." He got out of the car. "Do you know the priest?"

"Father Grimal works harder than anyone down here. If he doesn't slow down or get transferred, he's not going to see forty-five."

"Lead poisoning from a drive-by?"

Marne shrugged. "Coronary. It's hard to tell whether he's disappointed in God or thinks God is disappointed in him. He cares too much about everyone and everything. He's got to feel like he's hitting his head against a stone wall most of the time, but he keeps on going."

"Sounds like you've had some practice at the same thing."

Marne refused to look at him. Jake had a nasty habit of seeing too much. Instead, she checked the streets.

"This is a far cry from teaching a class of kindergartners in Atherton," Jake said softly.

She paused on the steps of the church. The manger scene at the entrance had seen better days. Joseph held a broken staff. Traces of a mustache and goatee lingered on Mary's scrubbed, serene face. The lamb beside the manger had no ears. The thick cluster of evergreen boughs couldn't hide the cinder block substituting for the cow's left hind leg. "This is where I belong. Where I can do the most good. You came along to help find Clarissa. I appreciate the help, but don't go poking around where you aren't wanted."

His hands raised in surrender. "Hell, it was a simple, honest observation. Last time I saw you, you were teaching a bunch of baby yuppies how to read. A blind man would notice the change."

"And an FBI agent would ask why, is that it?" She started up the steps. "Quit wondering and just accept it."

Jake snorted and reached for the door. "Sure, Marne. You know how much I love having other people's decisions crammed down my throat. Force-feeding leaves such a pleasant aftertaste."

"Sarcastic as ever, aren't you?" She reached into her pocket and brought out a roll of Life Savers. "Suck on a mint, then swallow. It'll sweeten your disposition."

"In that case, you'd better pop the whole roll."

Inside the church, the soft chords of "O Holy Night" wafted over the pews. The aroma of evergreen, candle wax, and incense filled the warm air with solemnity broken by the whispers of children.

They found Father Grimal directing a rehearsal of the Christmas Story on the altar steps. Each time Marne saw him, he looked older. The balding, wiry priest projected an aura of calm, though he was constantly on the move. His blue eyes brightened when he saw her. Their color never failed to surprise strangers because his skin was a rich chocolate brown. When he flashed a snow-white smile that would have made an orthodontist weep at its perfection, he captivated his audience.

"Have you decided to participate in our Christmas Eve pageant?" Father Grimal asked, catching Marne's hand in both of his.

A quick smile lit up her face. "I'm supposed to be heading for the hills as we speak, Father. But I've got a problem."

"I see. Is this man part of it?" Father Grimal teased.

Marne introduced Jake, then ignored him and explained what had happened to Angela.

The glow of a holiday smile melted from Father Grimal's generous features. The burden of man's inhumanity to woman settled on him hard enough to deepen the lines around his eyes.

Jake offered the picture of Clarissa Tomari. "This is a recent photo."

"Children change so fast . . . so much from a year and a half ago," the priest murmured. He snapped out of his introspection. Three loud claps of his hands silenced everything in the church.

"We have a sister who needs our help. Gather around." Adults and children closed ranks around him.

It never ceased to amaze Marne how he could command the hearts and spirits of those who took the time to know him. She caught Jake's rapt fascination with the priest dressed in frayed blue jeans and a black shirt with a clerical collar.

"He's the only person I know who has the Christmas spirit 370 days a year," she whispered. "He doubles up on a few of the high holy days."

The hint of a smile flickered and died on Jake's face. She hadn't seen him look so lost since the day she met him. At nine, she hadn't understood why Caroline left Jake behind when she divorced his drunken father. Today, she knew too well the choices and sacrifices women caught in a cycle of abuse faced. Some traded the survival of their daughters for their son, like Caroline had done. Others, like Angela, traded themselves.

But Caroline had not completely thrown Jake on the mercy of a man who had little. She'd waited until Jake had a chance of surviving, until it was almost too late for herself and the girls. After Caroline married her pro bono divorce attorney, Harrison Hudson, she encouraged, even bribed, Jake to visit. It had practically taken an act of God to get him to come the first time.

"Why are you looking at me as though you like me?" Jake asked warily.

"Just remembering."

"What?"

"The first Christmas you joined the York and Hudson families. Granny Grayson." She straightened. Father Grimal was breaking his pageant participants into groups.

"I think she knew," Jake whispered.

Marne switched thoughts. "Who knew what?"

"I think your Granny Grayson took one look at the tough-guy image I tried to hold on to, and knew you'd destroy it." A sad laugh rumbled from deep in his chest. "Damn, but I was scared when I stumbled up the walk of your fancy house with its manicured lawns, big rooms, matching furniture, gourmet food—the whole bit. Part of me was resentful, the other part glad was my mother had married into an extended family. A rich one. Even so, I felt like a toad invading a castle."

"It wasn't a castle. Just a house."

"Right." Jake studied the back of a pew. "She knew I wanted to run," he said with a softness at reliving an uncomfortable, twenty-year-old memory. "So she gave me a direction. She sent me to the castle princess who'd fled to the gazebo in the backyard."

"I was hardly a princess." He'd frightened her when he sat down beside her on the white bench. Thousands of tiny Christmas lights woven through the gazebo lattice had raced around them. It had been the last year of the Snow White and the Seven Dwarfs Christmas figures in the backyard. In a very real sense it had been the year Marne started seeing life's realities.

"Yeah, you were a princess. You shared your deepest, most painful secret with me that day."

"You made me tell you why I was crying."

"Then I wanted to cry with you. I didn't know Granny Grayson then, but I knew you loved her and didn't want her to die."

"And you held me while I cried on your shoulder." Marne closed her eyes, remembering how bitterly she had sobbed after overhearing her parents discussing the prognosis of Granny's cancer. At nine, she had thought it would go away, like a cold or the flu. Get a shot. Take a pill. Then everything would be all right. But it wasn't.

For a second Marne relived the warmth of Jake's embrace, the strength and security that emanated from the young boy. She had fallen in love with him right then.

Marne shook off the memory. Irritated that he could seduce her thoughts so easily, she stalked off to Father Grimal. They had a lot of ground to cover in a short time. The parishioners would do what they could to search for Clarissa. The organist had made photocopies of Clarissa's picture with Marne's cell phone number at the bottom. Marne gratefully took the flyers and headed out the door.

"I'll drive." Jake angled in front of Marne as they exited the church. "I don't suppose anyone has a recent picture of Julius Tomari."

"Lieutenant Peterson does. Why?"

"I haven't seen him for fifteen years. I'd like to be able to recognize him." He cast a trained eye up the street for loiterers.

At the car he opened the trunk and rooted around in one of his suitcases.

"What are you looking for?"

"This," he said softly, then withdrew a 9mm Glock and shoulder holster.

He put on the holster and loaded the Glock, stuck a second clip in his back pocket and a third in his jacket.

"We're looking for a little girl. Not a guerrilla training

camp,'' Marne muttered. ''Let's get moving.''

''Where's the nearest ATM?'' He adjusted the shoulder holster for comfort.

''Will this be a friendly withdrawal?''

''Get off my case or I'll show you how friendly I really am.''

Reflexively, Marne sank deeper into the seat. ''I didn't think rape was your style.''

Irritated, Jake started the car. ''What the hell are you talking about?''

''Could we get this show on the road? It's almost dark.''

''Yeah, and rush-hour traffic is building like a bitch in heat.''

The urge to scream in frustration crawled up her throat. He'd just described how being around him affected her hormone level.

A stiff, cold wind accompanied the early winter darkness. Christmas lights blinked at erratic intervals behind the barred windows of businesses lining the Great White Way. Anyone who wanted to score, whether it was drugs or a hooker, could find whatever they wanted along the eight-block stretch.

''If God wanted to take the temperature of this city, he'd stick the thermometer in here,'' Jake mumbled as he slid the car into a parking place a block from the apartment where Julius Tomari had rearranged his ex-wife's Christmas.

''Since when did you find religion?'' Marne zipped her jacket, then got out of the car.

''Nothing like a trip home to make a man thankful he left.'' Jake left his jacket open. Although she couldn't see the gun, he looked comfortable carrying it close to his heart.

Marne followed his gaze to a customized car vibrating with booming bass speakers and an indiscernible rap song. The car stopped beside Jake's rented Lincoln.

''Goldilocks,'' called a young black man through the open passenger window.

Marne tipped her head in recognition. "Boomer," she called back, then started forward.

The sound reverberating from the car ebbed to a low, distant thunder. Boomer grinned. The glint of his gold front tooth was nearly as bright as the diamond gleaming in the side of his broad nose. He adjusted his backward cap, his dark eyes never wavering from hers.

"Irritating comfort" was the best way she could describe the sensation of Jake's presence as she approached the car.

"What's this? You got you a white boy?" Boomer sized up Jake with the eyes of a deadly predator, which he was. "You need a real man, Goldilocks."

"She's got one," Jake said evenly.

Marne ignored the macho banter. She bent, then flashed a smile at the driver. "Hey, Roach. You guys cruising tonight, or working?"

"Both."

"Good." She unzipped her jacket and reached inside.

"That's it, baby, take it off. Show me whatcha got," Boomer encouraged.

"What I got is a picture." She pulled out a photocopy of Clarissa.

"Shee-it! I need more than that."

"That's all you're getting." Jake's hand flashed, catching Boomer's wrist when he reached for Marne's jacket.

"Back off, Jake," Marne snapped.

"Yeah, back off, white boy."

"You don't touch the lady. Look. Have a wet dream, but don't touch. Got it?"

"You tired of breathin'?"

Jake released him.

Boomer massaged his wrist and regarded Jake with respectful animosity. "Now *you* get somethin'. This be my turf. My street. I say who stays, who goes."

"Don't!" Marne warned Roach as he reached for the gun on the floor.

"We ain't takin' no dissing from him," Roach said, bringing up a chrome-plated .44.

Marne leaned closer, her heart hammering in her chest. "He's not dissing you."

"Gimme one good reason he oughta see Christmas." All the lightness was gone from Boomer.

Marne drew a breath, never taking her gaze from Boomer's flat brown eyes. "Because he's FBI. You do one of theirs, and they're going to be all over the street before you can change CDs."

"You shittin' me, Goldilocks?"

"No, I'm not. He's helping me look for this girl. Clarissa Tomari." She shoved the paper at Boomer.

Wary, Boomer glanced at the picture, then handed it to Roach. "What'd she do?"

"Julius Tomari put her mother in County as an early Christmas present," Marne said. "Clarissa escaped. I need to find her before he does."

"What's it to me?"

"If you were looking for your sister, I'd help." She had no leverage, no way of coercing Boomer to keep an open ear and an eye out for Clarissa. But everything was worth a try. "You see her, call me."

"Julius. He don't come on my turf."

"His kid might," Jake said.

"Do I look like San-tee Claws?" Boomer turned up the stereo and pointed down the street.

Marne stepped away.

Roach accelerated.

"Well, it was worth a shot. You never know with Boomer." She returned to the sidewalk. "At least he didn't throw the picture away."

"Punks with guns," he muttered.

"He got to you. I'm surprised." Jake had always been the personification of cool. She'd seen him angry twice, both times at her, and she didn't care for a three-peat.

"Yeah, well, guess there's no place like home for the holidays." He shoved his hands into his pockets and inclined his head in the direction of a brightly lit convenience store.

She'd always known Jake hated where he grew up, hated

the filth, the hopelessness. Fifteen years ago, he'd owned the street. He'd been the one in the car. "It isn't your home anymore, Jake."

"The past doesn't come off when you take a shower. It's part of you."

How well she knew.

The silver-and-green garland wrapped around the burglar bars over the convenience store's windows and doors danced in the wind. Gold-foil snowflakes hung across the top of the bulletproof glass encasing the counter. Red and green balls dangled from chunks of garland ringing the array of fish-eye mirrors strategically placed near the ceilings.

Marne spoke to the middle-aged Korean couple inside the bulletproof cage. They hadn't seen Clarissa, but they would watch for her. Before leaving, Marne taped a flyer on the door.

On the sidewalk, the wind bit colder. Marne brightened. "Come on." She grabbed Jake's sleeve. "I see Sister Mary Magdalene."

Jake watched with incredulity when Marne genuflected before a homeless woman pushing a shopping cart holding all her possessions. Sister Mary Magdalene wore a torn, dirty nun's headdress, a dress with a round black yoke, and a crucifix.

She had parked her cart under the harsh glare of the streetlight. A closer look at the mismatched manger scene resting in the folds of a stained blanket showed Mary was really a one-armed Barbie doll. Joseph was Han Solo.

The wanna-be nun had enough wrinkles to make her look older than God. On the street, that equated to around fifty. The yellow cast of her rheumy eyes and leathery skin promised someone else's cart would occupy this spot next Christmas. Cirrhosis or hepatitis, Jake guessed.

He scanned the street traffic while Marne spoke with the woman. The nightlife was emerging early in preparation for last-minute holiday parties. The later it got, the more active the trade. Across the street, a woman with small, colorful Christmas ornaments tied into her green hair extended Jake an invitation with a knowing smile. The scanty elf costume she wore revealed jingle bells on the garters that secured her green hose. Balanced on three-inch gold stiletto heels, she shivered against the wind as a shiny Mercedes stopped in front of her.

Jake kept an ear tuned to the conversation between Marne and the wanna-be nun. The street woman knew Julius—and feared him.

Across the street the Mercedes drove away with the Christmas elf in the passenger seat.

Christ, the more things changed, the more they stayed the same.

"The Baby Jesus takes care of His children." Sister Mary Magdalene opened the baby blanket wrapped around a teddy bear. She laid a trembling hand on Marne's. It was all Jake could do to keep from pushing the woman away from her. "I'll be an instrument of His kindness." The pseudo-sister clasped the Jesus-bear to the crucifix on her black yolk. "He will guide me tonight, as He guided me away from my sins."

The light went out of her eyes. She started pushing her cart down the street.

"Sister," Marne called softly. "The shelter is that way." She pointed in the opposite direction.

"Bless you, my child." Sister Mary Magdalene continued in the same direction she'd started in.

Jake caught Marne's arm and half led, half dragged her across the sidewalk. He pinned her against the closest building with his body. "How the hell do you know these people? Why? Why do you come down here?"

"To look for Clarissa," she answered in a voice so calm that it increased his unnameable agitation.

"Bullshit! You know these people. That doesn't happen overnight. They don't trust. And you know they're dangerous."

"So am I, Jake. Back off, or you'll find out just how dangerous." The hardness in her face belonged to a woman he didn't know. One who damn well could be as dangerous as she thought she was. Hell, he hoped so.

He eased the pressure of his body against her. "You don't belong here."

"Why? Because this isn't where I grew up? Because I didn't have my hand stamped with the rite of passage when I was born?"

How could he explain it? "If you wanted to punish me for something, you couldn't have picked a better way," he seethed. "I hate knowing you frequent these streets. Know these people. This life. Why, Marne?"

"I'm not trying to punish you, Jake. You're free to leave at any time."

"The hell I am. We need to find the girl. And I'd walk through hell before I let you pound these streets alone."

"I do it all the time. There are women down here who need help. My help. Someone to show them how to help themselves. It's what I've chosen to do with my life."

"Nobody chooses this place."

"Jake, Jake," she soothed, touching his face with her cold fingertips. "If I hadn't known you, seen the strides you made to grow over the years, felt the price you paid at every turn, I would have never come down here. I'd be as lost as most of the people around us."

"Oh, well, that makes everything fine." Christ, now he felt guilty for surviving.

"No place is all good or all bad. Not even the Great White Way." Her hand left his cheek, leaving him cold on the inside. "Now, let's find Clarissa. She has to be close by."

Close by, and far away, just like Marne. He backed off, no wiser, no more settled than he'd been a few minutes ago. His cell phone vibrated against his chest.

"Rimsa," he answered, pinning Marne in place with his gaze. He listened for a moment, then turned off the phone.

"Your contact?" Marne asked hopefully.

"He's not the most reliable man on the streets, but he'll be out most of the night." He took her arm and started down the street. "With three of his cronies. That gives us eight more eyes looking for Clarissa."

"Thank you, Jake."

"That doesn't mean they'll find her." He snorted. "Nor does it mean they'll be straight enough to see the ends of their noses in a few hours."

As they neared the place where Jake expected to meet the ghost he'd summoned, the Salvation Army quartet began playing "Joy to the World."

Some joy.

Some world.

# THREE

"Rimsa," called the bell ringer in front of the Salvation Army shelter. He was a stocky man, just under six feet, with brown-gray hair swept beneath a captain's cap. The cooling night had already pinched his face rosy enough to accent a permanent dimple in his left cheek. "Never thought to see your sorry hide down here again."

Few things in life had surprised Jake as much as seeing Larry Prine in a churchly uniform. During their teenage years, a knife had filled Larry's hand, not a bell.

"Damn," Jake hissed through his teeth. He extended his hand, then got another shock when Larry laid a cold, stainless-steel hook on his palm. "Damn," he breathed again, collecting himself.

"You always were an expressive S.O.B." Larry lifted the hook and laughed. "Car crash eight years ago."

"Damn, I'm sorry, man." Jake looked into clear hazel eyes, familiar but different than he recalled. Peace lived where anger had once dwelled.

"Merry Christmas, Larry," Marne said, worrying a

folded bill through the slit of the lid on the red collections kettle.

"Merry Christmas to you, Goldilocks. Thanks." His hazel eyes softened with the smile he gave Marne. "Are you with this renegade?"

"Until we find Clarissa Tomari." She gave him a flyer, then pulled another stack from inside her jacket.

"Any help we can give, it's yours." He motioned to the large black man playing trombone. "Show our guests Clarissa's pretty face."

"Sure." He tucked the horn under his beefy left arm and took the flyer.

"Instill some Christmas spirit. This little one is alone and very scared," Larry said.

"I'll give 'em my lost lamb speech, then offer a Holiday incentive." The ridge of Lashad's nose wrinkled when he grinned broad enough to reveal the absence of his upper-right eyetooth.

"I didn't hear that last part, Lashad."

"Right, Cap'n," he said to Larry, then winked at Marne.

"Thanks." Marne winked back. "I'll catch you before New Year's."

"No, she won't," Larry said. "It's on me."

The easy repartee excluded Jake. He was finally an outsider on the Great White Way, a status he'd spent most of his life trying to achieve. Now that he had, it didn't fit as comfortably as he'd anticipated.

Marne showed the picture to the remaining members of the quartet.

"You doing community service time for the holidays?" Jake asked Larry. He supposed it was better than hard jail time or the scams that Larry used to work. Safer than running drugs across San Francisco Bay. These days Boomer, or someone like him, controlled that gig.

"You could say that. I run the shelter. Have been for seven years," Larry said, the bell ringing, calling, pleading in his left hand. "We do some good work."

"Shit, like extorting me over the phone in return for

looking for a little girl? Real charitable, Larry.'' Jake
grinned, in spite of the idea.

"You're an outsider now, Jake. That makes you fair
game. But you're still an old friend, and I don't forget those
who pulled my fat out of the fire as many times as you did.
However, I hope you'll make a contribution to the cause,''
Larry said in earnest. "In memory of those who are no
longer with us.''

Jake didn't want to know who'd died, who was in jail,
or who'd blown his mind on bad drugs. "Sure.'' He
reached into his pocket for the cash he'd gotten at the ATM.
He pushed all two hundred through the narrow slot in the
Salvation Army red kettle.

Reflexively, he checked on Marne. She was talking with
a homeless man at the shelter entrance. Christmas lights
winked around the windows sprayed with fake snow.
"Noel" and snowflakes filled the window on the left side
of the door. A stenciled Santa Claus head filled the right.

"How come people only remember we get hungry at
Christmas? How come there ain't no special meals on Au-
gust tenth or May third?'' the homeless man demanded of
Marne while clutching his tattered hat.

"The shelter offers you a meal on those days, too, Burt,''
Marne said with the patience of a saint. "Now you can do
something good in return. We're looking for this little
girl.'' She shoved a flyer into his hand. "Look real hard at
her. If you see her, tell Larry right away, okay?''

"What'd she do?''

"Nothing. She's alone. Lost. Scared. And she needs her
mother.''

"Me, too,'' the man murmured.

"We have a lot to do here,'' Larry said, drawing Jake's
attention away from Marne. "Anytime you want to lend a
hand, Jake, it'd be appreciated.''

"It'd be a helluva commute from the East Coast.'' He
had no intention of getting caught up in someone else's
crusade to reform mankind. Not Larry's. Not Marne's.

"Maybe you ought to consider moving closer. That

woman you're with needs more help than most folks in the shelter," Larry said softly.

Everything in Jake became alert. "What're you telling me? Spit it out clean."

Larry shook his head in rhythm with the bell he never stopped ringing. "Something's troubling her. Something deep. Don't know what it is, but I know hurting when I see it. She's got it in spades. I always figured it was because of you."

Larry was one of the few who knew his ties to Marne and the families in Atherton, a life so remote to the way they grew up that it may as well have been Timbuktu. "You figured wrong."

"I knew that when you walked up with her. She's not the type to go back for seconds, if you know what I mean."

He did know. But if he had to move heaven and earth, she was coming back to him for seconds, or tell him why. "Thanks for the help, Larry. We still have a lot of street to cover."

"Sure thing. Merry Christmas, Jake Rimsa. You've done good."

He turned away. "So have you, Larry." *Damn good.*

The quartet switched songs. The trumpeter started a clear solo of "I'll Be Home for Christmas." Jake collected Marne and glanced over his shoulder as Larry touched his stainless-steel hook to the brim of his cap. "The Lord works in mysterious ways."

Jake couldn't help grinning. If Larry Prine could rebuild his life out of a disaster and find religion, there was hope for the Great White Way.

"It's been a long evening. How about some coffee?" Marne asked a couple of hours later. "There's a diner on the next block. We can get it to go."

"I could use some."

She looked up at Jake. It had been a hard night for him, but it seemed to get easier after his encounter with Larry.

Her cell phone rang. Hope and excitement that someone

had seen Clarissa shot through her. She fumbled it out of her jacket.

"Hello?"

"Are you okay? Where are you? Where's my brother? Why is his cell phone turned off?" Worry laced Alice's strident demands.

"Alice," she glanced at Jake, "we're fine, but you're on my shit list. As for your brother, he's helping with a problem that's come up. We'll be there as soon as we can."

"Thank God you two are all right. You both promised—"

"And we'll both be there for Christmas."

"But you're together again?"

Not dignifying the absurd question with an answer, Marne handed the phone to Jake. "Here, give your sister a lashing with a cloth belt before I reach through this phone and rip her head off."

"We'll be there when we get there," Jake said after listening a minute. "Meanwhile, don't call this number again, Alice. We need the line free."

Would wonders never cease? Jake actually taking a firm line with one of his sisters had to be seen to be believed.

"I'll tell you about it when we get there. Don't look for us before tomorrow afternoon." He punched an end to the conversation, then handed the phone back.

"Well, well, well," Marne said with open admiration. "The marshmallow has grown a crust."

"Marshmallow, my ass," he growled.

"When it comes to your sisters, big time. To everyone else, you're a hard-ass." She grinned into the teeth of the wind as they crossed the street.

"Except you, Marne. Let's get that coffee."

"You don't have to be a softie for me. I'm doing fine."

He stopped short and turned her around to face him. "Christ, there's isn't anything soft between you and me."

Her heart dropped to her stomach, then raced. "Let it go, Jake. It isn't going to happen."

"It's going to happen, Marne. We both know it. We're like this place. Like it or not, it gets in your blood and doesn't let go. We belong."

"Now you're admitting I belong here?" Better a fight than the line of intimacy he wanted to explore.

"Only if I'm with you."

"God, you have an ego the size of Alaska. I've gotten along fine without you, Jake. This is the way I want it. I've found my niche here."

"A few hours ago I'd have argued that. You're good with people. You seem to know what they need, what they want, how to reach them. What about me, Marne? You know what I need? What I want?"

"Yes," she breathed, fighting the heated tide of her body. "And the answer is no. I made that decision a long time ago." In a quick motion, she spun free. "I'm going for coffee. Coming?"

They passed a wino talking to a plastic Santa Claus waving and nodding on the warm side of a barred window at a bail-bond office. The wino lifted a paper-bag-wrapped bottle, then resumed chattering about going home for Christmas. The plastic Santa kept agreeing and waving him on his way.

A pair of big-haired blond hookers grinned at Jake as they passed in a miasma of floral perfume. One whistled. "Nice ass," crooned the other. They both laughed.

His scowl deepened. Marne frowned. Jake had a better-than-nice ass—and everything else. "Welcome to the meat market."

"I'm not for sale." He pushed the door of the diner open.

Steamy heat hit them with the force of a slap. The aroma of coffee, frying grease, and overcooked vegetables nearly overwhelmed her. A rap version of "The Night Before Christmas" blared from the kitchen grill area.

"You get the coffee. I'll cruise the tables," Marne said, then headed for a young Hispanic couple at the far end.

Ten minutes later, they were on the street again. The wind had eased. The cloud cover moving over the sky kept the night from getting colder.

"Where the hell could she be?" Marne sipped her coffee, strong and black. She savored its heat.

"She's not on the street or we'd have found her by now. None of your calls have paid off. She's hiding." Jake eyed a driveway between two buildings. "Where would she feel safe?"

"In her own bed in Boise," Marne mumbled.

"Call her family again. Ask if they've seen her."

"They'd call me." Marne started down the driveway. "They know I'm on the street looking for her."

"They trust you that much?"

"Yeah. Angela's grandmother and brother stayed home just in case Clarissa turned up there. The rest are at the hospital." Helluva way to spend the holidays. She kicked aside a bag of garbage that hadn't made the overstuffed, foul-smelling Dumpster, then called Clarissa's name and identified herself.

Nothing. She started back to the street. "By the way, Jake, thanks."

"For what?"

"For helping with this. It isn't your problem." And you hate roaming the streets you've done such a great job of leaving behind, she added silently.

"Goldilocks," called a nervous voice from the sidewalk.

"Yeah. That you, Burt?" She tossed her half-empty Styrofoam cup at the Dumpster. "Did you see her?"

"Not me. But someone did." He wrung his trembling hands.

Jake pulled a few dollars out of his pocket and shoved them into Burt's hands.

"Thanks, man," Burt said, his entire body nodding appreciation from the waist up.

"Where?" Marne demanded.

"Near your office."

"Shit!" She should have thought of that, should have anticipated it. Clarissa equated the office with her, and her with safety. So did Julius. "Thanks, Burt."

"I dunno if she's still . . ."

Marne didn't wait to hear the rest. Clarissa had been seen. It was a start. Hopeful, she ran, darting around people and obstacles with Jake hot on her heels.

"Where the hell's your office?" Jake called.

"Six blocks," she shot back.

"Go to the car." He caught her upper arm and diverted them through parked vehicles.

Dodging traffic, they crossed the street. The alarm on the rental car chirped once.

By the time Marne jumped into the passenger seat, Jake had the car started and was pulling away from the curb. A slight break in the endless stream of traffic crawling along the Great White Way was all Jake needed to flip a U-turn. Horns blared. Shouts rose over the din.

"Why the hell did you open an office down here?" Jake ground out between clenched teeth.

"Just drive," she snapped. "We need to get there before she moves on."

He ran a red light, swerving to avoid a pickup truck. "How much farther?"

"Next block. Halfway down. There. Where some creep has parked in front of the driveway." She held on to the door grip, her right foot pressing into the floorboard to vicariously help him accelerate and brake as he wove around the slow-moving cars.

The two-story building housing the Grayson Foundation on the bottom floor was dark. Marne was out of the car before it stopped. Desperation sharpened her call of Clarissa's name.

Other than the traffic, it was quiet on the fringe of the Great White Way. She darted down the drive lined with used fast-food containers, old newspapers, and unidentifiable refuse. The muted glow of a heavily screened light over the steel back door reached across the cement drive at an angle. As she rounded the end of the building, she heard a noise.

She wheeled, her senses sharp, her heart thudding hard against her ribs. A scuffle. Without thinking, she dashed toward the source of it, in the darkest corner of the parking alcove.

Dimly, she heard Jake shouting her name.

Movement in the corner brought her closer. She made

out the form of a man in a baggy coat clutching a child.

"Let her go!" Marne shouted.

A pipe arced through the space separating Marne from the man in the overcoat. Quick reflexes saved her from having her head bashed in. She swore, then dove for the man's midsection.

The child screamed.

The impact sent all three of them sprawling against the wall. The garbage cans toppled and rolled every which way as they spilled their contents.

Marne caught the back of Clarissa's sweatshirt and yanked her away from her captor. Before she could follow, a fist caught her shoulder, knocking her sideways. The momentum helped her roll away.

The next thing she knew, Jake was pounding the man into the pavement. "You . . . don't . . . touch . . . her." He landed a punch with each word.

She pulled at Jake's shoulders and nudged his ribs with her knee. "Let him up," she shouted. "You're killing him."

Bloody fist poised to deliver another blow, Jake froze.

"You're scaring Clarissa," she hissed. *And me.* Her breath came in unsteady pants until Jake relaxed his fist. Satisfied that he'd finished delivering his own form of justice, she approached the child huddled against the wall.

"Come on, baby girl. It's over. Let's go inside and get you warm." She pulled the girl up with trembling hands. In the dull light, she could see the terror in ten-year-old Clarissa Tomari's big, dark eyes. Though the child made no sound, her chin quivered uncontrollably.

Marne knelt and offered warmth and safety by opening her jacket. "Come on, baby. You're safe. I won't let anything happen."

Clarissa lunged for her, nearly knocking them both to the ground. Small, cold arms clamped around Marne's ribs like a vise. Soft sobs leaked from the face pressed against her cheek.

Relief so great it stung her eyes swept through Marne. She hugged Clarissa. "Did he hurt you?"

Clarissa shook her head no, then yes, then no.

She indulged in holding the child and letting the conflagration of emotion sweep through her. Rocking them both, she whispered, "You're safe. Safe." She wasn't sure who needed assurance more, her or Clarissa. The sharp tremors of adrenaline surging through her ebbed. The child was in one piece and so was she. This time, she'd taken on the devil and defeated him, with Jake's help. This time.

"Let's get inside." She kissed Clarissa's cheek. The death grip on her ribs eased.

"I'll take care of this garbage. Too bad it isn't Tomari." Jake lifted the cell phone away from his mouth. "What's the address here?"

Marne told him, faltering when she met the fury of an avenging angel with hardened features. She fumbled in her pocket for her keys. Clarissa held on to her left hand with both of hers. "Thanks, Jake."

He stared back for an instant before turning away and speaking into the phone.

Inside, Marne flipped on the lights and turned up the thermostat. She grabbed a blanket from the storeroom where the staff collected household goods for the women they helped get started in new places.

In her office, she wrapped Clarissa in the blanket and pulled her onto her lap. The child was cold and had a few scratches, but otherwise she was all right. Her mental and emotional state were another story.

"Where . . . my mom?" Fear of the answer trembled in Clarissa's small voice.

"She's at the hospital. Worried about you. I'll take you there in a little while." She picked up the phone and punched in the number for County.

Sirens screamed outside. Blue, red, and white strobe lights shot through the tilted blinds.

Marne spoke with the nurses' station, then Dr. Kulick. Angela was still in the recovery room after six hours of surgery.

"Ms. York?" asked the patrolman standing at the door.

Marne nodded, rocking Clarissa in the squeaky office chair.

"That the little girl you've been looking for? Clarissa Tomari?"

Clarissa recoiled against Marne. "Don't let them take me. Please." Long-lashed dark eyes pleaded harder than the frightened voice that was tearing a hole in Marne's heart.

"You're with me," she assured, then tightened her hold. "I'm taking her to County."

"We need her checked out," he warned. "Statements from her and you."

"At County, Patrolman Hayes," she said, reading the name below the shield on his jacket. "This child has been through hell today. She needs to see her mother, and her mother needs to touch her. To know she's okay." The tears streaming down Marne's cheeks came from nowhere and wouldn't stop.

Patrolman Hayes hesitated, then drew a breath. "I'll take you over. We'll get your statements there. Your friend will be at the station for a while."

Marne nodded. Jake was a friend. The kind of friend who walked through the ghosts of his own past to help her. If only he didn't ask too many questions, he'd be the best kind.

FOUR

Though it was after midnight, people still huddled in the hospital waiting rooms. Anxiety and fear formed invisible walls around the clusters of people waiting for news of a loved one.

Clarissa was traumatized, though okay physically.

Marne dealt with Child Protective Services and acted as the child's advocate. It took an hour to convince them that Clarissa would be better off in the hospital overnight.

She found an unexpected ally in Dr. Kulick, who thought that having her daughter close by would be an incentive for Angela Tomari. He ordered the girl hospitalized for observation.

By three A.M., everything was settled. The statements were done. Clarissa and her mother were asleep. Everyone but Angela's brother Vincent, who kept vigil over both, had gone home.

Weary to the core, Marne rose and tossed her empty coffee cup into the waste can.

"Let's get out of here." Jake pushed away from the wall

that he was supporting with his shoulder and uncrossed his arms.

How long he'd stood there Marne had no idea, probably since returning from the police station a couple of hours earlier. At the moment, he was as welcome a sight as a safe harbor after a storm. God, how she'd missed him, would miss him for the rest of her life. "Take me home, Jake."

Slipping easily into an old habit, she leaned against him and slid her hand around his waist when he put his arm around her shoulders. The emotional roller coaster she'd ridden since opening her door to him had finally crashed.

In the small hours of the morning, freeway traffic was as thin as it got during the holidays in California. Even so, they passed an accident before Jake turned down the exit ramp.

"God, I'm tired," she said, breaking the silence.

"Get your keys out. Bed is a block away."

"I've got a couch," she offered.

"I'll take it." He pulled up in front of her town house. A few die-hard neighbors had left their Christmas lights burning in the shrubs. Miniature lights ran around a Christmas tree in the window next to Marne's town house.

He switched off the ignition and pulled the trunk lever.

Marne drew a deep breath and released it slowly. The idea of Jake's spending what remained of the night on her couch felt too good. Too dangerous. Too exciting. She was out of her mind for offering.

He opened the car door for her. She looked up into the shadows of his impassive face and realized she'd been waiting for him, waiting for the old habits they'd forged with patience and youth.

She entered the house and withdrew her cell phone before removing her jacket and tossing it on the living room coffee table. Habits, she thought, like Jake and I were a habit all those years. Worse than cigarettes. Worse than crack. But oh so satisfying. So safe. So full of life.

For so many years they had been each other's touchstones, the balance that kept each of them on an even keel. And times like today made her miss him even more than all the lonely, empty nights since she'd cut him free.

She set the cell phone on the nightstand, but didn't turn around. Chaos laid siege to her reason and fired her blood with promise. The sensation of being alive in every part of her being made her dizzy.

"Marne, a blanket . . ."

The whisper of her name broke the dam restraining the desire she'd tried to ignore all day. Until he'd walked into her town house yesterday afternoon, she had thought it gone. Forever. Ripped out by the roots. Crushed into oblivion. But like him, it was back. Big. Powerful. Unstoppable.

The controlled strength of his hand on her shoulder became a wildfire of loss and need searing her heart. She turned slowly, her gaze searching his somber face, then his gray eyes for understanding.

"Don't say anything," she begged in a whisper. The shadow of his heavy whiskers prickled under her fingertips as they traced his jaw. The glide of her fingers traveling to the back of his neck then pulled until he lowered his head.

This is a mistake, she thought, rising on tiptoe to meet his mouth. *You're tired. Don't do this. Don't give in to it. A mistake!*

The touch of his lips on hers said it was her mistake to make, one she chose freely. Eagerly. To hell with the consequences.

The gentleness of his kiss made her want to weep for all the tender lovemaking they'd shared in the past, and all the lonely nights since. The caress of his hands on her shoulders bespoke reverence, making her feel fragile. God, she'd forgotten he was a master of patience and restraint—just what she couldn't afford.

One taste of him shattered the rigid walls of her defenses. Heart-pounding anxiety hammered out the tattoo: *Your turn. Your turn.*

She deepened the kiss. A starving soul greedy for nourishment, she plundered his mouth, taking, tasting, savoring, demanding that he respond in kind. And he did.

The power of his hunger sent a shiver of fear through

her. But she couldn't, wouldn't stop. He was salvation and damnation. She wanted him.

With one knee propped on the bed, she pulled him off balance, forcing him to catch himself and her as they tumbled. She eased away just long enough to turn off the light on the nightstand.

"Marne—"

The beast of isolation swaddled in loneliness roared encouragement when she silenced Jake by catching his lower lip with her teeth. She tore at his jacket, desperate to peel away the layers. For just a little while, she would touch him, remember all she'd lost, and experience it. For just a little while. Then she'd set him free, for his own good.

Straddling his hips, her chest heaving, she wound her fist in the front of his shirt and sat up. He followed, holding the kiss that was ravaging her mouth, burning her skin through her clothing with the sensation of his hands touching her everywhere. With his help, she got rid of his shoulder holster and weapon.

In the dim glow of the living room lamp, she saw reflected in his stormy gray eyes the hunger gnawing at every cell in her body. And something else. Something she refused to acknowledge.

"Shh-h-h-h," she whispered to the voice of reason warning her to stop.

When she could stand it no longer, she pulled his shirt over his head. God, he was gorgeous. Broad-shouldered and muscular, he symbolized power, strength. She alternately wanted to cover him in kisses and pound his hard, warm flesh with her fists.

"Don't stop now, Marne," he rasped, opening her jeans.

The whisper of reason grew fainter.

Adrift on a sea of chaotic emotions, she cast herself upon the tide of need and jerked loose the metal buttons fastening his fly.

The sensation of cool air on her breasts sent a burst of fear through her. Panicked, she pushed his hands away and pulled her shirt down. "Don't! Don't touch me," she hissed. Shivers crisscrossed the length of her spine, taunting, fading, then dying in the chaos.

Jake's hands slid down her ribs and rested on her hips. "What's going on here?"

"Give me this," she demanded through clenched teeth. His eyes narrowed. For a heart-stopping instant, she thought he would deny her. He wouldn't. She wouldn't let him. "Just give me this." She hated the plea in her softer tone. "No questions. No promises. Just this. Now."

Christ, she was wild, out of control in a way that startled him. He thought he'd seen all her moods, but he didn't know the woman straddling his hips, running her fingers through the hair on his chest, digging her short nails into his shoulders, and kissing him like a vampire.

For four years he'd ached to have her next to him, to be inside her, touch every sensitive part of her, experience the heat of her response, her passion for him. Now he had her. More accurately, she had him, was taking him, stoking the fire of his need, commanding his response with a desperation bordering on brutality.

Christ, he wanted her so badly, he'd give her anything she demanded, then offer more.

She shimmied out of her jeans and panties one leg at a time without breaking the ravenous, soul-consuming kiss.

He shifted when she pulled at his jeans. "Condom," he said against her mouth. He'd never made love with her without one. Now he shifted his weight to make his back pocket accessible.

"I'll do it." The awkward way she worried his wallet from his hip pocket was another reminder of how long it had been since they'd made love. Once she had the condom, she tossed the wallet over her shoulder.

Cold air hissed between his teeth when she put the condom on him. He exhaled a curse at the pleasure and pain shooting through him. Before he collected his thoughts, she grabbed his wrists and brought his hands beside his head. Her fingers laced in his and tightened to a death grip.

This was wrong. All wrong. His instincts demanded he put an end to her game.

He looked into her hard, wild, and angry eyes. Not the clear blue eyes of Marne York. It was another woman wearing her face, her body, using her personality.

And it was too late.

She lowered herself onto his erection carefully, slowly, as though it was painful.

Every muscle in his body tensed. Christ, he didn't want it this way. It was torture of the soul-eating kind to let her continue, and worse to stop.

He wrenched his hands free and reached for her.

A chop from the side of her fist stopped him. She leaned down, riding him hard, her breasts heaving, her shirt swaying. "Don't touch me."

"The hell I—"

Her upper body slammed into his chest. Her mouth on his shut him up. The stinging nips of her teeth on his lips added to the frenzy of lust consuming him.

The quickening tempo of her hips drew the willpower out of him. He grabbed her hips in a final attempt to control her furious possession.

Her orgasm triggered his.

They lay in a heap, trembling and panting. The perfume of desire clung to their sweaty bodies. Jake stared at the ceiling, not sure what the hell had just happened. His arms folded over her back, holding her close enough to indelibly imprint her body on his.

Immediately, Marne pushed away and climbed off him. Without a backward glance, she went into the bathroom and shut the door. The sound of the shower leaked into the silence.

Jake pushed himself up on an elbow. He was still wearing his jeans and shoes. This wasn't how it was supposed to be. This wasn't how people who'd once loved each other made love. But what they'd just done wasn't making love. She hadn't said she loved him, nor had he told her he had never stopped loving her.

"Shit!" He swung his legs over the side of the bed and undressed. "You want full-combat sex, Marne York. You got it. The door swings both ways."

He stormed the bathroom, then stopped cold.

In the middle of the tub Marne sat hugging her knees with her left arm, and holding her bowed head with her right hand. The shower beat down on her. She still wore her shirt. The red socks she hadn't bothered to remove bagged at her ankles. The bow of her back trembled from the silent sobs wracking her body.

Jake slid the glass shower door aside and climbed in behind her.

"Go away, Jake," she sobbed, lowering her head farther.

"I did that four years ago." He reached over her and turned off the water. "Now I'm back."

He hunkered down on the balls of his feet, his knees wide to accommodate her in the cramped tub.

"I don't want you back."

"You already got what you wanted tonight. Hell, that's as close as I've ever come to being raped. Whatever the hell it was, it's not happening again."

"I'm sorry," she sobbed, "so sorry I did that. Oh, God. To you. You didn't deserve it." She sniffed and lifted her head. "I'm so sorry," she whispered.

"Look me in the eye and say it."

"I can't."

He snorted. "Empty words you think you ought to say, Marne?"

She hugged her knees tighter. "Let me . . . let me shower."

"Soap and water won't wash it away." He reached around her and turned on the water.

"Alone."

"Don't worry, Princess. The toad isn't in the mood for a repeat performance."

"Please, Jake. Leave."

"No." He straightened up, caught her under the arms, and brought her to her feet. "You've done all the running and I've done all the leaving we're going to do. Four fucking years. Wasted." He turned her around. "You want to know what I did during that time?"

Blue eyes wide with torment, hair pasted to her forehead

and cheeks, her head shook in short, terse movements. "No."

"For two years I tried battering down your wall of silence, but it was tougher than I was. I spent the next year trying to lay every woman in Arlington and Washington, D.C. But none of them was you, Marne. Goddamn it! None of them was you."

She pounded his chest with her fist, each hit harder. Her jaw remained clamped, her angry eyes unblinking. Silence was the most effective, frustrating weapon he'd ever encountered. Marne had perfected it.

"Goddamn it, why wouldn't you see me? You fucking hid from me, from both families for a year. Drove everyone nuts. And when you came home, you had nothing to say. Screened your calls and wouldn't talk to me. Wouldn't answer an E-mail. You wouldn't even come to Christmas if I was going to be there. And you quit your goddamn teaching job. Did you even care what kind of hell you put me through?" The old wounds hadn't healed. Despite everything, he still loved her.

"Was he that great in bed, Marne? Was he worth distancing yourself from everyone you love, everything you'd worked for? Dreamed of?" At the moment, he couldn't stand to look at her.

She beat at his chest and shoulders with both fists, her teeth clenched, tears streaming down her cheeks.

He caught her wrists. "That's enough! I'm not the asshole who seduced and dumped you."

"I wasn't seduced!" she screamed. "I was raped!" She wrenched her hands free and stepped directly under the shower.

Torment the depth of which he'd not thought possible lived in her blue eyes. The impact charged her revelation with mind-numbing shock. Raped?

Ah, God, not Marne. Not idealistic, do-gooder Marne. His Marne.

"Look at me!" She grabbed the front of her shirt and opened it wide.

Water sluiced over the fine scars slashed across her ribs,

abdomen, and pelvic region. Rape wasn't the worst of it. She'd been tortured. With a knife slicing through her sweet, smooth skin. Very slowly, he sat down on the edge of the tub. Shock gripped him, then sorrow so enormous that it nearly stopped his heart.

The entire world had just turned upside down. "Jesus Christ."

She turned her back and removed her shirt, then braced her hand against the front of the white-tiled shower enclosure.

"Why didn't you tell me?"

He wanted to touch her, to gather her in his arms and promise it would be all right. But it wasn't all right. And he didn't know how to fix it.

"It was my fault."

"Bullshit!" Rage overwhelmed the softer emotions easier to handle than the sorrow and loss he didn't know how to cope with. He wanted to say the right thing. Help her. And didn't know how. "The hell it was your fault." Staring at the fine scars on her pale flesh, the urge to break something balled his fists.

"You don't know. You weren't there. You didn't go through the interrogations. The surgeries. The depositions." The trembling that had wracked her body steadied. She reached for the shampoo, squirted half the bottle on her head, and started to scrub. And scrub.

"I would have been beside you every step of the way." Was this how it felt to bleed to death internally? Couldn't be. That would hurt less.

"I didn't want you there." Shampoo lather coated her back, slipped over the curve of her buttocks and down her thighs like a white veil.

"What about what I wanted?" he shouted, the rage building. He'd have killed the guy. Still might. Oh, yeah. Once he located the bastard, he'd be in and out. A SEAL didn't forget how to annihilate the enemy without a trace. He'd kill the soulless bastard slowly. Painfully. With a dull knife. He wanted it more than anything.

She rinsed her hair and scrubbed soap across a soft

sponge. "You wanted a princess from Atherton. The perfect wife. A mother for your beautiful children. Well, she died in a Denver hotel room, Jake."

He could take damn near anything but her smart-mouth indifference. He spun her around, his insides as raw as if he had eaten ground glass. "I wanted *you*, Marne. God help me, I still do."

"Look hard at these scars. They don't wash off. They don't go away." She pushed free and scrubbed the scars on her abdomen. "I can't have your kids, Jake. I can't have anybody's kids."

"That was your thing, the reason you wanted to be a teacher." He wrapped his hand around the sponge. "I don't give a rat's ass about having kids."

"When you think about it in the morning, you will." She yanked the sponge away and continued washing. "Get on with your life, Jake. I'm rebuilding mine the best I can."

He wanted to shake her, to hold her, to cry with her, and vent his rage all at the same time. He did nothing, just watched the hard, protective layers she'd cultivated over the years rise into place. Of all the emotions assaulting his tired brain, he hated the helplessness the most.

She rinsed, then slapped the sponge at the center of his chest. "It's all yours." She wrung out her shirt and socks, then got out of the shower.

Hands braced against the front tiles, Jake stuck his head under the water. Sometimes life and shit imitated one another. Like now.

It was over. Really over.

Guilt gnawed at her.

How could she have let the demon out of its cage after all this time? Unleashed it on Jake?

Who else but him? Who else could she have trusted enough not to hurt her? She had never wanted anyone but him. Now she had used him, hurt him, and set them both free with the truth.

Marne pulled on her sweatpants and sleep shirt and climbed into bed.

"Don't think about it," she muttered, punching her pillow into shape.

Shutting down had worked in the past, but tonight, despite the bone-weary tiredness creeping through her bones, it didn't.

Curled on her side and facing the wall, she heard Jake leave the bathroom. The ensuing silence further relaxed her body. Fatigue turned her muscles to lead.

Each time she closed her eyes, she saw the horror in his face, the shock draining the color from his cheeks, the fine trembling of his limbs. And the hurting accusations in his eyes. That was the worst. Those eyes that had once feasted on her naked body with love, desire, and the sweet promise of forever.

Movement on the edge of the bed brought her alert.

Jake slid under the covers.

"The couch is in the other room," she said, scooting to the edge of the bed.

"I'm not."

She lacked the strength to argue. "Stay on your own side."

The bed bounced several times before he stilled. Silence filled the room. Sleep never seemed further away.

"One question, Marne."

She heard his head shift on the pillow, but said nothing.

"Do you love me?"

"It doesn't matter." The stinging in her eyes came and left in the time it took to clamp down her emotions. She would love him until she died.

"It matters. That's all that matters. The rest is workable." He turned again.

The weight of his hand on her shoulder reached into her soul.

FIVE

A few hours of sound sleep without the usual nightmares reliving the horrors of Denver had left her groggy but rested. An emotional hangover lingered from the confrontation in the shower. She burrowed deeper into the surrounding warmth, then realized it was Jake's body curled around hers. The twilight of sleep offered a false security. For just a moment, she would savor the press of his big, hard body against her backside.

"Keep your eyes closed," Jake whispered.

"Why?"

"We're going to do a little time traveling."

The caress of his fingers in her hair swept away the absurdity of his claim. The illusive peace of the moment, despite the source, was too rare to give up easily. Later, they would do battle and go their own ways. Later. "Are you going to teleport us to the mountains for Christmas Eve dinner? Traffic is going to be a bitch."

"There's no traffic where we're going. We've been there before. Just you and me."

She suspected that the two people he referred to wore

their faces but were different inside. The people they'd become would never go to the same places hand in hand. Their paths had taken opposite forks on the road they once traveled together. The old, naive dreams had died.

His warm breath kissed her ear with the whisper of a sweet memory that refused to stay buried. "We're going backward, to the first Christmas we made love. Remember?"

"The Christmas Granny Grayson died," she murmured, not liking the direction of this game. Christmas had always been the best and worst time of the year.

"This isn't about her. It's about us." The slow, sinuous glide of his hand over her arm had the same hypnotic effect as his voice.

"There is no *Us*," she murmured.

The kiss he placed below her ear bespoke his patience. "The Christmas morning I snuck into your room guaranteed there would always be an *Us*. Remember how quiet we had to be?"

She did remember, and smiled. It had been cold that Christmas, and rainy. The slow-moving clouds had wept while she and Jake had kept a vigil during Granny Grayson's last hours. By unspoken agreement, Jake had come to her room before dawn. She'd been waiting. "God, you looked so macho in your Navy uniform. I was seventeen and crazy in love with you."

"And eager to jump my bones."

When she'd made love with him for the first time that somber Christmas, Jake had been a life raft in a sea of loss. The presence of his strength, the depth of his love, had sustained her when cancer sucked the last breath from Granny Grayson.

"I'd wanted you for so long, Marne, and every day since." His hand slipped over her elbows and along the curve of her hip.

Echoes of a time when that was all it took for her to shimmy out of her panties tempted her, but she denied it. The sexual debacle earlier this morning had been enough. Too much. What had driven her to punish Jake?

"We were patient with one another then, and careful."

"You were both. I was neither." She had practically ripped the buttons off his fly in the rush to lose her virginity.

She had done the same thing last night, only with ignoble intent. Remembering the depths she'd sunk to made her want to put an end to his game.

The bar of his forearm across her hipbones stopped her from retreating.

"Not so fast. We haven't come to the good part yet." He drew her into the niche created by his heated body. "You've got your clothes on. Nothing is going to happen but memories."

She relaxed slightly. Memories were dangerous. Painful. Who knew that better than she? "Make your point, Jake. I've got places to go."

"You mean places to run?" He flipped her onto her back so she was in the shelter of his shoulders, his knees tucked under hers. "In those days, we ran to each other. We helped. We healed. Even during the years I was in the Seals, and we couldn't write, couldn't talk on the phone. We loved enough for all that."

Marne squeezed her eyes tight, snared by memories of a simpler time. "Your Seal years, my college years. I used to sit in my room and spin the globe with my eyes closed. When it slowed, I'd pick a spot with my finger, open my eyes, and wonder if that was where you were. What you were doing. If you were in danger. I prayed every night you'd come back."

"I always did. Always will."

The sting in her eyes started again when he kissed her forehead.

"We promised each other something that Christmas morning." He kissed her temple and slid his arm around her shoulder, drawing her even closer to him. "Remember?"

She did, with painful clarity.

"Before we made love the first time, we promised to

love each other until death parted us.'' He kissed her closed eyes.

A single tear leaked from the corner of her eye and rolled down her temple. He was tearing her apart with the lost dreams of a woman who'd died four years ago. The reverence of his lips soaking up her tears spawned more.

''We promised we'd marry.''

''And have children,'' she rasped, suddenly needing to break free of the haunting memories. ''That's no longer possible. The *us* we were is over.''

''No, it's not. There were no guarantees that we could have kids then. We just took it for granted. Maybe like we took each other for granted over the years.'' He cradled her face, his chest pinning her right arm between them.

''Game over, Jake.'' She opened her eyes and stopped struggling. The strain etched into his face denied that he'd slept. Sometime during the night he had shaved. Even so, his angular features had a gauntness she had never seen. An ever-changing kaleidoscope of emotion shone in his expressive, unblinking gray eyes.

''I love you, Marne York. We've got a helluva lot to work on, but we can do it. Unless . . .''

She didn't want to know *unless*. It didn't matter.

''Unless you don't love me—but I think you do,'' he said.

The way he cradled her head in his hands kept her from turning away. She could do damn near anything, except look him in the eye and lie about that. ''You love someone who doesn't exist.''

''I love someone who shut me out because she didn't think our love was strong enough to survive what happened.''

Unable to meet the love she saw on his face, she closed her eyes. ''I'm not strong enough. Too often, I wished he'd done a complete job and killed me. All of me.''

The tremor that shot through his body shook hers. ''Don't say that. Ever.'' Gone was the hypnotic bass voice. Anger ruled him now.

''I'll say what I want. It's my house. My bed. My life.''

"My heart, my love," he added.

Defiant, she stared up at him. "I quit my job because I couldn't pass a drug test, Jake. Think the taxpayers of Atherton want to send their five-year-olds to someone who can't provide a clear piss test?" The gauntlet was down. Time to go in for the kill. "For the year I was gone, I was in and out of hospitals. The last one was Betty Ford. That helped me enough to find a direction for my life, a way to empower myself. Have meaning. The Great White Way has been my salvation. People need me there. Women and children caught in a cycle of brutality and raped on a daily basis, one way or another."

Although he backed off slightly, the intensity of his gaze held her. "You've honed your defenses, Marne. It won't work this time."

"I don't know what you're talking about." Why wouldn't he back off?

"Did you forget what I do for a living now?"

She glared at him. How could she forget what she never knew the whole of? "You never spoke much about it, did you, Jake? What are you into? Computers? Security? Communications or something like that for the government?"

"Communications security. You have to know a little something about breaking security codes to build an effective one. I'm very good at both. Before you woke up, I spent a little time doing just that with some old police records. I made a few phone calls, too. It didn't take much to find out what happened in Denver four years ago. Your father pulled a lot of strings to keep it quiet, then got lucky when the bastard pleaded guilty. If he hadn't . . . I'd have known what happened. You couldn't have kept me away."

Her blood ran cold with anger, then hot with indignation. Jake was a pit bull when he wanted something. Using his contacts and skills, he'd pried into her secrets, probably even into the dark corners of her records. Everything in her stilled. Jaw clenched, she clung to the only weapon effective against him. Silence.

"He ran a scam on you, Princess. Probably targeted you the minute you walked into the convention. Stalked you for the next couple of days. Made sure you saw him, talked with you at the conference, in the elevator, and during the meals. He listened when you didn't even know he was there. By the time he made his move on you, he knew the jargon, felt your enthusiasm, your vitality. That's what he wanted to take from you. To rob you of."

The rapid beat of her heart hammered at her constricting chest. "Stop it."

"He invited you to the bar to talk about new teaching methods being discussed at the conference. Bought you a drink, then offered to walk you to your room, didn't he? Said you couldn't be too careful in a strange city."

The bloody night in Denver crashed through her tattered defenses, paralyzing her with its clarity.

"You offered him a copy of the materials from the afternoon seminar. And let him into your room."

Stupid. Deadly stupid to trust anyone.

"Don't," she pleaded.

"I know what happened, and why, Princess. But not why you shut me out. Why you closed the door on everyone."

"Not everyone," she confessed. "My parents knew. I asked them not to tell the others. They came to Denver instead of going to the Bahamas." How the hell could she tell him it was the uppers and downers of her mother's prescriptions that got her through the hearings? That the pain medication became addictive? Or the shrink she went to believed that all cures came in pill form? That like a worn-out sponge, she soaked it all up and the pain still didn't go away.

She was strong, but not that strong.

"I know it all. I pulled some strings, called in a favor, and got access to your file at Betty Ford," he said softly.

She closed her eyes in resignation. If he read her file, he did know it all. Every sordid detail. "Is nothing sacred to you?"

"You are."

The chaste kiss he placed on her lips started the tears in earnest. She tried to stop them, but she couldn't mend the broken dam.

There were few things that could beat him. Marne's tears were one; they stripped him to the bone. He held her, rocked her, encouraged her to cry it out, and told her he loved her for the next hour.

The grizzly images he'd pulled up on his laptop haunted him. The phone calls filled in the blanks.

In hindsight, it was easy to predict her downward spiral. Four years ago when he was part of a Navy Seal task force in the Middle East, she had been a lamb caught in the fist of evil. Now she courted evil and snatched the lambs free. Or tried to.

"There's something else," he whispered in her ear. "He won't be coming after you."

She became a writhing ball of snakes turning on him. "You can't kill him!"

Clink. The final piece fell into place, the one vexing him for so long. "Is that what you were afraid I'd do? Kill him?" Christ, she knew him too well.

"Promise me, Jake." Red-rimmed blue eyes awash in tears pleaded with him. "I couldn't stand . . ."

"He's already dead." *Unfortunately,* he added silently.

He released when she pushed again. "When? Where? How?"

"Last month. In prison, a week before he was going to be paroled."

"You're sure? No mistake?"

"I spoke to the warden a couple of hours ago. I'm sure."

She exhaled a deep breath she'd probably held for four years. Her visible relief that he hadn't killed the bastard, or had him killed, contrasted sharply with his disappointment at being cheated of the opportunity.

"Someone slipped a shiv through his ribs straight to his heart."

She collapsed onto her pillow. "My father got a letter saying he'd be paroled. I figured he'd look for me. Eventually. No one informed us that he was killed," she whispered. "It's really over, isn't it?"

"I don't think so. He's still the enemy. You give him power by letting him dictate your life. Until you give him up, he's alive. Bury him by coming back to me, Marne.'' It was a last-ditch effort, and he was botching it badly. He lacked her persuasiveness with words, and the means of imparting the lessons he'd learned in the school of hard knocks.

"I don't know if I can," she whispered.

"Do you want to?" Every nerve in his body braced for the answer.

"I can't go back." She touched his cheek in the special way she had of drawing tension away from him. "I love you, have always loved you. But love doesn't change or cure anything."

Relief eased the knots in his shoulders. The admission was enough to build on. More than he had hoped for last night.

"If only it was as simple as being seventeen for a few hours."

"It's a place to start. Try."

"I'm hardly the naive virgin I was then."

He shifted, drawing her close, loving the way her body flowed against his. "Not naive. Not virginal. The woman I love."

At a loss for words, freer than she had been in what seemed forever, Marne let the old desire that he sparked with a look roll through her. "You're already undressed."

"Yes, thank God. In a minute you will be too."

For a second she smiled, then remembered what she kept hidden beneath a long sleep shirt and sweatpants. Before she could object, his hands were sliding up her ribs and his mouth was coaxing her lips apart.

He worshiped her with his body, his mouth, his hands. He banished her fear, her self-consciousness with hot kisses and gentle touches.

When she cried at the beauty he created, he held her, but he never stopped touching, stroking, expressing what he couldn't put into words. He had always been better at showing than telling.

"This isn't how we did it," she said between hungry kisses. They lay face-to-face on their sides.

"Close enough," he murmured, hiking her thigh over his hip. "Unless you want to be on top."

In a flash, she understood that he had positioned them so she had an escape route at all times. And he was right. Like a room with an open door, she had no sense of entrapment. God, how she loved this man.

"Together forever," he whispered, repeating the promise they had exchanged the first time they made love.

"For now," she answered back, claiming him with the same possessiveness, unable to promise anything beyond the moment. This time when he entered her, there was no pain, only intense pleasure as she climaxed immediately.

And it wasn't enough. He wouldn't let it be. Within minutes, she wanted him as wild as she felt the moment he made them whole.

"Jesus, Marne." Like hers, his breath came in quick gasps. He gripped her buttocks and rolled onto his back.

She might be on top, but she wasn't in control. His hands splayed over her hips and buttocks as he lifted her. She moved with him, lost in the mounting sensation, unable to look anywhere but into his dilated gray eyes. Still he kept the tempo slow, never quite letting her have as much as she wanted.

"Jake," she pleaded, reaching for the magic he kept just out of reach.

"All of me, Princess. All of—"

She tightened the powerful muscles surrounding his erection, flexed again, and stole control. In exchange, she took them both to the special paradise that belonged only to them.

Time slowed while she floated in a place she had thought she would never be again. She lay on his chest, panting, listening to his breathing and the beating of their hearts. His arms were folded over her shoulders.

"I missed you, Princess."

The simple words touched her deeply. She curled her hands around his shoulders and hugged him. "Me, too. But no Christmas promises this year, Jake."

"All right."

"Speaking of which, we'd better get on the road if we're going to make the Sierras before dark." She sighed, wishing she could spend Christmas right here with him, but afraid in ways she hadn't considered. She laughed softly.

"What's so funny?" He stroked her back, buttocks, and thighs in a never-ending sweep.

"I thought I knew all the faces of fear."

"Are you afraid?"

"Scared to death. This doesn't change anything."

"It does for me."

"It doesn't change me. Who I am now. What I am and believe in."

"I'm not looking to change you, Marne, just understand you. Don't shut me out. Give me a little time. That's all I ask."

"I—" The warbling of her cell phone cut off her protest. Jake picked it up. "Two to one it's Alice."

"You talk to her. I'm getting in the shower." She gave him a long, wet kiss while the phone chirped two more times before she left him.

She darted into the bathroom and turned on the shower for a quick run-through. She had almost finished when Jake came in.

"Your phone's busy this morning. You probably want to take this one, Goldilocks," he said, offering her a towel and the cell phone.

She did a quick rinse, then stepped out of the tub. "Yeah?"

"Yo, Goldilocks, you got that FBI ape monitoring your phone? What'd you do? Bang him?"

"What's happening, Boomer? I passed the word we found Clarissa. You get it?"

"Yeah, I got it. Thought I'd give you a tip, though. Seein' as how you be so tight with the Feds an' all. Know what I'm sayin'?"

She did. Boomer was looking to buy a future favor. "What kind of tip?" She glanced up at Jake as he entered the bathroom carrying a fresh towel, comfortable with his nudity. Why not? He was a Class AAAA, ultra-prime male.

"Your buddy. Julius."

She dragged her eyes away from the sculptured hair pattern on Jake's torso. "What about him?"

"Two of my bros got the word he's lookin' for you. Hard. Gonna make you pay."

"You selling protection?" she asked warily.

"Shee-it, no. I don't need ta be mixin' it up with no homeboy turned Fed. Un-unh. Jest letting ya know, Goldilocks. It ain't safe for you down here." He hung up.

"What did he want?" Jake stepped into the shower.

"We have a little unfinished business. Make it quick. We need to talk to a cop about a wife-beater." She had an idea of how to get Julius Tomari behind bars.

She smiled at the steamy mirror. With a little luck he, too, would be home for Christmas.

SIX

Marne let Jake load her suitcase into the trunk of the Lincoln. Eventually they would head east into the Sierras, but her first destination was the hospital to check on Angela.

Clarissa's quiet presence went a long way toward easing the physical trauma that Dr. Kulick and his team had repaired. Angela stood a fair chance of spending Christmas outside the ICU.

Kulick was a hard-ass, but he had demonstrated that his heart was in the right place by going out on a limb and keeping Clarissa hospitalized. The sign-off by the Social Services caseworker was no small feat in the wake of tight budgets and service cutbacks.

In the lounge outside the ICU, Marne spoke privately with Angela's brothers. They took her warnings about Julius seriously. One of them would remain near Angela and Clarissa until Julius was picked up or until Angela was well enough to be secretly returned to Boise.

Satisfied she had done what she could, Marne checked in with the Grayson Foundation hot line. Things were quiet there. Thank God.

"Let's eat," she said on the way to the car in the hospital parking lot.

"About time. My stomach thinks my throat's been cut. Any place in particular?" Jake opened the car door for her.

She got in, smiling, amazed by how easily they fell into old habits. Maybe some things didn't change. But some did, irrevocably.

"The diner," she said when he started the car.

"That isn't on the way to I-80."

"I need to go to my office after we grab a bite." On the streets, traffic was snarled with last-minute shoppers desperate to complete their Christmas Eve rounds. Red-and-white candy-cane decorations hanging from the street-divider lampposts twisted in the breeze. The silver garland bows wrapped around the fasteners reflected the sunlight streaming through patchy clouds.

"You going to tell me what this is about? What the hell Boomer wanted?" He accelerated the car up the freeway entrance.

He would find out soon enough. Some arguments were better in public. This was one of them. "When we get to the diner."

He eyed her with an intensity that burned. "I still know of half a dozen places to eat where the food won't poison you."

"I happen to like the way Nateesha cooks my eggs." She smiled, knowing he was biding his time, not pressing her for answers. The hard set of his jaw revealed his concern about her wanting a final trip to the strip before they went to the family Christmas gathering. At least he wasn't bucking her. Yet.

"It's hard to ruin breakfast, but it can be done," he said, checking traffic on his left.

"If it'll make you feel any better, I'll ask her to make sure no one spits on your food before it's served."

"I love a woman with connections to the chef at a gourmet restaurant." He passed an eighteen-wheeler with snow chains dangling from the carriers beneath it.

"It's almost two. Nateesha is on for another half hour

or so.'' And Lieutenant Peterson was going to join them in fifteen minutes. When he did, Jake would go ballistic. Then, he could stay or go, but it wouldn't matter. She was seeing this through her way.

The Great White Way's nightlife was sleeping or holed up while the sun remained in the sky. Most of the clubs and bars were open, but no hawkers wasted time luring pedestrians inside. A gaggle of teenagers performed the strutting rituals of courtship in front of the convenience store run by the Korean couple.

Jake pulled behind a rarely seen street-sweeping truck moving slowly around parked cars near the diner.

''I see the mayor's found a new method of cleaning the so-called undesirable elements from the streets.''

Marne got out of the car. A homeless woman wearing a Santa Claus hat rocked against the wall of the diner. Stained polyester pants that might have been beige at one time hung from beneath a zipped parka stuffed with her possessions. One of her scuffed running shoes had no laces. Her heels locked a roll of blankets against the cracked, stucco wall.

Marne fingered the money in her jeans pocket. She put a fin into the woman's outstretched hand. ''Merry Christmas, Zelda.''

''Thanks, Goldilocks.'' A grin turned her face into a plane of fractured wrinkles. A line of stained teeth broken at the center flashed. ''You gotta good heart.''

Marne entered the diner. Zelda had been on the street so long, she'd never leave. It was home now. At times, she suspected Zelda No-Last-Name had lived a good life under a different name, in a better place. Things changed. Everybody had to be somewhere. But life on the Great White Way seemed harsher, more austere during the Christmas season.

She waved at Natecsha back in the kitchen area. ''Two of the usual,'' she called, then glanced at Jake. ''Clean.''

The tall black woman with more long cornrows than it seemed possible to fit on one head, loosed a belly laugh that drowned out a Mannheim Steamroller version of ''Hark! The Herald Angels Sing.''

"You got it, Goldilocks. Get your own coffee. The one on the left is fresh." Nateesha wiped her hands on a towel, then adjusted her apron.

"Make yourself at home." Marne gestured at the far corner booth, well away from the windows and the few patrons trying to appear oblivious while they sized up Jake. Strangers always drew attention, especially one who exuded the striking self-confidence Jake did.

"Give me a minute." He left her standing at the coffee-pots and headed for the kitchen.

Marne set two cups of coffee on the table at the back booth. A squeal from the kitchen brought heads up throughout the diner. Two young men wearing Boomer's colors rose from the counter and started for the grill area. Marne raced along the row of stools fixed in front of the long counter.

"I thought you be dead by now. Or livin' in some fancy neighborhood." Nateesha hugged Jake's neck. Her laughter boomed reassurance. "Ain't you a sight for Christmas!"

Marne gripped the counter and exchanged relieved glances with the young men returning to their meals. Damn him! Jake hadn't given any indication that he knew Nateesha. What astounded her was that he not only acknowledged her, he went out of his way to reacquaint himself.

"Marne. What's so damn important?"

The grin faded when she turned around. Lieutenant Peterson had traded his suit for gray Dockers, a burgundy cotton pullover, and a black windbreaker boasting a reptile on the breast pocket. She hadn't been sure he would keep the appointment, let alone be a few minutes early.

"Thanks for coming. Hungry?"

"Never hungry enough to eat here."

Marne shrugged. "Don't know why not." She headed for the booth she'd staked a claim on earlier.

Peterson slid in front of the second cup of steaming coffee, sniffed it, then took a sip. "You did a helluva job finding Clarissa Tomari. I read the reports. Looks like you got to her just in time to save her more grief."

"Thanks." *For nothing in the way of help doing it,* she added silently. "She's still at the hospital."

"So is the son of a bitch your ex-fiancé damn near pounded into the ground." He glanced down the long aisle of counter seats. "Who the hell is he, Marne?"

"I'm surprised you didn't check him out." More than surprised. Word had reached her that Gary Peterson had checked out everyone her work brought her into contact with. She didn't like it, but she couldn't stop him. It seemed a lot of trouble to go through for a woman who would never give him a tumble.

"I got as far as confirmation that he's FBI, then hit a stone wall. He's no run-of-the-mill agent, is he?"

Marne sat back and folded her arms. "I don't know what his job is, but no, Lieutenant. There's nothing run-of-the-mill about him. Nothing at all."

He leaned over the edge of the table, his arms circling his coffee cup. "He breezes into town for the holidays and you jump. That how it is?"

Marne shook her head.

"Does he have something on you? On one of the women you're protecting?"

"Not really, but thanks for the concern. When I need help with my personal life, I call the Psychic Friends Hotline."

"This is my town. If he's hassling you, I can help you out."

Yesterday, had she been planning the dangerous scheme rolling around in her head now, she might have accepted his offer to get Jake out of the way. Today, she suspected there was no way in heaven or hell Jake would be side-tracked.

She looked down the long aisle. Jake balanced two plates on his left arm and carried a cup and a coffeepot in his right hand. A jerk of his head told her to slide over. She didn't budge. No way was she going to be sandwiched between two men ready to bicker over a bone.

Jake set the plates and coffee down. "Move it, Peterson. My breakfast is getting cold."

Marne checked her watch and picked up her fork.

"Have you found Julius Tomari?" Jake settled across from Marne and attacked his food.

"What's it to you?" Peterson dragged his coffee into the U-shaped depth of the booth.

"Hey, do I detect police hostility directed at a concerned citizen?" Jake shoved a forkful of scrambled eggs and crispy hash brown potatoes into his mouth.

"We may issue a warrant for you, Rimsa. Assault."

Unfazed by the threat, Jake shrugged and kept eating.

"Of course, if we do, that'll put a wrench in your holiday plans. Know a good bail bondsman?"

"Still using your shield as a weapon?"

Though caught in the center, Peterson started to stand. "Look, you arrogant, overgrown punk—"

"You boys playing nice?" Nateesha picked up the coffeepot, topped off all three coffees. She ran her ringed fingers through Jake's thick black hair until he grinned at her.

"Great breakfast." Jake lifted a fork piled with potatoes and eggs.

"I spit in it when you weren't lookin'."

Jake winked at her, then examined the food on his fork. "So that's the secret sauce flavor. Tastes like ambrosia." He put the fork into his mouth.

Laughter bubbled up in Marne's throat, then rang clear when she couldn't contain it. She'd forgotten how infuriatingly cool and antagonistically charming he could be. She met Jake's raised eyebrows and devilish smile, and laughed harder.

"Well, damn. I didn't know Goldilocks knew how to laugh." Nateesha ruffled Jake's disheveled hair a final time. "You come back for special sauce anytime, Jake, just so's you make her laugh."

The sudden sorrow in his eyes quelled Marne's laughter. She sniffed, then picked up her fork again.

"You mind telling me why it was so damn urgent for me to meet you here?" demanded Peterson.

"Julius Tomari," she said, then shoved in another bite. "We've got an APB out for him."

"But you don't know where he is." She washed down the mouthful of food with a sip of coffee. "I got a tip."

Jake swore under his breath. His fork clattered on his empty plate. "Boomer. Goddamn it, Marne, why didn't you say so?"

"You could have called it in," Peterson said.

"It wouldn't work that way." She shoved the remnants of her breakfast away. "For openers, I don't know where he is, but I think I know how to catch him."

"It's a police matter," Peterson grumbled. "We'll get him."

"Before or after he gets another shot at Angela? Next time, Clarissa might not have a window to crawl out of. What then, Lieutenant? You think that little girl could survive the kind of beating he gave Angela?"

"Neither can you," Jake said softly. "No way, Marne. I'm taking you out of here. Peterson and his men better pick up Tomari before we get back, or I'll make it my business." Cold gray eyes glared at the lieutenant. "You don't want that, Peterson."

"Who the fuck do you think you are?"

"A mediocre cop's worst nightmare."

"Knock it off!" Marne slammed her cup into the saucer and sent coffee flying across the table. "Instead of fighting, help me."

"What the hell do you want?" Peterson demanded, red-faced.

"A present. I want Julius Tomari in jail for Christmas."

"I can't promise that."

"I can, if you'll work with me."

"Marne—" Jake started, his expression a thundercloud.

"Help me or stand quietly on the sidelines, Jake. This is my business." Every defense she'd cultivated over the past four years rose against the angry torment she read in his face.

"The hell it is."

She turned to Peterson. "Julius wants to make me pay for Angela's divorcing him, then testifying against him. You know he and I have a history. What you don't know is that he promised Angela I wouldn't see Christmas."

"Goddamn it, Marne!" Jake exploded.

"And you didn't mention it? What is it with you? You got a death wish?" Peterson demanded.

"More like a life wish. When I leave here, I'm going to my office." She turned her attention back to Jake. "Alone."

"When hell freezes over," Jake seethed. "You aren't going to be bait."

"He knows a hundred places to hide. The only way to catch him is to offer him something he wants. Me." She reached across the table and covered Jake's white-knuckled fist with her hand. "This is what I am now, what I do."

"It could work," Peterson mused. "If we set up a stake-out."

"It could get her killed, or beaten to a pulp."

"You can walk away, Jake. I can't. I'm doing this. You can help or get out of the way. Which will it be?" She'd backed him into a corner, forcing him to see who she'd become, forcing him to accept or reject it.

"We don't need him." Peterson withdrew a cell phone from inside his jacket and started punching in numbers.

Jake ignored the mouthy lieutenant. If Marne was scared, she didn't show it. Cold determination clung to her like a second skin.

The images he had accessed on his computer before dawn flooded back. Marne, her face beaten until she was barely recognizable. Her torso slashed and bleeding through the compression bandages. Innocence lost. Hell, she'd been lost for more than four years and fighting her way back since.

The woman who had rebuilt her life sat across the table, the same but wiser, harder, determined to save the lambs from the wolves. Who would save her?

"You know I'm not walking," he said evenly. Christ, if she had to do this, she damn sure wouldn't do it alone. Peterson couldn't even protect his own ass in a street fight. He damn sure couldn't protect Marne's. "We do this my way."

"Butt out, Rimsa," Peterson said. "This is my case. All your FBI badge gets you here is spit on your eggs." He slid sideways in the booth, putting his back to Jake, and spoke softly into the phone.

"Julius is a sneaky bastard. He won't come at you the way you think he will," Jake warned her.

"I keep a gun in the office."

"Do you know how to use it?"

"I go to the range once a month."

He studied her for a long moment before deciding she would shoot Julius if she had to. If she got the chance. "I'll be in the office with you. All we need is for him to show. You don't need to confront him."

The rosy color lovemaking had put in her cheeks faded. "I have no intention of confronting him. If it goes by the book, I won't even see him face-to-face."

Jake's breakfast turned into a rock in his stomach. "You've done this before."

She nodded. "A year ago. I'm better at defending myself now."

"We're good to go," Peterson interrupted. "I've got two cars setting up outside your office. We'll have a man on both sides of the street. We'll use radios and keep the channels open so we can hear everything inside. Sergeant Hill is setting up a surveillance team now. They'll be here in an hour." He consulted his notepad, then continued detailing the operation.

The plan Peterson outlined followed standard police procedure. Theoretically it should work. But the bad feeling Jake had about Julius Tomari wouldn't go away. Tomari had made his living by breaking and entering. Even as a teenager, he'd only dabbled in drugs and never the hard stuff. He'd had aspirations that required a cool head and clear thinking.

"What's Tomari's rap sheet look like?" Jake asked Peterson.

As Jake listened to the rundown of Tomari's arrests, the feeling in his gut tightened. Twice Tomari had been con-

victed of felony assault. The first time he had crippled a
fence who tried to cheat him. The second was Angela. Both
were crimes of passion and out of his element.

Tomari was a planner, and that bothered Jake. He'd had
plenty of time to plan how to get to Marne. Much as he
hated to admit it, she was right. They had to get him before
he got her. But he damn sure wasn't going to put her safety
in Peterson's hands.

Peterson had screwed around for more than two hours.
If this was his idea of instant response, the whole city was
in a world of shit. The tired winter sun was dangerously
close to the horizon by the time Jake parked behind the
Grayson Foundation. Before he cleared the car door to open
Marne's, she got out. When ensconced behind her defenses,
she ignored the niceties he extended.

There was nothing nice about the anxiety gripping his
gut. Nor was there anything he could do about her making
herself a target for Julius Tomari.

Under the circumstances, he preferred her intense and
hardened. She was with him; that made her as safe as she'd
ever be while near the strip.

"I want the building checked before she enters," he told
Peterson through the walkie-talkie. "Both floors and the
roof. He could be hiding in the flat portion with heating
equipment right now."

"The building is locked up." As though to demonstrate,
Marne turned the knob and pulled on the back door. It
didn't budge. Burglar bars secured the front door and all
the first-floor windows.

"I still want it checked. Got that, Peterson?" He slipped
the radio into his pocket, took the keys, and unlocked the
door. "Tomari hasn't avoided being caught by being
sloppy. He was cagey twenty years ago. He's better now.
They check the building before you go in."

"You're paranoid, but that doesn't make you wrong."
Marne put her hands in her jacket pockets and waited for
Peterson.

Jake spun her around, putting her back against the door.
Startlement widened her eyes. Her hands flew out of her

pockets in a spontaneous reaction to defend herself. With even quicker reflexes, he stopped her before she delivered a blow.

"I'm alive because I don't trust the other guy, Marne. That isn't paranoia. That's survival. What you're doing here is noble, but dangerous. Not taking every precaution is stupid."

"Stupid!" she snapped, her blue eyes ablaze with fury. "I don't—"

"The first rule of engagement is to respect your enemy. Neither you nor Peterson has given Tomari the respect he's due. He's counting on you selling him short. That's his advantage. Rearranging Angela's face is his sideline, not his bread and butter. Hell, he's probably watching this fiasco right now. Laughing his ass off. Waiting for the right moment."

Her gaze darted past him to the second-story windows of the buildings beyond the eight-foot cinder-block wall isolating the parking area.

The fear he'd hoped to instill to make her cautious never showed. "He won't get into the building, Jake. Lieutenant Peterson and his men will pick Julius up as soon as he's spotted."

"You think he's going to walk up to the front door? Are you intentionally being dense?"

Her angry glare flashed back at him. "Now I'm dense. Any more wisdom you care to impart before we get this show on the road?"

"Yeah. There's only one person here you can trust. You're looking at him."

"Lieutenant—"

"Has an agenda," he whispered into her ear.

"So do you." She pushed at his chest.

"Right. Keeping you safe." The sound of men coming down the drive forced him to back off.

She retreated the two steps down to the parking area.

Jake unlocked the door and pocketed the keys. "Check everything. Closets. Offices. Bathrooms," he told the two patrolmen. "Just like you'd do to protect your mother or your kid."

"Got it," said the second officer as he entered the building.

He would check it again before following the plan Peterson had laid out. He hated it. Hated the whole idea. Hated that Marne felt compelled to face the devil of her own past with a different face and not slay him.

"Jake?"

He quit trying to see behind the windows of adjacent buildings and looked at her. "Yeah?"

"I trust you."

"Wise move." Christ. He was the only one she could trust. The only one who'd seen why Tomari was such a damn good second-story thief. From the looks of his rap sheet, Tomari hadn't lost his edge; he'd honed it over the years.

"Trust me to know what I'm doing, will you?"

He trusted that she had something to prove to herself.

With the walkie-talkie channels open and everything they said being recorded in the surveillance van, he settled for nodding. What he trusted was that she thought she knew what she was doing.

After the patrolmen gave the all clear, he let Marne enter, then locked the back door and looked around. Shit. No security cameras. No alarm. The place was an invitation on a silver platter. He thumbed the radio. "We're in and ready to roll."

"You come out in fifteen minutes, Rimsa. If he's watching, he's not coming in with you there." Peterson was an officious prig. If he'd spent as much time researching Julius Tomari as he did picking out his wardrobe, he'd have a clue to what he was dealing with. Tomari didn't give a shit about Peterson's timetable. He had his own.

Jake's instincts nagged at him to stay with Marne and tell Peterson to go to hell. Something didn't feel right. For the life of him, he couldn't pinpoint it.

"Acknowledge, Rimsa."

He turned on the light in the storeroom and began a final

thorough check of the Grayson Foundation offices.

"Rimsa."

"Yeah, I hear you, Peterson," he barked into the speaker, then released the button and checked his watch. Fifteen minutes of protection for Marne. How long before Tomari showed? He'd wager his last nickel it'd be longer than a quarter of an hour.

"Got a building diagram?" he asked Marne after checking every nook and cranny of the cramped offices.

"No. Why?"

Although Jake was satisfied Tomari wasn't hiding in the offices, that didn't mean he couldn't get inside. Jake had already checked the offices on the second floor. The trapdoor to the heating equipment on the roof was locked from the outside.

"What are you doing?" Marne put her hand over his on the thermostat that he had turned up all the way.

"Checking the ducts. Where's your gun?"

She drew back the front of her jacket and showed him the butt of a .357 Smith and Wesson protruding from a holster clipped to her waistband. He extended his hand. "Let me check it."

"Give me some credit, Jake. I know about weapons."

"Humor me." He wiggled his fingers.

Glaring at him with open rancor, she removed the .357 from the holster and gave it to him.

He examined the load, silently approving of the hollow-point bullets, looked down the bore and nodded. It was clean and oiled. A good weapon, lethal enough to stop Tomari. He returned it to her.

The heat came on. He checked every vent and both air-intake ducts. All blew clear.

"Did you check under the sink in the bathroom?" she asked wryly.

"Yes."

"Time's up. You're out of there, Rimsa," Peterson ordered over the radio.

He checked his watch. "I've got two minutes." And intended to use them reminding Marne why she had to be careful. He stuffed the radio into his pocket. "Come here."

She took a step, then hesitated. Uncertainty replaced the coldness in her eyes. Before she regrouped, he slid his hand behind her neck and closed the distance between them.

What started out as a gentle kiss turned into screaming need within a few rapid heartbeats. The press of her warm, firm body against his cradled the erection straining his jeans. The sharp outline of her gun ground into his hip.

"Time's up. Get out," came Peterson's strident order.

He held her tightly, his mouth against her ear. "I'll be close by."

He released her, then walked out of her office. It felt like he was leaving a lamb in a lion's den. "Lock the door behind me."

Marne leaned against the steel door and threw the dead bolt.

Jake Rimsa was the most infuriating, domineering lone wolf she'd ever known. And she loved him. Had loved him even when she didn't want to draw another breath.

The Grayson Foundation was locked up tight. There was nothing to do now but wait—and hope Julius Tomari took the bait.

Marne wasn't good at waiting. She turned down the thermostat on the furnace. The early darkness of Christmas Eve had descended outside the windows. If Julius Tomari meant to keep his promise to Angela, he'd have to hurry.

She removed her jacket and turned on the office computer. After three games of Solitaire, she started pulling together the records for year-end tax preparation.

Jake drove away from the Grayson Foundation without looking at the undercover officers on the street. He stared straight ahead when he passed the ratty-looking surveillance van. Two blocks down the street, he turned right, pulled over, and parked the Lincoln. "I'm clear," he said into the radio.

"Good. Shut off your radio and answer your damn phone."

Jake snorted. Whatever Peterson had to say, he didn't

want Marne hearing it. He turned off the walkie-talkie and tossed it into the passenger seat. He took the phone from inside his jacket. It vibrated in his hand. ''What?''

''Let's get something clear, Rimsa,'' Peterson hissed. ''This is my turf. My operation. You stay the hell away, or I'll bust you for interference. Got that?''

''You're on record.''

''She's got me. She doesn't need you. Go back to the rock you crawled out from under.'' The line went dead.

Peterson had shown his ass, just as expected. Knowing the tactics Peterson used didn't make them any easier to swallow. There wouldn't be any more transmissions until it was over. Meanwhile, he'd eavesdrop. He turned on the walkie-talkie, then went to the trunk and retrieved the smaller of his two suitcases. Time to get ready to do the kind of work an ex–Navy Seal did best. It had never mattered more.

''Sounds like you're beating your keyboard to death,'' Peterson teased over the radio.

She checked the wall clock. Ten to six. A whopping seven minutes had passed since the last time she looked at it. ''Taxes,'' she muttered. ''Any sign of him?''

''The street's as quiet as a four-year-old waiting for Santa. We've got a long way to go until midnight. If he doesn't show by then, he's not coming.''

''He's got a little over six hours.'' Which was plenty of time. ''I need coffee.''

''Guess you'll have to make your own for now. When this is over, I'll take you someplace nice for dinner.''

Where he and Jake would dine on each other's bone marrow, she thought wearily. ''Is Jake with you?''

''He's, ah, keeping watch down the street.''

The uneasiness she'd felt since Jake left tightened its grasp. Jake would want to be in the thick of things. No one sidelined him, unless he allowed it. ''Right. He'll spot To-mari if he comes that way. Don't underestimate Jake, Lieu-tenant.'' Hadn't Jake said the same thing about Julius Tomari?

Raising her arms over her head, she stretched and pushed

away from the computer. On the way out of the office, she snagged the coffeepot.

She went down the hall to the bathroom and flipped the wall switch. No light. Not a flicker came from the temperamental fluorescent light in the ceiling. She flipped the switch off, then on, waiting for the transformer in the light fixture to catch. It had finally given up the ghost.

She propped the door open with her heel, stretched to the sink, and turned on the water.

A sweaty hand clamped over her mouth. A knife blade glinted in the hall light. The cold steel edge pressed against the side of her throat.

Terror gripped her. As the bathroom door swung shut, she saw Julius Tomari grinning over her shoulder in the mirror.

SEVEN

Jake scaled the eight-foot wall behind the two-story building housing the Grayson Foundation. If the man Peterson had watching the back of the building spotted him, he gave no indication on the walkie-talkie. Balanced atop the cinder-block barrier, Jake took aim at one of the two-by-six eaves behind the rain gutter ringing the angled portion of the roof, then fired the small weapon in his hand. The tip of the dart went deep into the two-inch-wide beam before quietly exploding three barbs. He pulled the nylon leader threaded through the end of the barbed shaft until the climbing rope filled his hand.

The sense of urgency gnawing at him increased with each pulse of the seconds changing on his watch. Once on the roof, he kept a low profile on the shingled, slanted portion. If Peterson and his men could see him, so could Tomari. The earphone plugged into the walkie-talkie remained silent.

The center of the roof was recessed and flat. The profiles of heating equipment and vents remained below the angled roofline.

His heart skipped a beat at the sight of the trapdoor for maintaining one of the two heating systems. A bolt cutter lay beside the broken lock that had once secured the access.

He was too late. Tomari was already inside.

The scream ringing in every cell in her body remained mute. With the knife at her throat and images of another man slashing at her body running through her brain, she couldn't move. It was Denver all over. This time Marne knew what to expect. Julius Tomari wouldn't rape her, but he'd damn sure do his best to kill her.

"Not so brave now, are you, you home-wrecking bitch?" Tomari seethed into her right ear.

The words barely registered through fear as thick as the darkness. Her chest heaving in fright, she tried to gather her wits. If she didn't do it quickly, she'd die on the bathroom floor. If she let that happen, Jake would hunt Julius Tomari down and kill him.

Jake.

God, if Tomari killed her . . .

"You ruint my life. Turned my wife against me with your meddling. You poisont Angela's mind. She'da never said a word in court if you hadn'ta forced her to."

Tomari's voice hissing in her ear conjured the image of a snake. Evil. Vile. Corrupt.

Fighting back the fear sending fine tremors through her body and weakening her knees, Marne swallowed hard. Over the last four years she'd died a thousand times. This time, she would do her damnedest to take her attacker with her. The edge of the blade bit into the soft flesh of her throat. The sting of a fresh cut turned her fear into cold, calculating determination.

"You gonna beg me for your life?"

That was what he wanted. Power. Fear. Homage to his superiority. She had begged in Denver. Pleaded. Did everything he demanded.

Now she remained silent, too aware of the blade against her sensitive throat.

"Answer me, bitch."

Left-handed, she touched the back of the hand holding the knife to her throat. Her bravery was rewarded by a slight easing of the pressure.

"Would it do any good?" she asked in a thin but steady voice. He might kill her, but she would deprive him of the satisfaction he sought by making her beg.

"What do you think?"

"I think Angela begged you not to hit her, and it didn't do her any good." She felt him tense against her. The arm across her breasts and holding her hard against his chest tightened. His fingers bit into the fleshy part of her upper right arm.

"You ain't Angela."

"No, I'm not." *Keep him talking, buy time.* Eventually Lieutenant Peterson would wonder where she was, maybe suspect Tomari's presence, and come into the building. They had all underestimated Julius Tomari. Especially her. In a flash, she realized it was Jake's presence that had made her feel invincible against Tomari's threat. But he wasn't here now.

"You're a smart man, Julius. Smart enough to get in here without being seen." Flatter his ego. The longer he talked, the longer she'd live.

"Smart enough to kill you and get away before anyone knows you're dead."

She swallowed the lump in her throat, relieved the knife blade didn't bite into her skin again. "Get away, maybe. But you won't get far." Streams of sweat gathered between her breasts and trickled down her abdomen.

"Who's gonna look for me? Peterson?" A snort that passed for disdain in the darkness blew hot garlic breath along her cheek.

She tried to moisten her dry lips with her sandpaper tongue. "Not Lieutenant Peterson." Her heart raced at the thought of Jake stalking the corners and alleyways of the city until he found Julius Tomari.

"Fuckin' right he's not coming after me. Maybe I'll go after him next. The bastard deserves killing."

Keep him talking. Keep him talking. ''Why? He's never arrested you.''

''He ain't gonna arrest me this time, neither.''

The hand holding the knife relaxed a fraction. She felt it but pretended not to notice.

''How can you be so sure?'' Her fingers tightened around the handle of the coffeepot in her right hand. She had almost dropped it when he grabbed her. Right now, it was the best weapon she had.

''None of your fuckin' business, bitch.''

''Okay,'' she said as lightly as she could manage. She could play the perversity game.

He was quiet for a moment.

She wasn't sure if he was debating whether to talk or get on with killing her. Given his history, he would want to knock her around first. Pound her into begging for her life. He was in for a surprise.

She wasn't Angela. And she damn sure wasn't the naive, defenseless woman who had attended a teaching convention four years ago.

Using the glow streaming through the windows from the streetlights, Jake navigated the layout of the second floor. He crept down the stairs, waiting for the undercover cop outside the main entrance to turn away.

In the foyer, the door accessing the Grayson Foundation was secure. It took him five seconds to pick the Tinkertoy locks in the knob and the dead bolt.

Careful not to cast any shadows on the window blinds, he stayed low. With each tick of the invisible clock in his head, his anxiety increased.

Where the hell was Marne?

Not in the waiting area. Not in her office. Not in any of the offices or the storeroom.

In the hallway, he listened at the bathroom door.

Silence.

Tomari couldn't have come and gone. The back door was still locked. He wouldn't have gone out the front, and he hadn't returned to the roof.

That left only one place he could be—in the bathroom with Marne.

Jake started to pull away from the bathroom door. Gripping the knob, he steeled himself for whatever awaited inside. Visions of Marne's battered body after the attack in Denver washed through his memory.

"It'll be pretty hard for me to beg if you cut my throat."

Jake froze. She was in there with Tomari. With a knife at her throat.

When he could move, he slipped to the back of the hall, well out of earshot of the bathroom. He stripped down to his black T-shirt and jeans. He removed his shoulder harness and checked the round in the chamber of the Glock.

From down the hall, voices sounded on the walkie-talkie in her office. Peterson had finally decided Marne had been out of touch too long.

"Answer me!" Peterson demanded. "Answer me, or I'm calling this off and coming inside."

Coldly, impassively, Jake returned to the bathroom door and listened for the moment of opportunity. When it came, he would kill Julius Tomari.

The arm around her chest eased away in the darkness. The knife remained at her throat. Marne stayed still, waiting to see what he'd do next.

A wild beam of light danced off the walls and nearly blinded her as it slashed across the mirror.

"I'm gonna watch you die, bitch. I'm gonna make you pay for destroying my family." Tomari reached around her to set the flashlight on the edge of the sink counter.

The moment the knife relaxed from her throat, Marne grabbed his wrist with her left hand and twisted away. Simultaneously, she brought the glass coffeepot in her right hand up with all her strength and slammed it into his face.

Tomari's strangled yell broke with the impact of her right knee slamming into his groin.

The door burst open.

Before she knew what was happening, she was yanked through the doorway. The momentum bounced her into the opposite wall. She landed hard on the floor. In a panicked retreat, she scrambled, half crawling, half running until she got her feet under her. The door to the foyer and freedom was her goal.

"I'm looking for an excuse to kill you, Tomari."

"Jake," she whispered, stopping in midflight. She turned, then gaped. His balanced stance and the Glock in his hand looked natural. Deadly. He'd been there for her all the time. Just waiting for her to make a move.

"You can give me an excuse, or you can kick the knife out here and back up against the wall with your hands over your head."

Bent at the waist, Tomari held his genitals. His agony turned to squinty-eyed relief as he regarded Jake. "Shee-it! Jake Rimsa? That you?"

"In the flesh and pissed as hell."

"Hell, Jake, you ain't gonna do nothin' to me." In a show of bravado, he straightened to an almost upright stance.

"Wrong again. Nobody touches my woman. Nobody threatens her. Hurts her without answering to me. Time to pay the piper, Tomari." Jake took a step into the bathroom.

The sound of metal skittering across the tile floor told him where the knife was. He reached for it with his left foot and flicked it into the hall.

"You can't do nothin' to me now. I ain't got a weapon." Tomari backed against the wall and lifted his hands. Blood welled from a cut on the left side of his face.

Commotion in the front of the building warned Jake the time of retribution was limited. "We're using street rules. Like old times."

Tomari's dark eyes widened. "There's cops outside. You won't kill me."

"But I want to. Just like you wanted to kill Marne. Like you wanted to beat Angela time after time. That's what counts, doesn't it? What I want to do, and to hell with what you want?"

"Look, Rimsa. You don't understand."

"Sure I do. Power feels good—when you're the one holding it."

"We got him," Peterson said from behind Jake.

"No, you don't. I do. And he hasn't been searched. He probably has another weapon on him. You always carried two, didn't you, Tomari?"

Tomari swore and turned his head toward the darkness.

"Check his right boot first. That's where he used to carry his switchblade. Check for a gun, too." He wanted to feel Tomari's fear in his hands, see it in his eyes, smell it in his sweat, then hurt him before he killed him. It damn near broke every bone in Jake's body to let the officers have Tomari.

"Peterson, you can't take me in," Tomari said in a cold voice. Two uniformed officers approached him cautiously.

"The hell I can't," Peterson snapped.

"Why can't he take you in?" Jake demanded, never taking his eyes off Tomari or the officers searching him. He wanted an excuse, but Tomari wasn't playing. The switchblade was in his boot. A .25-caliber Saturday night special was tucked into the back of his waistband.

"We made a deal. Break it, and I ain't testifying again."

"Blow it out your ass, Tomari." Peterson shone his flashlight on Tomari's face. "Three strikes. Looks like you got four going for you here." Peterson stepped back as the cuffs went on Tomari's wrists. "Read him his rights."

Jake lowered his weapon. It was over.

Marne was glad Jake had limited the time they spent at the police station giving statements. The deal Peterson and the district attorney had worked to let Julius Tomari out of prison early in exchange for testimony on a case they wanted to close made her sick. Angela would be paying the price long after the plastic surgeons who volunteered for the Grayson Foundation finished rebuilding her face.

It was nearly ten o'clock when Marne got into the car with Jake. Her phone rang.

"Your turn," Jake said, then started the car.

"Hello, Alice," Marne said into the phone. "We're leaving now. We'll be at the breakfast table." She let Alice gush her concern, her worry, and that of both families without interruption. When Alice paused to draw a breath, Marne continued. "We'll see you in a few hours."

The voice on the other end was silent for a moment.

"Call it a Christmas promise," Marne continued, studying the edge of the dashboard. "I, ah, haven't told you for a long time, but . . . I love that you care about me enough to rag on me when I need it, and forgive you when I don't. I love you, Alice. Good night." She hung up before Alice could respond.

"Guess we're driving up to the lodge now," Jake said with a chuckle. "We can't break a Christmas promise."

"No, they've been waiting." *For me, for a long time. Just like Jake has,* she realized. "I'll drive if you're tired."

"I'm not tired, just damn glad we don't have any loose ends hanging for the next couple of days. Tomari won't get bail."

"How can you be so sure? He hasn't been arraigned."

"I had a little talk with Peterson about where he'd be wearing that badge he likes so much if Tomari went free for even an hour."

Marne leaned against the plush seat. For the first time since Denver, the storm had stopped raging inside her. "I thought I was on my own with Tomari. When no one thought . . . You knew. You were there for me tonight, Jake."

"I've always been there for you, Marne. Just not close by, like I should have been. For that, I'm sorry."

"You have nothing to be sorry about. It's life. That's all. Some good. Some bad. Choices. Perceptions. It goes on." *And Jake is always there,* she realized. Waiting, ready to take her part, like tonight. Like this morning. Like twelve years ago. All she had to do was reach out and accept.

She looked out the window. Christmas lights on buildings and houses brightened the night. On the freeway, traffic was nearly nonexistent. So were the reasons for keeping him out of her life.

"Like distance?" she added softly. "You have your life. I have mine."

"Did you know there's an FBI office in Palo Alto just begging for a man of my talents with communication security?"

"No. Is there?" That was Jake, she realized in fresh amazement, an answer for everything.

"Let me put it this way—if they're not, someone else in the Bay Area is. I can change jobs, but I can't change loving you."

She studied him in the light from the dashboard and the passing cars. "I love you, too, Jake."

"That's all I need. I'm coming home for good, Marne."

"Then what?" Hope as bright as the Star of Bethlehem warmed her heart.

He studied her for a brief minute, then returned his focus to his driving. "Then we move on with our lives. Together. We work at keeping the Christmas promises we made each other."

She reached across the seat divider. His fingers closed around hers. Having him beside her felt right, the way it should be. "I'm willing to give it a try."

He stared straight ahead. "Is that a Christmas promise, Marne?"

She brought his hand to her smiling lips. "Yes, it is."

MIDNIGHT IN DEATH

J. D. Robb

The year is dying in the night.

—TENNYSON

The welfare of the people is the chief law.

—CICERO

# ONE

Murder respects no traditions. It ignores sentiment. It takes no holidays.

Because murder was her business, Lieutenant Eve Dallas stood in the predawn freeze of Christmas morning coating the deerskin gloves her husband had given her only hours before with Seal-It.

The call had come in less than an hour before and less than six hours since she'd closed a case that had left her shaky and exhausted. Her first Christmas with Roarke wasn't getting off to a rousing start.

Then again, it had taken a much nastier turn for Judge Harold Wainger.

His body had been dumped dead center in the ice rink at Rockefeller Center. Face up, so his glazed eyes could stare at the huge celebrational tree that was New York's symbol of goodwill toward men.

His body was naked and already a deep shade of blue. The thick mane of silver hair that had been his trademark had been roughly chopped off. And though his face was severely battered, she had no trouble recognizing him.

She'd sat in his courtroom dozens of times in her ten years on the force. He had been, she thought, a solid and steady man, with as much understanding of the slippery channels of the law as respect for the heart of it.

She crouched down to get a closer look at the words that had been burned deeply into his chest.

JUDGE NOT, LEST YOU BE JUDGED

She hoped the burns had been inflicted postmortem, but she doubted it.

He had been mercilessly beaten, the fingers of both hands broken. Deep wounds around his wrists and ankles indicated that he'd been bound. But it hadn't been the beating or the burns that killed him.

The rope used to hang him was still around his neck, digging deep into flesh. Even that wouldn't have been quick, she decided. It didn't appear that his neck had been broken, and the burst vessels in his eyes and face signaled slow strangulation.

"He wanted you alive as long as possible," she murmured. "He wanted you to feel it all."

Kneeling now, she studied the handwritten note that was flapping gaily in the wind. It had been fixed over the judge's groin like an obscene loincloth. The list of names had been printed in careful square block letters.

JUDGE HAROLD WAINGER
PROSECUTING ATTORNEY STEPHANIE RING
PUBLIC DEFENDER CARL NEISSAN
JUSTINE POLINSKY
DOCTOR CHARLOTTE MIRA
LIEUTENANT EVE DALLAS

"Saving me for last, Dave?"

She recognized the style: gleeful infliction of pain followed by a slow, torturous death. David Palmer enjoyed his work. His experiments, as he'd called them when Eve had finally hunted him down three years before.

By the time she'd gotten him into a cage, he had eight victims to his credit, and with them an extensive file of discs recording his work. Since then he'd been serving the eight life-term sentences that Wainger had given him in a maximum-security ward for mental defectives.

"But you got out, didn't you, Dave? This is your handiwork. The torture, the humiliations, the burns. Public dumping spot for the body. No copycat here. Bag him," she ordered and got wearily to her feet.

It didn't look as though the last days of December 2058 were going to be much of a party.

Tne minute she was back in her vehicle, Eve ordered the heat on full blast. She stripped off her gloves and rubbed her hands over her face. She would have to go in and file her report, but the first order of business couldn't wait for her to drive to her home office. Damn if she was going to spend Christmas Day at Cop Central.

She used the in-dash 'link to contact Dispatch and arrange to have each name on the list notified of possible jeopardy. Christmas or not, she was ordering uniformed guards on each one.

As she drove, she engaged her computer. "Computer, status on David Palmer, mental-defective inmate on Rexal penal facility."

Working. . . . David Palmer, sentenced to eight consecutive life terms in off-planet facility Rexal reported escaped during transport to prison infirmary, December nineteen. Man-hunt ongoing.

"I guess Dave decided to come home for the holidays." She glanced up, scowling, as a blimp cruised over, blasting Christmas tunes as dawn broke over the city. Screw the herald angels, she thought, and called her commander.

"Sir," she said when Whitney's face filled her screen. "I'm sorry to disturb your Christmas."

"I've already been notified about Judge Wainger. He was a good man."

"Yes, sir, he was." She noted that Whitney was wearing a robe—a thick, rich burgundy that she imagined had been a gift from his wife. Roarke was always giving her fancy presents. She wondered if Whitney was as baffled by them as she usually was. "His body's being transferred to the morgue. I have the evidence sealed and am en route to my home office now."

"I would have preferred another primary on this, Lieutenant." He saw her tired eyes flash, the golden brown darkening. Still, her face, with its sharp angles, the firm chin with its shallow dent, the full, unsmiling mouth, stayed cool and controlled.

"Do you intend to remove me from the case?"

"You've just come off a difficult and demanding investigation. Your aide was attacked."

"I'm not calling Peabody in," Eve said quickly. "She's had enough."

"And you haven't?"

She opened her mouth, closed it again. Tricky ground, she acknowledged. "Commander, my name's on the list."

"Exactly. One more reason for you to take a pass here."

Part of her wanted to—the part that wanted, badly, to put it all aside for the day, to go home and have the kind of normal Christmas she'd never experienced. But she thought of Wainger, stripped of all life and all dignity.

"I tracked David Palmer, and I broke him. He was my collar, and no one knows the inside of his mind the way I do."

"Palmer?" Whitney's wide brow furrowed. "Palmer's in prison."

"Not anymore. He escaped on the nineteenth. And he's back, Commander. You could say I recognized his signature. The names on the list," she continued, pressing her point. "They're all connected to him. Wainger was the judge during his trial. Stephanie Ring was APA. Cicely Towers prosecuted the case, but she's dead. Ring assisted. Carl Neissan was his court-appointed attorney when Palmer refused to hire his own counsel, Justine Polinksy served as jury foreman. Dr. Mira tested him and testified against him at trial. I brought him in."

"The names on the list need to be notified."

"Already done, sir, and bodyguards assigned. I can pull

the data from the files into my home unit to refresh my memory, but it's fairly fresh as it is. You don't forget someone like David Palmer. Another primary will have to start at the beginning, taking time that we don't have. I know this man, how he works, how he thinks. What he wants.''

''What he wants, Lieutenant?''

''What he always wanted. Acknowledgment for his genius.''

''It's your case, Dallas,'' Whitney said after a long silence. ''Close it.''

''Yes, sir.''

She broke transmission as she drove through the gates of the staggering estate that Roarke had made his home.

Ice from the previous night's storm glinted like silver silk on naked branches. Ornamental shrubs and evergreens glistened with it. Beyond them, the house rose and spread, an elegant fortress, a testament to an earlier century with its beautiful stone, its acres of glass.

In the gloomy half-light of morning, gorgeously decorated trees shimmered in several windows. Roarke, she thought with a little smile, had gotten heavily into the Christmas spirit.

Neither of them had had much in the way of pretty holiday trees with gaily wrapped gifts stacked under them in their lives. Their childhoods had been miseries, and they had compensated for it in different ways. His had been to acquire, to become one of the richest and most powerful men in the world. By whatever means available. Hers had been to take control, to become part of the system that had failed her when she was a child.

Hers was law. His was—or had been—circumventing law.

Now, not quite a year since another murder had put them on the same ground, they were a unit. She wondered if she would ever understand how they'd managed it.

She left her car out front, walked up the steps and through the door into the kind of wealth that fantasies were made of. Old polished wood, sparkling crystal, ancient rugs lovingly preserved, art that museums would have wept for.

She shrugged off her jacket, started to toss it over the newel post. Then, gritting her teeth, she backtracked and hung it up. She and Summerset, Roarke's aide-de-camp, had declared a tacit truce in their sniping war. There would be no potshots on Christmas, she decided.

She could stand it if he could.

Only marginally pleased that he didn't slither into the foyer and hiss at her as he normally did, Eve headed into the main parlor.

Roarke was there, sitting by the fire, reading the first-edition copy of Ycats that she'd given him. It had been the only gift she'd been able to come up with for the man who not only had everything but owned most of the plants where it was manufactured.

He glanced up, smiled at her. Her stomach fluttered, as it so often did. Just a look, just a smile, and her system went jittery. He looked so . . . perfect, she thought. He was dressed casually for the day, in black, his long, lean body relaxing in a chair probably made two hundred years before.

He had the face of a god with slightly wicked intentions, eyes of blazing Irish blue and a mouth created to destroy a woman's control. Power sat attractively on him, as sleek and sexy, Eve thought, as the rich fall of black hair that skimmed nearly to his shoulders.

He closed the book, set it aside, then held out a hand to her.

"I'm sorry I had to leave." She crossed to him, linked her fingers with his. "I'm sorrier that I'm going to have to go up and work, at least for a few hours."

"Got a minute first?"

"Yeah, maybe. Just." And she let him pull her down into his lap. Let herself close her eyes and simply wallow there, in the scent and the feel of him. "Not exactly the kind of day you'd planned."

"That's what I get for marrying a cop." Ireland sang quietly in his voice, the lilt of a sexy poet. "For loving one," he added, and tipped her face up to kiss her.

"It's a pretty lousy deal right now."

"Not from where I'm sitting." He combed his fingers through her short brown hair. "You're what I want, Eve, the woman who leaves her home to stand over the dead. And the one who knew what a copy of Yeats would mean to me."

"I'm better with the dead than with buying presents. Otherwise I'd have come up with more than one."

She looked over at the small mountain of gifts under the tree—gifts it had taken her more than an hour to open. And her wince made him laugh.

"You know, one of the greatest rewards in giving you presents, Lieutenant, is the baffled embarrassment they cause you."

"I hope you got it out of your system for a while."

"Mmm," was his only response. She wasn't used to gifts, he thought, hadn't been given anything as a child but pain. "Have you decided what to do with the last one?"

The final box he'd given her had been empty, and he'd enjoyed seeing her frown in puzzlement. Just as he'd enjoyed seeing her grin at him when he told her it was a day. A day she could fill with whatever she liked. He would take her wherever she wanted to go, and they would do whatever she wanted to do. Off-planet or on. In reality or through the holo-room.

Any time, any place, any world was hers for the asking.

"No, I haven't had much time to think it through. It's a pretty great gift. I don't want to screw it up."

She let herself relax against him another moment with the fire crackling, the tree shimmering, then she pulled back. "I've got to get started. There's a lot of drone work on this one, and I don't want to tag Peabody today."

"Why don't I give you a hand?" He smiled again at the automatic refusal he read in her eyes. "Step into Peabody's sturdy shoes for the day."

"This one's not connected to you in any way. I want to keep it that way."

"All the better." He nudged her up, got to his feet. "I can help you do the runs or whatever, and that way you won't have to spend your entire Christmas chained to your desk.''

She started to refuse again, then reconsidered. Most of the data she wanted were public domain in any case. And what wasn't was nothing she wouldn't have shared with him if she'd been thinking it through aloud.

Besides, he was good.

''Okay, consider yourself a drone. But when Peabody's got her balance, you're out.''

''Darling.'' He took her hand, kissed it, watched her scowl. ''Since you ask so sweetly.''

''And no sloppy stuff,'' she put in. ''I'm on duty.''

TWO

The huge cat, Galahad, was draped over the back of Eve's sleep chair like a drunk over a bar at last call. Since he'd spent several hours the night before attacking boxes, fighting with ribbon, and murdering discarded wrapping paper, she left him where he was so he could sleep it off.

Eve set down her bag and went directly to the AutoChef for coffee. "The guy we're after is David Palmer."

"You've already identified the killer."

"Oh, yeah, I know who I'm after. Me and Dave, we're old pals."

Roarke took the mug she brought him, watched her through the steam. "The name's vaguely familiar to me."

"You'd have heard it. It was all over the media three, three and a half years ago. I need all my case files on that investigation, all data on the trial. You can start by—" She broke off when he laid a hand on her arm.

"David Palmer—serial killer. Torture murders." It was playing back for him, in bits and pieces. "Fairly young. What—mid-twenties?"

"Twenty-two at time of arrest. A real prodigy, our Dave.

He considers himself a scientist, a visionary. His mission is to explore and record the human mind's tolerance to extreme duress—pain, fear, starvation, dehydration, sensory deprivation. He could talk a good game, too.'' She sipped her coffee. ''He'd sit there in interview, his pretty face all lit with enthusiasm, and explain that once we knew the mind's breaking point, we'd be able to enhance it, to strengthen it. He figured since I was a cop, I'd be particularly interested in his work. Cops are under a great deal of stress, often finding ourselves in life-and-death situations where the mind is easily distracted by fear or outside stimuli. The results of his work could be applied to members of the police and security forces, the military, even in business situations.''

''I didn't realize he was yours.''

''Yeah, he was mine.'' She shrugged her shoulders. ''I was a little more low profile in those days.''

He might have smiled at that, knowing it was partially her connection to him that had changed that status. But he remembered too much of the Palmer case to find the humor. ''I was under the impression that he was safely locked away.''

''Not safely enough. He slipped out. The victim this morning was dumped in a public area—another of Dave's trademarks. He likes us to know he's hard at work. The autopsy will have to verify, but the victim was tortured premortem. I'd guess Dave found himself a new hole to work in and had the judge there at least a day before killing him. Death by strangulation occurred on or around midnight. Merry Christmas, Judge Wainger,'' she murmured.

''And that would be the judge who tried his case.''

''Yeah.'' Absently, she put her mug down, reached into her bag for a copy of the sealed note she'd already sent to the lab. ''He left a calling card—another signature. All these names are connected to his case and his sentencing. Part of his work this time around would be, at my guess, letting his intended victims stew about what he has in store for them. They're being contacted and protected. He'll have a tough time getting to any of them.''

"And you?" Roarke spoke with studied calm after a glance at the list, and his wife's name. "Where's your protection?"

"I'm a cop. I'm the one who does the protecting."

"He'll want you most, Eve."

She turned. However controlled his voice was, she heard the anger under it. "Maybe, but not as much as I want him."

"You stopped him," Roarke continued. "Whatever was done after—the tests, the trial, the sentence—was all a result of your work. You'll matter most."

"Let's leave those conclusions to the profiler." Though she agreed with them. "I'm going to contact Mira as soon as I look through the case files again. You can access those for me while I start my prelim report. I'll give you the codes for my office unit and the Palmer files."

Now he lifted a brow, smiled smugly. "Please. I can't work if you insult me."

"Sorry." She picked up her coffee again. "I don't know why I pretend you need codes to access any damn thing."

"Neither do I."

He sat down to retrieve the data she wanted, moving smoothly through the task. It was pitifully simple for him, and his mind was left free to consider. To decide.

She'd said he wasn't connected to this, and that she expected him to back away when Peabody was on duty again. But she was wrong. Her name on the list meant he was more involved than he'd ever been before. And no power on earth, not even that of the woman he loved, would cause him to back away.

Close by, Eve worked on the auxiliary unit, recording the stark facts into the report. She wanted the autopsy results, the crime scene team and sweeper data. But she had little hope that she would get anything from the spotty holiday staff before the end of the next day.

Struggling not to let her irritation with Christmas resurface, she answered her beeping 'link. "Dallas."

"Lieutenant, Officer Miller here."

"What is it, Miller?"

"Sir, my partner and I were assigned to contact and guard APA Ring. We arrived at her residence shortly after seven-thirty. There was no response to our knock."

"This is a priority situation, Miller. You're authorized to enter the premises."

"Yes, sir. Understood. We did so. The subject is not in residence. My partner questioned the across-the-hall neighbor. The subject left early yesterday morning to spend the holiday with her family in Philadelphia. Lieutenant, she never arrived. Her father reported her missing this morning."

Eve's stomach tightened. Too late, she thought. Already too late. "What was her method of transpo, Miller?"

"She had her own car. We're en route to the garage where she stored it."

"Keep me posted, Miller." Eve broke transmission, looked over, and met Roarke's eyes. "He's got her. I'd like to think she ran into some road hazard or hired a licensed companion for a quick holiday fling before heading on to her family, but he's got her. I need the 'link codes for the other names on the list."

"You'll have them. One minute."

She didn't need the code for one of the names. With her heart beating painfully, she put the call through to Mira's home. A small boy answered with a grin and a giggle. "Merry Christmas! This is Grandmom's house."

For a moment Eve just blinked, wondering how she'd gotten the wrong code. Then she heard the familiar soft voice in the background, saw Mira come on screen with a smile on her face and strain in her eyes.

"Eve. Good morning. Would you hold for a moment, please? I'd like to take this upstairs. No, sweetie," she said to the boy who tugged on her sleeve. "Run play with your new toys. I'll be back. Just a moment, Eve."

The screen went to a calm, cool blue, and Eve exhaled gratefully. Relief at finding Mira home, alive, well, safe— and the oddity of thinking of the composed psychiatrist as Grandmom played through her mind.

"I'm sorry." Mira came back on. "I didn't want to take this downstairs with my family."

"No problem. Are the uniforms there?"

"Yes." In a rare show of nerves, Mira pushed a hand through her sable-toned hair. "Miserable duty for them, sitting out in a car on Christmas. I haven't figured out how to have them inside and keep my family from knowing. My children are here, Eve, my grandchildren. I need to know if you believe there's any chance they're in danger."

"No." She said it quick and firm. "That's not his style. Dr. Mira, you're not to leave the house without your guards. You're to go nowhere, not the office, not the corner deli, without both of them. Tomorrow you'll be fitted for a tracer bracelet."

"I'll take all the precautions, Eve."

"Good, because one of those precautions is to cancel all patient appointments until Palmer is in custody."

"That's ridiculous."

"You're to be alone with no one, at any time. So unless your patients agree to let you walk around in their heads while a couple of cops are looking on, you're taking a vacation."

Mira eyed Eve steadily. "And are you about to take a vacation?"

"I'm about to do my job. Part of that job is you. Stephanie Ring is missing." She waited, one beat only, for the implication to register. "Do what you're told, Dr. Mira, or you'll be in protective custody within the hour. I'll need a consult tomorrow, nine o'clock. I'll come to you."

She broke transmission, turned to get the 'link codes from Roarke, and found him watching her steadily. "What?"

"She means a great deal to you. If she meant less, you'd have handled that with more finesse."

"I don't have much finesse at the best of times. Let's have the codes." When he hesitated, she sighed and replied, "Okay, okay, fine. She means a lot, and I'll be damned if he'll get within a mile of her. Now give me the goddamn codes."

"Already transferred to your unit, Lieutenant. Logged in, on memory. You've only to state the name of the party for transmission."

"Show-off." She muttered it, knowing it would make him grin, and turned back to contact the rest of the names on Palmer's list.

When she was satisfied that the other targets were where they were supposed to be, and under guard, Eve turned to the case files Roarke had accessed.

She spent an hour going over data and reports, another reviewing her interview discs with Palmer.

Okay, Dave, tell me about Michelle Hammel. What made her special?

David Palmer, a well-built man of twenty-two with the golden good looks of the wealthy New England family he'd sprung from, smiled and leaned forward earnestly. His clear blue eyes were bright with enthusiasm. His caramel-cream complexion glowed with health and vitality.

Somebody's finally listening, Eve remembered thinking as she saw herself as she'd been three years before. *He's finally got the chance to share his genius.*

Her hair was badly cut—she'd still been hacking at it herself in those days. The boots crossed at her ankles had been new then and almost unscarred. There was no wedding ring on her finger.

Otherwise, she thought, she was the same.

She was young, fit. An athlete, Palmer told her. *Very disciplined, mind and body. A long-distance runner—Olympic hopeful. She knew how to block pain, how to focus on a goal. She'd be at the top end of the scale, you see. Just as Leroy Greene was at the bottom. He'd fogged his mind with illegals for years. No tolerance for disruptive stimuli. He lost all control even before the application of pain. His mind broke as soon as he regained consciousness and found himself strapped to the table. But Michelle . . .*

She fought? She held out?

Palmer nodded cheerfully. *She was magnificent, really. She struggled against the restraints, then stopped when she understood that she wouldn't be able to free herself. There was fear. The monitors registered her rise in pulse rate, blood pressure, all vital physical and emotional signs. I have excellent equipment.*

Yeah, I've seen it. Top of the line.

It's vital work. His eyes had clouded then, unfocused as they did when he spoke of the import of his experiments. *You'll see if you review the data on Michelle that she centered her fear, used it to keep herself alive. She controlled it, initially, tried to reason with me. She made promises, she pretended to understand my research, even to help me. She was clever. When she understood that wouldn't help her, she cursed me, pumping up her adrenaline as I introduced new pain stimuli.*

"He broke her feet," Eve said, knowing Roarke was watching behind her. "Then her arms. He was right about his equipment back then. He had elcctrodes that when attached to different parts of the body, or placed in various orifices, administered graduating levels of electric shock. He kept Michelle alive for three days until thc torture broke her. She was begging for him to kill her toward the end. He used a rope and pulley system to hang her—gradual strangulation. She was nineteen."

Roarke laid his hands on her shoulders. "You stopped him once, Eve, you'll stop him again."

"Damn right I will."

She looked up when she heard someone coming quickly down the corridor. "Save data, and file," she ordered just as Nadine Furst came into the room. Perfect, she thought, a visit from one of Channel 75's top on-air reporters. The fact that they wcre friends didn't make Eve any less wary.

"Out paying Christmas calls, Nadine?"

"I got a present this morning." Nadine tossed a disc on the desk.

Eve looked at it, then back up at Nadine's face. It was pale, the sharp features drawn. For once, Nadine wasn't perfectly groomed with lip dye, enhancers, and every hair in place. She looked more than frazzled, Eve realized. She looked afraid.

"What's the problem?"

"David Palmer."

Slowly Eve got to her feet. "What about him?"

"Apparently he knows what I do for a living, and that we're friendly. He sent me that." She glanced back down at the disc, struggled to suppress a shudder. "Hoping I'd do a feature story on him—and his work—and share the contents of his disc with you. Can I have a drink? Something strong."

Roarke came around the desk and eased her into a chair. "Sit down. You're cold," he murmured when he took her hands.

"Yeah, I am. I've been cold ever since I ran that disc."

"I'll get you a brandy."

Nadine nodded in agreement, then fisted her hands in her lap and looked at Eve. "There are two other people on the recording. One of them is Judge Wainger. What's left of Judge Wainger. And there's a woman, but I can't recognize her. She's—he's already started on her."

"Here." Roarke brought the snifter, gently wrapped Nadine's hands around the bowl. "Drink this."

"Okay." She lifted the glass, took one long sip, and felt the blast of heat explode in her gut. "Dallas, I've seen a lot of bad things. I've reported them, I've studied them. But I've never seen anything like this. I don't know how you deal with it, day after day."

"One day at a time." Eve picked up the disc. "You don't have to watch this again."

"Yes." Nadine drank again, let out a long breath. "I do."

Eve turned the disc over in her hand. It was a standard-use model. They'd never trace it. She slid it into her unit. "Copy disc and run, display on screen."

David Palmer's youthful and handsome face swam onto the wall screen.

"Ms. Furst, or may I call you Nadine? So much more personal that way, and my work is very personal to me. I've admired your work, by the way. It's one of the reasons I'm trusting you to get my story on air. You believe in what you do, don't you, Nadine?"

His eyes were serious now, professional to professional, his face holding all the youth and innocence of a novitiate at the altar. "Those of us who reach for perfection believe in what we do," he continued. "I'm aware that you have a friendly relationship with Lieutenant Dallas. The lieutenant and I also have a relationship, perhaps not so friendly, but we do connect, and I do admire her stamina. I hope you'll share the contents of this disc with her as soon as possible. By this time she should already be heading the investigation into the death of Judge Wainger."

His smile went bright now, and just a little mad at the edges. "Hello, Lieutenant. You'll excuse me if I just conclude my business with Nadine. I want Dallas to be closely involved. It's important to me. You will tell my story, won't you, Nadine? Let the public themselves judge, not some narrow-minded fool in a black robe."

The next scene slipped seamlessly into place, the audio high so that the woman's screams seemed to rip the air in the room where Eve sat, watching.

Judge Wainger's body was bound hand and foot and suspended several inches from a plain concrete floor. A basic pulley system this time, Eve mused. He'd taken time to set up some of the niceties, but it wasn't yet the complex, and yes, ingenious, system of torture that he'd created before.

Still, he worked very well.

Wainger's face was livid with agony, the muscles twitching as Palmer burned letters in his chest with a hand laser. He only moaned, his head lolling. Nearby, a system of monitors beeped and buzzed.

"He's failing, you see," Palmer said briskly in a voice-over. "His mind is moving beyond the pain, as it can no longer endure it. His system will attempt to shut down into unconsciousness. That can be reversed, as you'll see here." On screen, he flipped a switch. There was a high whine, then Wainger's body jerked. This time he screamed.

Across the room a woman shrieked and sobbed. The cage she was in swung wildly on its cable and was only big enough to allow her to crouch on hands and knees. A dark fall of hair covered most of her face, but Eve knew her.

Stephanie Ring was Palmer's.

When he turned, engaged another control, the cage sparked and shook. The woman let out a piercing wail, shuddered convulsively, then collapsed.

Palmer turned to the camera, smiled. "She's distracting, but I have only so much time. It's necessary to begin one subject before completing work on another. But her turn will come shortly. Subject Wainger's heart is failing. The data on him are nearly complete."

Using the ropes, he manually lowered Wainger to the floor. Eve noted the flex and bunch of muscles in Palmer's arms. "Dave's been pumping," she murmured. "Getting in shape. He knew he'd have to work harder this round. He likes to prepare."

Palmer slipped a perfectly knotted noose around Wainger's neck and meticulously slid the trailing end through a metal ring in the ceiling. Leading it down, he threaded it through another ring in the floor, then pulled out the slack until Wainger rose to his knees, then his feet, and began gasping for air.

"Stop it, will you?" Nadine leapt to her feet. "I can't watch this again. I thought I could. I can't."

"Stop disc." Eve waited until the screen went blank, then went over to crouch in front of Nadine. "I'm sorry."

"No. I'm sorry. I thought I was tough."

"You are. Nobody's this tough."

Nadine shook her head and, finishing her brandy with one deep gulp, set the snifter aside. "You are. You don't let it get to you."

"It gets to me. But this is for me. I'm going to have a couple of uniforms come and take you home. They're going to hang with you everywhere until Palmer's down."

"You think he'll come after me?"

"No, but why take chances? Go home, Nadine. Put it away."

But after she'd asked Roarke to take Nadine downstairs to wait for the escort, Eve finished watching the disc. And at the end her eyes met Palmer's as he moved toward the camera.

"Subject Wainger died at midnight, December twenty-fourth. You'll last longer, Dallas. We both know that. You'll be my most fascinating subject. I have such wonders planned for you. You'll find me. I know you will. I'm counting on it. Happy holidays."

THREE

Stephanie Ring's car was still in its permit slot in the garage. Her luggage was neatly stowed in the trunk. Eve circled the vehicle, searching for any sign of struggle, any evidence that might have been dropped and gone unnoticed during the snatch.

"He's got two basic MOs," she said, as much to herself as to the uniforms waiting nearby. "One is to gain entrance into the victims' homes by a ruse—delivery, repair, or service con; the other is to come on them in an unpopulated area. He spends time getting to know their routines and habits, the usual routes and schedules. He keeps all that in a log—very organized, scientific, along with bio data on each of them."

They weren't lab rats to him, she mused. It was personal, individualized. That was what excited him.

"In either case," she went on, "he uses a stunner, takes them down quickly, then transports them in his own vehicle. Security cameras operational in here?"

"Yes, sir." One of the uniforms passed her a sealed package of discs. "We confiscated them for the last three days, assuming that the subject may have stalked the victim previous to her abduction.''

Eve lifted a brow. "Miller, right?''

"Sir.''

"Good thinking. There's nothing more you can do here. Go home and eat some goose.''

They didn't exactly race away, but neither did they linger. Eve put the package in her bag and turned to Roarke. "Why don't you do the same, pal? I'll only be a couple of hours.''

"We'll only be a couple of hours.''

"I don't need an aide to do a pass through Ring's apartment.''

Roarke simply took her arm and led her back to the car. "You let the two uniforms go,'' he began as he started the engine. "Everyone else on Palmer's list is under guard. Why aren't you?''

"We covered that already.''

"Partially.'' He reversed and headed out of the garage. "But I know you, Lieutenant. You're hoping he'll shuffle the order and come after you next. And you don't want some big-shouldered uniforms scaring him off.''

For a moment she just drummed her fingers on her knee. In less than a year, the man had learned her inside and out. She wasn't entirely comfortable with that. "And your point would be?''

He nearly smiled at the annoyance in her voice. "I admire my wife's courage, her dedication to duty.''

"You tossed in 'my wife' to irritate me, didn't you?''

"Of course.'' Satisfied, he picked up her hand, kissed the knuckles. "I'm sticking, Eve. Deal with it.''

The pass through Stephanie Ring's apartment was no more than routine, and it turned up nothing but the tidy life of a single career woman who enjoyed surrounding herself with attractive things, spending her city salary on a stylish wardrobe.

Eve thought of the naked woman crouched like an animal in a cage, screaming in terror.

He's killing her now. Eve knew it. And she had no power to stop him.

When she was back in her home office, she reviewed the disc Palmer had sent Nadine. This time she willed herself to ignore what was happening and focus only on the surroundings.

"No windows," she commented. "The floor and walls look like concrete and old brick. The whole area can't be over thirty feet by twenty. It's probably a basement. Computer, pause. Enhance sector eight through fifteen. Magnify."

She paced as the computer went to work, then moved closer to the screen. "There, that's a stair tread. Steps, part of a railing. Behind it is some sort of—what is it—old furnace unit or water tank. He's found himself a hole. It has to be private," she continued, studying the view. "He can't do his work in a building where people might hear. Even if it's soundproofed, he'd risk someone poking around. Maintenance crew, repair team. Anything like that."

"Not an apartment or office building," Roarke agreed. "And with the steps it's not likely a storage facility. From the look of the furnace, it's a good-sized building, but far from new. Nothing built in the last fifteen or twenty years would have had a tank furnace installed. He'd want something in the city, wouldn't he?"

"Yeah, he'd want to be close to all of his marks. He wouldn't go for the 'burbs and even the boroughs aren't likely. Dave's a true urbanite and New York's his turf. Private home. Has to be. But how did he get his hands on a private residence?"

"Friends?" Roarke suggested. "Family?"

"Palmer didn't have a tight circle of friends. He's a loner. He has parents. They relocated after the trial. Went under the Victim and Survivor's Protection Act."

"Sealed files."

She heard the faintest trace of humor in his voice, turned to scowl at him. For a moment she wrestled with procedure. She could get clearance to access the Palmers' location.

And it would take at least two days to hack through the red tape for authorization. Or she could hand the problem to Roarke and have what she needed in minutes.

She could hear Stephanie Ring's screams echoing in her head.

"You'll have to use the unregistered equipment. Compuguard will have an automatic block on their file."

"It won't take long."

"I'm going to keep working on this." She gestured toward the screen. "He might have slipped up just enough to have let something identifiable come through."

"All right." But he crossed to her, framed her face in his hands. Lowering his head, he kissed her, long and slow and deep. And felt, as he did, some of the rigid tension in her body ease.

"I can handle this, Roarke."

"Whether you can or not, you will. Would it hurt to hold on to me, just for a minute?"

"Guess not." She slipped her arms around him, felt the familiar lines, the familiar warmth. Her grip tightened. "Why wasn't it enough to stop him once? Why wasn't it enough to put him away? What good is it if you do your job and it comes back this way?"

He held her and said nothing.

"He wants to show me he can do it all again. He wants to take me through all the steps and stages, the way he did before. Only this time as they're happening. 'Look how clever I am, Dallas.' "

"Knowing that, understanding that, will help you stop him a second time."

"Yeah." She eased back. "Get me the data so I can hammer at his parents."

Roarke skimmed a finger over the dent in her chin. "You'll let me watch, won't you. It's so stimulating to see you browbeat witnesses."

When she laughed, as he'd hoped she would, he went to his private room to circumvent Compuguard and officially sealed files.

She'd barely had time to review another section of the recording before he came back.

"It couldn't have been that easy."

"Yes." He smiled and passed her a new data disc. "It could. Thomas and Helen Palmer, now known as Thomas and Helen Smith—which shows just how imaginative bureaucrats can be, currently reside in a small town called Leesboro in rural Pennsylvania."

"Pennsylvania." Eve glanced toward her 'link, considered, then looked back at Roarke. "It wouldn't take long to get there if you had access to some slick transpo."

Roarke looked amused. "Which slick transpo would you prefer, Lieutenant?"

"That mini-jet of yours would get us there in under an hour."

"Then why don't we get started?"

If Eve had been more fond of heights, she might have enjoyed the fast, smooth flight south. As it was, she sat, jiggling a foot to relieve a case of nerves while Roarke piloted them over what she imagined some would consider a picturesque range of mountains.

To her they were just rocks, and the fields between them just dirt.

"I'm only going to say this once," she began. "And only because it's Christmas."

"Banking for landing," he warned her as he approached the private airstrip. "What are you only going to say once?"

"That maybe all these toys of yours aren't a complete waste of time. Overindulgent, maybe, but not a complete waste of time."

"Darling, I'm touched."

Once they were on the ground, they transferred from the snazzy little two-person jet to the car that Roarke had waiting. Of course, it couldn't be a normal vehicle, Eve mused as she studied it. It was a sleek black bullet of a car, built for style and speed.

"I'll drive." She held out a hand for the keycode the attendant had given him. "You navigate."

Roarke considered her as he tossed the code in his hand. "Why?"

"Because I'm the one with the badge." She snatched the code on its upward are and smirked at him.

"I'm a better driver."

She snorted as they climbed in. "You like to hotdog. That doesn't make you better. Strap in, ace. I'm in a hurry."

She punched it and sent them flying away from the terminal and onto a winding rural road that was lined with snow-laced trees and sheer rock.

Roarke programmed their destination and studied the route offered by the onboard computer. "Follow this road for two miles, turn left for another ten point three, then next left for five point eight."

By the time he'd finished, she was already making the first left. She spotted a narrow creek, water fighting its way through ice, over rock. A scatter of houses, trees climbing steeply up hills, a few children playing with new airskates or boards in snow-covered yards.

"Why do people live in places like this? There's nothing here. You see all that sky?" she asked Roarke. "You shouldn't be able to see that much sky from down here. It can't be good for you. And where do they eat? We haven't passed a single restaurant, glide cart, deli, nothing."

"Cozily?" Roarke suggested. "Around the kitchen table."

"All the time? Jesus." She shuddered.

He laughed, smoothed a finger over her hair. "Eve, I adore you."

"Right." She tapped the brakes to make the next turn. "What am I looking for?"

"Third house on the right. There, that two-story prefab, mini-truck in the drive."

She slowed, scanning the house as she turned in behind the truck. There were Christmas lights along the eaves, a wreath on the door, and the outline of a decorated tree behind the front window.

"No point in asking you to wait in the car, I guess."

"None," he agreed and got out.

"They're not going to be happy to see me," Eve warned him as they crossed the shoveled walk to the front door. "If they refuse to talk to me, I'm going to give them some hard shoves. If it comes down to it, you just follow the lead."

She pressed the buzzer, shivered.

"You should have worn the coat I gave you. Cashmere's warm."

"I'm not wearing that on duty." It was gorgeous, she thought. And made her feel soft. It wasn't the sort of thing that worked for a cop.

And when the door opened, Eve was all cop.

Helen Palmer had changed her hair and her eyes. Subtle differences in shades and shapes, but enough to alter her looks. It was still a pretty face, very like her son's. Her automatic smile of greeting faded as she recognized Eve.

"You remember me, Mrs. Palmer?"

"What are you doing here?" Helen put a hand high on the doorjamb as if to block it. "How did you find us? We're under protection."

"I don't intend to violate that. I have a crisis situation. You'd have been informed that your son has escaped from prison."

Helen pressed her lips together, hunched her shoulders as a defense against the cold that whipped through the open door. "They said they were looking for him, assured us that they'd have him back in custody, back in treatment very soon. He isn't here. He doesn't know where we are."

"Can I come in, Mrs. Palmer?"

"Why do you have to rake this all up again?" Tears swam into her eyes, seeming as much from frustration as grief. "My husband and I are just getting our lives back. We've had no contact with David in nearly three years."

"Honey? Who's at the door? You're letting the cold in." A tall man with a dark sweep of hair came smiling to the door. He wore an old cardigan sweater and ancient jeans with a pair of obviously new slippers. He blinked once, twice, then laid his hand on his wife's shoulder. "Lieutenant. Lieutenant Dallas, isn't it?"

"Yes, Mr. Palmer. I'm sorry to disturb you."

"Let them in, Helen."

"Oh, God, Tom."

"Let them in." His fingers rubbed over her shoulder before he drew her back. "You must be Roarke." Tom worked up what nearly passed for a smile as he offered Roarke his hand. "I recognize you. Please come in and sit down."

"Tom, please—"

"Why don't you make some coffee?" He turned and pressed his lips to his wife's brow. He murmured something to her, and she let out a shuddering breath and nodded.

"I'll make this as quick as I can, Mr. Palmer," Eve told him, as Helen walked quickly down a central hallway.

"You dealt very fairly with us during an unbearable time, Lieutenant." He showed them into a small living area. "I haven't forgotten that. Helen—my wife's been on edge all day. For several days," he corrected himself. "Since we were informed that David escaped. We've worked very hard to keep that out of the center, but . . ."

He gestured helplessly and sat down.

Eve remembered these decent people very well, their shock and grief over what their son was. They had raised him with love, with discipline, with care, and still they had been faced with a monster.

There had been no abuse, no cruelty, no underlying gruel for that monster to feed on. Mira's testing and analysis had corroborated Eve's impression of a normal couple who'd given their only child their affection and the monetary and social advantages that had been at their disposal.

"I don't have good news for you, Mr. Palmer. I don't have easy news."

He folded his hands in his lap. "He's dead."

"No."

Tom closed his eyes. "God help me. I'd hoped—I'd actually hoped he was." He got up quickly when he heard his wife coming back. "Here, I'll take that." He bent to take the tray she carried. "We'll get through this, Helen."

"I know. I know we will." She came in, sat, busied herself pouring the coffee she'd made. "Lieutenant, do you think David's come back to New York?"

"We know he has." She hesitated, then decided they would hear the news soon enough through the media. "Early this morning the body of Judge Wainger was found in Rockefeller Plaza. It's David's work," she continued as Helen moaned. "He's contacted me, with proof. There's no doubt of it."

"He was supposed to be given treatment. Kept away from people so he couldn't hurt them, hurt himself."

"Sometimes the system fails, Mrs. Palmer. Sometimes you can do everything right, and it just fails."

Helen rose, walked to the window, and stood looking out. "You said something like that to me before. To us. That we'd done everything right, everything we could. That it was something in David that had failed. That was kind of you, Lieutenant, but you can't know what it's like, you can't know how it feels to know that a monster has come from you."

No, Eve thought, but she knew what it was to come from a monster, to have been raised by one for the first eight years of her life. And she lived with it.

"I need your help," she said instead. "I need you to tell me if you have any idea where he might go, who he might go to. He has a place," she continued. "A private place where he can work. A house, a small building somewhere in New York. In the city or very close by."

"He has nowhere." Tom lifted his hands. "We sold everything when we relocated. Our home, my business, Helen's. Even our holiday place in the Hamptons. We cut all ties. The house where David—where he lived that last year—was sold as well. We live quietly here, simply. The money we'd accumulated, the money from the sales is sitting in an account. We haven't had the heart to . . . we don't need it."

"He had money of his own," Eve prompted.

"Yes, inheritance, a trust fund. It was how he financed

what he was doing.'' Tom reached out a hand for his wife's and clasped her fingers tightly. ''We donated that money to charity. Lieutenant, all the places where he might have gone are in the hands of others now.''

''All right. You may think of something later. However far-fetched, please contact me.'' She rose. ''When David's in custody again, I'll let you know. After that, I'll forget where you are.''

Eve said nothing more until she and Roarke were in the car and headed back. ''They still love him. After all he did, after what he is, there's a part of them that loves him.''

''Yes, and enough, I think, to help you stop him, if they knew how.''

''No one ever cared for us that way.'' She took her eyes off the road briefly, met his. ''No one ever felt that bond.''

''No.'' He brushed the hair from her cheek. ''Not until we found each other. Don't grieve, Eve.''

''He has his mother's eyes,'' she murmured. ''Soft and blue and clear. She's the one who had to change them, I imagine, because she couldn't look in the mirror and face them every morning.''

She sighed, shook it off.

''But he can,'' she said quietly.

FOUR

There was nothing else to do, no other data to examine or analyze, no other route to check. Tomorrow, she knew, there would be. Now she could only wait.

Eve walked into the bedroom with some idea of taking a catnap. They needed to salvage some of the day, she thought. To have their Christmas dinner together, to squeeze in some sense of normalcy.

The strong, dreamy scent of pine made her shake her head. The man had gone wild for tradition on this, their first Christmas together. Christ knew what he had paid for the live trees he'd placed throughout the house. And this one, the one that stood by the window in their bedroom, he'd insisted they decorate together.

It mattered to him. And with some surprise she realized it had come to matter to her.

"Tree lights on," she ordered, and smiled a little as she watched them blink and flash.

She stepped toward the seating area, released her weapon harness, and shrugged it off. She was sitting on the arm of the sofa taking off her boots when Roarke came in.

"Good. I was hoping you'd take a break. I've got some calls to make. Why don't you let me know when you're ready for a meal?"

She angled her head and studied him as he stood just inside the doorway. She let her second boot drop and stood up slowly. "Come here."

Recognizing the glint in her eyes, he felt the light tingle of lust begin to move through his blood. "There?"

"You heard me, slick."

Keeping his eyes on hers he walked across the room. "What can I do for you, Lieutenant?"

Traditions, Eve thought, had to start somewhere. She fisted a hand in the front of his shirt, straining the silk as she pulled him a step closer. "I want you naked, and quick. So unless you want me to get rough, strip."

His smile was as cocky as hers and made her want to sink in with her teeth. "Maybe I like it rough."

"Yeah?" She began to back him up toward the bed. "Well then, you're going to love this."

She moved fast, the only signal was the quick flash of her eyes before she ripped his shirt open and sent buttons flying. He gripped her hips, squeezing hard as she fixed her teeth on his shoulder and bit.

"Christ. Christ! I love your body. Give it to me."

"You want it?" He jerked her up to her toes. "You'll have to take it."

When his mouth would have closed hotly over hers, she pivoted. He countered. She came in low and might have flipped him if he hadn't anticipated her move. They'd gone hand to hand before, with very satisfying results.

They ended face-to-face again, breath quickening. "I'm taking you down," she warned him.

"Try it."

They grappled, both refusing to give way. The momentum took them up the stairs of the platform to the bed. She slipped a hand between his legs, gently squeezed. It was a move she'd used before. Even as the heat shot straight down the center of his body to her palm, he shifted, slid under her guard, and flipped her onto the bed.

She rolled, came up in a crouch. "Come on, tough guy."

She was grinning now, her face flushed with battle, desire going gold in her eyes and the lights of the tree sparkling behind her.

"You look beautiful, Eve."

That had her blinking, straightening from the fighting stance and gaping at him. Even the man who loved her had never accused her of beauty. "Huh?"

It was all she managed before he leapt at her and took her out with a mid-body tackle.

"Bastard." She nearly giggled it even as she scissored up and managed to roll on top of him. But he used the impetus to keep going until he had her pinned again. "Beautiful, my ass."

"Your ass is beautiful." The elbow to his gut knocked some of the breath out of him, but he sucked more in. "And so's the rest of you. I'm going to have your beautiful ass, and the rest of you."

She bucked, twisted, nearly managed to slip out from under him. Then his mouth closed over her breast, sucking, nipping through her shirt. She moaned, arched up against him, and the fist she'd clenched in his hair dragged him closer rather than yanking him away.

When he tore at her shirt, she reared up, hooking strong, long legs around his waist, finding his mouth with hers again as he pushed back to kneel in the center of the bed.

They went over in a tangle of limbs, hands rough and groping. And flesh began to slide damply over flesh.

He took her up and over the first time, hard and fast, those clever fingers knowing her weaknesses, her strengths, her needs. Quivering, crying out, she let herself fly on the edgy power of the climax.

Then they were rolling again, gasps and moans and murmurs. Heat coming in tidal waves, nerves raw and needy. Her mouth was a fever on his as she straddled him.

"Let me, let me, let me." She chanted it against his mouth as she rose up. Her hands linked tight to his as she took him inside her. He filled her, body, mind, heart.

Fast and full of fury, she drove them both as she'd needed to from the moment he'd come into the room. It

flooded into her, swelled inside her, that unspeakable pleasure, the pressure, the frantic war to end, to prolong.

She threw her head back, clung to it, that razor's edge.
"Go over." She panted it out, fighting to clear her vision,
to focus on that glorious face. "Go over first, and take me
with you."

She watched his eyes, that staggering blue go dark as
midnight, felt him leap over with one last, hard thrust. With
her hands still locked in his, she threw herself over with
him.

And when the energy slid away from her like wax from
a melting candle, she slipped down, quivering even as she
pressed her face into his neck.

"I won," she managed.

"Okay."

Her lips twitched at the smug, and exhausted, satisfaction
in his voice. "I did. I got just what I wanted from you,
pal."

"Thank Christ." He shifted until he could cradle her
against him. "Take a nap, Eve."

"Just an hour." Knowing he would never sleep longer
than that himself, she wrapped around him to keep him
close.

When she woke at two A.M., Eve decided the brief pre-
dinner nap had thrown her system off. Now she was fully
awake, her mind engaged and starting to click through the
information and evidence she had so far.

David Palmer was here, in New York. Somewhere out
in the city, happily going about his work. And her gut told
her Stephanie Ring was already dead.

He wouldn't have such an easy time getting to the others
on his list, she thought as she turned in bed. Ego would
push him to try, and he'd make a mistake. In all likelihood
he'd already made one. She just hadn't picked up on it yet.

Closing her eyes, she tried to slip into Palmer's mind, as
she had years before when she'd been hunting him.

He loved his work, had loved it even when he'd been a
boy and doing his experiments on animals. He'd managed

to hide those little deaths, to put on a bright, innocent face. Everyone who'd known him—parents, teachers, neighbors—had spoken of a cheerful, helpful boy, a bright one who studied hard and caused no trouble.

Yet some of the classic elements had been there, even in childhood. He'd been a loner, obsessively neat, compulsively organized. He'd never had a healthy sexual relationship and had been socially awkward with women. They'd found hundreds of journal discs, going back to his tenth year, carefully relating his theories, his goals, and his accomplishments.

And with time, with practice, with study, he'd gotten very, very good at his work.

Where would you set up, Dave? It would have to be somewhere comfortable. You like your creature comforts. You must have hated the lack of them in prison. Pissed you off, didn't it? So now you're coming after the ones who put you there.

That's a mistake, letting us know the marks in advance. But it's ego, too. It's really you against me.

That's another mistake, because no one knows you better.

A house, she thought. But not just any house. It would have to be in a good neighborhood, close to good restaurants. Those years of prison food must have offended your palate. You'd need furniture, comfortable stuff, with some style. Linens, good ones. And an entertainment complex—got to watch the screen or you won't know what people are saying about you.

And all that takes money.

When she sat up in bed, Roarke stirred beside her. "Figure it out?"

"He's got a credit line somewhere. I always wondered if he had money stashed, but it didn't seem to matter since he was never getting out to use it. I was wrong. Money's power, and he found a way to use it from prison."

She tossed back the duvet, started to leap out of bed when the 'link beeped. She stared at it a moment, and knew.

FIVE

Two teenagers looking for a little adventure snuck out of their homes, met at a prearranged spot, and took their new scoot-bikes for a spin in Central Park.

They'd thought at first that Stephanie Ring was a vagrant, maybe a licensed beggar or a chemi-head sleeping it off, and they started to give her a wide berth.

But vagrants didn't make a habit of stretching out naked on the carousel in Central Park.

Eve had both of them stashed in a black-and-white. One had been violently ill, and the brittle air still carried the smear of vomit. She'd ordered the uniforms to set up a stand of lights so the area was under the glare of a false day.

Stephanie hadn't been beaten, nor had her hair been cut. Palmer believed in variety. There were dozens of long, thin slices over her arms and legs, the flesh around the wounds shriveled and discolored. Something toxic, Eve imagined, something that when placed on a relatively minor open wound would cause agony. The blood had been allowed to drip and dry. Her feet speared out at sharp angles, in a parody of a ballet stance. Dislocated.

Carved into her midriff were the signature block letters.

LET'S KILL ALL THE LAWYERS

He had finally killed this one, Eve thought, with the slow, torturous strangulation he was most fond of. Eve examined the noose, found the rope identical to that used on Judge Wainger.

Another mistake, Dave. Lots of little oversights this time around.

She reached for her field kit and began the routine that followed murder.

She went home to write her report, wanting the quiet she'd find there as opposed to the postholiday confusion at Central. She shot a copy to her commander, then sent messages to both Peabody and Feeney. Once her aide and the top man in the Electronics Detective Division woke and checked their 'links, she was pulling them in.

She fueled on coffee, then set about the tedious task of peeling the layers from Palmer's financial records.

It was barely dawn when the door between her office and Roarke's opened. He came in, fully dressed, and she could hear the hum of equipment already at work in the room behind him.

"You working at home today?" she said it casually, sipping coffee as she studied him.

"Yes." He glanced down at her monitor. "Following the money, Lieutenant?"

"At the moment. You're not my bodyguard, Roarke."

He merely smiled. "And who, I wonder, could be more interested in your body?"

"I'm a cop. I don't need a sitter."

He reached down, cupped her chin. "What nearly happened to Peabody two nights ago?"

"It didn't happen. And I'm not having you hovering around when you should be off doing stuff."

"I can do stuff from here just as easily and efficiently as I can from midtown. You're wasting time arguing. And I doubt you'll find your money trail through Palmer's official records."

"I know it." The admission covered both statements, and frustrated her equally. "I have to start somewhere. Go away and let me work."

"Done with me, are you?" He lowered his head and brushed his lips over hers.

The sound of a throat being loudly and deliberately cleared came from the doorway. "Sorry." Peabody managed most of a smile. She was pale, and more than a little heavy-eyed, but her uniform was stiff and polished, as always.

"You're early." Eve rose, then slid her hands awkwardly into her pockets.

"The message said to report as soon as possible."

"I'll leave you two to work." Alone, Roarke thought, the two of them would slip past the discomfort faster. "It's good to see you, Peabody. Lieutenant," he added before he closed the door between the rooms, "you might want to check the names of deceased relatives. The transfer and disbursement of funds involving accounts with the same last name and blood ties are rarely noticed."

"Yeah, right. Thanks." Eve shifted her feet. The last time she'd seen her aide, Peabody had been wrapped in a blanket, her face blotchy from tears. "You okay?"

"Yeah, mostly."

Mostly, my ass, Eve thought. "Look, I shouldn't have called you in on this. Take a couple of more days to level off."

"Sir. I'd do better if I got back to work, into routine. Sitting home watching videos and eating soy chips isn't the way I want to spend another day. Work clears it out quicker."

Because she believed that herself, Eve moved her shoulders. "Then get some coffee, Peabody, I've got plenty of work here."

"Yes, sir." She stepped forward, pulling a small

wrapped box from her pocket, setting it on the desk as she went to the AutoChef. "Your Christmas present. I didn't get a chance to give it to you before."

"I guess we were a little busy." Eve toyed with the ribbon. Gifts always made her feel odd, but she could sense Peabody's eyes on her. She ripped off the red foil, opened the lid. It was a silver star, a little dented, a bit discolored.

"It's an old sheriff's badge," Peabody told her. "I don't guess it's like Wyatt Earp's or anything, but it's official. I thought you'd get a kick out of it. You know, the long tradition of law and order."

Absurdly touched, Eve grinned. "Yeah. It's great." For the fun of it, she took it out and pinned it to her shirt. "Does this make you the deputy?"

"It suits you, Dallas. You'd've stood up wherever, whenever."

Looking up, Eve met her eyes. "You stand, Peabody. I wouldn't have called you in today if I thought different."

"I guess I needed to hear that. Thanks. Well . . ." She hesitated, then lifted her brows in question.

"Problem?"

"No, I just . . ." She pouted, giving her square, sober face a painfully young look. "Hmmm."

"You didn't like your present?" Eve said lightly. "You'll have to take that up with Leonardo."

"What present? What's he got to do with it?"

"He made that wardrobe for your undercover work. If you don't like it . . ."

"The clothes." Like magic, Peabody's face cleared. "I get to keep all those mag clothes? All of them?"

"What the hell am I supposed to do with them? Now are you going to stand around grinning like an idiot or can I get on with things here?"

"I can grin and work at the same time, sir."

"Settle down. Start a run and trace on this rope." She pushed a hard-copy description across the desk. "I want any sales within the last week, bulk sales. He uses a lot of it."

"Who?"

"We'll get to that. Run the rope, then get me a list of private residences—upscale—sold or rented in the metro area within the last week. Also private luxury vehicles—pickup or delivery on those within the last week. He needs transpo and he'd go classy. The cage," she muttered as she began to pace. "Where the hell did he get the cage? Wildlife facility, domestic animal detention? We'll track it. Start the runs, Peabody, I'll brief you when Feeney gets here."

She'd called in Feeney, Peabody thought as she sat down at a computer. It was big. Just what she needed.

"You'll both want to review the investigation discs, profiles, transcripts from the Palmer case of three years ago. Feeney," Eve added, "you'll remember most of it. You tracked and identified the electronic equipment he used in those murders."

"Yeah, I remember the little bastard." Feeney sat, scowling into his coffee. His habitually weary face was topped by wiry red hair that never seemed to decide which direction it wanted to take.

He was wearing a blue shirt, so painfully pressed and bright that Eve imagined it had come out of its gift box only that morning. And would be comfortably rumpled by afternoon.

"Because we know him, his pattern, his motives, and in this case his victims or intended victims, he's given us an edge. He knows that, enjoys that because he's sure he'll be smarter."

"He hates you, Dallas." Feeney's droopy eyes lifted, met hers. "He hated your ever-fucking guts all along. You stopped him, then you played him until he spilled everything. He'll come hard for you."

"I hope you're right, because I want the pleasure of taking him out again. He got the first two on his list because he had a lead on us," she continued. "The others have been notified, warned, and are under guard. He may or may not make an attempt to continue in order. But once he runs into a snag, he'll skip down."

"And come for you," Peabody put in.

"Everything the others did happened because I busted him. Under the whack is a very logical mind. Everything he does has a reason. It's his reason, so it's bent—but it's there."

She glanced at her wrist unit. "I've got a meeting with Mira at her residence in twenty minutes. I'm going to leave it to Feeney to fill you in on any holes in this briefing, Peabody. Once you have the lists from the runs I ordered, do a probability scan. See if we can narrow the field a bit. Feeney, when you review the disc he sent through Nadine, you might be able to tag some of the equipment. You get a line on it, we can trace the source. We do it in steps, but we do it fast. If he misses on the list, he might settle for someone else, anyone else. He's been out a week and already killed twice."

She broke off as her communicator signaled. She walked to retrieve her jacket as she answered. Two minutes later she jammed it back in her pocket. And her eyes were flat and cold.

"Make that three times. He got to Carl Neissan."

Eve was still steaming when she rang the bell of Mira's dignified brownstone. The fact that the guard on door duty demanded that she show her ID and had it verified before entry mollified her slightly. If the man posted at Neissan's had done the same, Palmer wouldn't have gotten inside.

Mira came down the hall toward her. She was dressed casually in slacks and sweater, with soft matching shoes. But there was nothing casual about her eyes. Before Eve could speak, she lifted a hand.

"I appreciate your coming here. We can talk upstairs in my office." She glanced to the right as a child's laughter bounced through an open doorway. "Under different circumstances I'd introduce you to my family. But I'd rather not put them under any more stress."

"We'll leave them out of it."

"I wish that were possible." Saying nothing more, Mira started upstairs.

The house reflected her, Eve decided. Calming colors,

soft edges, perfect style. Her home office was half the size of her official one and must at one time have been a small bedroom. Eve noted that she'd furnished it with deep chairs and what she thought of as a lady's desk, with curved legs and fancy carving.

Mira adjusted the sunscreen on a window and turned to the mini AutoChef recessed into the wall.

"You'll have reviewed my original profile on David Palmer," she began, satisfied that her hands were steady as she programmed for tea. "I would stand by it, with a few additions due to his time in prison."

"I didn't come for a profile. I've got him figured."

"Do you?"

"I walked around inside his head before. We both did."

"Yes." Mira offered Eve a delicate cup filled with the fragrant tea they both knew she didn't want. "In some ways he remains the exception to a great many rules. He had a loving and advantaged childhood. Neither of his parents exhibits any signs of emotional or psychological defects. He did well in school, more of an overachiever than under-, but nothing off the scale. Testing showed no brain deformities, no physical abnormalities. There is no psychological or physiological root for his condition."

"He likes it," Eve said briefly. "Sometimes evil's its own root."

"I want to disagree," Mira murmured. "The reasons, the whys of abnormal behavior are important to me. But I have no reasons, no whys, for David Palmer."

"That's not your problem, Doctor. Mine is to stop him, and to protect the people he's chosen. The first two on his list are dead."

"Stephanie Ring? You're sure."

"Her body was found this morning. Carl Neissan's been taken."

This time Mira's hand shook, rattling her cup in its saucer before she set it aside. "He was under guard."

"Palmer got himself into a cop suit, knocked on the damn door, and posed as the relief. The on-duty didn't question it. He went home to a late Christmas dinner. When the morning duty came on, he found the house empty.''

"And the night relief? The real one?''

"Inside the trunk of his unit. Tranq'd and bound but otherwise unharmed. He hasn't come around enough to be questioned yet. Hardly matters. We know it was Palmer. I'm arranging for Justine Polinsky to be moved to a safe house. You'll want to pack some things, Doctor. You're going under.''

"You know I can't do that, Eve. This is as much my case as yours.''

"You're wrong. You're a consultant, and that's it. I don't need consultation. I'm no longer confident that you can be adequately protected in this location. I'm moving you.''

"Eve—''

"Don't fuck with me.'' It came out sharp, very close to mean, and Mira jerked back in surprise. "I'm taking you into police custody. You can gather up some personal things or you can go as you are. But you're going.''

Calling on the control that ran within her like her own bloodstream, Mira folded her hands in her lap. "And you? Will you be going under?''

"I'm not your concern.''

"Of course you are, Eve,'' Mira said quietly, watching the storm of emotions in Eve's eyes. "Just as I'm yours. And my family downstairs is mine. They're not safe.''

"I'll see to it. I'll see to them.''

Mira nodded, closed her eyes briefly. "It would be a great relief to me to know they were away from here, and protected. It's difficult for me to cope when I'm worried about their welfare.''

"He won't touch them. I promise you.''

"I'll take your word. Now as to my status—''

"I didn't give you multiple choices, Dr. Mira.''

"Just a moment.'' Composed again, Mira picked up her tea. "I think you'll agree . . . I have every bit as much influence with your superiors as you do. It would hardly serve either of us to play at tugging strings. I'm not being stubborn or courageous,'' she added. "Those are your traits.''

A ghost of a smile curved her mouth when Eve frowned at her. "I admire them. You're also a woman who can see past emotion to the goal. The goal is to stop David Palmer. I can be of use. We both know it. With my family away I'll be less distracted. And I can't be with them, Eve, because if I am I'll worry that he'll harm one of them to get to me."

She paused for a moment, judged that Eve was considering. "I have no argument to having guards here or at my office. In fact, I want them. Very much. I have no intention of taking any unnecessary chances or risks. I'm just asking you to let me do my work."

"You can do your work where I put you."

"Eve." Mira drew a breath. "If you put both me and Justine out of his reach, there's the very real possibility he'll take someone else." She nodded. "You've considered that already. He won't come for you until he's ready. You're the grand prize. If no one else is accessible, he'll strike out. He'll want to keep to his timetable, even if it requires a substitute."

"I've got some lines on him."

"And you'll find him. But if he believes I'm accessible, if I'm at least visible, he'll be satisfied to focus his energies on getting through. I expect you to prevent that." She smiled again, easier now. "And I intend to do everything I can to help you."

"I can make you go. All your influence won't matter if I toss you in restraints and have you hauled out of here. You'll be pissed off, but you'll be safe."

"I wouldn't put it past you," Mira agreed. "But you know I'm right."

"I'm doubling your guards. You're wearing a bracelet. You work here. You're not to leave the house for any reason." Her eyes flashed when Mira started to protest. "You push me on this, you're going to find out what it feels like to wear cuffs." Eve rose. "Your guards will do hourly check-ins. Your 'link will be monitored."

"That hardly makes me appear accessible."

"He'll know you're here. That's going to have to be

enough. I've got work to do." Eve started for the door, hesitated, then spoke without turning around. "Your family, they matter to you."

"Yes, of course."

"You matter to me." She walked away quickly, before Mira could get shakily to her feet.

SIX

Eve headed to the lab from Mira's. From there she planned a stop by the morgue and another at Carl Neissan's before returning to her home office.

Remembering Mira's concern about family, Eve called Roarke on her palm-link after she parked and started into the building.

"Why are you alone?" was the first thing he said to her.

"Cut it out." She flashed her badge at security, then headed across the lobby and down toward the labs. "I'm in a secured facility, surrounded by rent-a-cops, monitors, and lab dorks. I've got a job to do. Let me do it."

"He's gotten three out of six."

She stopped, rolled her eyes. "Oh, I get it. Shows what kind of faith you have in me. I guess being a cop for ten years makes me as easy a fish as a seventy-year-old judge and a couple of soft lawyers."

"You annoy me, Eve."

"Why? Because I'm right?"

"Yes. And snotty about it." But his smile warmed a little. "Why did you call?"

"So I could be snotty. I'm at the lab, about to tackle Dickhead. I've got a few stops to make after this. I'll check in."

It was a casual way to let him know she understood he worried. And he accepted, in the same tone. "I've several 'link conferences this afternoon. Call in on the private line. Watch your back, Lieutenant. I'm very fond of it."

Satisfied, she swung into the lab. Dickie, the chief tech, was there, looking sleepy-eyed and pale as he stared at the readout on his monitor.

The last time she'd been in the lab, there'd been a hell of a party going on. Now those who'd bothered to come in worked sluggishly and looked worse.

"I need reports, Dickie. Wainger and Ring."

"Jesus, Dallas." He looked up mournfully, hunching his shoulders. "Don't you ever stay home?"

Since he looked ill, she gave him a little leeway. Silently she opened her jacket, tapped the silver star pinned to her shirt. "I'm the law," she said soberly. "The law has no home."

It made him grin a little, then he moaned. "Man, I got the mother of all Christmas hangovers."

"Mix yourself up a potion, Dickie, and get over it. Dave's got number three."

"Dave who?"

"Palmer, David Palmer." She resisted letting out her impatience by cuffing him on the side of the head. But she imagined doing it. "Did you read the damn directive?"

"I've only been here twenty minutes. Jesus." He rolled his shoulders, rubbed his face, drew in three sharp nasal breaths. "Palmer? That freak's caged."

"Not anymore. He skipped and he's back in New York. Wainger and Ring are his."

"Shit. Damn shit." He didn't look any less ill, but his eyes were alert now. "Fucking Christmas week and we get the world's biggest psycho-freak."

"Yeah, and Happy New Year, too. I need the results, on the rope, on the paper. I want to know what he used to carve the letters. You get any hair or fiber from the sweepers?''

''No, wait, just wait a damn minute.'' He scooted his rolling chair down the counter, barked orders at a computer, muttering as he scanned the data. ''Bodies were clean. No hair other than victim's. No fiber.''

''He always kept them clean,'' Eve murmured.

''Yeah, I remember. I remember. Got some dust—like grit between the toes, both victims.''

''Concrete dust.''

''Yeah. Get you the grade, possible age. Now the rope.'' He skidded back. ''I was just looking at it, just doing the test run. Nothing special or exotic about it. Standard nylon strapping rope. Give me some time, I'll get you the make.''

''How much time?''

''Two hours, three tops. Takes longer when it's standard.''

''Make it fast.'' She swung away. ''I'm in the field.''

She stopped at the morgue next, to harass the chief medical examiner. It was more difficult to intimidate Morse or to rush him.

No sexual assault or molestation, no mutilation or injuries of genitalia.

Typical of Palmer, Eve thought as she ran over Morse's prelim report in her head. He was as highly asexual as anyone she'd come up against. She doubted that he even thought of the gender of his victims other than as a statistic for his experiments.

Subject Wainger's central nervous system had been severely damaged. Subject suffered minor cardiac infarction during abduction and torture period. Anus and interior of mouth showed electrical burns. Both hands crushed with a smooth, heavy instrument. Three ribs cracked.

The list of injuries went on until Morse had confirmed the cause of death as strangulation. And the time of death as midnight, December twenty-fourth.

She spent an hour at Carl Neissan's, another at Wainger's. In both cases, she thought, the door had been opened,

Palmer allowed in. He was good at that. Good at putting on a pretty smile and talking his way in.

He looked so damn innocent, Eve thought as she climbed the steps to her own front door. Even the eyes—and the eyes usually told you—were those of a young, harmless man. They hadn't flickered, hadn't glazed or brightened, even when he'd sat in interview across from her and described each and every murder.

They'd taken on the light of madness only when he talked about the scope and importance of his work.

"Lieutenant." Summerset, tall and bony in severe black, slipped out of a doorway. "Do I assume your guests will be remaining for lunch?"

"Guests? I don't have any guests." She stripped off her jacket, tossed it across the newel post. "If you mean my team, we'll deal with it."

He had the jacket off the post even as she started up the stairs. At his low growl of disgust she glanced back. He held in his fingertips the gloves she'd balled into her jacket pocket. "What have you done to these?"

"It's just sealant." Which she'd forgotten to clean off before she shoved them into her pocket.

"These are handmade, Italian leather with mink lining."

"Mink? Shit. What is he, crazy?" Shaking her head, she kept on going. "Mink lining, for Christ's sake. I'll have lost them by next week, then some stupid mink will have died for nothing." She glanced down the hallway at Roarke's office door, shook her head again, and walked into her own.

She was right, Eve noted. Her team could deal with lunch on their own. Feeney was chowing down on some kind of multitiered sandwich while he muttered orders into the computer and scanned. Peabody had a deep bowl of pasta, scooping it up one-handed, sliding printouts into a pile with the other.

Her office smelled like an upscale diner and sounded like cops. Computer and human voices clashed, the printer hummed, and the main 'link was beeping and being ignored.

She strode over and answered it herself. "Dallas."

"Hey, got your rope." When she saw Dickie shove a pickle in his mouth, she wondered if every city official's stomach had gone on alarm at the same time. "Nylon strapping cord, like I said. This particular type is top grade, heavy load. Manufactured by Kytell outta Jersey. You guys run the distributor, that's your end."

"Yeah. Thanks." She broke transmission, thinking Dickie wasn't always a complete dickhead. He'd come through and hadn't required a bribe.

"Lieutenant," Peabody began, but Eve held up a finger and walked to Roarke's door and through it. "Do you own Kytell in New Jersey?"

Then she stopped and winced when she saw that he was in the middle of a holographic conference. Several images turned, studied her out of politely annoyed eyes.

"Sorry."

"It's all right. Gentlemen, ladies, this is my wife." Roarke leaned back in his chair, monumentally amused that Eve had inadvertently made good on her threat to barge in on one of his multimillion-dollar deals just to annoy him. "If you'd excuse me one moment. Caro?"

The holo of his administrative assistant rose, smiled. "Of course. We'll shift to the boardroom momentarily." The image turned, ran her hands over controls that only she could see, and the holos winked away.

"I should have knocked or something."

"It's not a problem. They'll hold. I'm about to make them all very rich. Do I own what?"

"Did you have to say 'my wife' just that way, like I'd just run up from the kitchen?"

"So much more serene an image than telling them you'd just run in from the morgue. And it is a rather conservative company I'm about to buy. Now, do I own what and why do you want to know?"

"Kytell, based in New Jersey. They make rope."

"Do they? Well, I have no idea. Just a minute." He swiveled at the console, asked for the information on the company. Which, Eve thought with some irritation, she could have damn well done herself.

"Yes, they're an arm of Yancy, which is part of Roarke Industries. And which, I assume, made the murder weapon."

"Right the first time."

"Then you'll want the distributor, the stores in the New York area where large quantities were sold to one buyer within the last week."

"Peabody can get it."

"I'll get it faster. Give me thirty minutes to finish up in here, then I'll shoot the data through to your unit."

"Thanks." She started out, turned back. "The third woman on the right? The redhead? She was giving you a leg shot—another inch of skirt lift and it would have been past her crotch."

"I noticed. Very nice legs." He smiled. "But she still won't get more than eighty point three a share. Anything else?"

"She's no natural redhead," Eve said for the hell of it and heard him laugh as she shut the door between them.

"Sir." Peabody got to her feet. "I think I have a line on the vehicle. Three possibles, high-end privates sold to single men in their early to mid-twenties on December twentieth and twenty-first. Two dealerships on the East Side and one in Brooklyn."

"Print hard copies of Palmer's photo."

"Already done."

"Feeney?"

"Whittling it down."

"Keep whittling. Roarke should have some data on the murder weapon inside a half hour. Send what he has to me in the field, will you? Peabody, you're with me."

The first dealership was a wash, and as she pulled up at the second, Eve sincerely hoped she didn't have to head to Brooklyn. The shiny new vehicles on the showroom floor had Peabody's eyes gleaming avariciously. Only Eve's quick elbow jab kept her from stroking the hood of a

Booster-6Z, the sport-utility vehicle of the year.

"Maintain some dignity," Eve muttered. She flagged a salesman, who looked none too happy when she flipped out her badge. "I need to talk to the rep who sold a rig like this"—she gestured toward the Booster—"last week. Young guy bought it."

"Lana sold one of the 6Zs a few days before Christmas." Now he looked even unhappier. "She often rounds up the younger men." He pointed to a woman at a desk on the far side of the showroom.

"Thanks." Eve walked over, noting that Lana had an explosion of glossy black curls cascading down her back, a headset over it, and was fast-talking a potential customer on the line while she manually operated a keyboard with fingernails painted a vivid red.

"I can put you in it for eight a month. Eight a month and you're behind the wheel of the sexiest, most powerful land and air unit currently produced. I'm slicing my commission to the bone because I want to see you drive off in what makes you happy."

"Make him happy later, Lana." Eve held her badge in front of Lana's face.

Lana put a hand over the mouthpiece, studied the ID, cursed softly. Then her voice went back to melt. "Jerry, you take one more look at the video, try out the holo run. If you're not smiling by the end of it, the 7000's not the one for you. You call me back and let me know. Remember, I want you happy. Hear?"

She disconnected, glared at Eve. "I paid those damn parking violations. Every one."

"Glad to hear it. Our city needs your support. I need information on a sale you made last week. Booster. You were contacted earlier today and confirmed."

"Yeah, right. Nice guy, pretty face." She smiled. "He knew what he wanted right off."

"Is this the guy?" Eve signaled to Peabody, who took out the photo.

"Yeah. Cute."

"Yeah, he's real cute. I need the data. Name, address, the works."

"Sure, no problem." She turned to her machine, asked for the readout. Then, looking back up at Eve, she narrowed her eyes. "You look familiar. Have I sold you a car?"

Eve thought of her departmental issue, its sad pea-green finish and blocky style. "No."

"You really look— Oh!" Lana lit up like a Christmas tree. "Sure, sure, you're Roarke's wife. Roarke's cop wife. I've seen you on screen. Word is he's got an extensive collection of vehicles. Where does he deal?"

"Wherever he wants," Eve said shortly, and Lana let out a gay laugh.

"Oh, I'm sure he does. I'd absolutely love to show him our brand-new Barbarian. It won't be on the market for another three months, but I can arrange a private showing. If you'd just give him my card, Mrs. Roarke, I'll be—"

"You see this?" Eve took out her badge again, all but pushed it into Lana's pert nose. "It says 'Dallas.' Lieutenant Dallas. I'm not here to liaison your next commission. This is an official investigation. Give me the damn data."

"Certainly. Of course." If her feathers were ruffled, Lana hid it well. "Um, the name is Peter Nolan, 123 East Sixty-eighth, apartment 4-B."

"How'd he pay?"

"That I remember. Straight E-transfer. The whole shot. Didn't want to finance. The transfer was ordered, received, and confirmed, and he drove off a happy man."

"I need all the vehicle information, including temp license and registration number. Full description."

"All right. Gee, what'd he do? Kill somebody?"

"Yeah, he did."

"Wow." Lana busily copied the data disc. "You just can't trust a pretty face," she said and slipped her business card into the disc pack.

SEVEN

Peter Nolan didn't live at the Sixty-eighth Street address. The Kowaskis, an elderly couple, and their creaky schnauzer had lived there for fifteen years.

A check of the bank showed that the Nolan account had been opened, in person, on December 20 of that year and closed on December 22.

Just long enough to do the deal, Eve thought. But where had he gotten the money?

Taking Roarke's advice, she rounded out a very long day by starting searches on accounts under the name of Palmer. It would, she thought, rubbing her eyes, take a big slice of time.

How much time did Carl have? she wondered. Another day, by her guess. If Palmer was running true to form, he would begin to enjoy his work too much to rush through it. But sometime within the next twenty-four hours, she believed he'd try for Justine Polinsky.

While her machine worked, she leaned back and closed her eyes. Nearly midnight, she thought. Another day. Feeney was working his end. She was confident they'd have a line on the equipment soon, then there were the houses to check. They had the make, model, and license of his vehicle.

He'd left a trail, she thought. He wanted her to follow it, wanted her close. The son of a bitch.

It's you and me, isn't it, Dave? she thought as her mind started to drift. How fast can I be, and how clever? You figure it'll make it all the sweeter when you've got me in that cage. It's because you want that so bad that you're making mistakes. Little mistakes.

I'm going to hang you with them.

She slid into sleep while her computer hummed and woke only when she felt herself being lifted.

"What?" Reflexively she reached for the weapon she'd already unharnessed.

"You need to be in bed." Roarke held her close as he left the office.

"I was just resting my eyes. I've got data coming in. Don't carry me."

"You were dead out, the data will be there in the morning, and I'm already carrying you."

"I'm getting closer, but not close enough."

He'd seen the financial data on her screen. "I'll take a look through the accounts in the morning," he told her as he laid her on the bed.

"I've got it covered."

He unpinned her badge, set it aside. "Yes, Sheriff, but money is my business. Close it down a while."

"He'll be sleeping now." She let Roarke undress her. "In a big, soft bed with clean sheets. Dave likes to be clean and comfortable. He'll have a monitor in the bedroom so he can watch Neissan. He likes to watch before he goes to sleep. He told me."

"Don't think." Roarke slipped into bed beside her, gathered her close.

"He wants me."

"Yes, I know." Roarke pressed his lips to her hair as much to comfort himself as her. "But he can't have you."

•　•　•

Sleep helped. She'd dropped into it like a stone and had lain on the bottom of the dreaming pool for six hours. There'd been no call in the middle of the night to tell her Carl Neissan's body had been found.

Another day, she thought again and strode into her office. Roarke was at her desk, busily screening data.

"What are you doing?" She all but leapt to him. "That's classified."

"Don't pick nits, darling. You were going too broad last night. You'll be days compiling and rejecting all accounts under the name Palmer. You want one that shows considerable activity, large transfers, and connections to other accounts—which is, of course, the trickier part if you're dealing with someone who understands how to hide the coin."

"You can't just sit down and start going through data accumulated in an investigation."

"Of course I can. You need coffee." He looked up briefly. "Then you'll feel more yourself and I'll show you what I have."

"I feel exactly like myself." Which, she admitted, at the moment was annoyed and edgy. She stalked to the AutoChef in the kitchen, went for an oversized mug of hot and black. The rich and real caffeine Roarke could command zipped straight through her system.

"What have you got?" she demanded when she walked back in.

"Palmer was too simple, too obvious," Roarke began, and she narrowed her eyes.

"You didn't think so yesterday."

"I said check for relatives, same names. I should have suggested you try his mother's maiden name. Riley. And here we have the account of one Palmer Riley. It was opened six years ago, standard brokerage account, managed. Since there's been some activity over the last six months, I would assume your man found a way to access a 'link or computer from prison."

"He shouldn't have been near one. How can you be sure?"

"He understands how money works, and just how fluid it can be. You see here that six months ago he had a balance of just over $1.3 million. For the past three years previous, all action was automatic, straight managed with no input from the account holder. But here he begins to make transfers. Here's one to an account under Peter Nolan, which, by the way, is his aunt's husband's name on his father's side. Overseas accounts, off-planet accounts, local New York accounts—different names, different IDs. He's had this money for some time and he waited, sat on it until he found the way to use it."

"When I took him down before, we froze his accounts, accounts under David Palmer. We didn't look deeper. I didn't think of it."

"Why should you have? You stopped him, you put him away. He was meant to stay away."

"If I'd cleared it all, he wouldn't have had the backing to come back here."

"Eve, he'd have found a way." He waited until she looked at him. "You know that."

"Yeah." She let out a long breath. "Yeah, I know that. This tells me he's been planning, he's been shopping, he's been juggling funds, funneling into cover accounts. I need to freeze them. I don't think a judge is going to argue with me, not after what happened to one of their own."

"You'll piss him off."

"That's the plan. I need the names, numbers, locations of all the accounts you can connect to him." She blew out a breath. "Then I guess I owe you."

"Use your present, and we'll call it even."

"My present? Oh, yeah. Where and/or when do I want to go for a day. Let me mull that over a little bit. We get this wrapped, I'll use it for New Year's Eve."

"There's a deal."

A horrible thought snuck into her busy mind. "We don't have like a thing for New Year's, do we? No party or anything."

"No. I didn't want anything but you."

She looked back at him, narrowing her eyes even as the

smile spread. "Do you practice saying stuff like that?"

"No." He rose, framed her face and kissed her, hard and deep. "I have all that stuff on disc."

"You're a slick guy, Roarke." She skimmed her fingers through her hair and simply lost herself for a moment in the look of him. Then, giving herself a shake, she stepped back. "I have to work."

"Wait." He grabbed her hand before she could turn away. "What was that?"

"I don't know. It just comes over me sometimes. You, I guess, come over me sometimes. I don't have time for it now."

"Darling Eve." He brushed his thumb over her knuckles. "Be sure to make time later."

"Yeah, I'll do that."

They worked together for an hour before Peabody arrived. She switched gears, leaving Roarke to do what he did best—manipulate data—while she focused on private residences purchased in the New York area, widening the timing to the six months since Palmer had activated his account.

Feeney called in to let her know he'd identified some of the equipment from the recording and was following up.

Eve gathered her printouts and rose. "We've got more than thirty houses to check. Have to do it door-to-door since I don't trust the names and data. He could have used anything. Peabody——"

"I'm with you, sir."

"Right. Roarke, I'll be in the field."

"I'll let you know when I have this wrapped."

She looked at him, working smoothly, thoroughly, methodically. And wondered who the hell was dealing with what she often thought of as his empire. "Look, I can call a man in for this. McNab——"

"McNab." Peabody winced at the name before she could stop herself. She had a temporary truce going with the EDD detective, but that didn't mean she wanted to share her case with him. Again. "Dallas, come on. It's been so nice and quiet around here."

"I've got this." Roarke shot her a glance, winked at Peabody. "I have an investment in it now."

"Whatever. Shoot me, and Feeney, the data when you have it all. I'm going to check out the rope, too. He likely picked up everything himself, but it would only take one delivery to pin down his hole."

After three hours of knocking on doors, questioning professional parents, housekeepers, or others who chose the work-at-home route, Eve took pity on Peabody and swung by a glide cart.

In this neighborhood the carts were clean, the awnings or umbrellas bright, the operators polite. And the prices obscene.

Peabody winced as she was forced to use a credit card for nothing but coffee, a kabob, and a small scoop of paper-thin oil chips.

"It's my metabolism," she muttered as she climbed back into the car. "I have one that requires fuel at regular intervals."

"Then pump up," Eve advised. "It's going to be a long day. At least half these people aren't going to be home until after the five o'clock shift ends."

She snagged the 'link when it beeped. "Dallas."

"Hello, Lieutenant." Roarke eyed her soberly. "Your data's coming through."

"Thanks. I'll start on the warrant."

"One thing—I didn't find any account with a withdrawal or transfer that seemed large enough for a purchase or down payment on a house. A couple are possible, but if, as you told me, he didn't finance a car, it's likely he didn't want to deal with the credit and Compuguard checks on his rating and background."

"He's got a damn house, Roarke. I know it."

"I'm sure you're right. I'm not convinced he acquired it recently."

"I've still got twenty-couple to check," she replied. "I

have to follow through on that. Maybe he's just renting. He likes to own, but maybe this time he's renting. I'll run it through that way, too.''

"There weren't any standard transfers or withdrawals that would indicate rent or mortgage payments.''

She hissed out a breath. "It's ridiculous.''

"What?''

"How good a cop you'd make.''

"I don't think insulting me is appropriate under the circumstances. I have some business of my own to tend to,'' he said when she grinned at him. "I'll get back to yours shortly.''

Palmer had purchased, and personally picked up, a hundred twenty yards of nylon rope from a supply warehouse store off Canal. The clerk who had handled the sale ID'd the photo and mentioned what a nice young man Mr. Dickson had been. As Dickson, Palmer had also purchased a dozen heavy-load pulleys, a supply of steel O rings, cable, and the complete Handy Homemaker set of Steelguard tools, including the accessory laser package.

The entire business had been loaded into the cargo area of his shiny new Booster-6Z—which the clerk had admired—on the morning of December 22.

Eve imagined Palmer had been a busy little bee that day and throughout the next, setting up his private chamber of horrors.

By eight they'd eliminated all the houses on Eve's initial list.

"That's it.'' Eve climbed back in her vehicle and pressed her fingers to her eyes. "They all check out. I'll drop you at a transpo stop, Peabody.''

"Are you going home?''

Eve lowered her hands. "Why?''

"Because I'm not going off duty if you're starting on the list of rentals I ran.''

"Excuse me?''

Peabody firmed her chin. Eve could arrow a cold chill up your spine when she took on that superior-officer tone.

"I'm not going off duty, sir, to leave you solo in the field with Palmer on the loose and you as a target. With respect, Lieutenant."

"You don't think I can handle some little pissant, mentally defective?"

"I think you want to handle him too much." Peabody sucked in a breath. "I'm sticking, Dallas."

Eve narrowed her eyes. "Have you been talking to Roarke?" At the quick flicker in Peabody's eyes Eve swore. "Goddamn it."

"He's right and you're wrong. Sir." Peabody braced for the explosion, was determined to weather it, then all but goggled with shock.

"Maybe," was all Eve said as she pulled away from the curb.

Since she was on a roll, Peabody slanted Eve a look "You haven't eaten all day. You didn't even steal any of my oil chips. You could use a meal."

"Okay, okay. Christ, Roarke's got your number, doesn' he?"

"I wish."

"Zip it, Peabody. We'll fuel the metabolism, then star on the rental units."

"Zipping with pleasure, sir."

EIGHT

It began to snow near midnight, fat, cold flakes with icy edges. Eve watched it through the windshield and told herself it was time to stop. The night was over. Nothing more could be done.

"He's got all the cards," she murmured.

"You've got a pretty good hand, Dallas." Peabody shifted in her seat, grateful for the heat of the car. Even her bones were chilled.

"Doesn't matter what I've got." Eve drove away from the last rental unit they'd checked. "Not tonight. I know who he is, who he's going to kill. I know how he does it and I know why. And tonight it doesn't mean a damn thing. Odds are, he's done with Carl now."

It was rare to see Eve discouraged. Angry, yes, Peabody thought with some concern. And driven. But she couldn't recall ever hearing that quiet resignation in her lieutenant's voice before. "You covered all the angles. You took all the steps."

"That's not going to mean much to Carl. And if I'd covered all the angles, I'd have the son of a bitch. So I'm

311

missing one. He's slipping through because I can't pin it."

"You've only had the case for three days."

"No. I've had it for three years." As she pulled up at a light, her 'link beeped. "Dallas."

"Lieutenant, this is Detective Dalrymple, assigned to observation on the Polinsky residence. We've got a mixed-race male, mid-twenties, average height and build. Subject is on foot and carrying a small sack. He used what appeared to be a key code to gain access to premises. He's inside now."

"I'm three blocks east of your location and on my way." She'd already whipped around the corner. "Secure all exists, call for backup. Doesn't make sense," she muttered to Peabody as they barreled across Madison. "Right out in the open? Falls right into our laps? Doesn't fucking make sense."

She squealed to a stop a half a block from the address. Her weapon was in her hand before she hit the sidewalk. "Peabody, the Polinsky unit is on four, south side. Go around, take the fire escape. He comes out that way, take him down quick."

Eve charged in at the front of the building and, too impatient for the elevator, raced up the stairs. She found Dalrymple on four, weapon drawn as he waited beside the door.

"Lieutenant." He gave her a brief nod. "My partner's around the back. Subject's been inside less than five minutes. Backup's on the way."

"Good." She studied Dalrymple's face, found his eyes steady. "We won't wait for them. I go in low," she added, taking out her master and bypassing the locks.

"Fine with me." He was ready beside her.

"On three. One, two." They hit the door, went through high and low, back to back, sweeping with their weapons. Music was playing, a primitive backbeat of drums behind screaming guitars. In the tidy living area, the mood screen had been set on deep reds and swimming blues melting into each other.

She signaled Dalrymple to the left, had taken two steps

to the right herself when a naked man came out of the kitchen area carrying a bottle of wine and a single red rose.

He screamed and dropped the bottle. Wine glugged out onto the rug. Holding the rose to his balls, he crouched. "Don't shoot! Jesus, don't shoot. Take anything you want. Anything. It's not even mine."

"NYPSD," Eve snapped at him. "On the floor, face-down, hands behind your head. Now!"

"Yes, ma'am, yes, ma'am." He all but dove to the rug. "I didn't do anything." He flinched when Eve dragged his hands down and cuffed them. "I was just going to meet Sunny. She said it would be okay."

"Who the hell are you?"

"Jimmy. Jimmy Ripsky. I go to college with Sunny. We're on winter break. She said her parents were out of town for a few days and we could use the place."

Eve holstered her weapon in disgust. The boy was shaking like a leaf. "Get him a blanket or something, Dalrymple. This isn't our man." She dragged him to his feet and had enough pity in her to uncuff him before gesturing to a chair. "Let's here the whole story, Jimmy."

"That's it. Um"—cringing with embarrassment, he folded his arms over his crotch—"Sunny and I are, like, an item."

"And who's Sunny?"

"Sunny Polinsky. Sheila, I guess. Everybody calls her Sunny. This is her parents' place. Man, her father's going to kill me if he finds out."

"She called you?"

"Yeah. Well, no." He looked up with desperate gratitude when Dalrymple came in with a chenille throw. "I got an E-mail from her this morning and a package. She said her parents were going south for the week and how I should come over tonight. About midnight, let myself in with the key she'd sent me. And I should, um, you know, get comfortable." He tucked the throw more securely around his legs. "She said she'd be here by twelve-thirty and I should, well, ah, be waiting in bed." He moistened his lips. "It was pretty, sort of, explicit for Sunny."

"Do you still have the E-mail? The package the key came in?"

"I dumped the package in the recycler, but I've got the E-mail. I printed it out. It's . . . it's a keeper, you know?"

"Right. Detective, call in your partner and my aide."

"Um, ma'am?" Jimmy began when Dalrymple turned away with his communicator.

"Dallas. Lieutenant."

"Yes, ma'am, Lieutenant. What's going on? Is Sunny okay?"

"She's fine. She's with her parents."

"But—she said she'd be here."

"I think someone else sent you that keeper E-mail. Somebody who wanted me to have a little something extra to do tonight." But she sat, pulled out her palm-link. "I'm going to check out your story, Jimmy. If it all fits, Detective Dalrymple's going to arrange for a uniform to take you home. You can give him the printout of the E-mail—and your computer."

"My computer? But—"

"It's police business," she said shortly. "You'll get it back."

"Well, that was fun," Peabody said when Eve resecured the door.

"A barrel of laughs."

"Poor kid. He was mortified. Here he was thinking he was going to have the sex of his dreams with his girl, and he gets busted."

"The fact that a rosebud managed to preserve most of his modesty tells me that the sex of his dreams outruns the reality." At Peabody's snort, Eve turned to the elevator. "Sunny backed up his story about them being an item. Not that I doubted it. The kid was too scared to lie. So . . . Dave's been keeping up with the social activities of his marks. He knows the family, the friends, and he knows how to use them."

She stepped out of the elevator, crossed the lobby. "For an MD in a maximum lockup, he managed to get his hands on plenty of data."

She paused at the door and simply stood for a moment looking out at the thin, steady snow. "You got off-planet clearance, Peabody?"

"Sure. It's a job requirement."

"Right. Well, go home and pack a bag. I want you on your way to Rexal on the first transport we can arrange. You and McNab can check out the facilities, find the unit Palmer had access to."

The initial rush from the idea of an off-planet assignment turned to ashes in her mouth. "McNab? I don't need McNab."

"When you find the unit, you'll need a good electronics man." Eve opened the door, and the blast of cold cooled the annoyed flush on Peabody's cheeks.

"He's a pain in the ass."

"Sure he is, but he knows his job. If Feeney can spare him, you're the off-planet team." She reached for her communicator, intending to interrupt Feeney's sleep and get the ball rolling. A scream from the end of the block had her drawing her weapon instead.

She pounded west, boots digging into the slick sidewalk. With one quick gesture, she signaled Dalrymple to stay at his post in the surveillance van.

She saw the woman first, wrapped in sleek black fur, clinging to a man with an overcoat over a tux. He was trying to shield her face and muffle her mouth against his shoulder. The pitch and volume of her screams indicated he wasn't doing a very good job of it.

"Police!" He shouted it as he saw Peabody and Eve running toward them. "Here's the police, honey. My God, my God, what's this city coming to? He threw it out, threw it out right at our feet."

It, Eve saw, was Carl Neissan. His naked and broken body lay face up against the curb. His head had been shaved, she noted, and the tender skin abraded and burned. His knees were shattered, his protruding tongue blackened. Around his neck, digging deep, was the signature noose. And the message carved into his chest was still red and raw.

WOE UNTO YOU ALSO, YE LAWYERS!

The woman's screaming had turned to wailing now. Eve tuned it out. With her eyes on the body, she pulled out her communicator. "This is Dallas, Lieutenant Eve. I have a homicide."

She gave Dispatch the necessary information, then turned to the male witness. "You live around here?"

"Yes, yes, this building on the corner. We were just coming home from a party when—"

"My aide is going to take your companion inside, away from this. Out of the cold. We'll need her statement. I'd appreciate it if you'd stay out here with me for a few minutes."

"Yes, of course. Yes. Honey." He tried to pry his wife's hands from around his neck. "Honey, you go with the policewoman. Go inside now."

"Peabody," Eve said under her breath, "take honey out of here, get what you can out of her."

"Yes, sir. Ma'am, come with me." With a couple of firm tugs Peabody had the woman.

"It was such a shock," he continued. "She's very delicate, my wife. It's such a shock."

"Yes, sir, I'm sure it is. Can I have your names, please?"

"What? Oh. Fitzgerald. George and Maria."

Eve got the names and the address on record. In a few minutes she would have a crowd to deal with, she knew. Even jaded New Yorkers would gather around a dead, naked body on Madison Avenue.

"Can you—sir, look at me," she added when he continued to stare at the body. He was going faintly green. "Look at me," she repeated, "and try to tell me exactly what happened."

"It was all so fast, so shocking." Reaction began to set in, showing in the way his hand trembled as he pressed it to his face. "We'd just come from the Andersons'. They had a holiday party tonight. It's only a block over, so we walked. We'd just crossed the street when there was a squeal of brakes. I barely paid attention to it—you know how it is."

"Yes, sir. What did you see?"

"I glanced back, just out of reflex, I suppose. I saw a dark car—black, I think. No, no, not a car—one of those utility vehicles. The sporty ones. It stopped right here. Right here. You can still see the skid marks in the snow. And then the door opened. He pushed—he all but flung this poor man out, right at our feet."

"You saw the driver?"

"Yes, yes, quite clearly. This corner is very well lit. He was a young man, handsome. Light hair. He smiled . . . he smiled at me just as the door opened. Why, I think I smiled back. He had the kind of face that makes you smile. I'm sure I could identify him. I'm sure of it."

"Yeah." Eve let out a breath, watched the wind snatch it away as the first black-and-whites arrived on the scene. You wanted to be seen, didn't you, Dave? she thought. And you wanted me to be close, very close, when you gave me Carl.

"You can go inside with your wife, Mr. Fitzgerald. I'll be in touch."

"Yes, of course. Thank you. I—it's Christmas week," he said with honest puzzlement in his eyes. "You live in the city, you know terrible things can and do happen. But it's Christmas week."

"Joy to the world," Eve murmured as he walked away. She turned around and ordered the uniforms to secure the scene and prepare for the crime-scene team. Then she crouched beside Carl and got to work.

NINE

Eve spent most of the next thirty hours backtracking, searching for the step she was sure she had missed. With Peabody off-planet, she did the work herself, rerunning searches and scans, compiling data, studying reports.

She did personal drop-bys at both the safe house where Justine and her family were being kept and Mira's home. She ran checks on their security bracelets to confirm that they were in perfect working order.

He couldn't get to them, she assured herself as she paced her office. With them out of reach, he would have no choice but to come for her.

Jesus, she wanted him to come for her.

It was a mistake, she knew it was a mistake, to make it a personal battle. But she could see his face too clearly, hear his soft prep-school voice so perfectly.

But you see, Lieutenant Dallas, the work you do is nothing more than a stopgap. You don't change anything. However many criminals you lock up today, there'll be that many and more tomorrow. What I'm doing changes everything. The answers to questions every human being asks.

How much is too much, how much will the mind accept, tolerate, bear, if you will, before it shuts down? And before it does, what thoughts, what impulses go through the mind as the body dies?

Death, Lieutenant, is the focus of your work and of mine. And while we both enjoy the brutality that goes with it, in the end I'll have my answers. You'll only have more questions.

She only had one question now, Eve thought. Where are you, Dave?

She turned back to her computer. "Engage, open file Palmer, H3492-G. Cross-reference all files and data pertaining to David Palmer. Run probability scan. What is the probability that Palmer, David, is now residing in New York City?"

Working. . . . Using current data the probability is ninety-seven point six that subject Palmer now resides in New York City.

"What is the probability that subject Palmer resides in a private home?"

Working. . . . probability ninety-five point eight that subject Palmer is residing in a private home at this time.

"Given the status of the three remaining targets of subject Palmer, which individual will he attempt to abduct next?"

Working. . . . strongest probability is for target Dallas, Lieutenant Eve. Attempts on targets Polinsky and Mira are illogical given current status.

"That's what you're hoping for."

She turned her head. Roarke stood in the doorway between their offices, watching her. "That's what I'm counting on."

"Why aren't you wearing a tracer bracelet?"

"They don't have one that goes with my outfit." She straightened, turned to face him. "I know what I'm doing."

"Do you?" He crossed to her. "Or are you too close to this one? He's gotten to you, Eve. He's upset your sense of balance. It's become almost intimate between you."

"It's always intimate."

"Maybe." He brushed a thumb just above her left cheekbone. Her eyes were shadowed, her face pale. She was, he knew, running on nerves and determination now. He'd seen it before. "In any case, you've interrupted his work. He has no one now."

"He won't wait long. I don't need the computer analysis to tell me that. We've got less than forty hours left in the year. I don't want to start the new one knowing he's out there. He won't want to start it without me."

"Neither do I."

"You won't have to." Because she sensed he needed it, she leaned into him, closed her mouth over his. "We've got a date."

"I'll hold you to it."

When she started to ease back, he slid his arms around her, brought her close. "I'm not quite done here," he murmured, and sent her blood swimming with a hard and hungry kiss.

For a moment that was all there was. The taste of him, the feel of him pressed against her, the need they created in each other time after time erupting inside her.

Giving herself to it, and to him, was as natural as breathing.

"Roarke, remember how on Christmas Eve we got naked and crazy?"

"Mmm." He moved his mouth to her ear, felt her tremble. "I believe I recall something of that."

"Well, prepare yourself for a review on New Year's Eve." She drew his head back, framing his face as she smiled at him. "I've decided it's one of our holiday traditions."

"I feel very warmly toward tradition."

"Yeah, and if I feel much warmer right now, I'm not going to get my job done, so . . ."

She jumped away from him when her 'link beeped and all but pounced on it. "Dallas."

"Lieutenant." Peabody's face swam on, swam off again, then came shakily back.

"Peabody, either your transmission's poor or you've grown a second nose."

"The equipment here's worse than what we deal with at Central." The audio came through with a snake hiss of static. "And I don't even want to talk about the food. When you're planning your next holiday vacation, steer clear of Rexal."

"And it was top of my list. What have you got for me?"

"I think we just caught a break. We've tracked down at least one unit Palmer had access to. It's in the chapel. He convinced the padre he'd found God and wanted to read Scripture and write an inspirational book on salvation."

"Glory hallelujah. Can McNab access his files?"

"He says he can. Shut up, McNab." Peabody turned her head. The fact that her face became a vivid orange could have been temper or space interference. "I'm giving this report. And I'm reporting, sir, that Detective McNab is still one big butt ache."

"So noted. What does he have so far?"

"He found the files on the book Palmer used to hose the preacher. And he *claims* he's working down the levels. Hey!"

The buzzing increased and the screen blurred with color, lines, figures. Eve pressed her fingers to her eyes and prayed for patience.

McNab's cheerful, attractive face came on. Eve noted that he wore six tiny silver hoops in one ear. So he hadn't decided to tone down his look for a visit to a rehabilitation center.

"Dallas. This guy knows his electronics, so he took basic precautions with his personal data, but—take a hike, She-Body, this is my area. Anyway, Lieutenant, I'm scraping off the excess now. He's got stuff tucked under his praise-the-Lord hype. It won't take me long to start picking it out. The trouble, other than your aide's constant griping, is transmitting to you. We've got crap equipment here and a meteor storm or some such happy shit happening. It's going to cause some problems."

"Can you work on the unit on a transport?"

"Ah . . . sure. Why not?"

"Confiscate the unit, catch the first transpo back. Report en route."

"Wow, that's iced. Confiscate. You hear that, She-Body? We're confiscating this little bastard."

"Get started," Eve ordered. "If they give you any grief, have the warden contact me. Dallas out."

Eve drove into Cop Central, making three unnecessary stops on the way. If Palmer was going to make a move on her, he'd do it on the street. He'd know he would never be able to break through the defenses of Roarke's fortress. But she spotted no tail, no shadow.

More, she didn't feel him.

Would he go for her in the station? she wondered as she took the glide up to the EDD sector to consult with Feeney. He'd used a cop's disguise to get to Carl. He could put it to use again, slip into the warrenlike building, blend with the uniforms.

It would be a risk, but a risk like that would increase the excitement, the satisfaction.

She studied faces as she went. Up glides, through breeze-ways, down corridors, past cubes and offices.

Once she'd updated Feeney and arranged for him to consult with McNab on the unit en route, she elbowed her way onto a packed elevator to make the trip to Commander Whitney's office.

She spent the morning moving through the building, inviting a confrontation, then she took to the streets for the afternoon.

She recanvased the houses she and Peabody had already hit. Left herself in the open. She bought bad coffee from a glide cart, loitered in the cold and the smoke of grilling soydogs.

What the hell was he waiting for? she thought in disgust, tossing the coffee cup into a recycling bin. The sound of a revving engine had her glancing over her shoulder. And she looked directly into Palmer's eyes.

He sat in his vehicle, grinned at her, blew her an exaggerated kiss. Even as she leaped forward, he hit vertical lift, shot up and streaked south.

She jumped into her car, going air as she squealed away from the curb. "Dispatch, Dallas, Lieutenant Eve. All units, all units in the vicinity of Park and Eighty respond. I'm in ground-to-air chase with murder suspect. Vehicle is a black new-issue Booster-6Z, New York license number Delta Able Zero-4821, temporary. Heading south on Park."

"Dispatch, Dallas. Received and confirmed. Units dispatched. Is subject vehicle in visual range?"

"No. Subject vehicle went air at Park and Eighty, headed south at high speed. Subject should be considered armed and dangerous."

"Acknowledged."

"Where'd you go, where'd you go, you little son of a bitch?" Eve rapped the wheel with her fist as she zipped down Park, shot down cross streets, circled back. "Too fast," she muttered. "You went under too fast. Your hole's got to be close."

She set down, did her best to bank her temper, to use her head and not her emotions. She'd let the search run another thirty minutes, though she'd already decided it was useless. He'd had the vehicle tucked away in a garage or lot minutes after she'd spotted him. After he'd made certain she'd spotted him.

That meant canvases of every parking facility in three sectors. Public and private. And with the budget, it would take days. The department wouldn't spare the manpower necessary to handle the job any quicker.

She stayed parked where she was, on the off chance that Palmer would try another taunt. After aborting the search, she did slow sweeps through the sectors herself, working off frustration before she drove home through the dark and the snarling traffic.

She didn't bother to snipe at Summerset, though he gave her ample opportunity. Instead, scooping up the cat, which circled her legs, she climbed the stairs. Her intent was to take a blistering-hot shower, drink a gallon of coffee, and go back to work.

Her reality was to fall facedown on the bed. Galahad climbed onto her butt, kneaded his way to comfort, curled up, and went on guard with his eyes slitted on the door.

That's how Roarke found them an hour later.

"I'll take over from here," he murmured, giving the cat a quick scratch between the ears. But when he started to drape a blanket over his wife, Eve stirred.

"I'm awake. I'm just—"

"Resting your eyes. Yes, I know." To keep her prone, Roarke stretched out beside her, stroked the hair away from her cheek. "Rest them a bit longer."

"I saw him today. The son of a bitch was ten feet away, and I lost him." She closed her eyes again. "He wants to piss me off so I stop thinking. Maybe I did, but I'm thinking now."

"And what are you thinking, Lieutenant?"

"That I've been counting too much on the fact that I know him, that I've been inside his head. I've been tracking him without factoring in one vital element."

"Which is?"

She opened her eyes again. "He's fucking crazy." She rolled over, stared at the sky window and the dark beyond it. "You can't predict insanity. Whatever the head shrinkers call it, it comes down to crazy. There's no physical, no psychological reason for it. It just is. He just is. I've been trying to predict the unpredictable. So I keep missing. It's not his work this time. It's payback. The other names on the list are incidental. It's me. He needed them to get to me."

"You'd already concluded that."

"Yeah, but what I didn't conclude, and what I'm concluding now, is he's willing to die, as long as he takes me out. He doesn't intend to go back to prison. I saw his eyes today. They were already dead."

"Which only makes him more dangerous."

"He has to find a way to get to me, so he'll take risks. But he won't risk going down before he's finished with me. He needs bait. Good bait. He must know about you."

She sat up now, raking her hair back. "I want you to wear a bracelet."

He lifted a brow. "I will if you will."

A muscle in her cheek jumped as she set her teeth. "I phrased that incorrectly. You're *going* to wear a bracelet."

"I believe such things are voluntary unless the subject has committed a crime." He sat up himself, caught her chin in his hand. "He won't get to you through me. That I can promise. But if you expect me to wear NYPSD accessories, you'll have to wear a matching one. Since you won't, I don't believe this conversation has a point."

"Goddamn it, Roarke. I can slap you into protective custody. I can order taps on all your communications, have you shadowed—"

"No," he interrupted, and infuriated her by kissing her lightly. "You can't. My lawyers will tap-dance all over your warrants. Stop." He tightened his grip on her chin before she could curse him again. And this time there was no light kiss, no flicker of amusement in his eyes. "You leave here every day to do a job that puts you in constant physical jeopardy. I don't ask you to change that. It's one of the reasons I fell in love with you. Who you are, what you do, why you do it. I don't ask you to change," he repeated. "Don't you ask me."

"It's just a precaution."

"No, it's a capitulation. If it was less, you'd be wearing one yourself."

She opened her mouth, shut it again, then shoved away and rose. "I hate when you're right. I really hate it. I'm going to take a shower. And don't even think about joining me and trying anything because I'm not too happy with you right now."

He merely reached out, snagged her hand, and yanked her back onto the bed. "I dare you to say that again in five minutes," he challenged and rolled on top of her.

She didn't say anything in five minutes, could barely speak in thirty. And when she did finally make it to the shower, her blood was still buzzing. She decided it was wiser not to comment when he joined her there. It would only appeal to his competitive streak.

She kept her silence and stepped out of the shower and into the drying tube. It gave her a very nice view. She let herself relax enough to enjoy it, watching the jets of water pulse and pound over Roarke as the hot air swirled around her.

She was back in the bedroom, just tugging on an ancient NYPSD sweatshirt and thinking about coffee and a long evening of work when her palm-link rang. Vaguely irritated with a call on her personal, she plucked it up from where she'd dumped it on the bedside table.

"Dallas."

"It was nice to see you today. In person. Face-to-face."

"Hello, Dave." With her free hand, she reached in her pocket, switched her communicator on, and plugged in Feeney's code. "Nice vehicle."

"Yes, I like it very much. Fast, efficient, spacious. You're looking a bit tired, Lieutenant. A bit pale. Overworked, as usual? Too bad you haven't been able to enjoy the holidays."

"They've had their moments."

"Mine have been very rewarding." His handsome face glowed with a smile. "It's so good to be back at work. Though I did manage to keep my hand in while I was away. But you and I—I'm sure we'll agree—know there's nothing like New York. Nothing like being home and doing what we love best."

"Too bad you won't be able to stay long."

"Oh, I intend to be here long enough to see the celebration in Times Square tomorrow night. To ring in the new year. In fact, I'm hoping we'll watch it together."

"Sorry, Dave. I have plans." From the corner of her eye, she watched Roarke come out of the bath. Watched him keep out of range, move directly to the bedroom computer, and begin to work manually.

"I think you'll change them. When you know who else I've invited to the party. I picked her up just a little while ago. You should be getting a call shortly from the guards you'd posted. The police haven't gotten any smarter since I've been gone." He let out a charming laugh. "I took a little video for you, Dallas. Take a look. I'll be in touch later to tell you what you need to do to keep her alive."

The image shifted. Eve's blood iced as she saw the woman in the cage. Unconscious, pale, one slim hand dangling through the bars.

"Transmitted from a public 'link," Roarke said from behind her. "Grand Central."

Dimly she heard Feeney giving her the same information through her communicator. Units were already on their way to the location.

He'd be gone. Of course they knew he'd already be gone.

"He has Mira." It was all she could say. "He has Mira."

TEN

Panic wanted to win. It crawled in her belly, snaked up her throat. It made her hands shake until she balled them into fists.

It wanted to swallow her when she moved through Mira's house, when she found the broken security bracelet on the floor of the office.

"He used laser tools." Her voice was steady and cool as she bagged the bracelet. "He anticipated that she'd be wearing one and brought what was necessary to remove it."

"The MTs are taking the guards in. The two from outside were just stunned. But one of the inside team's in bad shape." Feeney crouched down next to her. "Looks like Palmer got in the back, bypassed the security system like a pro. He hit the one guard in the kitchen, used a stunner to take him out quick and quiet. From the looks of the living area, the second one gave him more trouble. They went a round in there. Mira must have been up here. If she had the door closed and was working, she wouldn't have heard anything. Room's fully soundproofed."

"So he takes out the security, four experienced cops, waltzes right in, dismantles her bracelet, and waltzes out with her. We underestimated him, Feeney." And for that she would forever blame herself. "He's not what he was when I took him down before. He's studied up, he's learned, he's gotten himself into condition. He made good use of three years in a cage."

"She knows how his mind works." Feeney laid his hand on her shoulder. "Mira knows how to handle this kind of guy. She'll use that. She'll keep her cool and use it."

"No one knows how his mind works this time around. Thinking I did was part of the problem all along. I fucked up here, Feeney, and Mira's going to pay for it."

"You're wrong. The only fucking up you're doing is thinking that way now."

"I thought he might use Roarke as bait. Because if he's been studying me he knows that's where he could hit me the hardest." She made herself breathe slow as she got to her feet. "But he knows me better than I figured. He knows she matters to me."

"And he'll count on that messing you up. You gonna let it?"

"No." She breathed in again, exhaled. "No. I need McNab to shake something loose. What's their ETA?"

"Midday tomorrow. They had some transpo delays. The transmissions are full of blips, but I got that he's dug into some financials."

"Shoot whatever you've got to my home unit. I'll be working from there."

"We'll want to tap your palm-link."

"Yeah, he'll have figured that, but we'll do it anyway." She met Feeney's eyes. "We take the steps."

"We'll get her back, Dallas."

"Yeah, we will." She turned the sealed bracelet over in her hand. "If he hurts her, I'm taking him out." She lifted her gaze again. "Whatever line I have to cross, I take him out."

When she walked outside, Roarke was waiting. She hadn't argued when he'd come with her and could only be grateful that he was there to drive home so her mind could be free to think.

"Feeney's going to be sending me data," she began as she climbed into the car. "Financials. You'll be able to extrapolate faster. The sweepers will go through Mira's house, but he won't have left much, if anything. Anyway, it's not a question of IDing him. Peabody and McNab won't be back until midday tomorrow, so we'll be working with whatever they can send us while they're en route."

"I took a look at the alarms and security. It's a very good system. He used a sophisticated bypass unit to take it out without triggering the auto. It's not something your average citizen can access easily. I can help you trace the source."

"Doesn't matter at this point. Later we can deal with it. It's just another thread he left dangling, figuring I'd waste time pulling it and getting nowhere."

She rubbed at the headache behind her eyes. "I've got uniforms canvasing. One of the neighbors might have seen or heard something. It's useless, but it's routine and we might get lucky."

She closed her eyes, forced herself to think past the fear. "She's got until tomorrow, midnight. Dave wants some tradition and symbolism. He wants to welcome in the new year with me, and he needs her to get me there."

Her voice was too cool, Roarke thought. Too controlled. He'd seen the hint of panic in her eyes, and the grief. He let her hold in both as they arrived home, as she walked directly up to her office and called up all necessary files.

She added hard-copy data to the investigator's board she'd set up. And when she shifted Mira's photo from one area to the other, her fingers shook.

"Eve." He took her shoulders, turned her around. "Let it out."

"Can't. Don't talk to me."

"You can't work around it." He only tightened his grip when she tried to jerk away. "Let it out. Let it out," he said in a gentler tone. "I know what she means to you."

"God." She wrapped her arms around him, curling her

hands up over his shoulders as she pressed her face into his neck. "Oh, God. Hold on. Just for a minute, hold on."

Her body shook, one hard wave of shudders after another. She didn't weep, but her breath hitched as he held her close. "I can't think about what he might do to her. If I think about it, I'll lose it."

"Then remember she's strong, and she's smart. She'll know what she has to do."

"Yeah." Her 'link signaled incoming data. "That'll be the financials."

"I'll start on them." He eased her back. "He won't win this round."

"Damn right."

She worked until her eyes and mind went blurry, then fueled up with coffee and worked some more. At just after two A.M. Feeney shot her more data. It told her that he, Peabody, and McNab were all still on the job.

"Basically," Roarke said, "this is just confirming what we already have. The accounts, the transfers. You need to find more. You need to look from a different angle." He glanced up to see Eve all but swaying on her feet. "And you need to sleep."

She would have argued, but it would have wasted time. "We both do. Just a little while. We can share the sleep chair. I want to stay close to this unit."

The caffeine in her system couldn't fight off exhaustion. Moments after closing her eyes, she fell into sleep. Where nightmares chased her.

Images of Mira trapped in a cage mixed and melded with memories of herself as a child, locked in a room. Horror, pain, fear lived in both places. He would come—Palmer, her father—he would come and he would hurt her because he could. Because he enjoyed it. Because she couldn't stop him.

Until she killed him.

But even then he came back and did it all again in her dreams.

She moaned in sleep, curled into Roarke.

It was the smell of coffee and food that woke her. She sat up with a jerk, blinked blindly in the dark, and found herself alone in the chair. She stumbled into the kitchen and saw Roarke already taking food from the AutoChef.

"You need to eat."

"Yeah, okay." But she went for the coffee first. "I was thinking about what you said, looking at a different angle." She sat, because he nudged her into a chair, and shoveled in food because it was in front of her. "What if he bought or rented this place he's got before he got to New York? A year ago, two years ago?"

"It's possible. I still haven't found any payments."

"Has to be there. Somewhere." She heard the ring of her palm-link from the other room and was on her feet. "Stay in here, do what you can to trace."

Deliberately she moved behind her desk, sat, composed her face. "Dallas."

"Good morning, Lieutenant. I hope you slept well."

"Like a top, Dave." She curled a hand under the desk.

"Good. I want you rested up for our date tonight. You've got, oh, let's see, just over sixteen and a half hours to get here. I have every confidence in you."

"You could tell me where you are, we can start our date early."

He laughed, obviously delighted with her. "And spoil the fun? I don't think so. We're puzzle solvers, Dallas. You find me by midnight and Dr. Mira will remain perfectly safe. That's providing you come to see me alone. I'll know if you bring uninvited guests, as I have full security. Any gate-crashers, and the good doctor dies immediately and in great physical distress. I want to dance with you, Dallas. Just you. Understood?"

"It's always been you and me, Dave."

"Exactly. Come alone, by midnight, and we'll finish what we started three years ago."

"I don't know that she's still alive."

He only smiled. "You don't know that she's not." And broke transmission.

"Another public 'link," Roarke told her. "Port Authority."

"I need the location. If I'm not there by midnight, he'll kill her." She rose, paced. "He's got a place, one with full security. He's not bullshitting there. He'll have cameras, in and out. Sensors. He didn't have time to set all that up in a week, so either the place came equipped with them or he ordered them from prison courtesy of the chaplain."

"We can access tax records, blueprints, specs. It'll take time."

"Time's running out. Let's get started."

At two she received word that Peabody and McNab had landed, and she ordered them to bring the unit to her home office. He was close, she thought again, and none of them should waste time working downtown.

The minute they walked in, she began outlining her plan of attack. "McNab, set up over there. Start checking out any financials, transfers, transmissions, using the chaplain's name. Or a combo of his and Palmer's. Peabody, contact Whitney, request a canvas of all private garages in the suspect area. I want uniforms, every warm body we can find, hitting the public parking facilities with orders to confiscate and review all security tapes for the past week."

"All, Lieutenant?"

"Every last one."

She swung around and into Roarke's office. Using his auxiliary unit, she called up data, shot it to screen. "I've got the residences of Palmer's targets in blue," she told Roarke. "We run from mid to upper Manhattan, heaviest population on the East Side. We need to concentrate on private homes in this ten-block radius. Unless something jumps out at you, disregard anything that doesn't fit this profile."

She rolled her shoulders to relieve the tension, closed her eyes to clear her mind. "It'll have a basement. Probably two stories in addition to it. Fully soundproofed and most likely with its own vehicle storage area. I've got them looking at public storage, but I'm betting he has his own. He wants me to find him, goddamn it, so it can't be that hard. He wants me to work for it but not to fail. It's just personal for him, and without me . . .''

She trailed off, whirled around. "He needs me. Jesus. Check my name. Check deeds, mortgages, leases using my name.''

"There's your new angle, Lieutenant," Roarke murmured as he set to work. "Very good.''

"Toss it on screen," she asked even as she moved to stand behind him and watch. As her name popped up with a list of liber and folio numbers she swore again. "How the hell did he get all that property?''

"That's not his, it's yours.''

"What do you mean mine? I don't own anything.''

"Properties I've transferred into your name." Roarke spoke absently as he continued the scan.

"Transferred? What the hell for?''

He skimmed a finger lightly over her wedding ring and earned a punch in the shoulder. "You're welcome.''

"Take it back. All of it.''

"It's complicated. Taxes. Really, you're doing me a favor. No, there's nothing here that isn't yours. We'll try a combination of names.''

She wanted, badly, to seethe, but she didn't have time.

They found three listings for the name David Dallas in Manhattan.

"Get the property descriptions.''

"I'm working on it. It takes a moment to hack into city hall.''

Barely more than that for Roarke, Eve noted as the data flashed on screen. "No, that's downtown. Sex club. Try the next." She gripped the back of his chair, straining with impatience. "That's just out of the target area, but possible. Hold that and run the last. I'll be damned." She almost whispered it. "He reverted to type after all. That's his parents' house. He bought their place.''

"Two and a half years ago," Roarke confirmed. "Using the name David Dallas. Your man was thinking ahead.

Very far ahead. We'll find accounts in that name, or an account that he had and closed."

"Five blocks from here. The son of a bitch is five blocks from here." She leaned down, kissed the top of Roarke's head, and strode back into her office. "I've found it," she announced, then looked at her wrist unit. "We've got seven hours to figure out how to take him down."

She would go in alone. She insisted on it. She agreed to go in wired. Agreed to surveillance and backup at half-block intervals surrounding the house. For luck she pinned on the badge Peabody had given her, then waited with growing impatience as Feeney checked the transmitter.

"You're on," he told her. "Nothing I found on the video disc had equipment that can tag this pretty little bug. We've got a decoy so he'll think he's found one and deactivated it."

"Good thinking."

"You got to do it this way." He nodded at her. "I'd do the same. But you better understand I hear anything I don't like, I'm coming in. Roarke." He stepped back as Roarke came into the room. "I'll give you a minute here."

Roarke crossed to her, tapped a finger on her badge. "Funny, you don't look like Gary Cooper."

"Who?"

He smiled. "*High Noon*, darling Eve, though the clock's turned around on this one. We have a date in a couple of hours."

"I remember. I've got a present coming. I can do this."

"Yes." He kissed her, softly. "I know. Give my best to Mira."

"You bet. The team's moving into place now. I have to go."

"I'll see you soon."

He waited until she was gone, then walked outside himself and climbed casually into Feeney's unit. "I'll be riding with you."

Feeney scratched his chin. "Dallas won't like it."

"That's a pity. I spent the last few hours studying the

schematics for the security on the Palmer house. I can by-pass it, by remote.''

"Can you, now?" Feeney said mildly.

Roarke turned his head, gave Feeney a level look. "I shouldn't need more than twenty minutes clear to manage it.''

Feeney pursed his lips and started down the drive. ''I'll see what we can do about that.''

She went in at ten. It was best, she'd decided, not to cut it too close to the deadline. The old brownstone was lovely, in perfect repair. The security cameras and sensors were discreetly worked into the trim so as not to detract from its dignity.

As she walked to the door she was certain Palmer was watching. And that he was pleased. She gave the overhead camera a brief glance, then bypassed the locks with her master.

She closed the door at her back, heard the locks snick automatically back into place. As they did, the foyer lights flashed on.

''Good evening, Dallas.'' Palmer's voice flowed out of the intercom. ''I'm so pleased you could make it. I was just assuring Doctor Mira that you'd be here soon so we could begin our end-of-year celebration. She's fine, by the way. Now, if you'd just remove your weapon—''

''No.'' She said it casually as she moved forward. ''I'm not stripping down for you, Dave, so you can take me out as I come down the stairs. Let's not insult each other.''

He laughed. ''Well, I suppose you're right. Keep it. Take it out. Engage it. It's fine. Just remember, Doctor Mira's fate is in your hands. Come join us, Lieutenant. Let's party.''

She'd been in the house before, when she interviewed his parents. Even if the basic setup hadn't come back to her, she'd taken time to study the blueprints. Still, she didn't move too quickly, but scanned cautiously for booby traps on the way through the house.

She turned at the kitchen, opened the basement door. The sound of cheering blasted up at her. The lights were on bright. She could see streamers, balloons, festive decorations.

She took her weapon out and started down.

He had champagne chilling in a bucket, pretty canapés spread on silver trays on a table draped with a colorful cloth.

And he had Mira in a cage.

"Lieutenant Dallas." Mira said it calmly, though her mind was screaming. She'd been careful to call Eve by her title, to keep their relationship professional, distant.

"Doctor." Palmer clucked his tongue. "I told you I'd do the talking. Lieutenant, you see this control I'm holding. Just so we understand each other right away, if I press this button, a very strong current will pass through the metal of the doctor's temporary home. She'll be dead in seconds. Even with your weapon on full, I'll have time to engage it. Actually, my nervous system will react in such a way to the shock that my finger will twitch involuntarily, and the doctor, shall we say, is toasted."

"Okay, Dave, but I intend to verify that Doctor Mira is unharmed. Are you hurt, Doctor?"

"No." And she'd managed so far to hold back hysteria. "He hasn't hurt me. And I don't think he will. You won't hurt me, will you, David? You know I want to help you. I understand how difficult all this has been for you, not having anyone who appreciates what you've been working to achieve."

"She's really good, isn't she?" he said to Eve. "So soothing. Since I don't want to show her any disrespect— you'll note I didn't remove her clothing for our little experiment—maybe you should tell her to shut the fuck up. Would you mind, Dallas?"

"Dave and I need to handle this, Dr. Mira." Eve moved closer. "Don't we, Dave? It's you and me."

"I've waited for this for so long. You can see I've gone to quite a bit of trouble." He gestured with his free hand. "Maybe you'd like a drink, an hors d'oeuvre. We have a celebration going on. The end of the old, the birth of the new. Oh, and before I jam that wire you're wearing, tell the backup team that if anyone attempts entry, you both die.''

"I'm sure they heard you. And they already have orders to hold back. You said to come alone,'' she reminded him. "So I did. I always played it straight with you.''

"That's right. We learned to trust each other.''

"Why stop now? I've got a deal for you, Dave. A trade. Me for Mira. You let her out of there, you let her go, and I'll get in. You'll have what you want.''

"Eve, don't—'' Mira's composure started to slip.

"This is between me and Dave.'' She kept her eye on him, level and cool. "That's what you want, isn't it? To put me in a cage, the way I put you in one. You've been thinking about it for three years. You've been planning it, working for it, arranging it step by step. And you did a damn good job this time around. Let her go, Dave. She was just bait, you got me here by using her. Let her go and I'll put down my weapon. I'll get in, and you'll have the kind of subject you've always wanted.''

She took another step toward him, watching his eyes now, watching them consider. Desire. "She's a shrink, and she's not in the kind of condition I'm in—mental or physical. She sits at a desk and pokes into other people's minds. You start on her, she'll go down fast, give you no satisfaction. Think how long I'll last. Not just hours, days. Maybe weeks if you can hold the outside team off that long. You know it's going to end here, for both of us.''

"Yes, I'm prepared for that.''

"But this way, you can get your payback and finish your work. Two for one. But you have to let her out.''

Music crashed out of the entertainment unit. On screen the revelers in Times Square swarmed like feverish ants.

"Put down the weapon now.''

"Tell me it's a deal.'' She held her breath, lifted her weapon, aimed it at the center of his body. "Tell me it's a deal or I take you down. She goes, but I live. And you lose all around. Take the deal, Dave. You'll never get a better one.''

"I'll take the deal.'' All but quivering with excitement,

he rubbed a hand over his mouth. "Put the weapon down. Put it down and move away from it."

"Bring the cage down first. Bring it down to the floor so I know you mean it."

"I can still kill her." But he reached out to the console, touched a switch. The cage began to sway and lower.

"I know it. You've got the power here. I've just got a job. I'm sworn to protect her. Unlock the cage."

"Put the weapon down!" He shouted it out now, raising his voice over the music and cheers. "You said you'd put it down, now do it!"

"Okay. We've got a deal." Sweat slid down her back as she bent to lay the weapon on the floor. "You don't kill for the hell of it. It's for science. Unlock the cage and let her go." Eve lifted her hands, palms out.

On a bright laugh, he grabbed up a stunner, jabbed the air with it. "Just in case. You stay where you are, Dallas."

Her heart began to beat again when he put the control down, hit the button to release the locks. "Sorry you have to leave the party, Doctor Mira. But I promised this dance to the lieutenant."

"I need to help her out." Eve crouched to take Mira's hand. "Her muscles are stiff. She wouldn't have lasted for you, Dave." She gave Mira's hand one hard squeeze.

"Get in, get in now."

"As soon as she's clear." Eve remained crouched, pushed Mira aside. As she used her body as a shield, she had time to register a movement on the stairs, then her clinch piece was in her hand.

"I lied, Dave." She watched his eyes go round with shock, saw him grab for the control, lower the stunner. The crowd cheered wildly as her blast took him full in the chest.

His body jerked, a quick and obscene dance. He was right, she noted, about the finger twitch. It depressed convulsively on the control even as he fell onto the cage.

Sparks showered from it, from his quaking body as she dragged Mira clear and curled herself over her.

"Your jacket's caught fire, Lieutenant." With admirable

calm, Roarke bent over and patted out the spark that burned the leather at her shoulder.

"What the hell are you doing here?"

"Just picking up my wife for our date." He reached down gently and helped Mira to her feet. "He's gone," Roarke murmured, and brushed tears from her cheeks.

"I couldn't reach him. I tried, for hours after I woke up in that . . . in that thing. But I couldn't reach him." Mira turned to Eve. "You could, in the only way that was left. I was afraid you'd—" She broke off, shook her head. "I was afraid you'd come, and afraid you wouldn't. I should have trusted you to do what had to be done."

When she caught Eve in a hard embrace, pressed her cheek against hers, Eve held on, just held on, then eased away, awkwardly patting Mira's back. "It was a team effort—including this civilian this time around. Go spend New Year's with your family. We'll worry about the routine later."

"Thank you for my life." She kissed Eve's cheek, then turned and kissed Roarke's. And didn't begin to weep again until she was upstairs.

"Well, Lieutenant, it's a very fitting end."

She followed Roarke's gaze, studied Palmer, and felt nothing but quiet relief. "To the man or the year?"

"To both." He stepped to the champagne, sniffing it as he drew it from the bucket. "Your team's on the way in. But I think we could take time for a toast."

"Not here. Not with that." She took the bottle, dumped it back into the bucket. On impulse, she took the badge off her shirt, pinned it on his. "Routine can wait. I want to collect on my present."

"Where do you want to go?"

"Just home." She slid an arm around his waist, moving toward the stairs as cops started down. "Just home, with you." She heard the crowd erupt with another cheer. "Happy New Year."

"Not quite yet. But it will be."